A THRONE OF RUIN AND ROSE

ALSO BY KATHERINE ANN

A THRONE OF RUIN AND ROSE

THE SHADOW SERIES
BOOK ONE

KATHERINE ANN

BROOKHAVENPUBLISHING

NOTE FROM THE AUTHOR

THIS STORY IS INTENDED FOR MATURE AUDIENCES ONLY (18+).
IT EXPLORES DARK AND TRAUMATIC THEMES THAT MAY BE
DISTRESSING FOR SOME READERS. READER DISCRETION IS
ADVISED.

HOW TO USE A QR CODE LIKE THE ONE BELOW: OPEN YOUR
SMARTPHONE CAMERA AND POINT IT AT THE SQUARE CODE, THEN
TAP THE NOTIFICATION LINK THAT POPS UP.

YOU CAN FIND A FULL LIST OF TRIGGERS HERE

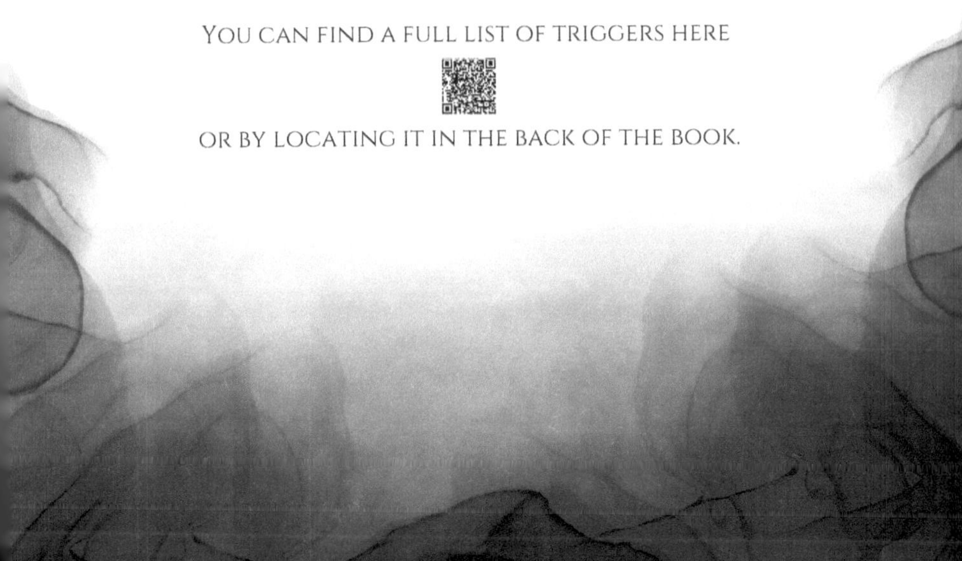

OR BY LOCATING IT IN THE BACK OF THE BOOK.

For those who survived what was never meant to be survived—not quietly, not gently, but stubbornly. May your crown never tilt.

A THRONE OF RUIN
AND ROSE

PROLOGUE

Before they were called gods, they were creations, shaped by divine hands that believed order and obedience were balance.

Forged as instruments and not equals, *Life* and *Death* were given purpose but denied choice—power but no mercy. Their alliance was not seen as devotion, but as defiance, one that tilted the balance their creators had so carefully engineered.

Torn from the world they had shaped, the gods were bound to the stars and the night sky, cast high above the realms as punishment and warning. Never allowed to touch again, yet forced to watch as the world they left behind paid dearly for the act they had committed.

Devastation on a scale the realms had never known

tore through the land. The war that followed their absence was so great it drowned kingdoms in blood and grief, until nearly all life was wiped from existence.

But something was left behind among the ruins and ash—an ember waiting to ignite, so small and quiet that no one thought to fear it.

CHAPTER ONE

THERE IT WAS. I breathed quietly, drawing the cracked skin of my bottom lip between my teeth as I inched closer to the overgrown patch of clover. The thumping of my heart, loud in my ears—a reminder that this place wasn't meant for the likes of me or any Mortal.

Impenetrable darkness, as ancient as time itself, lingered along the edges of my eyesight, making me feel as if I would be swallowed whole by it as I took another soft step closer.

I had never prayed to the forgotten gods before, but starting now didn't seem like a bad idea.

Sweat beaded on my forehead and rolled down my face in the unforgiving heat as I focused on the eerie sensation of something watching me, creeping up my spine.

Drawing an idle circle along the hilt of my blade with my thumb, I readied myself for what was sure to come next.

"Riven," my name was whispered softly.

I pressed my lips into a tight line, recognizing the voice.

It was a trick. The forbidden wood was known for them, luring Mortals into their depths until they had lost themselves completely or became a meal for the wicked Faye creatures that bordered our realm... and that was only *if* the shadows didn't take them first.

"Riven!" Finley screamed, the sound of it shrill and grating to my ears. Any doubt she was a figment of my imagination was long gone as I set my eyes on her tiny figure peeking out from behind a petrified tree trunk.

I jerked my head to the tendrils of smoky darkness surrounding me as if testing or teasing my form. Never had they come so close before.

The clover would have to wait. I had drawn too much attention in my hesitation. A mistake that had proven fatal to many before me.

I lunged toward Finley before the tendrils could strike, yanking her forward by the arm and locating the small stones I'd used to mark the trails leading toward the village.

We jumped over a thorned bush, dodging low-hanging branches rotted from the inside out as we went, my bony legs aching with the effort of dragging along a second person.

"Riven," Finley gasped, her feet tangling beneath her. "Riven, I can't go much further."

"Yes, you can." I dug my fingers into her bicep, keeping her close as we barreled past another stone marker with the shadows snapping at our heels.

Relief rushed me when daylight filtered through the darkness ahead, casting distorted figures across the forest floor.

The tree line was just within reach.

I wrapped my arm around Finley's shoulders and pulled her to me, leaping through a gnarled wall of thorns and dead brush that tore into our skin before we smacked face-first into the hard ground in a mess of sweaty limbs and heaving chests.

The bright sun bore down on us—a welcome sight compared to the dark, dead forest we had come from.

"What—" I managed after the burning in my lungs was no longer agonizing, and the shaking in my limbs had begun to wear off. "What in the hell do you think you were doing following me in there?"

"Me?" She propped herself up with her arms to face me, her cheeks bright red and glistening, as she brushed away the golden hair stuck to her damp forehead. "You're the one who left me at the mercy of your father."

I rolled onto my side, unsure if I wanted to shout at her for following me in or hug her for being… well, for being Finley. I shook my head and got to my feet, tugging her upright before the wood could decide to pull us back in.

"It's not safe in there," I reminded her as I plucked a small stick from her tangled waves and tossed it aside.

She fussed, batting at my hand. "Your father would have up and died if he knew what you were up to."

"You're not going to tell him, are you?" I bit my lip a bit nervously. "He can't know this is where I get them from."

"It depends." She looped her arm around mine, guiding us toward Terling. "Will you *finally* say yes to Knox so I can stop hearing about how amazing you are over breakfast, or are you still hung up on *he who shall not be named*? You know he's not real, right?"

"You know I can't." I pulled at one of the many curls that had fallen from my plaited braid, going out of my way to ignore the last part of her question. "As much as I'd love to be your sister-in-law, you know my father has other plans for me."

The faint scent of pollen reached my nose when she rested her head on my shoulder. "I know. But a girl can dream, right?"

We continued down the path in silence, passing by a few tiny shops selling useless trinkets and Faye-repelling potions I was certain came from the fountain in the village center. A few herbs mixed in, and even the wealthy were convinced of its potency.

I, however, would never dare waste what little coin we had on it when we needed every bit for the garden. Providing stew was far more important than protection from the Faye when the creatures only seemed to come on the Red Moon.

Even then, the animal blood across the threshold did more than some dirty laundry water in a glass vial… most of the time.

My chest tightened as my thoughts drifted to the family targeted only a few moons ago. I wouldn't have wished their fate on even my worst enemy.

"I won't tell… Though, you should probably wipe your face before he sees you."

I slowed to a stop, running my fingers across the ash I had forgotten about before rubbing it the rest of the way off with the sleeve of my tunic. "Thank you. That would have been a pain to explain."

"No problem." She smiled, the thick red and blonde

lashes lining her pale blue eyes making them pop more than usual as we continued on. "What do you think they are?"

"The shadows?" I raised a brow. "I don't know."

We had been told our whole lives they were lost spirits rejected from the Veil, but the truth was, I wasn't so sure we knew the first thing about what resided in the forbidden wood.

The thought bothered me as we arrived outside Alma's, where she waited with an armful of clean pots that needed to be filled and returned to her.

"Riven, my gods. What have you done to yourself?" She heaved the load onto the rickety serving table outside her shop and grimaced, prodding at my clothes and hair. "And Finley, too? You both need baths. You look like you've crawled around in the dirt."

"Riven was just showing me how to set some snares by the wood," Finley giggled, releasing my arm and giving Alma a quick peck on her full, pink-hued cheek as I let the worry that she might let my whereabouts slip roll off my shoulders and gathered up the pots.

CHAPTER TWO

THE SETTING SUN blanketed brush roofs and worn cobblestone pathways in soft magentas as the towns-people began lighting lanterns outside their shops and homes.

New parents swaddled their babes tightly to their chests, many listening to the barkeep play a melody on his harmonica while watching with reverence as children giggled and danced in uneven circles to the tune.

Alma wiped down the serving table beside me and passed off pots to Finley to be brought inside and washed for tomorrow, while I filled the final small bowls and handed off spoons to what remained of the line.

"Thank you, miss," an elderly woman rasped, her

unfamiliar face cloaked in shadow as she took the bowl from me.

I reached out to give her a spoon, jerking back when my hand brushed her gray, withered one—the brief contact sending a dreadful jolt shooting through me.

"Careful, dear," Alma said when I nearly stepped on her toes.

The stranger nodded her thanks and disappeared into the evening crowd while I stared after her, absently retrieving another bowl and filling it for the next in line —a small boy with a moon-white face caked in dirt beneath an uneven cap.

"Phineas, it's good to see you." I smiled, hoping he'd be here. "How is your mother doing? Stronger today?"

The two were regulars in this line.

His mother was always so happy to see me and Fin, constantly boasting about Phineas and how quickly he was growing into a man.

I remember he once spent an entire evening with me going on about the chin hair he had acquired overnight. I didn't have it in me to tell him it was just a smudge. He learned later that it was, and my, did that boy pout about it for weeks.

Still, he was a welcome presence on the days Fin was stuck indoors sewing. I'd listen to the wild tales he'd tell me while I reset my traps.

Eventually, he stopped joining me.

By the third time I caught him in line by himself this year, I realized it was because his mother, like many others, wouldn't be around much longer.

"She's not doing well, miss. I'm afraid she won't last the week." He dipped his head, something most did in shame for admitting their hardships.

I bit my lip and looked around, adding the final helpings to his bowl once I knew no one else would join the line and knelt before him.

"You are strong. You *both* are." I reached into the satchel hanging at my side and pulled out one of my last coins and a clover folded into an old cloth. Slipping it into his vest pocket, I said, "The clover will help her. The coin is for whatever you may need to ease the coming days."

"Thank you, miss." He nodded, his eyes a little less gray than they had been moments ago, as I watched him wander into the crowd with his meal.

My back ached as I stood, reaching out to pick up the final empty pot.

"Let me get that for you." Knox shooed my hands away with his much larger, overly tanned and calloused ones.

"I can do it, you know." I grinned, welcoming the smell of cedar that always seemed to follow him wherever he went. It was a scent he carried with him even when we were little.

"Yes, but you don't have to do it all. I'm happy to help."

I crossed my arms over my chest and raised a brow. "I don't need any help."

"Yes, you do," Finley added from the threshold of Alma's shop, where she dried her hands meticulously against her top skirts. "We all see it. Take a break, Riven. No one would blame you if you did."

Except there wasn't time for a break. Not if I wanted to keep the village fed and my father well. The Red Moon would be here in a few days, and I still needed to get more clover from the wood before the lockdown. The longer I waited, the more unpredictable the shadows became.

Lilac loomed in the air as I considered what had happened this morning. They had never come so close before. It was as if—

Knox brushed his shoulder against mine, passing by to hand the final pot to his sister and taking my outlandish thoughts with him. When he returned, he pointed in no particular direction.

"This is because of you and your father. They would understand if you took a day or two. Fin and I will serve while you spend time at home. You should be with him while you still can—" His green eyes widened, recognizing the mistake he had made. "I didn't—"

"No," I stopped him, fighting the frown that was etching itself into the corners of my mouth as I spoke. "I know. It's fine."

We were all trying to come to terms with the fact that my father wouldn't be here much longer. Between the headaches and the memory loss, I expected that day to come sooner rather than later, and so did he.

It was why he had a hidden marriage contract tucked away in a desk drawer with only one blank signature line. He was waiting for the day when he had no choice but to sign it—an agreement that would place my life in the hands of a wealthy merchant on the other side of Terling.

I'd never want or need for anything after his death… but that was not the life for me.

I looked around at my home, unable to see a future outside of this.

"I need to check snares in the morning," I redirected him. "Any chance you'll be up for some—"

A loud bell sounded across the cobblestone pathway before I could finish, and my heart sank.

"Town of Terling. Before you, kneels Robert Jones. Guilty for the crimes of stealing and assaulting a shop-keeper." The judgment maker stuck the elderly man in the side with his waxed boot, forcing him to fall onto his side as people began to gather. "How do you plead?"

"It was for my wife, sir. She's skin and bone." The man got back to his knees with some struggle and pressed his palms together in a plea. "Please, Jeremiah. You know I didn't mean to hurt anyone. I just needed bread for my wife. She's in a bad way."

Knox grasped my arm firmly when I began to move forward, pulling my eyes away from the scene of a well-fed, well-bred man in a nice tunic with slicked-back hair, standing above a man whose tattered shirt barely covered his emaciated ribcage.

"*Don't*. It's not worth it, Riven." He squeezed tighter as if he thought he could keep me in place. "You'll only make it worse."

"We can't let this happen," I said tightly.

"Riven, please," Finley begged.

But the man on his knees wouldn't survive the night —not with what was to come. The scent of his death clung to the air, to me, confirming it. His only crime was being poor and hungry, like most of us.

I shook Knox's hand off with stinging eyes, only to be yanked back into the broadness of his chest, where he shielded me from what was about to happen.

"Think of your father."

My jaw flexed, and I twisted my fingers into his

tunic, pressing my face against him until I couldn't breathe.

He was right. If I tried to stop this, the penalty would be death for anyone involved.

Death. I closed my eyes, the lilac in the air choking my lungs as Knox ran long strokes down my back, and Finley stared at the ground, unmoving.

Whack—Whack—

Two hands. Not one. He lost *both* of them.

"Let's get you home," Finley said quietly.

It took everything in me to pull myself away from her brother. *Everything* in me to move from the spot we stood in.

I scooted my boots against the ground, unable to understand how someone so privileged could pass judgment without knowing or caring about our struggles. It wasn't right. I pressed my palm against my thin frame, knowing what it was like to be starving. We all did.

Knox dropped his hand to the hollow of my back and guided me forward when I stopped moving, more focused on the clusters of people we wove through—people who found entertainment in the man's punishment. *Actual* entertainment.

My hands balled into tight fists at my sides as condemning chants rang out.

I wanted to scream. Scream at them. Scream for the man who only wanted to help his wife.

These people, who had offered me kindness just moments ago, had turned rabid and disgraceful.

They were no better than the Faye we feared so much for their wicked ways—no better than the death they wished upon the man they shouted at.

"Just look ahead," Finley whispered. "There will be no trace of what happened tomorrow."

There never was, but that didn't stop the bile from rising in my throat with each leaden step we took. It didn't ease the guilt that churned within me for not doing anything to stop it.

We had gone days without a punishment. I didn't know why I let myself think there wouldn't be one today.

I stood at the edge of a darkened moor, staring into the inky black depths surrounded by dead, rotten limbs and slick moss.

I don't know at what point I was swept away with sleep. Only that my eyes had been heavy with tears and my heart sore, like it was most evenings, when Knox walked me home after Jeremiah passed his sentences.

The air around me was stale. Not even insects dared venture here. Not even the presence of my raven.

I gawked, unable to pull my eyes away, hypnotized by what lay beneath the glassy surface, looking back at me.

It was my reflection... but it wasn't. My high cheekbones and full lips. The light speckling of freckles across the bridge of my nose and under my eyes. My eyes... they weren't the deep brown I was born with. Instead, they were nearly as black as the water before me.

I reached for the reflection despite every instinct telling me it was time to leave, and my attention slid to the silver armor I wore, wrapping my arms in intricate displays of a forgotten battle encrusted in blood, new and old, before falling to my hand, which was also wrong.

My pale fingers were too long, thin and delicate, and my skin too shimmery.

Riven, *the water whispered, drawing my eyesight back to its decaying world.*

The sound was soft and sweet, eerie and dark, pulling me closer until I found myself kneeling on one ironclad knee, almost able to touch it.

The heavy presence in my chest told me, now. Now *was my chance.* Run.

The tips of my fingers rippled the water, my reflection distorted by the soundless waves as a hand, twisted and knobby, greeted mine, pulling me under before I had a chance to breathe the rancid air.

Underneath the murky surface, I found myself in a weightless descent to the bottom—surrounded by darkness that came to life, watching me from afar.

My limbs stiffened in the cold, penetrating my suit. I couldn't fight or move. Not even to the surface that bubbled above me. So close, yet so far away.

The chosen one, *the darkness whispered.* The chosen one has finally come to rid our world of the false gods.

My lungs burned beneath the pressure of the water as the last of my air choked its way from my chest, rising in a giant pocket that danced in the light above me. I closed my eyes and wished for one final breath to scream with, desperately begging my arms to move and my legs to push from the bottom—but they refused to budge.

Crippling pain shot through my deflated lungs, and I was pulled to the surface and onto the moss at the water's edge by hands that I often found myself yearning for in the darkest parts of my dreams.

I collapsed onto the bank, sputtering grainy water as I searched for him, knowing he'd be gone—just like he always was. And in a nauseating flash, I was no longer next to the moor but standing in the middle of a field of fallen soldiers.

The carnage was like nothing I had ever seen in my life.

"What—" My throat stung, and my lips trembled as I took in the sight. A place I had been before, but it wasn't like this. "What is this?"

The past, *the breeze whispered into my ear.* The *future.*

I blinked, unable to take in the full brunt of what lay before me—the bodies that were piled atop one another, drenched in thick blood, their ruined armor bearing crests I had never seen before while torn flags of various colors jutted from the ground on wooden poles, flapping lazily in the dry heat alongside corpses of horses in matching armor, sprawled on their backs and sides.

And in the middle of it all, stretching as far as the eye could see, was a great crack in the earth that split the battlefield for miles.

I was looking at the aftermath of a slaughter.

Shock drove me a step back, and I lost my footing on the slick ground, tumbling down the backside of the steep hill. I covered my head as much as my armor would allow and kicked out, trying, hoping to catch something solid enough to stop my descent.

With no luck, I hit the bottom.

Metal thudded and sharp pain tore through me as I

pressed my palm firmly against my side, staring up at the cardinal-hued sky while my breath hissed through my teeth.

Get up, *that voice that wasn't entirely my own* commanded. Get up now.

CHAPTER THREE

I JOLTED awake from the nightmare in a cold sweat long before the sun rose and slipped from my covers, careful not to wake my father, who was still well and asleep in the bed next to mine.

Leaving our final clover by the book on his side table, I readied myself for the day and kissed him on the forehead before securing my satchel and dagger into their usual places at my side and thigh.

With a handful of ash from the fireplace, I made my way out the front door and to what remained of the creek to apply the thick coating over my eyes, using the reflection of the dwindling water to make sure I stayed far enough from my lashes.

I had done this more than enough to know it burned

like the fire it came from if I didn't—and instead of camouflaging you from the spirits in the wood, it rendered you useless in their presence.

When I was finished, I made quick work of the trail I had marked, gathering as much clover as my satchel would hold before I could draw any unwanted attention to myself.

By the time I returned from the forest's edge, the sun had begun to rise, peeking over the morning clouds and marking another day closer to the moon.

Readjusting the thin strap on my shoulder, I padded lazily down the path, skirting the wood with the words from my nightmare etched into the back of my mind— exhausted from the lack of sleep I had been getting.

Between the bad dreams and my father's late-night fits, pushing myself day in and day out with little food and water, maybe Fin and Knox had been right about me needing a break. Though, I couldn't help the knot that formed in my stomach for admitting it.

We all needed a break, not just me. Mine could wait as long as it needed to.

I wiped the sweat from my brow and headed for the traps I had set. The last two days, they had been empty, and I didn't expect much from them today because of the drought.

It was driving the small game deeper into the wood

and drying up what streams we had left near the village. Our garden would surely come up barren by the end of the next month if it kept up this way.

With what little coin we had left to pay for the village tithe, keep ourselves fed, and the others—my chest tightened.

We were cutting it too close this month.

I could sell more animal hides to strangers passing through the village, but I needed full traps to do so. Otherwise, I'd be left to rely on my poor bow and arrow skills on the other side of Terling, where women hunting was just as frowned upon as women wearing trousers.

I dropped my gaze to the dark blue pants that hugged my thin legs and the worn knee-high boots with mismatched laces and holes starting on the sides of the soles unable to remember a time I had ever dressed in the usual skirts Terling expected of their women.

Thankfully, my father had never enforced the dress code on me.

Lilac filled my lungs as the dirt path came to an end, and I spotted my first snare beneath a lingering, dried bush of browning leaves—triggered but empty.

I knelt to reset it, leaving behind a few fragrant berries I had collected from the wood as bait.

A few feet further, the next one held a furry creature

with a snapped neck. I collected it, then moved to the final traps, which were also full.

It wasn't a feast, but it was something to add to the stew in the coming days.

I threaded each tiny ankle with a thin string and bone needle, attaching the bundle to the loop on my bag before heading in the direction of home while I tried my best not to feel guilty, especially when there were villagers on the wealthy side of Terling who dared to hunt for sport, leaving carcasses behind for the birds to eat.

My stomach ached with hunger, reminding me that some death was necessary and not all of us had a choice in the matter.

I ran my thumb over the warm fur. The least I could do was make it quick for them.

Knox came into view when I rounded the wooden path, and a smile I couldn't stop spread across my face as I quickened my pace, trying not to look too eager to see him.

"What's the old man up to?" I asked as I hopped across the small creek and slipped between the petrified posts that needed replacing, undoing the knot and setting the bundle on the garden table alongside my satchel.

"He and Fin are off looking for water," he began inspecting my catch. "You did good."

"Let's hope they last longer than the last batch." I

looked over at the fading fruits and vegetables, which mirrored so many of the other gardens.

We were one of the smallest Mortal villages on this side of the wall—maybe smaller now with the annual drought going on. Serving meals during this time was something my mother and father did routinely before I was born, and something we've continued since I was old enough to carry a full pot on my own. I was proud to do it with him, even if that meant needing to learn something I was terrible at in order to keep doing so.

"Will you teach me to use your bow and arrows?"

His eyes narrowed. "You already know the answer to that."

I did, but I still hated asking him under the circumstances.

It was easy to see how much it weighed on him and my father that I had taken over the job of hunting for our families, though calling it that was generous.

My father couldn't do it safely anymore after last year's boar-hunting accident, and Knox… well, after what had happened, it was safe to say his right hand would never be the same. It was a permanent injury, much like the one my father's knee had sustained that day.

My nose scrunched as I thought of the grotesque sight, their twisted limbs barely hanging on by the skin.

It haunted my dreams often.

"The line has been getting longer in the evenings, or I wouldn't ask." I picked at the table, trying my best to fight off the heat rising in my cheeks. It wasn't often I had to ask for help. When I did, getting the words out was a chore.

"You know you just have to say the words, and I'll be there for you. *Always*." He stepped closer and leaned down to touch his forehead against mine, his short brown hair falling forward and tickling my brow.

I cleared the tightness from my throat and put some distance between us, not wanting to go down that road again, regardless of how good it felt to be close to someone.

"If I could do it with a sword or my dagger, I wouldn't need your help." I began picking at the table again, a poor attempt to distract myself.

"Now that I believe. But only because I was the one who taught you." He angled against the table and crossed his arms over his chest.

My fingers stilled, and I laughed aloud when his words sank in.

His brows knitted together and he stood straighter. "Shall I remind you?"

"No amount of reminding will do you any good." I

smiled. "I was clearly the one who taught *you* how to wield a sword."

He turned and picked up two of the rusty, blunt practice swords we often used before tossing me one.

"Prove it," he challenged with a teasing smirk.

I caught it by the handle and twisted it in a fluid movement to direct it at his chest. "Gladly."

In a quick motion, he knocked my blade away from him with the beat-up edge of his own. We sidestepped away from the table and playfully struck at one another. Edge to edge, the metallic clang rang out, sending dull vibrations down my wrist and to my elbow.

Another loud clash of metal and I had him nearly backed into the side of the cottage.

"Looking a little trapped," I taunted, my words greeted with a quick glance behind me.

I turned my head to see what had caught his attention, and he took advantage of the distraction, kicking out and knocking me onto my back. The breath left my lungs on impact with the ground, and I groaned, dropping my weapon at his feet.

"Rule number one. *Never* take your eyes off your opponent," he crooned. "Faye or Mortal. You're small. *Quick.* Let that be your advantage. Backing them into a wall won't do you much good unless you have muscle on your side."

"Thanks for the reminder." I rolled my eyes and got up to dust the dirt from my pants.

He caught me by the elbow and pulled me closer, stealing away any space between us as he swept my unbound curls over my shoulder, allowing me a rare glimpse of the scarring on his hand when he did.

"Knox." My breath caught.

I raised my hands to his chest, wanting his embrace more than I should, as I flexed my fingers against the muscle hidden beneath his shirt, remembering how good they had felt against my bare skin.

He leaned in, brushing his lips against my cheek with a cruel sweetness that spun my heart into uneven beats. "Do you remember when we would sneak off at night? We'd go to your favorite spot and name the stars for what seemed like hours."

I shook my head. Not because I didn't remember, but because I wished he would forget.

"You'd let me hold you like this." He nuzzled his face into my neck, and the scent of cedar hit me in an intoxicating wave. "Why did you stop? Stop letting me in? Stop letting me touch you?"

The answer wasn't simple.

We didn't have the luxury of being reckless anymore. We were adults with adult problems. When would our next meal come? How many mouths did we need to feed this week? How would we pay the tithe this month? And then there was the marriage contract my father had written out for a man who wasn't Knox, but for some stranger I'd likely never be able to let myself love.

"Meet me there tonight?" he asked. "Please."

I carried in the last batch of vegetables and meat for my father to add to the massive pot boiling over the fire, then sat down in the chair next to Finley while she counted coin from the pouch she kept tucked within the sash tied around her waist.

"Ten," she said with a wide smile, setting them aside in a pile on the tea table between us. "Six from my father and four from Knox for the wood. It should be enough for what the garden needs and then some."

I nodded, more concerned with how I had left things with her brother only hours ago. It wasn't often he stormed off the way he did when I turned him down on his offer. I cared about him… so damned much. I just cared for my father more and respected his choices even more than that.

Finley muttered my name, and I dragged my gaze from the fire to find her watching me, a puzzled expression on her face as she said, "I asked if you were okay."

"I'm fine." I cleared my throat and sat up straight. "Just tired."

"Did you have another one of those dreams about the man with the raven?"

"What man?" My father shot me a look that made my face flush.

"No," I clarified, staring at the uneven stone beneath my boots, half expecting to see the carnage from the battlefield that had woken me so early today. "Just a bad dream."

"I think your father's stories are finally getting to me, too." She laughed. "It's a good thing they aren't real. Otherwise, I'd be praying to the forgotten gods more often."

There was a long moment of silence in the room before Fin looked at my father, stirring absentmindedly as if he were in a world all his own. "Right, Glendin?"

"You two have nothing to fret about. The Old Kingdom has been gone for thousands of years. The stew is just about done, and then—" He looked over at me from his short stool in front of the pot. "Then—I think maybe..." The frustration grew on his face as he fought to remember what he was about to say.

"Then we will fill the pots Alma sent and take them to her shop," I supplied.

"Yes, now I remember. Eranthe, can you hand me my boots?"

Both mine and Finley's mouths gaped open and snapped closed just as fast.

"Father." I stood and went to his side, placing my hand gently on his shoulder. "It's me, *Riven.*"

He looked over my face, taking in my features.

"*Riven.* Right." He glanced back to the pot with saddened eyes. "You look just like her."

CHAPTER FOUR

The line was longer today. My back and feet had begun to spasm enough that Fin took my place outside, serving with Alma, while I sat inside, washing the pots and bowls they were done with until my fingers ached.

I had thought angry scrubbing might ease my frustration some, since Fin wasn't fond of sparring or swords, and sneaking off to the drinkery wasn't an option after she nearly burned the place down the last time we were there together.

I hadn't let her drink since.

I sighed through my nose and started on the next dish. It had been hours since I'd seen Knox around. I had hoped he would be done punishing me for turning him down by now. He had to see how silly this was when there was so much more to worry about.

My frown deepened as I stared down at the bucket of recycled water, considering the shape my father was in today.

He had never called me by my mother's name before.

I tossed my scrub brush into the bucket and wiped away the sweat at my temple. Maybe it was me being silly. Knox was a proper match. He wasn't a wealthy merchant, but he cared for me. We had more than enough history with one another for this to work. I needed to swallow my pride and bring the contract up to my father when his mind was clear this evening.

If he was so willing to make it, maybe he would consider a change in terms. Or rather, a change in groom.

The stack of clean dishes had grown taller than me by the time I placed the last one on top and joined Fin outside, where only a dozen or so people were still in line. "Have you seen your brother?"

"No. I think he said something about shooting his bow. Though, if you ask me, it's a waste of time. He hasn't been able to pull back the string on that thing since the accident." She handed off a bowl.

"The soil is just too dry to grow anything in." One of Alma's friends took a spoon from her hand.

"We're all struggling, Lou. We will get through this."

Alma smiled at him before turning to serve the man and woman standing close behind him. They were sallow, their bodies reduced to skin and bone compared to the last time I had seen them. After what they had lost on the Red Moon, I wasn't surprised. There was almost always an adjustment period for those targeted by the Faye.

"Henry." Alma touched the man's bony shoulder. "It's been a while, my friend."

He nodded but had no words for her. A man who was once so full of life and excitement for the future now looked vacant and empty, his eyes as dark as his wife's. They were just going through the motions now.

Understanding that this wasn't the time to catch up, Alma handed him and his wife a bowl of stew and watched as they disappeared into the evening crowd.

"That is what you ladies should be worrying about… not boys. The Red Moon is coming, and with it, those wretched creatures." She reached into her apron pocket and pulled out two small amber glass vials wrapped in black thread before shoving them toward us. "I want you two to take these. Place the contents at your threshold after you finish painting it. It will help keep them away."

I didn't have the heart to tell her the vials were mostly for show, nor did I have the heart to accept one. Each tiny glass bottle easily cost as much coin as Finley had set on the table earlier today.

"That's very generous, but I'm not sure—"

"Oh, hush." She stopped me with a sharp look. "You will take it and do as I say."

Finley stifled a laugh with her fingers and dropped hers into her apron pocket.

"You don't understand now because you're young. One day, you will." She grazed the front of her dress with her hand before serving another bowl to the next villager in line.

It was easy to forget that she had also been affected by the Faye's visits. Long before I was born, but just the same as the others.

Even if it didn't happen every Red Moon, it happened enough.

It was the reason we called it the Red Moon. Eight babes in my lifetime from our village alone, missing in the middle of the night. After a while, the tally begins to add up.

"My father will be thankful for the added protection. As am I." I offered her a small smile of gratitude and dropped it into my pocket.

"It looks like there's one more group left." Finley stood on her toes and looked at the bottom of the final pot, her golden braid falling over her shoulder as she did. "Good thing, too."

"I'll get them." I stepped in, dipping the ladle to

scrape what lingered at the bottom, filling each bowl while she and Alma began wiping down the serving table with damp cloths and stacking the remaining dishes to take inside.

Tired. I was so *damned* tired and ready for this drought to end.

"Thief!" A cry rang out. "Thief!"

No.

I dropped the ladle and quickly moved through the people drawn to the man holding a small child by the collar of his tunic.

"Unhand that child!" I demanded, my heart galloping as I pushed through to the front of the crowd he had coaxed into a frenzy. "He is no thief!"

"Oh?" The man grinned crookedly at Phineas, who twisted and turned desperately, attempting to get away from him. "Explain this then?" He held up a coin between two fingers for all to see.

"It's mine." Phineas pulled against his captor.

"I gave that to him. Just yesterday," I amended. "His mother is sick." My eyes darted around for someone to confirm they had seen the handoff. "You." I pointed to a shopkeeper who was only a few feet away when I put it into his pocket. "You saw me give it to him."

The man dropped his head, not wanting to be a part of this.

"You see. A thief!" he accused again, turning my stomach into knots while I looked for another face. *Any* face that could have seen me giving him the coin.

The crowd began to part for the one person I despised most in Terling, and my knees nearly buckled.

"What is your grievance?"

"This child tried to pay for bread with a stolen coin. I worked hard on that bread. I will not be taken advantage of by a thief."

Phineas wiggled loose, only to be snatched up by Jeremiah's leather-gloved hands.

"He is no thief. I gave him the coin," I repeated. Desperate for anyone to listen.

A cold glimmer of amusement flicked across Jeremiah's angular features, sending a shiver of disgust down my spine. "You just *gave* this boy a coin? In the middle of a drought?"

"I did." I stood as tall as I could for five feet and clenched my fists at my side. "You will not take his hand for my mistake."

"Does that mean you're offering your hand in his place?" He laughed darkly, not bothered by the fact it was a child he so callously spoke about.

I pressed my lips into a thin line to keep them from trembling, hoping someone would step in.

"Yes," I whispered when no one spoke up. Not even

those I had given the clothing off my back for. "Yes, I will."

Jeremiah let Phineas go and gestured to the wooden stand that stood only a foot from the ground. I waited for the boy to completely disappear into the crowd before I took my first step, my knees shaking beneath me.

The world went silent as I climbed onto the makeshift stand, keeping my eyes straight ahead and using every ounce of willpower I had to keep from vomiting.

Instead of the butcher's block, I was ushered once more by the judgment maker to the tall column that was erected just beside it—the whipping post.

When I hesitated, Jeremiah shoved me forward with a broad hand on my back, pressing my front flush against the jagged and marked-up wood where he bound my wrists with twine on the other side.

I rested my forehead against the rough grain and exhaled quietly. It was the only sound I could latch onto as I accepted my fate, and the small shakes in my knees turned into tremors.

When Jeremiah finished the final knot, he stopped just behind me and yanked my unbound hair from my neck, twisting it and letting it fall over my shoulder before he ripped violently at the laces on the back of my leather binding.

"I've waited for this day," he leaned in so that only I could hear him, "for any chance to knock you from that high horse you always seem to be riding. It's too bad my brother isn't here to see this."

A single, restrained tear fell down my cheek.

I wouldn't break. Not for him.

When he finished pulling my laces away, he let my binding fall to his feet and tore my worn tunic from nape to hem, revealing the untouched skin on my back.

"I'm going to enjoy this," he mumbled with rotten breath. "It's been a long time coming."

The scent of leather hit me at the same time as the whip, forcing a startled gasp from my lips.

One welt across my shoulder blades quickly became more as I held my breath, digging my nails into the wood where my hands were bound.

He lashed out again, and it felt like shards of glass cutting into me, leaving a stinging heat in their wake that webbed out in every direction.

Another smack of the whip, and murmurs began to erupt from the crowd.

I bit my lip as he hit me relentlessly, *spitefully*, drawing the faint taste of blood into my mouth as I hugged the post with everything I had.

It would be over soon, I told myself, repeating it

under my breath like a prayer of devotion. "It's almost over."

"My gods, no!"

I recognized Alma's voice just before a loud clash of dishes hit the ground, and another smack rang out.

The world began to move around me, and my grip on the post started to slip. Black spots filled my vision, and my knees went out.

It felt like a bolt of lightning struck my lower back, and I clenched my teeth, the ache in my jaw nothing compared to the fire searing across my spine.

When the next ill-placed whip landed, a raspy gasp tore from my throat.

"She's had enough!"

"Let her go!" The villagers shouted at Jeremiah, who struck me even harder for their protests.

Gags and whimpers erupted from the mass as he continued until my skin began to numb—taking on a strange sort of tingling I couldn't describe until I let my head slump, realizing my knees hadn't buckled.

My boots *slid* out from beneath me.

Jeremiah snapped my head backward from the post, his breathing labored as he gritted his teeth against one another. "Have you had enough?"

I should have said yes. I *should* have begged him to stop.

"Fuck you and your brother." I sucked in a breath and forced myself back up from my knees. Something only a fool would have done.

"So be it," Jeremiah said bitterly before dropping my hair and stepping back, landing a hard lash against my raw flesh.

Warm, wet blood filled my boots to the top, and the flesh on my back—it felt wrong. *Loose.*

The copper smell in the air turned my stomach and I retched to the side of the post, my face burning as I lifted my gaze to the crowd—a sea of pale faces that refused to meet my eyes.

Alma stood colorless as ever, just a few feet away from me, while two villagers held her back... or up. I think they might have been holding her up as I looked for Fin under weighted lids, hoping she was still in the shop washing dishes.

Relieved when I didn't see her, my eyes fell to the steady trickle of crimson dripping into the soil beneath the stand before I closed them entirely, pretending for a moment that I was sitting by the crackling fire back at the cottage while my father told me a story of magic—pretending until what came next felt real.

A clap of thunder that was loud enough to shake the earth split across the land... or maybe it was my knees again.

Hang on. Please hang on.

With another violent tremor, my senses nearly left completely.

A roof to my side caved in, sending debris into the air and scattering the crowd for cover as gray clouds approached.

Another shift of the soil beneath me had me falling to my knees, this time greeted by the silent warmth of darkness.

CHAPTER FIVE

It was all that I could remember as I fought consciousness. The screams for help and the names that were being called out as people searched for their loved ones in the chaos. It was as bad as any nightmare, this one feeling as real and raw as the rest of them that always found me in my sleep.

"Is she awake yet?" Knox's voice was rough as it cut through the dark.

"No. Not yet," my father answered, an immeasurable soreness gnawing at me while I listened, struggling to open my lids.

"She's healing fast. It's only been two days—"

"It's the clover," my father cut him off.

My eyes fluttered with another pitiful attempt to open them.

"I'm so sorry, Glendin. I should have been there. If I had been, I could have stopped this. I could have—"

There was a pause, then the sound of a chair groaning at my side.

"You brought her home. That's what matters."

I let their voices fade, let the remnants of a foreign place creep in as I fell deeper into the darkness. It was only a dream—a bad dream. And yet the place I found myself in felt so real, like a home I had never seen before but somehow knew was mine, one that eased the pain.

"Why here?" I looked out over the mountains draped in velvet night. It wasn't the field of purple I had become accustomed to or the raging waterfalls that drowned out my thoughts and worries.

This place was new.

I filled my lungs with its earthy scent, thankful he got to me before the nightmares could.

My fingers moved first, then my toes.

I flexed each digit back and forth until the feeling had returned in them, and then I inhaled deeply, as if it were the first breath I had taken in a long time.

When I found enough strength, I cracked my eyes open to the dimly lit cottage, finding my father sleeping in a chair pulled beside me. His soft snores filled the room as I tried to remember what had happened, taking my time as I sat up and inched closer to the edge of my bed.

Every movement I made was a sting or throb—a reality that what had happened to me wasn't just a bad dream after all. Still, I felt the wounds should have hurt more than they did.

I dangled my feet and stood, dizzy and nauseous, weakly gripping every surface I could reach as I made my way to what could scarcely be considered a mirror.

When I reached the tarnished silver, I was grateful it was all we owned and that we couldn't afford anything more as I looked into it, certain that a clearer image would be worse than the one that stared back at me.

My skin was paler than normal, my eyes sunken into dark circles, and my curls bound into a long braid that hung lifelessly over my shoulder—something my father must have done for me while I slept.

My chest tightened as I prepared for what I would see on my back, beginning to turn when a black bird flew through the cracked window, startling both me and my father as it flapped its massive wings around the cottage

—knocking over stacks of books and sending baskets of vegetables tumbling to the floor.

My father stumbled upright and shooed the bird away, not yet realizing I was no longer in the bed next to him until he laid his tired eyes on it—and then me, standing in nothing but a shift made from one of his better tunics.

"Thank the gods!" He rushed to my side as fast as his leg would allow and placed his hands around my arms, taking care not to touch my back before pulling me into a hug. "You're awake. My daughter is awake."

I tried to swallow back the dryness in my throat as I let myself melt into him, remembering only bits and pieces. "What happened?"

His dull eyes were shadowed by prominent, bushy gray brows as he stepped away.

He brushed a loose strand of hair from my ear and went to the tea table to pour water into a cup for me. I took it eagerly, drinking it down to the last drop, needing every bit of the relief it offered my throat.

"You wouldn't believe me if I told you. Come, have a seat so I can look you over."

Doing as he asked, I let my tunic drop enough to expose my back.

The bed slumped as he sat behind me, running his

fingers through a tin of green clover mashed into a thick paste that smelled of earth.

"This may burn a little," he warned.

The cold concoction touched my sore skin, drawing a hiss through my teeth and sending pebbles over me.

The raven, now perched on a wooden ceiling beam, cried out with a rustling of its feathers. Its caw loud enough to call *Death* himself near.

"Oh, hush," my father growled at the bird.

"Alma seems to be rubbing off on you after all of these years." I bit my lip, stifling a whimper as he peeled away a stretch of old clover from my puckered flesh to replace it with new.

"I tell you. That damned bird hasn't left your side in the two days you've slept."

Two days?

I tilted my head up, observing it from below its perch.

Its eyes were filled with white flames as it studied me with a certain amount of intelligence I wouldn't expect from an animal, its black-feathered head tracking my father's every movement as if it would nip one of his fingers off if he touched me in the wrong way.

Perhaps it was a creature of the wood.

"A bad omen, maybe?—You said I had been asleep for two days?" I glanced toward the front door of our cottage, cracked just enough to allow in some lighting from the moon.

The threshold had already been painted red with an offering of blood, and at the base lay the contents of herbs from the vial Alma had given to me.

Tonight was the Red Moon.

My father's hands stilled on my back, confirming our thoughts were the same on the matter.

I pulled my knees to my chest and rested my cheek against them, unable to feel any remorse for where my thoughts led me next. "Maybe Jeremiah will be the first to be struck down by whatever is coming."

The rubbing motion of his fingers slowed to a stop. "Jeremiah is—he's dead, Riven."

"*Dead?*" I scrunched my brows. "*How?*"

"I've only got bits and pieces to go by." He started on a stretch of skin lower on my back, the old paste sticking as he peeled it away.

I jolted, sitting up straighter and biting down on my knuckles to keep from crying out at the sensation.

"I'm so sorry, my love. I'm almost done, and then you can rest."

"Is Finley okay? *Alma?*" I questioned through hot tears that had begun to gather.

"They made it out safely." He closed the tin and set it on the table next to us. "Look at me, Riven."

I wiped my eyes and turned to face him.

"What happened was not your fault. I know you, and I know you will find some way to put the blame on yourself. Don't."

"What happened?"

He raked his fingers through his short beard, as he often did when deep in thought, and sighed heavily before bringing his sluggish gaze back to mine. "A storm erupted over the wall in the Faye Realm. It was strong enough to make the ground shake in the village. Buildings fell… not everyone made it out."

It felt like my heart was being squeezed by a vise. *How many had died?* "I thought I imagined it."

"I don't want you to blame yourself for their deaths."

I fought back the urge to do just that as I placed my hand over the ache in my chest, attempting to swallow the impossibly large lump in my throat.

They wouldn't have been there if it wasn't for me.

"Those people were there because they wanted to be. Nothing more, nothing less. It was Finley who got Knox. They carried you home, and I—" His voice cracked. This man who had been strong my entire life. Who I had never seen shed a tear was breaking apart before me. "I couldn't believe what I was seeing."

"I'm okay," I said, cupping his hands in mine. "I'm fine."

He shook his head and ran a thumb over my knuckles. "You're just as brave as your mother was."

"And as stubborn as my father," I added, hooking my arm around his, not meaning to burden him when he already had so much to worry about.

My frown deepened when I spotted the clover tin. *How much had he used on me in the last two days?*

"I'll go on a run for more clover tomorrow."

"Like hell you will. *Rest.* You are healing remarkably fast, but not that fast."

"What about the stew?" I asked, angling myself toward him. "People still need to eat. Now more than ever. We need to get out there and help them rebuild."

"The stew can wait. So can rebuilding. I am in no hurry to feed or help those who would turn their backs on my daughter when she needed them most."

I winced at his words.

"They had no choice." I was angry, too, but I knew it was misplaced. It was me or them. I didn't blame them for not stepping in. If they had, it would have only made things worse for everyone. Jeremiah would have made an example of them.

"Everyone has a choice, Riven. Try to get some more rest. I'll make you something to eat." He reached for his cane and stood, pulling back the blankets and ushering me to get under.

Settling onto my stomach, I rested my face against the pillow and watched him move around our small cottage—aware that our houseguest was inching closer to my bed with each passing second.

My lids grew heavy, and I nuzzled into my pillow with a yawn, feeling a light brush of feathers against my skin as the sheet was drawn over my shoulders, lulling me into a deeper, much-needed rest.

My knees buckled beneath me as the whip struck against my skin once more, and the world shuddered with me this time.

Clouds darkened over the forbidden wood, and streaks of bright light webbed down from the angry clusters.

Rain.

I had hoped for rain to wash the evidence away. My father rarely made it into town anymore. But this? I didn't want him to see this.

Another rumble, and the stand beneath me cracked in two, dropping me like a rag doll from a dog's maw. Shops and homes, big and small, collapsed around me as people scattered, their screams of terror nearly smoth-

ered by the dust and debris churning in a thick haze through the air.

Panic swelled in my throat. I couldn't move—not with my arms stretched tight in their binds, my body half-dangling from the sagging column.

Calloused hands grasped me by my face.

"I'm going to get you out of here. Just hang on." Knox began frantically picking at the twine digging into my wrist when another shop fell, pelting us with rock and splintered wood.

"No," I gasped. It was only a matter of time before the rest of the scaffold went down. "Run. Just run."

The storm's violence had intensified, destroying everything around us.

"Fin, hand me that piece of glass!"

Fin? No, no, no. She couldn't be here for this.

My head rolled back with another wave of darkness as he struck the rope with the jagged shard, freeing my hands.

I awaited the drop to the ground. It might have been kinder than the pain that followed when he caught me—his fingers digging into the slippery slope of my back, ripping a pitiful scream from my throat as my leaden eyes settled on Jeremiah, his body impaled through the stomach on a jagged board nearby while a raven pecked out the whites of his eyes.

A final gruesome image before I lost consciousness altogether.

Hang in there, Riven. Please hang in there.

I awoke hours later, drenched in sweat and unable to get the horrific images from my sleep out of my head.

Rubbing my eyes, I tilted my head to where my father slumbered deeply in the chair between our beds, a half-open book forgotten on his lap and a small bowl of stew with two pieces of dried meat resting on the side table.

My mouth watered at the sight.

I pushed off the sheet that covered me and climbed out of bed, swiping back the damp strands of hair that framed my face and retrieving a salty piece of meat.

My stomach ached with every slow bite I swallowed, reminding me it had been a while since I had gone so long without something to eat.

At least after two days of sleep, I was no longer exhausted.

I moved my shoulders to test the soreness in my back, surprised to find the pain gone and the skin mostly normal when I reached behind me to prod it with my fingertips.

There were sensitive welts, but nothing more.

The cottage door flung open, startling me as a warm breeze swirled dry dirt and cracked leaves across the stone floor at my feet.

I darted forward to close it, only to be stopped by a giant mass of feathers that dropped from the ceiling, landing in front of me and cocking its head this way and that.

"Shoo." I flicked my wrists at the thing. "Get out of here."

Another strong breeze made its way through the door, and a small figure on the other side of the dried creek bed caught my attention.

"*Phineas*?" I narrowed my eyes. It couldn't be. No one was allowed to leave their homes during the Red Moon.

The raven flew into my face, batting at me with its wings. By the time I pushed it out of the way, Phineas was no longer standing by the creek but much further away.

I ground my teeth. Leaving him out there would be a death sentence, and I didn't just get the whipping of my life for this kid to be eaten by a Faye on a Red Moon.

I quickly slid on my trousers, binding, and boots, tightened the laces over the loose tunic I wore, and strapped my blade into place on my thigh.

With a final glance at the snoozing man beside my bed, I stepped out into the silvery night.

CHAPTER SIX

I CALLED for Phineas from the tree line, my voice cutting through the stillness of the night as I scanned the shadows, cursing beneath my breath when I realized I'd forgotten ash.

I touched the clean skin on my face and forced down the fear gnawing at my stomach, knowing there was no time to return to the cottage. I had never stepped into the wood without it before, but tonight, I had no choice.

I breached the wall of twisted thorns and dead branches, a pit forming in my stomach as my boots crunched over a thick layer of brittle leaves and debris, long abandoned by the drought.

Wisps of murky black shadow coiled around me,

their tendrils shifting but not striking while I passed with careful steps, tracking the boy deeper into the wood—farther than I had ever gone before.

Not even the moonlight penetrated this part of the forest's canopy.

"Phineas," I whispered as he darted out of sight, my voice tangling in my throat when something rustled in the nearby brush.

My pulse raced as I pulled my dagger from its sheath, positioning it in front of me while I waited, edging toward panic.

I drew in a shallow breath, trying to stay composed, knowing that if I wanted to bring him home—if I wanted to get home myself—I had to keep calm.

My hands trembled as I focused on my surroundings, the darkness too thick to make anything out. If I was being stalked by a predator—or worse, a *Faye*—I was as good as dead.

I glanced back at the void I had come from and moved forward, unable to leave him—hating that I even considered it when he needed me.

He was just a boy. There had to be a reason he entered the wood on his own. Maybe he had been following something. *Food.* With his mother sick and his father gone, surely that was what he was doing.

Another rustle snagged my attention, and I froze.

Please don't be a Faye. Please don't be a Faye.

I might have had a chance against a boar or maybe even a large, vicious squirrel, but *not* a Faye.

Air whipped around me when a creature shot from behind a trunk and knocked me onto my ass, while feathers I recognized all too well flapped in my face.

"You damned bird!" I hissed through my teeth. "I almost killed you."

I glared at the creature as I got back to my feet, hardly able to see where its wings began and ended in the dark. Fortunately for me, the *eerie* glow from its eyes told me exactly where it stood.

I put my knife back in its place and knelt, not wanting to waste any more time as I pivoted forward, brushing the ground with light fingers until I found a child-sized boot print.

"If you're coming, let's go," I muttered to the bird, feeling slightly silly afterward.

We started in the direction of the print while the raven flew above me, close enough that, if I wanted to, I could reach out and touch it—or *wring* its neck for costing me precious time.

I jumped over a fallen log, my feet slipping out from under me and sending me sliding down an embankment on my side. Soil and leaves slid between my fingers as I dug in, trying to stop myself from landing in whatever waited for me.

My hip struck something hard, twisting my body before my head hit the bottom with a crack that reverberated through my skull.

Colors burst to life behind my eyelids, my ears ringing as I lay still. A minute went by—maybe more—before I opened my eyes and reached for the sharp pain to see how bad it was.

I winced when my fingers grazed a sticky gash in my scalp, then pressed against my hip. It hurt, but it wasn't broken.

Turning onto my side, I felt around with my palms. The surface felt like damp slate—possibly part of a dwindling creek bed.

Phineas moved through the trees only a few paces away, and I lurched forward onto my feet, breathing through the massive throb in my head as I sprinted after him on wobbly legs.

I dipped and dodged jagged branches that tugged at my hair and clothes, pushing myself harder than I ever had before, while the raven stayed with me through every leap and bound.

My breathing became ragged, and the pulsing in my head intensified as I continued, running until I found myself in a clearing that glittered in the moonlight.

"Phineas," I said a little too loudly, hoping I was close enough that he could hear me.

He couldn't be much further ahead. We could find shelter until the morning sun, when we had a better chance of finding our way home.

If it was food he was after, I would take Knox's bow out first thing. I wouldn't let him starve, and he had to be starving if he was driven to this madness.

If he didn't already have a mother, I'd berate him all the way home for this. She probably had no clue what he was up to right now. Though I imagined I would have done the same if the situation called for it.

I just wished he had come to me before pulling something like this.

I stopped when I lost him again and rested my hands on my knees while I attempted to catch my breath, each inhale stinging with the rapid rush of air.

The bird settled nearby on the ground, picking at its feathers like the last few miles had been nothing but a minor inconvenience for it, while I wiped the sweat from my forehead with the back of my hand.

Morning would be here soon. I had to keep going.

The ground changed beneath my boots with my next step, no longer firm but springy.

Before I could move back, it gave out with a loud wooden crack that echoed through the lingering night.

This time, I only fell a few feet, landing in a shallow pit that reeked of decay. Not lilac, but the putrid stench that came long after, when death had worn out its welcome.

The walls and ceiling of the cavern were woven with sinuous roots and ivy that glittered like something from one of my father's books—illuminated by the silvery rays pouring down from above me.

Mystified by my surroundings, I began to reach for a long, gleaming strand—but my arm didn't budge.

I tensed, attempting again with the same result.

Realizing I was stuck in a bed of stickiness, the odd string holding me captive, I worked it loose until my arm slid free, freezing when something shifted in the patches of darkness near my legs.

The raven circled erratically overhead, and I decided I had overstayed my welcome. Pretty or not, it was time to go.

I snatched my dagger from its sheath and sawed at the silken binds restraining me, shredding what was left near my arm and moving to the sticky pieces at my waist when it finally dawned on me where I was.

My palms slicked with sweat as a long claw, lined with tiny barbed hairs, emerged into the light—followed by two more, each easily the size of my arm.

This wasn't a scenario from my father's books, but

from the horror stories villagers told their children to make them behave.

Just a little further. My eyes widened, and my chest tightened as the skull-weaver inched closer.

I yanked one leg free. *One more,* I told myself. *Just one more leg.*

The skull-weaver exhaled, and it became apparent where the overwhelming scent had come from, as black dots of various shapes and sizes began crawling toward me atop the sticky web.

"Shit, shit, *shit!*" I cut through the last strand and hauled myself toward the opening, tugging at weak roots that couldn't hold me.

I tried again, digging the toes of my boots into the wall and heaving myself over the lip as pain erupted over my thighs.

Scrambling to my feet, I swatted at the creatures— crushing some beneath my palms while others dropped to the ground and fled back to their colony.

I changed my mind about giving Phineas an earful. He would *never* hear the end of this.

A gust of wind ruffled my braid over my shoulder, and I flinched when the sensation mimicked tiny legs crawling across my skin.

"Thanks for the help," I said sarcastically as the raven landed at my feet, tugging strands of webbing from my hair before sliding my dagger back into its sheath. "We need to get going—we've been in the same spot for far too long."

A glance back at the pit I had just fought my way out of was more than enough to get me moving again, though a bit slower than before.

My joints were stiff, and my head was still pounding from the knot behind my ear. If there was any clover left when we made it back to the village, I'd need one or two to chew on until I felt better. If not, I shuddered slightly with the thought I'd need to come back to this gods-forsaken place.

I blinked away the blurriness encroaching on my vision as everything seemed to come alive before me, the trees swaying closer while I fought back the urge to vomit.

Each step felt like the ground tilting beneath my boots, shifting on its own as I dragged myself forward, reaching out to steady myself when the world suddenly turned upside down.

For a moment, I was among the stars and the moon, staring in awe at the treetops below me.

Then, I was on my face with a hard thud, inhaling the festering smell of the forest floor with flimsy breaths.

I couldn't move, not even to offer a snarky remark to the bird flying circles above me.

Time seemed endless as I imagined myself home again, lying on my stomach and watching my father prepare dinner for us. It would have been our first meal —just the two of us—in longer than I could remember, and I missed it. I had slept through it.

My stomach ached as I pictured him asleep in the chair beside my bed and the horror he must have felt when Knox and Fin brought me home unconscious and shredded to ribbons.

Knox. I closed my eyes, conjuring up the scent of cedar, a much better alternative to the soil in my nose.

I imagined him like I so often did, dirty, sweaty, *shirtless.* Chopping wood outside his cottage with an all-too-knowing grin on his face while I watched from afar, propped up on our porch and pretending to rope together pieces of the snares I planned to set that day.

He knew as well as I did that I didn't need to. I simply enjoyed the show he put on for me.

Exhaling softly into the leaves, I remembered that I never got the chance to ask my father about the marriage contract. Now, I didn't think I'd get that chance.

I supposed none of that mattered now that I was face-down in the middle of the forbidden wood, unable to move. There was no need to worry about a future that would never come to pass.

The soreness in my bones deepened into a relentless

throb and my limbs grew impossibly stiff the longer I lay still—cold, even—hardly feeling the tiny feet that landed on my shoulder, or the surprisingly soft beak that rubbed against my cheek.

I didn't know why the bird insisted on staying with me, but I didn't complain. I was grateful not to be alone.

CHAPTER SEVEN

THE SKULL-WEAVER'S limerick played on repeat in my head for what felt like hours.

After all these years, I had nearly forgotten it—*funny,* considering it was one of the ones that had stood out to me most as a child.

As an adult, I came to believe that the stories of what lurked in the deepest parts of the wood were just as much of a farce as the forgotten gods we no longer prayed to— or at least, that's what I had told myself until now.

There were renderings of the creatures in books that had slipped through the cracks—tomes from an age-old history the council had worked tirelessly to erase.

They were easy to dismiss when they only seemed to exist in outlawed texts.

Once, I had glimpsed an illustration that depicted the creatures with long, sharp nails used to strip flesh from bone. They had black, depthless eyes that lured you closer to their gangly, humanoid bodies, and were said to be capable of destruction with a mere snap of their fingers—or so the texts claimed.

But no one truly knew, and the council preferred to keep us in the dark about what existed beyond our borders, for reasons no one ever dared to question.

Of course, those who entered the wood in desperation for food and were fortunate enough to return were smart enough never to speak of what they had seen, for fear of the council's wrath.

And those who were visited on the Red Moon didn't have the heart to recall what had happened.

Neither were ever quite the same afterward.

They whispered to themselves when no one was looking and stared into the tree line as if they could see something on the other side that the rest of us couldn't.

In time, they either took their own lives or fell into the hands of Jeremiah—both paths leading to the same fate of an untimely death.

The stories my father told me about what resided beyond our borders were different, though.

They were tales passed down in his family for generations—stories of a time when Mortals and Faye were equals in an ethereal realm of beauty and riches before a great wall was built to separate us from the Old Kingdom.

Even the wealthiest side of Terling didn't compare to what he described: a whole race that thrived in luxury while Mortals withered away, their skin tough as leather and their bones brittle from starvation.

People begged in the streets for moldy bread and tainted water just to survive.

No. I couldn't bring myself to believe in the Faye as he did, not when I had seen firsthand what they were capable of on the Red Moon.

We all had, even if it was never openly spoken about.

Whatever existed beyond our borders was exactly as the texts had described—*monsters.*

The raven curled itself against me.

I wanted to shoo it away, to tell it to fly off and save itself. It had to know that staying here with me was a death sentence. If the shadows or the skull-weaver didn't come to finish the job, then surely a wicked Faye with an unyielding appetite for Mortal flesh would.

I blinked against the grittiness in my eyes from being open so long and imagined what the wall might look like. I had traveled so deep into the wood, it had to be close.

The raven ruffled its feathers against my neck, and a

strange feeling rolled over me—tugging me in a direction away from here.

I followed the mental tether to a landscape of lush greenery and darkened mountains speckled with rock, rising higher than anyone could ever climb.

A deep chasm, bathed in starlight, split them down the middle, where water cascaded with such force it roared into a glistening lake below.

In the distance, twinkling lights flickered in shades of orange and yellow.

And the scent—my mouth watered. It was decadent. Fresh and earthy, yet also spicy and sweet.

My lids fluttered lazily. My entire body felt like ice beneath a slow-setting fever that burned my skin.

It was the skull-weaver's poison.

I had gotten out of several bad situations in my life, but this didn't seem to be one of them.

Perhaps that was why he had taken me back to the place from my dreams. He was giving me a chance to feel at peace one more time.

A faint flame caught my attention from afar, peeking through the contorted trunks and dense brush. I was certain it was the fever playing tricks on me—until it came close enough to touch, if I had been able to move.

"Well, now," an aged voice said, setting my bird into an uproar. "This just won't do."

The moon was hardly visible in the purple hues of encroaching dawn, its light washing over the forest as I forced myself to swallow, unsticking my tongue from the furry feeling against the roof of my mouth.

I drew in a deep breath and turned my head toward the warmth at my side, where a small fire burned—and then I remembered…

"Phineas!" I shot up, startled when I saw that I wasn't alone.

"Hush, girl. You'll wake the shadows," a female with a deep, gravelly voice snapped from beneath a hood.

I watched carefully as she dropped a handful of ingredients into a cup, stirring them before making her way around the fire to sit on the stump next to me.

"Drink this." She extended the concoction for me to take. "It will rid you of any poison left from the bites."

My eyes narrowed on the withered hands gripping the cup tightly. I had seen this woman before. *Served* her. "Who are you? Why are you helping me?"

She set the cup down in the dirt beside me when I hesitated, and pulled back her maroon hood, revealing wild white hair and a smooth yet wrinkled complexion. Her eyes were milky with age, her lips thin and pale, creasing at the corners as she said, "It depends on who you're asking. Some say I'm the whispers they hear in the wind. Others believe I'm the bringer of curses and death."

"Which is it then?"

Her mouth curved into a brittle smirk. "To you? An ally."

"Why are you in the forbidden wood?"

"It is my home." She picked up a stick and poked at the fire. "Now, drink. You were bitten numerous times."

I reached down and picked up the cup, holding it under my nose and smelling the greenish liquid before taking a test sip.

Clover. I sighed with relief, gulping the rest down my throat, nearly choking myself in the process.

I was so thirsty. It could have been poisoned, and I'm not sure I would have cared.

The stiffness in my joints and the pain in my head disappeared almost immediately, offering me the first bit of reprieve I'd had since entering this damned wood.

"You're looking for something?" The woman leaned in closer and propped her bony elbows atop her cloaked knees.

Pulling the now-empty cup from my lips, I nodded. "Someone."

"Yes." She grinned again and pointed toward the

wood. "He's that way. He's been looking for you too. For some time, I'd say."

I slid my gaze in the direction she pointed and abandoned the cup.

My legs wobbled as I stood, eager to get to Phineas so that we could finally go home. "Thank you for your aid. I will not soon forget it."

I let myself adjust to the lingering darkness around us, leaving the mysterious woman behind and stepping back into the dense foliage.

It didn't take long before the raven swooped down to hover over me, then flew ahead as if checking for obstacles I'd most likely fall into.

Rolling my eyes, I smirked, deciding the creature was beginning to grow on me as I leapt over a fallen log and pushed my way through an endless stream of trees— so tall no one would believe me if I told them.

My thighs burned and sweat dampened my skin as I pressed forward until I came to a halt on an overgrown dirt path, once wide enough for wagons and horses.

I turned in place, scanning for any potential traps or signs of Faye before continuing down the trail, where saplings and weeds sprouted from the grainy dirt.

The road widened the farther I went—until it ended, and I stood at the edge of the wood.

My lips parted as I stared out at vibrant green hills

and clusters of trees bathed in the warm hues offered by the morning sky.

A flock of cream-colored birds flew in tandem in the distance, dancing within the light that peeked through impossibly large clouds.

Below, dew clung heavily to the blades of green grass, and a light mist hung in the low dips and valleys, untouched by the pollution of man.

I dragged my attention away from the land and to Phineas, who had breached the tree line.

When I raised my foot to cross over the misshapen stones and go after him, my ears began to buzz, my lungs seized, and a metallic sweetness stung my senses.

"What in the hell?" I gripped my chest with a startled gasp and stumbled back.

My companion dropped down beside me, shaking its head and flapping its midnight feathers. No doubt a warning, I had no choice but to ignore if it meant reaching Phineas.

I looked at the sky. The moon had almost completely vanished, along with any trace of night. We would be safe from the Faye on our way home, at least... *hopefully*.

Holding my breath, I tried again.

I stepped over the ankle-high line of rock, triggering another awful metallic burst on my palate that disappeared once I had crossed over completely.

Phineas broke into an all-out run toward a grove of trees, and I went after him, not caring who or *what* saw us as I left the bird behind.

I had been after this boy for hours. Injured and bitten. My stomach ached with hunger, and I was parched with thirst. And we *still* had to worry about how we would find our way back home after all of this.

He better have one hell of an excuse.

I followed him down a hill, digging my heels in so I wouldn't slide in the morning condensation that blanketed the grass.

"Phineas, stop!" I shouted, losing sight of him in the grove of trees.

CHAPTER EIGHT

STAIRS LAY SUBMERGED in a crystal-clear lagoon, leading up to a cracked stone landing surrounded by fluted pillars and the remnants of a broken glass dome—hidden beneath the dense canopy I had followed Phineas into.

The weathered marble was drenched in sparkling light, smothered by ivy threaded with vibrant pink and white roses that crept over every inch of its surface.

At its center stood a half-crumbled statue of a woman, her hand clasped over her heart—*forgotten*.

Like the wood, this place was utterly silent.

Not even the water dared to ripple in my presence as I skirted the lagoon's edge and made my way to the far side, where the greenery thinned to reveal an ancient wall and a rusty gate that barely clung to its hinges.

Beyond it, another structure waited, abandoned to time.

A streak of red darted across my vision and into the side entrance that hardly looked solid. I barked a curse and slipped through the gate, navigating rubble and debris as I bolted down the overgrown path after the boy, drawing my dagger when I reached the spot where he had vanished.

My grip tightened around the hilt as I inched into the dim space, whispering Phineas's name while steadying myself with one hand against the rough stone.

My voice echoed back, and I hesitated—for the briefest moment—considering turning away and leaving him to figure this out alone.

Children went missing in the forbidden wood all the time. By now, we had to be close enough to the wall for the Faye to scent us, and though I didn't know exactly how it worked, no one would fault me for returning empty-handed.

The thought made bile rise in my throat. How could I contemplate something so hideous?

His mother would never forgive me if I left him—I'd never forgive myself.

I was letting my fear get the better of me. He had to be confused and turned around. He knew I was coming for him—the woman in the wood had said so herself.

Leaving him wasn't an option, even if he didn't know it.

The wall left my hand, and the passageway split into two paths. One was dark and musty, and the other was lit toward the end. That was the path I took, hoping Phineas had done the same.

The closer I got to the light, I recognized it as a lit candle, followed by a second and a third sitting in a thick pool of wax that dripped down the recess of the eroding wall it sat in.

I made my way up block stairs that gave way to daylight and a pointed archway at the top, my breath catching as I took in the circular courtyard below.

Arches like the one I stood beneath repeated around the chamber's edge, framed by fluted columns and whitewashed stone banisters climbing with the same ivy and roses from the lagoon.

Among the soft blades of grass, a faint dusting of rock and shimmering glass from the shattered ceiling glittered, leading up to what resembled a throne carved from the same gold-veined stone as the rest of the dwelling.

My heart skipped with the realization that I was standing in the ruins of a once-great castle.

Fin was going to lose her shit when I told her about this.

I jerked my head toward the sound of footsteps and followed them through a narrow opening and down a long corridor, stopping beneath an archway nestled next to more stairs, illuminated by daylight that diffused down from a glass ceiling much like the one before.

This one was still intact.

The massive iron-welded panes domed high above the room, mimicking the first in everything but shape—*clearly,* there was a theme in this place.

I froze when I heard tense voices down below.

Peeking around the edge of the archway and over the banister, I saw dozens of men and women sitting in high-backed chairs positioned around a man who reclined in a carved seat of jagged obsidian—a throne as out of place in this room as he was.

"And what makes you think we will go along with this?" A man with short brown hair and deep bronzed skin thick with muscle stood. His voice boomed with authority over the room. "What makes you think we will give our fealty over to you so easily?"

"What makes you think you have a choice?" the man on the throne responded, stroking a pale finger over the jagged scar traveling from the top of his left eyebrow down to his cheek.

A woman, decorated with inky designs on her rich brown skin and long silken black hair twisted into a braid, stood next to him, her hands clasped tightly in front of her emerald floor-length gown. "I agree with Phelan. How do we know you are who you say you are? The gods have been gone for some time now, as has the Old Kingdom. Some would go as far as to consider them a tall tale."

Phelan quirked his lips to the side before sitting back down in his seat, and the man on the throne took the floor next, fixing the sleeve of his pristine white tunic while he eyed the woman. "Let me remind you of the one true power. The rightful power your ancestors before you were all so quick to forget after the Great War."

His eyes darkened to an impossible shade, and the room fell silent.

Without warning, that same sweet, metallic feeling from before unfurled over me with such force, I thought I might curl onto the ground and vomit.

I pulled myself behind the safety of the archway and cupped my hands over my ears—the buzzing so loud that I thought I might scream.

My lungs felt like they would collapse in on themselves if it lasted a second longer.

Closing my eyes tightly, I swallowed back the bile creeping up my throat, the base of my skull prickling with the sensation that was slow to fade.

When it disappeared completely, I sucked in a deep

gulp of air, steadying myself as much as I could before it happened again.

The woman was seated when I glanced back around, and any trace of amusement or doubt in the room had vanished.

Had they felt it, too?

I wasn't sure what I walked into, but I was certain I wasn't meant to be here witnessing it. Nor did I want to go through another round of crippling suffocation again.

Phineas wasn't here.

I could backtrack my steps and go in a different direction until I found him… hopefully without getting caught.

I began to turn toward the stairs, only to find myself stuck, my boots refusing to budge even as I reached down and tugged at them. My eyes narrowed with alarm when nothing visible seemed to be holding me in place.

"Now that this is settled, our honored guest has finally arrived," the man with the scar announced.

When I looked up from my boots, I found his attention wasn't the only one on me.

"I—" My voice was tight as I straightened, nervously running my hands over the wrinkles of my tunic. "I'm sorry. I didn't mean to interrupt. I'm looking for someone. A boy."

"This boy, you mean?" The man dressed in all white

waved his hand, and Phineas appeared in front of him. My jaw went slack. "He's simply a figment meant to bring you to me."

With another roll of his hand, the image of Phineas rippled like a drop of water in a puddle before disappearing without any trace.

I clamped my mouth closed and glanced around the room at the people, unfazed by what had unfolded.

They were exquisitely dressed, sophisticated in their movements—thin, with straight backs and clean skin, flawless in every aspect.

I thought back to each path I took in the wood and out of it.

I hadn't passed over the wall... had I?

I touched the tender spot behind my ear, wincing when my fingertips made contact with the swollen scalp. *Maybe I hit my head harder than I thought I did.*

"How?" I asked, finally. "*Why?*"

"Magic." He scoffed, as if that answered all my questions.

Boots scuffed lazily against the stone at the top of the stairwell where Phelan appeared, surveying me from head to toe as if I were an oddity he'd never seen before.

The binding that held me in place unraveled as I took a step back, bumping into the vine-wrapped banister when I did.

He was beautiful—in an *alarming* sort of way. Tall with broad shoulders. A faint trace of frown lines etched into his stony features as he looked down at me.

With a tilt of his head, he jerked his stubble-covered chin toward the other end of the walkway, urging me to follow him.

It was then that I saw them. The small movement of misplaced hair exposed the delicate points of his ears. Not Mortal—*Faye*.

I sucked in a sharp breath, my eyes widening on the creature that moved with the fluidity and grace my father spoke of so ardently.

The grasp on my dagger was tight enough that the wooden handle beneath the leather creaked underneath the pressure.

Phelan looked nothing like the renderings in the sketchbooks—no hunched back, gangly limbs, razor-sharp teeth, or claws…

Yet I knew in my gut he was just as deadly as they had portrayed.

"Do I scare you, Mortal?" He turned when I didn't follow, raising a thick, dark brow. "Keep your dagger if it makes you feel better. You cannot harm us with it."

"I wouldn't be so sure about that," I said tightly before taking a wary step forward and sheathing the blade, silently praying to the forgotten gods to protect me as I followed the male down the spiral steps toward the main floor, where the others waited.

Some of the creatures were what I imagined true royalty to look like, while others were hardened and muscular with signs of conflict left behind on their skin and long elegant swords strapped at their waists.

I dragged my eyes away from theirs and stopped in front of the man... the *male*—close enough now to truly see him.

He was more than the jagged pink scar marring his pale face.

His coal-colored hair hung in limp strands that spilled over squared shoulders, and in the sharp ridge of his brow and the hollow of his cheeks lingered the traces of a male who might once have been handsome.

"I thought you would be taller. What is your name, girl?"

I considered my next words carefully as I tightened my fists at my sides. If these were indeed Faye, all they needed was a name to trick and enslave.

A name was as strong as any bind.

"Eranthe," I lied.

The male narrowed his eyes and smirked. Depraved and unkind. A smirk that made my knees want to tremble. "Lie to me again, and it will be the last thing that you do."

I bit down on the inside of my cheek, standing straighter.

"Do you normally threaten your *honored* guests?" I questioned unevenly as I eyed the exits of the room.

Two sets of gargantuan doors I doubted I'd be fast enough to make it to. Grand spiral stairs in each corner of the room that led up to the second-floor walkway I just came from… and a *shit* ton of Faye.

I wasn't going anywhere. Not right now.

"Your name?" the male growled through clenched teeth.

"My name… is *Riven*," I shot back, resisting the urge to cower.

"Now, that wasn't so hard, was it?"

He turned, ascending the three stairs to the crooked throne before sitting upon it.

"You can call me Demetrius. Though, I prefer Commander." He paused. "Do you know why I've brought you here, Riven?"

Without giving me a chance to answer, he continued, "You have something that is rightfully mine. Something that should have been given to me thousands of years ago. I have earned it ten times over."

He leaned forward, the blunt tops of his ears showing through the black panels of his hair.

"You are mistaken." I pinned my focus on him. "I don't have anything that isn't mine."

"Oh?" he countered. "But I can smell it on you."

I pinched my brows together, unable to hide the apprehension on my face as I began to back away from him. "Again, I say, you are mistaken, Commander."

In an explosion of movement, he stood before me, seizing my head tightly between two hands and lifting until a ragged scream ripped from my throat.

Pain—sharp, searing pain threaded with metallic—threatened to tear me apart from the inside out.

My vision blurred as he dangled me in the air, unbothered as I kicked my legs into his stomach, ripping at his tunic with my nails until it was nothing more than pieces.

This was no dream.

I wasn't passed out in a creek bed from hitting my head.

This was real—and I was fucked.

Demetrius released me, and I dropped to the floor, landing on my hip with a force that felt as if it would shatter.

Sweat and tears gathered on my face as I crumpled over, inching away while my heart pounded painfully in my ribcage, beating at an unbearable rate.

I tried to lift myself—tried to wedge my leg beneath me—only to collapse.

My cheek smacked against the ground, and a shuddering breath escaped me.

Every ounce of my strength was gone.

"If you don't give it to me willingly, I'll have to take it by force."

I twisted onto my back with a shriek, locking my jaw and clenching my fists when it felt as if I were being crushed by an invisible force—as if my spine were being ripped out through my chest.

My vision began to spot as I screamed, *begging* for anyone to help me. To stop this.

CHAPTER NINE

A FLURRY of commotion erupted around me, shouts breaking out across the room while I focused on the hard floor beneath my limp body, fighting to steady my breathing.

My lips prickled as I gasped up at the glass dome, my gaze lingering on the beams of sunlight that shone through.

The rapid pulse of my heart filled my ears and drowned out the discord as I drifted in and out, letting my eyes rest while I conjured things that would bring me comfort, hoping and praying they would help me get through this.

I imagined Knox sitting beside me on a blanket,

tossing ripe berries into his mouth with laughter while Finley picked at the spring flowers in her favorite dress.

I thought of my father sitting near the fire, warming his toes as he smoked a tobacco pipe after a long winter day—Alma's sweet rolls on the table beside him, made every Solstice.

The rhythm in my chest began to even out as I dragged myself over to my side. I didn't know what was happening, only that Demetrius's concentration was no longer on me.

If I could get up while they were distracted, I could make it back to the stairs—to the tunnels.

I slid my elbow beneath me and tried to lift myself again when the room began to spin—my chin smacked the floor, and I bit into the flesh of my tongue.

My mouth filled with the tang of blood as I settled on staying in place, concentrating on the patchy shapes of color as their movements came to a halt instead.

"I was wondering when you would show up," Demetrius spoke, his words muffled. "It seems you like to make an elaborate entrance, much like myself."

I squinted at the fuzzy dark figure stepping closer, kneeling to cup my jaw in the warmth of his hand.

His fingers burned like flames licking against my skin as he tilted my face upward, a low hum rumbling from him that sent every tiny hair on my body rising in response.

"I don't appreciate being summoned, Demetrius," he muttered, his voice like a balm, laced with velvet night.

"Good. So, you know who I am, and I know who you are." Demetrius sighed. "We have much to discuss."

I closed my eyes and let myself melt in the male's hand, no longer having it in me to hold my own weight as his thumb smoothed over the blood trailing down my chin, offering me a shred of comfort before he removed it.

"There is only one thing I am here to discuss with you," the male said sharply before standing. "I want her for myself."

Demetrius roared with laughter. "The girl is mine, as is the power she holds."

"She is nothing more than Mortal trash. She holds no power. You cannot keep us here, Commander," the strong voice of a female hurled back. "We are kings and queens. Do you not think our kingdoms will come looking for us if we do not return?"

"I will say this only once, Feronia—she is anything but Mortal trash. And for those of you who haven't realized it yet, you hold no power here. Your magic and titles became useless the moment you stepped into these ruins. You cannot harm me, you cannot stop me, and you cannot leave until I will it. We remain until she forfeits her power. Only then will we enter a new era of reign—one that each of you will witness firsthand. You will recognize me as King, or you will suffer the consequences. That includes you, *Alekxander Nightfall*. Test me again, and I don't care how old you are—your head will sit on a pike beside my throne."

A slight breeze brushed against the sweat on my cheek, lifting the damp curls stuck to my temple as a hand wrapped tightly around my ankle. It squeezed painfully with fingers that were contorted and sharp before dragging me across the stone, my arms trailing lifelessly above my head.

"Make her comfortable, Vassal. We may be here for a while."

I scrunched my nose when a rotten smell hit me and opened my eyes to the warm darkness stirring at the edges of my vision.

My head throbbed as I wiped the straw from the drool on my mouth and blinked into the cavernous space of brick and mortar—a single cell bound by iron slats and a rusty lock.

Groaning through the ache in my bones, I pushed

myself upright and let my gaze adjust to the dying flicker of the candle burning just beyond the bars.

There was no bed, no wash tub, no bucket… I sucked my bottom lip between my teeth and pulled my knees to my chest, unwilling to believe it.

None of this felt real.

I went over everything I could remember: Phineas was a figment. Magic existed. Faye, too. I had something in my possession that was thousands of years old, and it belonged to the Commander.

There was a conversation. I barely heard any of it— just bits and pieces.

The room was so tense, and then… I gingerly touched my jaw, dropping my hand to my thigh to feel for the hilt of my dagger and patting my only two pockets next. Both were empty.

I wore nothing in my hair—not even the tie I had arrived with. It must have fallen out at some point.

I glanced around my cell again, and my throat grew tight.

This had to be a mistake. It *had* to be. I slid my feet underneath me and stood, wobbly and bruised, able to see other cells like my own—four more on the opposite wall, each with flat beds hanging from chains and doors closed with padlocks.

"Hello?" I whispered into the empty space.

A tear ran down my cheek, dripping from my blood-crusted chin as I rested my forehead against the metal bar and gripped the iron posts firmly with each of my hands.

I had to find a way out of here. My father needed me. He needed clover, and I was the only one who could get it.

My lips trembled.

He'd be worrying himself sick about me by now, wondering what happened and where I went off to in the night. Knox and Fin, too.

The dungeon door scraped against the floor, and I stumbled back a step from the cell bars, wiping away the dampness on my face and pulling my dagger with a sniffle.

It might not be able to kill them, but maybe it would be what I needed to get free.

I'd aim for the heart. That would hurt anyone, regardless of who… or *what* they were.

The male figure stopped at the edge of the light, the glow from the candle revealing a slight tilt of his head as he studied me from where he stood in front of the open door.

All I had to do was strike true and run for it. I could do this. I *had* to do this if it meant I'd see my home again.

I adjusted my grip on the blade, the hilt creaking

beneath my fingers as I held it tightly. "Are you going to show yourself or just gawk at me eerily from the shadows like a creep?"

"So eager to get yourself killed," he purred, and my lips twitched with disgust as the sound traveled the length of my spine.

"I could say the same to you," I countered with a raw throat, knowing damn well I had never killed anything other than an animal before.

He stepped into the pulsing light, and my lips parted as the darkness came with him, wafting around his body as if it were somehow a part of him.

His eyes slid over me with a painful slowness that set me on edge as he pressed his hands into his pockets, undoubtedly considering me a puny Mortal in comparison.

I wondered if Faye also had terror-filled stories of us or if they simply enjoyed the thrill of tricking and eating us when we mistakenly traveled too far into the wood.

Beautiful or not, I wouldn't let them fool me... any more than they already had.

"The Commander requests your presence." He pulled a ring of old keys from his pocket and unlocked my cell door, unbothered by the dagger in my hand. "Let's not leave him waiting—"

I leapt from the balls of my feet when the door swung

wide, slamming it into his chest before darting for the stairs. Taking two at a time, I reached the top and headed down a massive corridor lit by gilded candelabras and sconces.

The walls towered high above me, lined with detailed tapestries of rust and navy, the space strewn with furniture and art I could have stared at for hours if I weren't in the middle of a grand escape.

Accents being the least of my worries, I slipped into the first room I came across, relieved to find a window cracked open inside.

My hands trembled as I closed the door behind me, snatched up a short stool, and shoved it beneath the ledge.

Gods, I was almost free.

I had just begun to climb when I was yanked back by my arms and slammed against a shelf, hissing through my teeth as the wooden slats dug into my bare shoulder blades—a wall of muscle pinning me in place.

This male—this *thing*—wasn't even bothered by the wound seeping cardinal red from his exposed chest as he caught my wrists, gripping them both in his hands and securing them to my sides so I couldn't move.

"Let go of me!" I demanded through my teeth, attempting to squirm free.

His fingers bit deeper into my skin, keeping me in

place as his lips quirked to the side with amusement at my absurdly pointless effort.

"Do you know who I am?" His breath tickled my face as he leaned closer, his lazily buttoned tunic revealing more of the damage I'd done.

"No," I panted wildly, not giving a damn about who he was as I met his silver-flecked eyes with my own, their severity like nothing I'd ever seen.

"Let me go," I snapped, regaining myself. "You disgusting—"

The shadows around him flared to life, caressing broad shoulders and a muscular frame that had me clamping my mouth closed.

His jaw hardened as he followed my jerky movements with his own, keeping me tucked in place against the shelves.

"You don't want to go out there," he said evenly.

"And why the hell not, you prick," I seethed, knowing my father would be damned proud that I fought until my last breath.

He leaned closer, his grin disappearing into a blank façade.

"What you'll find out there is much deadlier than what lives in the wood. Especially at night. If you don't run into a diamoria first, you'll likely run into something that prefers to take its time with its meals."

I pinched my lips together and forced my eyes from the hold of his to the opening of the window. The wood wasn't far from here. I'd made it through the night in it, on a Red Moon, no less. I could do it again.

"I'd rather take my chances out there than in here."

"I'm sure you would," he drawled felicitously. "Though no one can leave. The Commander has spelled the ruins until you give him what he wants."

His hands slipped from my wrists, and he stepped away to open the door, gesturing for me to go through it.

I glanced back toward the pane lit by the silver rays of the night, not sure I'd get another chance like this one.

"Shall we?" he urged, arching a groomed black brow that matched the mess of rough waves and unruly curls swept back from the ivory planes of his face.

"I don't have what he wants," I said tightly. "*Please*... just let me go."

His gaze went vacant and cold as it dropped to the floor at my feet. "I can't do that. Even if I wanted to, I couldn't."

CHAPTER TEN

DEMETRIUS LOUNGED on his obsidian throne, his golden-leafed crown askew atop his head and his legs crossed at the ankles as he absently picked at his cuticles.

The memory of the pain he could inflict with such little effort lingered as we entered the room, where the murmurs of the mingling Faye quickly fell silent.

Their shoulders tensed as they inched back, pressing into the walls, casting nervous glances and muttering snide remarks in our direction.

I was no stranger to the brazen thoughts and words of others. They hurt, but it was nothing I couldn't handle.

It didn't take long before I realized, though, it wasn't just me receiving their unkind welcome, but also the male escorting me, wearing a pretentious smirk, as if he were enjoying the reaction he'd garnered from them.

"Took you two long enough." Demetrius's gaze flicked up from his hand, settling on the mostly healed wound across the male's chest. "I don't like to be kept waiting, Alekxander."

"Apologies, my king." Alekxander leaned against a column beside the throne, leaving me to stand alone under the full weight of the Commander's glare.

"Are you hungry, Riven?" he asked, running a finger over the jagged pink scar on his face.

I stared at one of the roasted pigs laid out on a platter, a red apple stuffed in its mouth and steam rising from its back. The long table around it was laden with cooked vegetables and sticky fruits that permeated the air with the scent of fresh herbs and spices.

My mouth watered. I had never seen so much food in one place, even during the solstice. It took all I had not to react.

"I ate before I came. Thanks anyway," I said bluntly.

"I wasn't offering. I was simply asking." A smile tugged at his lips. "Have you had a change of heart after your little nap? Will you forfeit what is rightfully mine so we can be done with this?"

My nostrils flared as I glared up at him, realizing the Faye here had lost their minds.

"Nothing I have belongs to you. You can ask me the same question as many times as you like. My answer will remain the same."

"Pity. I had hoped this would go smoother for both of us." He snapped his fingers, and light instrumentals filled the room—an upbeat tune emanating from thin air as if riding a wave of *magic*.

"Why so tense, everyone?" He chuckled to himself as he scanned over the elegantly dressed creatures, his smile turning wicked. "It's a celebration. *Celebrate.* You'd think I was holding them captive or something."

The room erupted into loud laughter and conversation at his command—any trace of discontent vanishing as the Faye dug into the feast before them, draining and refilling their goblets.

I couldn't help but watch, envy creeping in because they didn't have to worry about rationing for the coming weeks.

"It was a joke," Demetrius sighed dramatically. "Do they not have those in the Mortal Realm?"

His jaw clenched when I didn't answer, the humor leeching from his face as he began again, "Do you like what I did with the place? It's a simple glamour."

"Fit for a king," I responded dryly, keeping my expression blank, though my knees shook.

If this were to be my last day, I wouldn't waste it on small talk.

"If you're going to kill me, get it over with. If not, let me go."

"If it were as simple as that, you'd already be dead." He rested his elbow on the stone armrest, casting a lingering glance at Alekxander, who twirled my blade between his ring-clad fingers, ignoring him. "Why don't we make this easy on each other and save the drama for another day?"

"Fine," I breathed. "Start by telling me exactly what of yours you think I have."

"Your power. It's old. Potent," he spat, straightening. "*Stubborn.* Not like the others I've taken. You can give it to me, or I can try to pull it from you again—if you recall, it didn't go well for you last time."

"*Power?*" I laughed, drawing the attention of the room, Alekxander's included. "I'm a Mortal from a poor village. Don't you think I would have chosen a life better than a shack if I had power? I'd eat more than scraps—" I snapped my mouth closed. This wasn't the time for sarcasm, but enough was enough. "I'm not who you think I am. I can't give you what I don't have. Release me."

"Or what?" he mocked. "Will you scowl at me some more?"

My face flushed as the room laughed obnoxiously at my expense.

"What do you think, Alekxander?" he asked. "Should we release her?"

I flicked my gaze to the male, unmoving. If it weren't for the way his jaw flexed when our eyes met, I might've believed he wasn't breathing.

"I thought not. As I said before. I can be very convincing—Vassal." Demetrius snapped his fingers, and a nightmare of a creature appeared at the bottom of the stairwell.

The Faye scattered from its path, and my eyes widened as I silently thanked the gods I wasn't hydrated enough to piss myself.

Its arms dragged along the ground, ending in long, clawed fingers blackened with grime while its contorted body strained beneath membranous skin stretched tight over jagged bone.

It sniffed the air through gaping slits, its mouth widening to reveal twin rows of razor-sharp teeth dripping with anticipation as it moved toward me.

Before I could react, bony knuckles slammed into my ribs, the force splintering through my middle and folding me into a knee that cracked against my nose with a sickening crunch.

My mouth filled with copper as I collapsed to the

floor, hands cupped over my face, flinching when it raised its leg to strike again.

Demetrius lifted a hand, and it stopped.

"I suggest you reconsider. I don't need your power to reign. I want it. For that reason alone, you are still alive."

I stared at the meager portion of molded bread lying on my cell floor next to a clay cup that held no more than two sips of discolored water.

It was a game Vassal and I had been playing… only I was losing.

If I ate what was brought to my cell, fungus and all, it would bring me a new one the next day, covered in more. If I didn't—or couldn't stomach it—the bread stayed in my cell until it was gone.

We'd been doing this for a week now… at least, it felt like it had been a week.

I tried to track time by the meals I received and the candles that were replaced, but it wasn't exactly accurate.

The bread in front of me had been here for at least two days… I think. It was brought in while I slept, and since that happened often, it made it nearly impossible to tell.

I picked up the cup and sniffed at the water, heaving out a mouthful of spit when the putrid smell hit me.

It would have been vomit, except I didn't retain enough to do so.

Tossing the liquid toward the corner of the room, where I had discovered a drain beneath the hay a few days ago, I set the cup back down with a sigh and rested my head against the filthy wall.

A steady drip of water came from a few cells down—each plop irritating the throb within my skull as dull pain radiated from the bridge of my nose.

I was thankful it hadn't broken from the impact of Vassal's knee as I slid my fingers through the laces of my binding, loosening them and lifting the hem of my tunic to check how much my ribs had progressed since the attack.

My body was still tender, my skin still purplish-blue. The only real improvement was the absence of a rattle when I inhaled.

The binding helped with that.

I dropped my hem back down and retightened the laces, hissing through my teeth when I tugged them a little too roughly.

I should have been in worse shape than I was.

My injuries were healing remarkably fast, probably

because I had stayed still for so long, crumpled in the corner of my cell.

Still, they hurt like hell.

Gods, what I'd give for some clover.

My chest constricted as I remembered how my father had looked before I left the cottage—peaceful, sitting at my bedside with a book on his lap.

I wondered if he thought I had run away because of what happened, or if he believed I somehow blamed him for it.

I wondered, too, if the others had noticed my absence. If they had started rebuilding the town, if Phineas's mother was still alive, if the clover I had given him had helped her at all, or if there was enough food to go around—enough water in the creek.

It would be Fin and Alma running things now, since I wasn't there with them.

It was nothing they couldn't handle—Knox would have to be the one setting the snares from now on. I'd shown him how to do it not too long ago. He struggled a bit with his right hand, but he didn't have much choice now that I was gone.

If Fin needed to, she could help him. She had seen me do it a dozen times or more when Phineas wasn't there to accompany me.

No. I couldn't keep doing this to myself—this damned rotation of grief.

Every time I thought it was over, it restarted: denial, acceptance, anger.

I'd even prayed to the forgotten gods while on my knees, forehead pressed to the dirt of my cell.

They didn't answer.

I shook my head, feeling like an idiot now that I had the time to think it over. It was apparent it had been a Faye trick. I didn't see Phineas's face once while I chased him, and I was close enough multiple times that he would have had to hear me calling out for him.

But that woman in the wood... I huffed a laugh, immediately regretting it as I pressed my hand to my side, realizing how ridiculous it all seemed.

If she wasn't a figment of my imagination, like Phineas, then she had to be in on it. She told me he had been looking for me too. Or maybe I just heard what I wanted to hear.

Maybe Terling was better off without me there.

Dammit. There I went again. I was beginning to lose track of which stage I was in.

I reached for the jagged rock I'd been chipping away at and tucked it into my boot before running my fingers through the knots in my hair, tying it back into a loose braid with a piece of lace I had cut from my binding using the makeshift weapon.

It wouldn't be Knox-approved, but it was better than nothing.

My stomach gnawed at itself as I glanced back to the moldy bread, and for a moment, I could almost taste my father's stew.

Thick brown liquid rich with flavor, seasoned with herbs from our garden. Potato chunks and beans. *No, meat.* Meat and potatoes. I groaned. If I didn't find a way out of here, I was going to drive myself mad.

CHAPTER ELEVEN

GETTING up from where I sat in the hay, I pressed my palms against the brick in my cell, looking for signs of weakness in the structure as I ran my fingertips over the rough mortar.

I had passed so many tunnels when I arrived that I was certain at least one ran behind these walls. If I could find a way through, I could make it out before anyone noticed.

There was little to work with as I picked at the loose pieces of mortar, most of my fingernails already broken down to the quick.

I could practically hear Alma chastising Fin and me about taking care of them. *Your appearance is of the utmost importance if you wish to marry someday,* she would always say after we'd spent time in the garden, pruning back leaves and digging away soil.

I grimaced at my dirty clothing, torn and splotched with sweat and dried blood in shades of gray and rust browns. If only she could see me now. I shook my head and resumed what I was doing.

Of course, what would be waiting for me outside these walls if I did make it out? A *diamoria?* I wasn't sure my rock would stand much of a chance against whatever monstrosity that was.

My skin pebbled as I wondered what else could be out there. What could be bad enough that a *Faye*, of all creatures, felt the need to warn me away from it?

The dungeon door scraped loudly against the floor, sending my heart to my throat. I quickly hid my hands, and when no one entered, I moved closer to the candlelight.

"Who's there?" I whispered, my body tense as I scanned the empty space, flinching when the lock clicked and my cell door opened.

When I was sure no one awaited me at the dungeon door, I took a cautious step out of my cell and darted for the stairs, climbing until I reached the top.

Wall sconces lined the empty corridor, casting a warm light over the low-hanging decorative banners I hadn't allowed myself to look at before, but I did now, taking in the thoughtfully woven threads of rust and navy.

One depicted a male and a female, separated among the stars while another showed a young child with golden strands of hair, seated upon a throne draped in ivy and rose.

Further down was a battle, a female on horseback fearlessly riding to the front of the line where swords were drawn and shields raised.

They reminded me of the stories my father had read to me as a child—flowing from page to page without missing a single detail.

On the opposite side, the banners continued.

A shooting star struck the center of the battlefield, splitting a crack so wide—I had seen this before. Not only seen, but *stood* on the very hill spun into the next banner.

The female with long golden hair had fallen to her knees before something I couldn't put into logical thought or words. A being of pure *light*. Chains wrapped around her arms and torso, tethering her to the ground as she fought against them.

How was this possible? My brows pinched. *How could I have dreams of a place and time I had never been before?*

I dropped my head, the scent of decay filling my nose

and souring my stomach as I recalled the bodies. It felt as if I were being dragged back to that hill. I didn't understand. I didn't understand any of this.

Voices echoed down the corridor, bouncing off unopened doors and high-arched walls as I hurried into the nearest room with a window, praying no one had seen me outside my cell.

Unlike before, the chamber was lit, a space nearly twice the size of my entire cottage. Shelves lined the walls, crammed with books that smelled of old pages and dust, and off to the side, a sitting nook with four chairs and a short table littered with open tomes waited.

Owning a book on the poor side of Terling was a feat, but an entire room of them was as unheard of as the matching furniture that hadn't been pieced together with rope and remnants of other furniture.

When the voices grew louder, I made a move for the window. Using the same stool as before, I quickly climbed onto it and reached for the worn latch holding the frosted panes closed against the night.

I pressed against the underside of the bronze lever, but my finger didn't move to flick it over.

My eyes narrowed as I tried again with the same result. "What in the—"

"Well, what do we have here?"

I jumped, nearly falling off the stool before turning to

see two Faye staring at me—a male and female with slender faces and hair that reminded me of Finley's.

The look in their eyes was anything but friendly as they unlinked their tanned arms from one another, closed the door behind them, and prowled closer.

"She looks Mortal to me." The female scrunched her pointed nose.

I slid off the stool and backed away.

There were no other exits in the room, and going through the window seemed out of the question, leaving me with only one option.

I reached for the sharp rock I had hidden in my boot. The pointed edge jutted out from between my fingers as I raised my arm, skipping my eyes between the two.

"Smells like it, too," the male hummed with delight, inhaling my scent through his nose and cornering me into the shelved wall. A true testament to how this week was going.

His mouth curled into a glossy smile as he took in the rock in my hand—holding it tight enough it cut into the pillows of my fingers. "Tell me, Sibble. Do you think we will be rewarded if we bring her to the Commander in pieces for escaping her cell? Or should we leave her whole?"

I paled as she returned to his side, tilting her head to rest on his shoulder while she ran a soft caress down his arm, reminding me of a field cat that caught a mouse. "I think pieces."

"Please," I said, my voice shaking.

He lashed out, grabbing my wrist and twisting it until a crack vibrated down to my elbow, causing me to drop the rock with a loud shriek.

"The fact that he thinks this thing holds any power at all is hysterical," Sibble laughed bitterly.

"Now, sister. We don't want to offend the new *king*."

He twisted again, and tears filled my vision as I latched onto his arm, trying to keep him from turning it any further. But his hold was solid and immovable.

"When he lifts the magic keeping us here..." he began again, and I cried out as another crack rippled down my arm. "If the girl is still alive, we'll take her for ourselves—see if what he claims is true. For now, we keep him happy. Let's leave her in one piece."

"What about the Dark Faye?" Sibble looked up at him beneath her heavy lashes. "He's the one we should be worried about, Erik. He wants her, too. You heard what the others were saying. If we get our power back when the magic is lifted, so does he."

A laugh left the male as he released my arm, and I dropped to my knees, cradling the sore limb against me.

My bottom lip trembled as I took in the damage— bruises already blooming in dark splotches where the tips of his fingers had bitten into me with impossible strength.

"Alekxander Nightfall is nothing more than an annoyance. Our ancestors drove the Dark Faye back once before. It can be done again. Just wait, sister. We will be back in the good graces of Viktor before you know it."

Sibble's full lips pulled upward as she waltzed over to a decanter and filled two crystal glasses, Erik watching as she inspected the hem of her silken dress.

I pushed myself from my knees while he was distracted and ran toward the closed door with everything I had—stopped by a crushing pain that erupted in my sternum.

My limbs flung outward in weightless suspension as Erik's arm slammed into my chest with impossible speed, knocking the air from my lungs.

A breathless sound tore from my throat as I hit the stone floor, gasping up at the two in horror.

"Where do you think you're going? The fun has just begun." Erik knelt in front of me, the scent of lilac filling the air like it always did when death was near.

Inky black shadows began to pour out from the crack underneath the door and Sibble dropped her glass, its contents spilling across the floor as she ran to her brother, twisting her fingers into the shoulder of his sapphire doublet and cowering behind him when he stood.

The soles of my boots scraped against the floor as I tried desperately to scoot myself away from the mass of velvety tendrils, afraid to find out what would happen if they touched me.

Pressing myself against the shelves until it hurt, I slumped onto my elbow, unable to take more than a shallow breath in. The pain in my sternum was so severe it was all I could do to stay upright.

They were scared—and I knew I should be too.

The door flung open, nearly cracking in two with the force of shadow that filled the room, dimming the sconces until they were nearly extinguished.

Sibble's scream was no more than a gargle as the blurred figure began to move in calculated motion between them, violently tearing them to pieces while I watched.

I cupped my hands over my mouth, stifling my whimpers when a severed head rolled forward, stopping inches from my leg. There wasn't enough air in my lungs; I couldn't scream or move—only stare in shock as my body trembled.

I was next.

I was going to die. Here and now.

Tears ran down my cheeks, mixing with blood that

wasn't mine, as I tugged at my tunic, desperate for air before I met the same fate as Sibble and her brother.

The chaos ended as abruptly as it had begun, and amid the stillness stood Alekxander, his chest rising and falling in sharp, deliberate pulls of air.

His eyes were closed and his head tipped back, the shadows clinging to him retreating into the folds of his black clothing—so subtle they were nearly invisible.

The blood wasn't.

Crimson beaded at the tips of his messy hair, rivulets tracing the lines of his throat, dripping down to saturate the collar of his tunic.

Pools of it gathered at his feet, spreading outward in thick, widening halos of red that glimmered faintly under the faltering candlelight.

I drew my eyes away, regretting it when I saw Erik's fate. Impaled on a candelabra, his limbs were twisted and strewn across the room—both arms and a leg discarded to the far corner, where most of Sibble's remains had been left in a fleshy mess.

"Please," I mouthed, unable to speak from both fright and the terrible pain in my sternum that Erik had left me with, certain he had broken something inside of me.

In a blur of movement, the Dark Faye was crouched in front of me, close enough that I could taste their deaths on his exhales.

"Don't look at them," he said, his voice hoarse as he lifted my chin with a slick knuckle, bringing my focus back to him. His otherworldly gaze traveled over my face—my body. "Look at me."

The feeling of his skin against mine was nauseating.

"You're all monsters," I managed to get out on a strangled breath.

He flinched... as if my words to him were somehow far worse than what he had just done. Far worse than what he was about to do.

I closed my eyes and readied myself, hoping he would make it quick.

"*Every* single one of you," I finished, clenching my teeth.

He dropped his knuckle from my chin and reached down to the laces of my binding, threading his fingers through them and tugging.

The tight leather fell to the ground beside me before I fully understood what he was doing, and when the squeezing pain eased, I took a small, much-needed breath as he stood.

He relaxed his shoulders, dragging a hand through the wet hair that had fallen over his brow and tucking it behind a pointed ear, pierced at the top with two golden cuffs that reflected the gruesome scene in the room as he muttered, "The Commander wishes to see you."

CHAPTER TWELVE

I KEPT my gaze low while Demetrius gorged himself on fruit and wine from a red velvet settee, strewn with naked Faye who shamelessly caressed one another while he observed, taking part in it himself.

When it became too much, and the heat in my cheeks grew unbearable, I looked past the Commander and what he was doing to the female in his lap.

Flesh parties were sparingly whispered about among the villagers in Terling. Mainly around the drinkery late at night, where more questionable men paid women to undress in front of them, among other things.

It was a detested profession they chose with reluctance to pay the impossible tithe, knowing it could end with life in the dungeon or at the noose if they were caught.

I imagined it was much like this. Wanton and provocative.

Alekxander shifted, unimpressed. And I couldn't help but stiffen, reminded of the room we had just left—and of what he could do with his bare hands when unprovoked.

The dried blood on my skin was beginning to itch, and the loose ringlets of my curls had hardened into a coppery crisp as I forced myself to raise my chin, maintaining the space between us while I considered what Sibble had said.

He wants her, too.

He could have killed me… but he didn't.

"Yes—*Yes!* Oh, *yes!*" The female in the Commander's grasp arched her head back, and I caught a glimpse of her eyes, heavy and tired, as she rocked her hips against his hand.

His other hand tangled in her plaited white braid, a thin chain of gold woven through it. The same chain draped over the fullness of her ivory breasts and shoulders, adorned with silver gems that dangled as she moved.

I wasn't ignorant of the intimacy between a man and

a woman, but… it had never been anything like this with me and Knox.

When swallowing became impossible, I forced my gaze toward Alekxander, who now lounged in a decorative high-backed chair—his focus fixed entirely on me rather than on what was happening in the alcove around us.

The silver in his eyes burned with the intensity of a steel flame as he stared back, my body suddenly too tight as I cleared my throat.

"Amazing, isn't it?" Demetrius shoved his fingers into her mouth, letting her suck on them to his content before dismissing her.

She slumped to the floor beside a rugged-looking male propped up on pillows, the same hazy glaze in his eyes.

"It's looked down upon in the Divine Kingdom to enjoy such things." He turned his attention from her and toward us, a grimace twisting his face as he looked me over. "What in the Divine hell happened to you two?"

"There was a slight delay," Alekxander spoke, turning his cold stare on the Commander. "I took care of it."

Demetrius took a red grape into his mouth and crushed it between his teeth, letting the juice drip down his chin as he chewed obnoxiously. "If you keep killing members of my court, there won't be any left for me to rule. It's bad enough I had to replace my Vassal with yet another from my armies."

"If your court would stop insulting me," he growled through his teeth. "Then maybe they wouldn't need to be replaced."

"I knew I'd like you." Demetrius unhooked his legs from one another and sat up, dismissing the others from the draped-off alcove we were in. "The feared Dark Faye. Alekxander Nightfall himself. Allying with you will prove to be a very wise decision. It's a shame you're all that's left... the Army of Exodus at my side—just imagine what I could do with that."

Alekxander pulled a clump of Erik from his shoulder and flicked it to the ground in front of the Commander. "Death is not something to be easily wielded, my king."

"Yet here you are. The High King of Shadow and Death." He narrowed his beady black eyes on Alekxander, expressionless in his seat and covered in as much blood as I was, if not more.

My mouth went dry. That *couldn't* be possible…

"Are you not thankful for the fraction of power I granted you back as a show of good faith?" Demetrius continued. "I can take it away just as easily as I gave it. You'd do well to remember that."

His attention slid back to me. "No matter. You're the

one I wanted to speak with. Do you know why I've been sent here, Riven?"

I dragged my eyes away from the Dark Faye and silently regarded the Commander.

"Arwen sent me. He was infuriated to find the blonde bitch had another trick up her sleeve. He couldn't come himself for fear the others would find out—another missed detail on his behalf. So he sent me to kill you, to keep his hands from getting any dirtier than they already were."

He snatched up his goblet from the short table at his side, muttering something beneath his breath before slurping it down.

"The Commander of the greatest Divine Armies of all time... sent to kill a young girl because he didn't have the gall to do it himself." He shook his head, speaking more to himself than to me.

"Who—" I cleared the dry pain from my throat and tried again. "Who is Arwen, and why would he want me dead?"

A vile grin pulled at his mouth as he set his goblet down, making me instantly regret asking the question.

"Do you know nothing of this world's history?" His scarred brow rose, tilting the gilded crown atop his head even more. "It seems the ignorance of the Mortals has rubbed off on you."

Asshole.

My cheeks flushed with embarrassment. The knowledge I had was limited to what I had heard around the village and the stories I grew up with. Our world's history wasn't something we glorified. It was the opposite.

Still, none of that covered a male named Arwen, a blonde bitch, or a Commander of a Divine Army—but *Death.* I fought the urge to glance back at Alekxander. My father often spoke of Life and Death when he would tell stories about the forgotten gods and the Old Kingdom.

Much like Life, he was beautiful and kind—a shepherd and protector when we are at our most vulnerable.

Bile rose to my mouth when I recalled the sounds of flesh tearing and bone breaking only moments ago. Alekxander was only *one* of those things.

"I thought not." Demetrius leaned back, straightening his ivory shirt trimmed with silver and plucking another grape from the vine.

"When this world was created, it was to prove to the council that it could be done—a world with balance and free of chaos. After much trial and error, as I mentioned, it failed. Arwen forged what he called a God of Death and a Goddess of Life from his own essence, meant to keep that balance. Your *forgotten* gods, from whom today's high-born Faye are descended," he clarified.

My eyes widened as I slid them between not one, but *two* impossible beings.

"It worked for a time, but against his command, they fell in love—something frowned upon where I'm from. You can imagine how things turned sour in the world when they let their duties fall to the side, placated by their emotions. By the time Arwen discovered what was happening, it was too late. He knew he could not present his failed attempt to the Divine Kingdom, so he came to me—his little brother who cleans up all his messes.

"We made a plan together to right what he had done before the council could take notice. However, when we got here, he couldn't do it. Despite being a failure, he cared for his creations like they were his children. Instead, he bound them as punishment to the stars and the night sky—casting them above, never to take form again. Never able to touch one another, but close enough to feel the pain and loss each one suffered.

"That was their punishment. What he didn't know was that Azrail and Evaline had conceived a child in their time together—hidden away by magic." His face went vacant. "Hair and skin spun from light. She was the most beautiful thing to exist, able to wield both of their power; her strength rivaled even Arwen's."

Shifting in his seat, he reached again for his goblet.

"The Great War was the first time I had ever seen him get his ass handed to him. She almost won. It wasn't long before we returned that the council caught wind of what we had been up to. It took a while, but he finally convinced them that he had taken care of it. Of course, that is not entirely the case—now, is it?" He eyed me over the rim of his goblet.

"They'll cast him out of the kingdom when they find out you exist. Which, again, is why I'm here—to get rid of you. Of course, time is a funny thing where I come from. I figure there is more than enough of it for me to have a little fun at his expense."

I chewed my lip as he took another piece of fruit into his mouth, the stone beneath my feet seeming to shift an inch or two as I watched him eat it.

"You've got the wrong girl. I'm twenty-four. I was born to both a Mortal mother and father. This has nothing to do with me."

"I thought so, too, until I laid my eyes on you. You're an exact replica of her, aside from the hair and skin." His nostrils flared. "You smell like her, too."

"This is ridiculous. I know nothing of what you say. I am a Mortal. From the *Mortal* Realm." My teeth ground against one another as I pleaded for him to listen to reason.

"You are a weapon!" He snapped forward, cheeks reddening as his face twitched into a toothy sneer.

I stepped back, my hand going to the empty sheath on my thigh.

"A promise fulfilled. Retribution on my kind for taking what belonged to her. Nearly six thousand years have passed since the Great War, her threat long forgotten until a little over a week ago when the ground shook so hard even the Divine Kingdom felt it. I can feel her power pulsing off you, and I want it. I *deserve* it. Arwen would have fallen on the battlefield if it hadn't been for me. He should be here now, cleaning up his own mess."

He set his goblet down and pushed his hair behind his ears. "You see, Riven. You die either way. Either by relinquishing your power to me willingly or by me extracting it from you once you're weak enough for me to do so. Fighting back is pointless."

I pinched my lips together and shook my head. Dried flakes of blood fell from my skin, landing on the floor at my feet as I blinked away the wall of tears I had been holding back.

There was nothing left I could say to convince him he was wrong about me. That I had *nothing* to do with this.

I wasn't a weapon. I wasn't even considered special where I came from.

My only skills were with my hands, and even that was overshadowed by unnatural clumsiness. If I had truly been created by the daughter of Life and Death, then I was nothing more than a cruel joke.

"I had hoped our little talk might convince you to do the right thing and hand it over. I'm not surprised, though. Honestly, I was looking forward to some push-back from you for the sake of added entertainment during the Summer Solstice celebrations." He picked a stray thread from the hem of his cuff. "I've sent scouts out to search for something that will change your mind in the event we didn't see eye to eye on this. Until they return, I need some things done, starting with the rose garden. It needs to be pruned back for the arrival of our guests."

"No." I lifted my chin, harnessing what tiny shred of bravery I had left in spite of the uneasy look Alekxander shot me.

"*No?*" His eyes narrowed, and the air in the room grew thick. "You're my prisoner, Riven. You'll do as you're told either by myself or my guests." He picked a grape from its barren stem and tossed it to the floor, the fruit rolling to the toe of my boot. "And you must be awfully hungry by now. Finish the garden, and if I'm feeling altruistic this evening, I'll have my Vassal find you some bread that isn't as molded."

"How considerate of you." My lips twitched as I stepped on the plump sphere, crushing it into the stone with a twist of my ankle.

If I was to die either way, I'd spend what was left of my time making him regret he had ever lured me here.

I turned to leave the alcove without being dismissed, stopped before I could make it a foot toward the gauzy drapes separating us from the other Faye, who lounged lazily near the wine and food in the throne room.

"I suggest you consider your next moves *very* carefully." Alekxander's eyes burned into mine with the warning as his grip tightened on my arm.

CHAPTER THIRTEEN

I STUDIED the small crimson droplets at my feet, my mind racing as I considered the Commander's words and the impossibility of it all while I rubbed the glistening tips of my ruby-red fingers together, wondering if it was even blood I was looking at.

Was I even real? A weapon... An object to be wielded. By whom?

If I was what the Commander claimed, then I would know. I'd *feel* it—or my father would have told me...

Wouldn't he have?

I ground my teeth, refusing to let them get in my head as I pulled back the dead branches I'd cut, tired from wandering endless halls and winding stairs for hours in search of this damned courtyard.

The thorns from the rose bush bit into my fingers as I started on a different section, trimming back the thin, weak growth with rusted shears while I glared at the colossal doors I had somehow missed when entering through the side of the ruins—propped open with large decorative vases that held more variations of the vibrant pink and white roses I'd been shearing most of the day.

I had tried to run through them multiple times this morning when I didn't have an audience watching me, taking a different approach with each attempt to find a way around the magic Demetrius used.

It was odd. I could go to the doors if I wanted, but the moment I thought about going past them, I was stuck in place—just like in the library. I could touch the lock, but nothing more.

I separated a piece of limp, dead branch and snipped it off diagonally, giving it a chance to regrow in the future. Doing the same with two more, I cut and pulled until the rose bush was as pristine as the others.

Prisoner or not, like my father, I took pride in my workmanship.

My throat tightened and I stalled, wondering if he was okay without me there to take care of him.

A deep ache twisted my chest as I glanced up at the clouds and inhaled, the warmth of the evening sun washing over the high walls of the courtyard, warming my cheeks.

I hoped that he wasn't waiting for me.

Now that I knew Demetrius's intentions—my *fate*—I knew coming home wasn't in the cards. It wouldn't keep me from trying, though.

A thorn stuck into the side of my thumb with a stinging prick, and I yanked my hand back from the branch with a wince.

"It looks like she's been chewed up and spit out by a diamoria."

I bit the inside of my cheek and listened. This wasn't the first group of Faye to comment on my scars today— just the loudest.

"She certainly can't heal herself. If she could, she wouldn't have those disgusting marks."

I shifted my braid over my shoulder to cover my back, fighting the tight feeling that crept up my throat. I hadn't seen the scars yet, but I could feel them—and that was enough to know they were repugnant, something I'd have to live with for the rest of my life, however short it might be.

"Or is it common in the Mortal Realm to show off such afflictions?" he continued.

I grimaced at the Faye I recognized from the alcove,

thankful that he was now wearing clothes on his pale body.

"Give her a break, Dorian." The male to his left scoffed into his cup.

"Don't tell me you feel bad for her, Enver?" Dorian laughed, and Enver stiffened at his side. "A *Mortal.* Far worse than a half-breed."

Dorian turned to me. "You should consider yourself lucky. Most Mortals that come this far are usually flayed and eaten."

"So, I've heard." I went back to pruning with a roll of my eyes, stopping when his statement settled in. "*Wait…* there are Mortals in the Faye Realm? *Alive?* Where?"

"A few," Enver answered. "Kept as slaves by creatures with no sense of right and wrong. *Death* would be a kinder ending for them."

I stared at the male with long silver hair twisted into small braids and knots decorated with tiny golden cuffs. His green eyes were piercing. More vibrant than Knox's as they focused on me.

If there were Mortals here, maybe I could find them. Maybe we could help each other escape.

Dorian tilted his head with a teasing grin.

"Some of those creatures are arriving outside these walls over the next few days. No slaves, thankfully. There's enough Mortal *stench* with you around." He crossed his arms over his chest—a shade or two paler than Enver's. "We'll see how long you'll last then. If we're lucky, this will be over swiftly for all of us."

"Ew, you're speaking with it?" the blonde from the alcove muttered as she strolled past me and toward Dorian and Enver, who were casually propped against a column with drinks in their hands.

"The Commander requests us in his chambers." She gave Dorian a handful of red berries.

"I would be shocked if he didn't."

My stomach growled as I watched him toss them into his mouth and chew, swaying when I felt faint.

I should have swallowed my pride and eaten that damned grape from the floor instead of crushing it.

"What are you looking at?" The blonde snapped her gaze to mine.

"No one is in the mood for your shit, Siobhan," Enver muttered against the rim of his goblet, taking a sip, unbothered as she slid her icy stare to him.

"What in the hell is your problem?" She shot back.

"Seriously?" Dorian's brow rose. "He's always a dick."

My jaw tightened as I returned to work, clearing away the dead branches I had trimmed and piling them into the wheelbarrow before moving on to another patch of withered growth while they carried on.

If there were truly Mortals in this realm, I'd need to find a way to free them.

I glanced back at the entrance when the three of them had finally sauntered off, knowing I'd need to free myself first—make it home to warn the others about what was happening on this side of the wall.

Maybe I could convince some of them to come back to help.

I moved toward the doors, but my boots instantly rooted in place.

For fuck's sake!

There had to be a way out of this damned castle.

I slammed the shears down onto the rock garden ledge and bit my lip.

This was only my first day out of the dungeon. Demetrius made it sound like I had weeks before his scouts returned. I'd use whatever time I had to my advantage and keep trying until I figured it out.

The sound of tiny wings fluttered violently, pulling my gaze to where my shears lay beneath the bush.

I stepped back, realizing what I had done, then snatched them up, tossing them into the wheelbarrow and gently cupping my hands beneath the body of… I wasn't quite sure as I stared down at it—limp with a crushed wing held between two glowing hands.

"Gods," I murmured as tiny fingers gripped my

thumb, pulling it to its crumpled wing. "I'm so sorry I did this to you."

I positioned the creature into one palm and gently massaged the thin, effervescent membrane until it perked back up.

The creature sat up in my hand, straightening the leaf pinned around its body, and without any other warning, it bit down on my finger with razor-sharp teeth hidden beneath its humanoid features.

I sucked in a sharp breath and yanked my hand back with a yelp, resisting the urge to shove my dirty finger between my lips to soothe the sting as it flew off.

"You get used to them," a high-Faye female, accompanied by two high-Faye males, said from the gravel path beside me as I rubbed the bead of blood against my pants.

"A beautiful day, isn't it?" she asked, adjusting the skirts of the fitted red gown that plunged at the neck, revealing a span of warm, tawny skin that the three of them shared. A compliment to the ethereal brown eyes that blinked back at me while she awaited a response.

"Yes," I said quietly, going back to my chores before she could sink her claws into me... or *teeth*.

"For the record, not all of us are out to get you." She clasped her hands at her waist and frowned. "Being lured from your home like that... I can only imagine how you must feel."

I gave her my attention again as she gestured toward the Faye at her left, his dark hair tapering at the sides and curling over his brow in tight ringlets. "This is my husband, Adrean, the High King of Flame. And our War Chief, Bellinor." She motioned toward the male opposite him—thicker, taller, and far more muscled than her husband—his short hair revealing the full scope of his pointed ears.

"The pleasure is ours." The High King inclined his head toward me, as did Bellinor.

"My name is Seraphine—" She scrunched up her nose, surveying the tattered laces of my binding and blood-soaked tunic. "What happened to your clothes?"

"Uhm…" I looked down at myself, unable to help but rub the soreness Erik left me with from my wrist. "Alekxander."

"The High King of Nightfall." She crossed her arms over her chest, where a golden emblem stitched into a thick leather bracelet reflected the sunlight. "I heard two members of Tide were killed earlier today."

"If only that was all. The Dark Faye made a spectacle with their bodies. Left them up for everyone to see the repercussions of speaking against the Commander," Adrean supplied, and my stomach churned.

No one deserved such a gruesome fate… But my throat tightened, and I hated that maybe—*just maybe*—they did deserve it.

Maybe what they were planning to do to me was far worse than what was done to them, even if they had intended to keep me alive.

I hated that I even had that thought when it should have been guilt and remorse for them that resided there instead.

What did that say about me?

"Typical." Bellinor rested a broad hand on the hilt of the long sword sheathed at his side. His arm was cuffed in the same bracelet Seraphine wore. "We've been rid of them for nearly two hundred and fifty years. Thought they were extinct until the High King decided to make an unexpected appearance."

"What do you mean?" My brows pinched as I looked at him, certain he could slice me in two with little effort.

"They disappeared during the War of Light and Dark. Those who returned did so with wild and inconclusive tales about what had happened. It was ruled a victory on our part. Valiant and swift."

"Though some of us digress." Adrean rested his hand on his wife's shoulder. "Our history is riddled with war. Mostly for power and territory. Light and Dark was one of many cleansings."

"It's easy to hate what you don't understand," Seraphine said, sadness behind her eyes as she held my gaze. "Not all of them were bad."

"You wouldn't be saying that if you'd seen the mess he left behind this morning." Bellinor scowled.

"Maybe so, but don't be so quick to forget our father's teachings, Bellinor. We are all one. Be it by the drop of water on a leaf or the wind that kicks up the flame. In the end, it is *Death* that is our shepherd. Not our enemy.

"Don't be so quick to forget our father's *fate,* Seraphine," Bellinor clipped out, the look of regret on his face was instant when she recoiled from him.

"I'm sorry," he breathed. "Please excuse me."

Gravel crunched beneath his boots as he stomped off, leaving us to stare after him.

"I'm sorry. I shouldn't have prodded."

"He'll be okay." Seraphine lifted her chin some. "We were young during the war. What seems like so long ago for some of us is still considered fresh for others."

"It wasn't our intention to fill your afternoon with stories of woe. Our apologies, Riven," Adrean offered with a warm smile.

"I—you're apologizing to *me*?" My brows raised, garnering a snicker from the High King of Flame.

"I had hoped to give you some great speech about

holding on and how you weren't in this alone, but it seems I've failed at that." Seraphine wiped her hands against her skirt. "We shouldn't keep you from your duties any longer. The Commander is already in a mood. Apparently, someone squashed a grape he offered her this morning."

CHAPTER FOURTEEN

"Have you finished yet?" The High King of Nightfall asked as he slouched against the archway across from me.

There was no sign of what had happened this morning as I looked up at him from my knees, watching him drag a ring-clad hand through the raven-black waves that brushed the tops of his cheekbones.

I waited, though not entirely certain for what exactly —*confirmation*, maybe? That what had happened was real and not something I had imagined in my hunger or distress… but I knew it was real as I sucked my bottom lip between my teeth. Because not only had Bellinor told me what Alekxander had done after the fact—I could still taste the blood left behind.

He moved forward when I didn't answer, and I shot to my feet, leaving behind the clippings I had been picking up. My hand inched over my thigh, reaching on instinct for the dagger now sheathed at *his* waist, mostly hidden by the sable doublet he wore.

I grasped at air, and he tracked the movement, his brows creasing as he said, "You're afraid of me."

"Terrified," I admitted.

Of him. Of the Commander. Of the others. This *damned* place I was in.

Only an idiot wouldn't be.

His eyes drifted back up to mine, and I became painfully aware that we were the only two in the courtyard.

"Is it true?" The words were out before I could stop them. "That you're all that's left?"

There was a glimmer of amusement on his face as he hesitated. "I am the only one of my kind, *yes*."

"And the others? The High Kings and Queens. They're truly descended from the forgotten gods?"

"So many questions." His mouth kicked up in a lazy smirk as he slid his hands into his pockets. After a quiet moment of studying me, he nodded. "What Demetrius says is true."

"And you?" I already knew the answer. I could smell it in the air as soon as he had entered the courtyard.

"How is it possible? How is any of this possible?" I had so many questions, but there was only one that mattered. "Why did you—they didn't deserve to die like that."

I backed away when he bent at the waist to pick up what I hadn't, adding the handful of clippings to the others before turning to face me again. "It seems I've forgotten how offensive death can be for Mortals."

I pressed my lips into a harsh line, thankful he regarded me for what I was and not what the Commander wanted me to be. "It seems you've forgotten more than that."

He looked away and ran the tip of his tongue over the edge of a canine. "Perhaps."

"What is it you want?" I asked, not caring if I had offended him.

"So many things." He inhaled deeply and tucked his hands into his pockets. "For now, though, you following me downstairs will have to suffice."

We walked the length of the corridor in silence, and I stopped just short of where I had stood the first time I looked up at the banners, their meaning far heavier now as I scanned their surface.

I let out an unsteady breath and closed my eyes.

How was I supposed to explain to him, or *anyone*, that I had been there? That I dreamed of the same hill so often it had rooted itself deep within my chest? How could I explain it when I didn't even understand it myself?

A faint sensation of soft fingers brushed the nape of my neck, and I shrugged away the phantom touch, tossing a glare at the Dark Faye when I was certain it had somehow come from him despite the distance between us.

"Would it be so bad to consider the truth?" he muttered with a tilt of his head.

"The truth?" I laughed bitterly, surprising myself with the boldness. "That I'm not a Mortal. I'm a weapon created by the daughter of the forgotten gods to exact an age-old revenge I have *literally* nothing to do with. That I'm going to die here. Alone. And I'll never see my father or the Mortal Realm again."

The truth?

I didn't know why or what connection I had to that battlefield. But it had to be simpler than that.

Maybe I had seen a painting as a child before bumping my head playing and had forgotten about it. It was only natural that a few pieces of their history would have survived the purging that took place long before my birth, and that I'd fixate on the colors and lifelike renderings until it became a part of me.

Because the alternative—the alternative meant my entire life was a lie. That I was like them, a monster—and *that* I wouldn't accept.

I hadn't said the rest aloud, but Alekxander bristled as if he'd heard it—as if he'd debated saying something more but stopped himself.

His jaw tightened, and he nodded toward another opening that led to a narrow staircase.

I followed him down into a room where massive fireplaces, built into the stone wall at the opposite end, bellowed with flames, and four metal pots, brimming with liquid, beckoned to be stirred.

The table closest to me was dusted with flour and piled high with tarts of every shape and size, while tiny cakes towered together, topped with ripe berries and drizzled in frosting.

Next to it was an identical spread of sorted vegetables, ready to be skinned and diced.

Potatoes were fluffed in massive bowls, with pools of liquid butter and gravy. Fruit jams and jellies sat beside rolls, ready to be pulled apart, while nearby, two pigs, waiting for slaughter, tugged at their ropes in a futile attempt to reach the baskets of apples and oranges shoved to the side.

My mouth watered at the sight.

The warmth of the room was comforting, and the scent of the food was overwhelmingly delicious. There was so much of it that I couldn't help the groan that escaped me when my stomach began to ache.

Of course, the Commander would send me *here* of all places.

Faye, dressed in off-white aprons, buzzed back and forth with their heads down, mixing, pouring, sprinkling, and rolling before noticing us standing at the door.

They were different from the Faye in the main castle. Average-looking. If it hadn't been for the pointed ends of their ears sticking out from beneath beige kitchen caps, I'd almost have thought they were Mortal.

"We've been waiting for you, dear," a lesser female Faye said with a thick accent I hadn't heard before.

She smiled widely as she approached, as if my being here were the best part of her day—a stranger she had not yet met.

Caught off guard by her candor, all I could do was blink.

She reminded me of Alma. Short and plump with pink cheeks that crinkled at the corners of her blue eyes and graying hair that was pinned back tightly from her pallid face.

I glanced back toward the doorway, half expecting to see Fin come through it with a basket of flowers. My chest caved in a little when she didn't, and I wondered if this was a part of the Commander's glamour to torture me further.

"You're skin and bone, girly. Come here. Let me have a look at ya." She wrapped her fingers around my biceps, and I knew then that it wasn't a glamour.

Her grasp was as real as the air filling my lungs, which was almost worse.

"Kora will keep an eye on you," Alekxander said as he meandered toward the doorway, lingering for a moment. "Help her with what she needs around the kitchen, and don't draw any more attention to yourself than you already have."

"Now, none of that," she dismissed him with a click of her tongue against her teeth. "She's going to be just fine down here with us. Won't ya?"

"Kora." He raised a brow as if in warning. "I mean it. Put her to work."

"Very well then. Can't grind wheat with dirty hands. You'd best wash up." She ushered me to a bucket, handing me a bar of animal fat and ash to scrub with while he watched, leaving when he was satisfied.

It took all the restraint I had not to climb into the tub as I ran the slick clump between my fingers and under my nails, wincing when the cuts and gashes left behind by the rose bushes stung violently.

Mortal, after all. I huffed, recalling what Dorian had said about my back and not being able to heal myself. This was further proof Demetrius had gotten it wrong.

"The Wildlings will be arriving soon. We'll need to get dinner served promptly so they don't get riled up," Kora announced to the room, pointing to a spot on my wrist I had missed.

"On it!" A fair-skinned female stationed at the table of sweets shouted over the sounds of pans clanging and pots boiling.

I focused on the dull red and brown suds dripping from my hands into the bucket below, afraid I might faint if I looked at another platter of food being prepared.

"What are Wildlings?" I asked, dipping my arms to my elbows and letting my sore fingers soak in the luke-warm water before drying them on the cloth Kora passed me.

"Creatures that reside on the outskirts of the lands. They don't adhere to court rules like the rest of the low-born or lesser-Faye. It's a wonder they've been invited at all." She snorted as I followed her to a table with a flat bowl indented on the top. "I imagine most of them will stick to the wood. The worst of them, anyway. They don't typically like to mingle."

The tiny hairs on the back of my neck rose when I thought of the creature Alekxander had warned me about —and then what Enver and Dorian had said in the courtyard.

I rubbed my thumb over the serrated toothmarks left behind on my finger.

Was that what had bitten me? A Wildling?

Kora motioned to the bundles of grain left out and ambled over to the mound of vegetables.

"Pluck the dried heads and put them on the table. You'll use the stone to grind them down into the bowl. When you finish, you'll need to sieve and winnow. Come find me if you need any help."

She returned to the mayhem of the kitchen, and I did as she instructed, sitting down on the stool and picking up a bundle of wheat before snapping the dried heads from their stalks between two fingers and tossing them into the bowl.

When the bowl was filled with the first batch, I reached for the smooth stone she had pointed to and began grinding it against the golden flakes, separating the pieces from one another.

The motion sent a twinge of pain through my arm as I shifted my gaze between the tables being cleared and Kora, who swayed effortlessly from station to station, keeping everything running smoothly before disappearing with one of the pigs to the back room and returning without it.

A fate I would soon meet myself.

I couldn't let myself think about Demetrius's plans as I pushed and pulled the stone, my muscles burning with each grinding pass over the wheat. I had never made flour from scratch before, nor had I ever thought it would take this much effort, but I was in no position to refuse— as much as I wanted to. I needed to bide my time for as long as possible until I could figure out a way around the magic keeping me here.

I frowned, wishing that Fin were sitting next to me. I imagined her telling me stories of her day to pass the time, like she always did when we'd do chores together.

Who she had met in the town square, and which village man she secretly had a crush on at the moment. She'd debate making the first move or resign herself to a quiet life with her pet cat, Oliver—a cat she had yet to acquire.

Of course, she'd never do something like that. She was too hardheaded and hell-bent on a man with a fortune, like the rest of the women in Terling.

I pinched my lips together, pausing my work and choking back a sob that took me without warning.

For a moment, it felt real, as if I'd turn my head to find her staring at me with doe eyes.

I wiped the tears sliding down my cheeks before anyone could see them and continued to grind the wheat.

I couldn't break. Not here. Not yet. I had to stay strong. For Fin. For my father. For Knox. If I cried, they would report it back to Demetrius, and I couldn't give him the satisfaction. I wouldn't.

Kora sat down on the barrel next to me, and my teeth clenched together.

The ache in my chest turned into a terrible burn I tried and failed to fight off as I dropped the stone and clasped a hand over my mouth, closing my eyes and squeezing them tight.

I hadn't expected it to hit me so hard. To hurt worse than any physical injury inflicted upon my body or mind. It was my heart that cracked. So loudly, I could almost hear it.

I willed it back together, silently praying the gods would take pity on me. That they would turn it to steel for as long as I resided on this side of the wall. That they would let me show strength where what I had left dwindled.

"Riven, dear. It's okay." Kora placed a hand on my shoulder.

My lashes were heavy with tears as I looked around the empty kitchen, where pots continued to boil and dough sat in tight balls on the counters, waiting to be rolled out when the others returned.

I didn't know where they'd gone, but I was glad they were—because one look at Kora and her familiar face was all it took for me to crumble.

My body shook, and my vision blurred with the onslaught of tears as I unclasped my hand from my mouth. And for the first time since being here, I let myself truly cry.

Loudly. *Unabashedly.* For the things I lost. For the people I loved. For what was still to come.

I cried until the burning in my chest became too much to handle, and then I gasped like a child who had lost everything all at once.

A child who watched as her life was reduced to nothing but embers.

Kora wrapped me into her ample arms and pushed the wet strands of hair from my face, much like Alma would have done. Only she didn't lecture me on how unbecoming this was for a woman. She held me in silence until it all poured out, not owing me the kindness or care but taking it upon herself to comfort me anyway.

A Faye comforting a Mortal, when all I had done since entering this kitchen was silently judge her and the others for being what they were.

What the hell was wrong with me?

I shuddered. "I can't do this."

"You can," she said, twirling a piece of my hair around a finger and tucking it behind my ear. "You can because you must. You are not alone. I promise ya that, girl."

"I am, though. I'll never see my home again. My friends or my family. I'm going to die here. I'm scared." The confessions continued to come with strangled breaths while she sat still, listening to each one until I was nothing more than a sopping mess of salty tears and grime.

When I saw that I had stained her dress and apron with blood and dirt, I quickly sat up and apologized.

She glanced down and laughed, catching me off guard just as she had before.

"You owe no one an apology, sweet girl." She collected a cloth napkin from her apron, setting it on the table and untying it. "I was waiting until the end of your shift to sneak this over to you, but I think now is just as good. Get some food on your belly. All will be right when you have a clear head."

My eyes widened at the fresh bread and mold-free clumps of cheese before I reached out, stopping myself just as I was about to pick up a cube.

Kora's brows pinched. "Well, go on, girl. There are

no tricks here. You'll need all the nourishment you can get if you plan to defeat the Commander."

I began to question what she meant, but food took precedence. Picking up a piece of cheddar, I held it under my nose, savoring the scent before pushing it into my mouth.

It was sharp and earthy. Even better than the cheese in the Mortal Realm.

I chewed it slowly as Kora got up to fill a clay cup to the brim with a frothy liquid she had been stirring over the fire, just before my emotions got the best of me.

"Here." She sat back down and handed it over. "This will help with your injuries, as well as—"

"Clover?" I asked eagerly as I watched the swirls of spice I didn't recognize mix with those I did.

She nodded, and I blew into the fragrant steam before sipping the warm liquid.

"Clover is a Faye spice. How do you know what it is?"

"There is a man that lives near my village in exile. Before I found it grew in wild groves in the forbidden wood, I'd travel to him to buy it. He'd sell it as a potion that would cure all that ailed you. People would spend all they had left on it."

Though, I didn't know it was a *Faye* spice.

"Were you not afraid to enter the wood?" Her forehead creased. "There are creatures in there three times your size."

"Yes," I mumbled. "I didn't have much choice. My father became ill not long after a hunting accident. It's the only thing that seems to help him, and we can't afford it otherwise." I set the cup down and took a breath. "Why are you being kind to me? I thought Faye hated Mortals."

She smiled warmly, taking a breath herself. "What stories have you been told about us, girl?"

"Nothing pleasant." My mind immediately went to the missing babes on the Red Moon—to the Mortals that disappeared in the wood or returned only to be a shell of themselves.

She nodded. "Unfortunately, there are creatures out there that would make sport of Mortals. Wildlings that venture out during the moon, when magic is the most unstable. Keep your wits about yourself, and you'll be okay."

She scooted more cheese toward me with a long glance at my collarbones, jutting out further than they should.

"You said *if* I planned to defeat the Commander—" I backtracked.

"*If* indeed."

CHAPTER FIFTEEN

Another week.

I had been away from home for another week.

Sighing in defeat, I rested my chin on my knuckles and stared off, unsure of what tactic to try next after exhausting just about every angle of escape.

I searched for weak spots. *Loopholes.* There were none.

The closest I had come to tasting my freedom again was standing between the two aged posts of the gate I entered through upon my arrival, unable to go any further than what my chores allowed.

It was a twisting feeling to be right on the edge but unable to move forward.

I wasn't sure how much longer I'd be afforded the luxury of leaving my cell, so I did with it what I could, taking my time with the tasks assigned to me—thankful to be away from the castle and the creatures within it, *thankful* for the chance to feel the warm breeze lifting my hair and the fresh dirt under my nails.

Of course, it didn't take long before I crossed paths with a *Wildling*.

It was so still while it watched me work that I almost missed its eyes boring into me from the tree line. Call it a lesson learned: backing away slowly didn't make you invisible to them.

My shoulder twinged with the lingering pain it left me with that day. If it hadn't been for Alekxander hearing my scream... I hadn't been far from the castle since.

Instead, I took my chances with the high-Faye— stoking their fires, bringing them meals, and scrubbing their floors. Anything to avoid Demetrius and his Vassal.

So long as I kept my head down like the lesser-Faye servants, they hardly noticed my presence. Though head down or not, if they scented any trace of fear, they took it as an invitation to torment me.

I did what I could to save it for when I was alone in my cell, not responding when they lashed out... most of the time.

The sister to the High King of Tide arrived a few days ago with a caravan of fancily dressed guards from their court. As soon as I laid my head down to sleep in my cell, she summoned me to her quarters to fluff pillows and stir tea, while her ladies-in-waiting took it upon themselves to point out my obviously human flaws and stench.

I flicked the edge of my thumb over the corner of a card.

A few weeks ago, I would have been awe-struck to know I was in the presence of royalty, let alone a Faye— that they existed, and the land beyond the wall was real and not made up.

Not anymore.

They hadn't been any more hideous to me than the others were. They simply rubbed me the wrong way— each one beautiful and entitled. It wasn't fair, and maybe that made me a bit childish for thinking so, but one of their silver bracelets could feed the entire kingdom of Terling lavish meals for months.

So, when she began complaining about my poor servant skills and how bland the food Kora made her was, there was no containing myself. Any sense of pride or accomplishment I felt after was ripped to pieces by her venom-coated tongue.

What was worse was that when I left her room,

cheeks inflamed and knees shaking with embarrassment, the others had heard, too.

I kept my head high and my eyes low as I retreated to my cell, and only then—when the heavy wooden door closed, the small table was shoved against it, and the candle lit—did I tuck myself into the shadows that waited for me behind the safety of the bars and weep, just as I did every night.

When I was finally swept away with exhaustion—able to forget that it was a bed of straw I lay my head on and not the goose-feather pillow I'd had since I was a babe—I would dream of standing on a balcony, gazing over towering mountains and a vibrant blue lake, listening to the sounds of a flourishing city below and the gentle swaying of water lapping against rocks.

I was never alone in those dreams. Someone was always there, standing just out of view, watching me from the shadows—my *raven*.

The places I dreamed of, I eventually realized, weren't something I conjured, but something he did. They were a gift. A way to protect me from the world when I couldn't protect myself.

He had done it for years, whisking me away when life became too much to bear—too crude with starvation and death—taking me to rolling fields of purple and glistening lagoons of crystal-clear water, where I would roam for hours, cataloging the smells and textures of his world.

Fin was the only person I had ever told about him. She was also the only one I'd ever told about the lilac—a scent that seemed only I could smell when death was near, an affliction I'd had since I was little.

We were both pretty sure I was going mad, and maybe I was. Maybe the visions he sent me—the places he took me—were just a coping mechanism, something entirely made up on my part.

Another *battlefield*, this one leading me somewhere other than death.

Sometimes, I'd pretend it was her who stood there with me, regardless of how silly it felt. I'd tell her I finally made it to a real castle once lived in by the only true Queen our world had ever seen, according to Kora, that was.

She was Azrail and Evaline's daughter.

During a time when there was no such thing as a Mortal Realm, she ruled it all. Everything was equal and just, how it was meant to be. How my father's stories often described it.

I kept my injuries hidden, of course, and lied a little about how warmly the Faye welcomed me over the last few weeks.

With Knox, I was entirely too honest, telling him the

truth about everything aside from Demetrius's plans to kill me, because he is a mad being of Divine blood who has it in his head that I'm a weapon out to get him and his brother.

I explained how the high-Faye were descendants of the original Light Faye, created by Azrail and Evaline to govern the lands in their absence, that they were killed off during the Great War, and their mantle was passed down to their heirs. That they were real.

They all have giant egos now, coddled to within an inch of their lives. They've completely forgotten what it means to be Faye, Kora had said in a wild rant when I asked her about them.

I told him about Alekxander and what he was—I still didn't really understand it myself, and I didn't want to be in a room with him long enough to ask.

Mostly, though, I told him I didn't know how much more I could take—how hard all of this was and that I missed him so much it hurt.

When my father stood just out of reach, I reminded him that I loved him and that I'd be home soon. I told him his stories about the Faye were right because I knew he'd be excited to hear it—to know that what had been passed down to him was rooted in a beautiful truth of wild chaos.

It hadn't necessarily been a lie.

The Faye Realm was enchanting and wicked, pulling me under its spell and chewing me up. And while my father's stories weren't entirely wrong, the villagers' stories weren't entirely right either.

Other times, I ignored the man inhabiting the shadows in my dreams, using what I had left to focus on taking my next breath. I twisted the raven's feather he'd left me to find between two fingers and forced in the sweet air I knew wasn't real.

When I managed to pull myself from the deep slumbers, afraid I'd find one of the lesser-Faye or Wildlings leering at me from the other side of my cell bars if I slept too long, I threw myself back into my chores, using them to learn everything I could about the creatures and their realm—anything that might help me gain the upper hand before I returned to the kitchen with Kora and the others, the only place in the castle that brought me any semblance of normalcy.

"Your turn," Isra crooned, eager to lay down his next card. The *winning* card, by the looks of it.

I rubbed the heaviness from my eyes and decided to lay down the pawn, nearly jumping from my seat when Rowan slammed her fist down on the makeshift table we were using.

"Cheater!" she barked at him as he leaned back, brushing a phantom lock of reddish-brown hair from his eyes and gathering it into the usual ponytail he wore at the nape of his neck.

He wasn't as old as Kora, but more like my father. The lines on his light-hued face looked out of place.

"Just because I'm better than you at this game doesn't make me a cheater." He gave her a smug grin. "You just need to pay better attention."

Rowan mumbled something under her breath, forcing a laugh from him.

"To be honest, you nearly had me in the first round."

"Bullshit. I know a liar when I see one." She crossed her arms over her chest, placing a booted foot on the table's edge while she watched him gather his winnings into a small satchel tied under his apron.

Two coins from her. One from Albert, who had been walking back and forth between the card game and stirring the pots so that they wouldn't boil over—and nothing from me.

Not money anyway.

"If only Faye could lie, sweetheart."

I scrunched my brows and leaned forward to stack up the rest of the deck. "Faye can't lie?"

"Eh." Rowan shrugged. "We're cunning enough with our words that we don't need to."

"Here they come." Albert placed a hand on Isra's shoulder with a snicker before sitting back down in the chair sandwiched between the two. "All of the questions she's been brimming with since the last time we saw her."

For a moment, I considered keeping my mouth clamped closed just to spite him. I couldn't.

I turned toward Kora. "You said there had only ever been one Queen. Isn't Seraphine one? Phelan's wife, Vanira, too?"

Their courts seemed to treat them as such, anyway.

"Yes and no. They are queens the same way the kings are kings—heirs to the thrones the original Light Faye left behind in their kingdoms. But they'll never be heirs to the realms like Fallon was."

"Oh." I picked at the edge of the table. Hearing her name made my chest ache a little, just as it did when Azrail and Evaline were mentioned.

Knowing that they were once as real as I was and not just one of my father's stories about the Old Kingdom was... a lot to swallow.

"Why were the gods forgotten? I mean, they created the Faye, right?"

"They've been gone for thousands of years, girl," she answered, taking the deck from my hands and putting it into a nearby drawer. "History tends to bury itself over time. There are a few who keep their story alive. Most prefer to pretend they never existed and that their powers weren't a gift but their right."

"What is it the Mortal Realm teaches?" Rowan asked, quirking a silver brow in my direction as she wiped away a scuff on her leather boot before setting it back on the ground.

"They don't." I dropped my gaze from her golden-green eyes to the now-empty table.

She wasn't like Isra or Albert, who were ordinary to the eye, or Kora, who often made me feel like I was staring at a Mortal when we spoke.

She could blend in with the high-Faye upstairs if she wanted to.

Thankfully, she didn't act like them, though she sometimes reminded me of myself when I'd catch her fidgeting with the dress she wore, as if she'd prefer pants to skirts.

"It's forbidden to learn about the Faye Realm," I continued. "People have been hanged for less in my village."

Loud drums sounded from the main corridor above, signaling that another caravan had arrived.

I stood with a sigh and returned to my cutting board to finish chopping potatoes into cubes while Isra started on the onions and carrots across from me and Albert drifted nearby, scratching the white scruff on his chin as he replaced the pots with new ones.

"We really aren't that bad once you get to know us." Isra tossed a piece of carrot at me with a grin.

There was truth in what he said.

It was a truth I had realized days ago when I caught myself letting my guard down in their company, even looking forward to it—something I had never thought would be possible before now.

"I'm going to go see which court just arrived. Be right back." Rowan threw her apron down at her station and disappeared through the door.

Nearly every room of the castle was filled at this point. I wasn't entirely sure how many more guests it could take, though it helped that they brought their own servants and goods with them.

"Maybe it's more of Terrene." Albert glanced toward Isra. "I've been *dying* to get my hands on some of their spices to try."

"*Spices*." Kora laughed, emptying the debris she'd just swept up into a bin to be tossed. "It's their wine I'm looking forward to trying."

"That makes two of us," Isra agreed, and I couldn't help but smile at how they fit so perfectly with one another.

"What the Commander doesn't know won't hurt

him." Kora breezed by me, sliding a napkin of cheese and bread into my pocket when she did.

Gods, she'd never truly know how grateful I was for her.

Rowan leaped back into the room. "The Royal Advisor from House of Tide finally made it. He's yummy, too."

"Adelram?" Kora clicked her tongue. "Everyone knows he and the High King's sister have a thing."

"Everyone except the High King." Both Albert and Isra snorted with laughter.

"Eh. He's too arrogant for my liking anyway." She wiggled her fingers at her side. Something I had noticed most of them doing absentmindedly.

"Why do you do that thing with your hands?" I wiped my palms over the apron I wore and mimicked the motion with my own. "I've seen the high-Faye do it too."

"Sometimes we forget," Rowan said, raising her hand and balling it into a fist with a frown. "When you've had magic your whole life, it's odd to know it's gone."

"It isn't gone." Kora took a pot from Albert and came to her side. "So long as the elements still flow through this land, our magic will never leave us."

"Is that how it works then? You're connected to the elements?"

Kora nodded. "Each province has its own element.

It's our purpose to keep them alive. Without us, the currents would no longer flow. The wind would cease, forests would wither, and flame would be no more. Life as we know it would end. So, it's only fair to assume that our magic is not gone—just out of reach."

CHAPTER SIXTEEN

We worked in silence for the next hour while Kora's words to Rowan played on repeat in my head, my ribs tightening with guilt each time I glanced their way.

I hated that they were in this position because of me. I hated that the only way their magic would be returned and they could leave these ruins was upon my death.

I wondered if they resented me for it.

They had every right to, but I was scared. I didn't want to die for someone's mistake. I just wanted to go home.

"Riven..." Alekxander said my name from the threshold behind me, and my hands stilled on the table.

My time in the kitchen had come to an end, which

meant I was another day closer to Demetrius's scouts returning.

"It's time to go back to your cell."

I wanted to refuse. I wanted to turn around and throw something hard at his head. To tell him how much I hated him for his wickedness.

I didn't.

Demetrius's protection didn't reach far, and it would be only a minor inconvenience if I died before giving him what he asked for. So I stayed my tongue, letting the retorts I had for the High King of Nightfall die where they began.

With a sleight of hand, I slid the kitchen knife I had been using into my sleeve and turned to face him, not meeting his eyes with my own as I walked through the door he leaned against, not bothering to say goodbye to the others as they silently watched me go either.

I didn't want it to be known they were kinder to me than necessary. I was afraid it might put a target on their backs if it were.

We had done this dance enough that I no longer needed his guidance to return to my cell—though he came anyway, walking behind me with such stillness, I sometimes forgot he was there.

Maybe it was his punishment for the Vassal he killed, despite his position next to the Commander. A way to show the rest of the Faye that even though Alekxander was the one the castle seemed to fear the most, it was *him* that did Demetrius's bidding. A pet easily controlled.

And if the High King of Shadow and Death could be controlled, what hope did the rest of them have other than to fall in line behind him?

What hope did I have?

I refused to let myself wallow in that painful truth as I took the final stair into the cavernous corridor, where the giant double doors to the throne room stood open, revealing Faye sprawled across ornate furniture, deep in drunken conversation as they gorged on fruits and cheeses.

It seemed every night was an excuse to dress up and gossip.

It was their chance to flaunt their wealth and observe how the other courts lived. Rowan had said as much when she returned with a crate of empty wine bottles before I left for my cell last night.

It wasn't common practice for them to leave their provinces to mingle. They usually sent emissaries in their place when new agreements needed tending because they were too afraid that another court might uncover their weaknesses or steal their secrets.

Things were simpler in the Mortal Realm.

There was wealth, and there was poverty. Fed and unfed.

The wealthiest convened once a month to sign off on updated regulations and decide what the tithe would amount to, while the taxes we paid went to fixing roads and replacing street lanterns—the fine print of it all? It wasn't *our* roads and lanterns.

Only the wealthy part of the village was kept up with a fool's promise that the poor side would reap the benefits of what remained.

Only nothing ever remained.

I stopped, my feet rooted in place when I noticed there were more than just the Faye I had become accustomed to wandering the corridor.

"They're Wildlings," Alekxander said, his mouth twitching with amusement as my eyes widened on a creature no more than a few feet tall that sauntered by.

Its leathery green skin was bunched into folds, its nose elongated with warts, and it had pointed ears with thick hair sticking out from the canals in wiry tendrils.

"*Goblins*," I whispered, shifting my gaze to more of the creatures gulping ale beneath a buffet table in the throne room.

There were some like the one I had encountered in the garden flying above us, and others that stood as tall as a cottage, their skin like tree bark, riddled with brightly colored beetles living in their branches.

A creature with the body of a young boy and the legs of a deer sharpened his antlers on a column, while another with the wings of a vibrant blue butterfly mingled with more like herself, sticking close to the table of sweet cakes.

Among them moved a few draped in thick blankets of moss, lumbering as slowly as snails with bright red mushrooms growing from their shoulders while they trailed the scent of damp earth.

I stared in awe as a stray tear slid down my cheek, wiping it away before anyone could see.

My whole life, I had listened to my father's tales of fantastical creatures inhabiting the other side of the wall. Creatures that weren't twisted and malevolent like the one I crossed paths with days ago but bewildering and mythical.

Not one of them did I believe.

It was easier to hate what lived beyond the border. To fear them and not consider that there could be more than the beasts that roamed the forbidden wood, but something more magical—more magical than even the Faye.

It felt as if an invisible thread in my chest was pulling me toward them as I began to take a step, halting when

Alekxander snatched my arm, effectively sobering me of my awe as I snapped my gaze to his.

Sparks. *Tingling.* Invisible sparks skittered up and down the arm he held, deepening into my bones and stealing the breath from my lips.

I narrowed my eyes, dropping them to where his fingers twisted into my worn tunic sleeve—just barely brushing my skin.

"Let. Go. Of. Me," I demanded through my teeth.

"High King of Nightfall," Morgan greeted Alekxander, glancing past me as though I weren't standing between them.

He released my arm and tucked his hands into his pockets, the sensation disappearing almost instantly.

What in the hell was that?

I had felt it before—the first time he held my chin in his hand, when I'd embedded my blade into his chest, and then again in the library.

In fact, I'd felt it *every* time we touched.

"Morgan," he regarded her sternly, though his gaze remained locked on me.

"It seems you've picked up a stray." She swayed her hips seductively, unbothered by the scrutiny she was receiving from the creatures in the corridor for her boldness in approaching Alekxander.

"Not hard, considering the castle is now full of them.

At least the disgusting ones are smart enough to stay outside, like the dogs they are."

I bit my tongue hard enough to draw blood. Any thoughts I had about the invisible sparks I felt were long gone as I glared at her.

"You didn't take me up on my offer," she continued. "Maybe tonight you will?"

Alekxander broke his concentration on me then, looking her over from top to bottom with an erotic caress of his eyes that made my throat tighten.

He didn't miss a single detail of the revealing gown that left her full breasts on display, or the way her hair cascaded down her back in tight waves the color of wet sand.

Even her face was unnervingly symmetric, with a button nose and full lips that complemented the heart shape of it.

Aside from her *shining* personality, she was flawless like the rest of them.

"Now, if I wanted a whore in my bed," he drawled sententiously. "I'd choose one with more class."

"Excuse me." She gawked in disbelief. "Do you know who I am?"

Alekxander raised his raven-black brows and straightened his stance in a regal manner as if to remind her who he was. "I don't care who you are."

She flicked her eyes toward me, the next best thing to toy with. "Don't you have a fireplace to clean, *slave*?"

I tensed when she reached for me, the warmth of her sun-kissed skin draining from her face when Alekxander caught her wrist.

"She belongs to the Commander," he said with an unnerving calmness that sent a shiver through me. "Touch her, and you'll be the next body I leave as a warning."

"He said we couldn't aid her in any way. He didn't say anything about hurting her."

She twisted her lips into a pout when she spotted her brother skimming fruit from a table nearby and called his name.

The High King of Tide's fingers stilled over a bowl of fuzzy orange spheres, and after a slow sip from his goblet, he joined us. "Dare I ask?"

"The High King just threatened to kill me." She yanked her arm out of Alekxander's grasp.

"Hmm." He smirked. "And I'm sure he was completely unprovoked."

"That's it?" She hissed through her teeth. "That's all you're going to say to him?"

"I apologize immensely for my sister's behavior, Riven. She tends to forget her place among kings and queens."

Heat stung my cheeks. I wasn't sure why he was apologizing to me—a prisoner.

"Go be toxic somewhere else, Morgan. The grownups need to speak now." He waved her away, and on instinct I went as well, needing to discard the knife tucked against my arm, along with the clover and cloth I had acquired in the hope that, should I be attacked again, I'd be prepared—or as prepared as one could be for that sort of thing.

"Not you," he motioned for me to stop, and my throat tightened as I glanced down to conceal the silver edge.

"I'd like it very much if you'd join us. I have some things I need to discuss with Alekxander, and I imagine you could use the fresh air."

I looked him over with caution, expecting Alekxander to insist on depositing me back in my cell.

"She'd love to," he said instead, and I snapped my head in his direction as he strolled into the corridor with relaxed shoulders, letting thick, glittering shadows ripple out from around him when the creatures in his path didn't clear fast enough.

When I didn't follow, he stopped with a sigh and turned to face me. "Shall we?"

Viktor lifted his hand, gesturing for me to go ahead, and hesitantly, I did.

The High King of Tide stayed by my side as we

passed Phelan and his wife, who shared space on a sofa while she scrutinized her gown, toying with the loose straps that slipped off her cream-colored shoulders.

Sitting across from them on a tufted bench was her identical copy, staring down her straight nose as she twirled the silver emblem they both wore around their necks between two claw-like nails.

"I see the Commander let his favorite pet out of its cage," Phelan said, breaking off from his conversation with Vanira as he leaned back onto the sofa with an ill-mannered smirk.

"Ignore them." Viktor guided me into one of the vacant alcoves strewn with tasseled pillows.

He took a seat next to Alekxander, unstrapping the longsword at his waist and angling it against his chair before offering me the seat beside him.

I sat in a way that kept the worst of the filth on my clothes from transferring to the cushions and dragged my attention to the opening of the alcove, trying to follow their conversation without being too obvious.

My Mortal ears caught only bits and pieces as they spoke among themselves, my attention divided between the Faye and Wildlings who resumed their mingling.

The conversation between Alekxander and Viktor seamlessly faded into the background as I let myself be once again drawn in by their ethereal beauty... and that feeling—that *tug* in my chest—grew the longer I marveled, still not entirely able to wrap my head around what I was seeing.

A low buzz began in my ears as I met the gaze of a creature spinning in circles with another, growing louder with each passing second.

The Wildling beside her locked eyes with me as if I had called her name, and the one a few paces over stumbled in his steps, doing the same.

Some of the Faye, too.

I scrunched my brows. They weren't offering their usual snide glances and mock glares I was becoming used to, but something else. Something *different*...

"Do you feel that?" I blurted without thought.

Viktor offered a tense smile before running his fingers through his sun-bleached hair and setting his goblet down. He didn't answer me, nor did Alekxander when I looked at him—his knuckles lazily pressed to his mouth as he watched me fidget beneath the odd feeling in my chest.

"Riven," Seraphine beamed, and I felt the closest thing to relief since leaving the kitchen as she plopped down on a bench with her husband in tow, Bellinor not far behind. "I was wondering when I'd see you again. You weren't out in the courtyard today."

"We must have just missed each other." The lie rolled

off my tongue, the buzz in my ears slow to disappear as I forced my attention to her.

There was a short window to roam the halls today. I spent it committing every staircase and archway I could to memory, learning the pathways until I knew them like I knew the one to my cell.

"I suppose so." She drank from her cup, and I let my shoulders slump a bit when she didn't press any further.

CHAPTER SEVENTEEN

T̲ʜᴇʏ ᴡᴇʀᴇ on their third jug of red wine, passing it around and refilling their cups as if it were nothing more than water.

Viktor had offered me a full goblet not long after we sat, only for Alekxander to snatch it for himself before I could reach out and take it—which was probably for the best, since I was a lightweight, and I doubted anyone I sat with would be kind enough to toss me in my cell if I blacked out.

Seraphine, maybe.

She tilted her head back with laughter when Adrean whispered into her ear.

A land of thieves and assassins, Rowan told me. Though looking at Seraphine now, I could hardly see it. I wondered if it was true that she could forge an inferno with the palms of her hands.

"How did you two come to meet?" I asked, curiosity getting the better of me.

Adrean smoothed a wrinkle from her crimson velvet dress, leaving his broad hand resting on her knee. "Her father would often bring her to the fields where we trained, dressed in warrior leathers and wielding a set of two flaming swords. She was impossible to miss."

"Don't let the dress fool you." She smiled with full ruby lips, nudging him playfully with her shoulder. "And if I recall, you were terrible with a blade during those formations."

"I was," he laughed. "During the War of Light and Dark, I was selected to stay behind and keep an eye on her. I was technically only training to be in the Troops of Inferno, so I didn't make the cut to go."

"He's been stuck with me since." Seraphine trailed her fingertips over Adrean's cut jaw.

"Hardly stuck."

Bellinor clicked his thumb against the emblem he wore around his forearm. The disdain gleaming in his eyes was unmistakable as he focused on Alekxander, who ignored him completely while swirling the contents of his cup.

I followed the Dark Faye's line of sight to the High

King of Wind. Phelan, arrogantly staring right back at him.

The tension between the three was palpable.

Kora had told me Phelan's kingdom was built into the side of cliffs, where clouds parted and birds stretched their wings.

I imagined it must be a freeing feeling to be that high up, able to look down on the realm and the beasts that dwelled within it.

The King's knuckles turned white, and I had no doubt he'd use his magic on Alekxander if he had access to it.

A chill ran the length of my spine with the thought, and I returned my gaze to Viktor, who was now asking Seraphine about one of the other recently arriving caravans.

He was tall and lean, with muscle hidden beneath his white linen pants and tunic. The hems, beautifully decorated with crystal azure, glinted in the candlelight when he moved.

I could almost taste the salt from the sea on my tongue when I looked at him.

I had seen it once as a child when my father and I traveled to one of the farther villages to sell pelts. From a distance, but it was enough to etch itself into my memory —the scent of it, the sound of waves crashing against mossy rocks at the water's edge. I swore to Fin that when we got older, I would take her to see it.

I still would. I just had to make it home first.

"I'm curious, Riven. What is the Mortal Realm like?" Adrean asked candidly.

"Uh…" I hesitated, not exactly sure how to answer.

"What did you do back home?" Seraphine urged.

"I worked with my hands, making traps mostly," I rasped. "It's how we fed the village I lived in."

"Could they not feed themselves?" Adrean refilled his goblet with wine before passing the jug over his shoulder to Bellinor.

"No. Not really." I chewed the inside of my cheek. "Terling is one of the poorer villages. My mother and father started doing it before I was born, and when I was old enough to carry a pot, I began helping my father. The droughts kill off everything. People become ill when they're malnourished."

"You'd help the very people who had you strung up and beaten within an inch of your life?" Alekxander asked sharply, his voice hoarse as he braced his elbows on his thighs.

It was the first time he had spoken to anyone other than Viktor since we sat down.

"My father raised me to do for others what I would want done for me if I were in need." I glared at the male.

"I don't expect you to understand that sentiment, High King."

His lips thinned as he shifted his lethal gaze from Phelan, pinning it on me instead.

"Your father sounds like a good man," Seraphine cut in before he could respond.

"Our father was a good man, too," Bellinor said, and Adrean stiffened. "Remember, Seraphine? Or have you already forgotten?"

"You know I haven't." She glared over her shoulder at him.

"We're all so curious about where the Dark Faye have been all these years," Bellinor continued. "And exactly where it is you've been hiding your court."

"What court?" Alekxander replied bluntly.

"The Commander of Nightfall's armies disappeared without a trace during the war. We thought your kind *extinct*. They aren't, though. Are they?"

Alekxander broke his concentration then, turning his deadly stare to Bellinor without answer.

"This isn't the time to strategize, Bellinor," Adrean dismissed his war chief. "We are on the brink of a great change in our world's history. For the first time since Fallon roamed our world, we have the chance to put things right—the way they were always meant to be."

Each of them slid their eyes to me.

"Oh, I'm not—I—" My binding felt a little too tight, and the alcove we were in felt a little too small as I shifted beneath their attention. "I'm not who Demetrius thinks I am."

Viktor smirked. "I think we can all agree that even though the Commander is mad, he's at least right about you. Anyone with half a brain can sense it when you walk into the room."

He stretched out his fingers. "It's like something that has been missing for so long clicking back into its place."

"No." I sat straighter. "He isn't."

"How do you figure?" He rested his hand back down on his knee.

"Look at me."

"We are." Seraphine's brown eyes gleamed.

I shook my head. "I'm no weapon. Not some great change either. I'm just Riven. A Mortal trapped in a realm of monsters that refuse to listen."

"There are monsters in your realm, too, Riven." Viktor sipped from his cup. "Maybe our realms are more alike than you've considered."

Vibrations rippled through the stone floor, and dishes slid off tables outside the alcove, shattering as an explosion violently ripped through the castle.

My heart lodged in my throat as I jumped to my feet

with the others, jerking my head around and searching for any sign of collapse nearby or anyone who might need help.

Dust filled the air in thick clouds, and the Faye in the main room were no longer sipping wine and dancing carelessly, but were scattering to shield themselves.

Bellinor positioned himself in front of Seraphine and Adrean. "It sounded like it came from one of the abandoned wings."

"Well," Viktor laughed. "Just when I thought things in this place were getting dull."

"Riven," Seraphine said my name, drawing my gaze to her as she asked if I was okay.

"I'm—" I glanced down at the trickle of blood staining my fingers, the result of my nails cutting into my palm from clutching my fists so tightly.

Another rock tore through the castle, and I felt as though I might faint.

I squeezed my eyes closed as chaos erupted outside the alcove, remembering the sights and sounds of Terling so vividly that it felt as if I were back there, hanging from the post by my wrists.

I couldn't inhale. I couldn't—my heart faltered as warm fingers gently cupped either side of my face.

Knox.

But it wasn't his emerald eyes that breathed life back into my paralyzed limbs when my lids opened.

Move. My body screamed the command at me as I ripped myself away from Alekxander, forgetting everything but my destination.

The shrieks from the Commander's Vassal entered the throne room just as I reached the archway leading to the safety of my cell—just as I was yanked back by my braid and slammed into a rigid corner.

My skull was smashed against the wall, pinned by a large hand.

Not claws. Not Vassal, then.

The sediment cleared just enough for me to recognize the disgust on Dorian's face before his mouth went to my ear. "You're nothing more than Mortal trash. You can mingle with as many of us as you'd like. It doesn't change that."

I yanked my knee into his crotch, and he barked out in pain, releasing his grip just long enough for me to bolt for the stairs.

I didn't stop until I had shut myself in the dungeon, my back pressed against the furthest wall as I waited for him to come after me, standing for so long that my limbs turned numb.

The sounds from above had long since faded by the time I let myself slump to the ground, pulling my knees to my chest while I kept the blade from my sleeve close, my fingers aching with how tightly I gripped it.

I had been here too long, biding my time while I searched for a weakness in Demetrius's magic—allowing them the upper hand as they starved me, as they abused me, and laughed at me.

I had let them underestimate me.

No more.

They didn't know what I was capable of or what I was willing to do when the time came.

They didn't know *me*, but they would.

CHAPTER EIGHTEEN

THE COMMANDER

My fingers gripped the ledge of the window, each roll of Siobhan's tongue sliding against the underside of my cock, sending a tight thrill to my balls.

I embraced the feeling, letting my head fall back and allowing it to gather and intensify.

I needed this. I *deserved* this.

For thousands of years, I've given the council every piece of me, never amounting to anything more than Arwen's little brother.

I brought my gaze back to the opened window and took in the massive hills and far-off tree lines, lit with torches.

It was all mine—the Faye Realm, the Mortal Realm. This world was *mine*, and I'd rule it ruthlessly.

My brother had it all in the palms of his hands, and he let it wither away.

I wouldn't.

I would take it for all it's worth, and when the council finally decides to make a move on him, I'll hand it over—a husk. Another mess of my brother's that I've cleaned up.

They'll have to recognize me then.

I growled through my teeth and dropped my hand from the ledge, lacing my fingers through soft blonde locks and yanking Siobhan's mouth off my length. "Am I your king?"

"Yes," she blubbered hoarsely through tears. "Yes, you are."

Humming with satisfaction, I shoved her head back down, pressing myself into her throat. Her reddened eyes bulged, fingernails slicing into my thighs as she fought instinctively to push me away.

Power. That was what I had—over her, over Alekxander, over the entire damned realm.

It was an intoxicating feeling, one I had been starved of my entire life.

I groaned, lodging myself deeper before pulling back just enough to let her gasp. Then I filled her mouth again.

She'd let me suffocate her if I wanted to.

I wrapped a finger around a lustrous strand of her hair and grunted. It wasn't the right shade. No matter how close it looked, she'd never be *her*.

My teeth ground together with the painful realization that I'd never feel her body against mine again, never feel her fight for her life the way she had on the battlefield.

I closed my eyes and groaned through each pulsing wave of pleasure, remembering the phantom sting of her blade slicing across my face as hands batted me away.

The scent of blood filled my nose as Siobhan shredded my flesh, and I withdrew from her mouth, reaching down to seize her by the arm before yanking her up from her knees.

Her breathing was sloppy and wet as I brushed away the sopping mess on her face. "Do you want more?"

"Yes," she cried, and a jolt of excitement shot through me.

I tossed her on the bed, no longer imagining Fallon with her legs spread in front of me—but Riven. Alive. *Real*. And I wanted her. *Every* piece of her as I plunged into her tightness.

Her *power*. Her *body*.

I imagined her just as she had been when my magic brought her to me—soil clinging to her skin, blood trickling from the cut on her head, her pulse wild and pounding before she had even made it up the stairs.

Pulling out, I flipped her onto her knees, thrusting to my base as I yanked her long strands to the side and ran a hand up her spine. I could almost feel the welts left behind on her skin, *feel* the ripple of need rising within her the deeper I went.

I saw it in her eyes, just as it had been in Fallon's—an ember easily stoked. She could deny it until her last breath, but I knew she felt her power calling to her. She could end worlds with it, wield Chaos itself if she wished. Yet she resisted. For what reason? To be good? Kind? *Mortal*?

I yanked her head back and growled into her ear. "I want you to scream."

Her whimpers filled the room as I pulled myself free and slid my slick cock into her ass without warning.

Her body tensed, fighting against me as she did what I asked, taking every rough thrust I threw at her until that pleasure built, ready to tear through me just as plates fell from tables and smashed onto the floor of my room, wine spilling and staining the fur rug as the castle shook.

My release erupted in thick, powerful spurts that shuddered through me before I shoved Siobhan off me, grabbed my pants, and pulled them on, leaving her to clean herself up.

I pushed open the doors of my chamber and stepped into the throne room, where Faye and Wildlings gathered in confusion as dust rose around them in choking swirls.

"What in the Divine hell is going on out here!" I demanded, my voice a power all in itself.

No one answered.

"It seems there was an explosion in one of the abandoned wings." Alekxander strolled over with his hands tucked into his pockets, the hint of a smirk at the corner of his mouth. "One of the castle walls is down."

"Who?" I bent my fingers at my side, letting the tang of power fill the air as my Vassal sought out the culprit in the crowded room, crawling down walls and raking through the Faye with loud snarls.

They knew what to do without me saying the word— my very own creations. All I had to do was think it, and it was done.

"Bring them to me when you find them." I turned with a grimace, and Alekxander followed me back to my rooms, closing the doors behind him.

There was no sign of Siobhan as I picked up the white tunic I had discarded on the floor and pulled it over my head.

"Where were you?" I asked, eyeing him.

My irritation only grew as I grabbed the goblet that had fallen from the table, filled it to the brim with the finest Faye wine I could get my hands on, and tossed what remained of the bottle at the wall, shattering glass across every surface.

"Escorting your prisoner back to her cell like a good boy," he answered, not skipping a beat. "Or would you have her roaming the halls while you slept—or *fucked*?"

He glanced toward the sheets and pillows that had fallen from my bed. "She'd have a dagger to your neck before you could blink."

I swallowed a deep gulp of the amaranthine liquid.

He wasn't wrong, though he seemed to underestimate how much I wanted just that. I wanted to see how far she was willing to go. How much pain she could take before she lay broken in my hands.

"Let her roam," I growled. "Send her out in the damned wood with the Wildlings if you must."

"They'd kill her, and then you wouldn't have her power."

"I don't need her power. I *want* it." I paced back and forth in front of the open window, noting the growing number of torches along the tree line.

I could go right now and take her from the dungeon, tie her to my bedpost, and keep pieces of her as trophies. She'd buckle then.

"Fuck!" I slammed my fist down onto the hardwood

surface of my desk, leaving it in a pile of splinters at my bare feet.

I didn't understand it. I had pulled power from several different creatures. Most of them I didn't even have to touch. Riven's power, though—*Fallon's* power. It wouldn't burn out like the others.

I could use it for eons.

If I could just get my Divined damned hands on it.

"Take away her food and water. Double her tasks. I want her weak enough for me to take what's mine. I want her to beg me for death." I had seen the way some of the Faye had looked at her. The Wildlings, too. As if she sparked something in them. I needed to crush it before it could gain traction.

"Consider it done." Alekxander knocked away some of the dust from his black tunic. "Have your minions found it yet?"

"No, but they will."

He nodded before settling into a low-backed chair.

"It's a shame." I sat across from him, balancing my drink on my knee. "Conveniently lost around the time of Light and Dark, with no mention of what happened to it."

He raised a brow. "It's a sentient box. I imagine it goes where it wishes. When you find it, you can ask it what happened."

"And what did happen, Alekxander? You've been dancing around my questions since your arrival here. It's becoming tedious."

His head tilted. "For an all-knowing creature, you don't seem to know much."

I didn't deign to answer him with more than a growl.

I knew enough to force him into allying with me. The Dark Faye existed despite what he had led the others to believe. I could feel them, though where they were I didn't know—a location he wouldn't disclose until it was time. With my word, I would save his kind for last.

My word wasn't worth much.

Unlike the Faye, I could lie, and he knew that.

I looked the male over. He had been quick with his words since his arrival, cunning even. We wanted the same thing—Riven's power. I knew what I had to gain from taking it, but what was it he had to gain?

My eyes narrowed.

He was stronger than the Light Faye. His power was concentrated, not spread out over the other elements. Giving him back even a small fraction of it had been a betting game on my part.

I had been waiting to see how he'd use it, having my Vassal keep an eye on him. He hadn't disappointed me yet. In fact, he intrigued me. The High King of Nightfall

—willing to hand over his own kind simply to be in the presence of power.

Maybe he was more like me than I'd considered: *ruthless*. A defect my mother always told me I was born with. It was the reason I was so good at being the Commander of the Divine Armies.

He was a worthy opponent. One to keep close, though he wasn't the only one I had my eye on. The High King of Wind, Phelan, also seemed to have some promise—lurking around corners and building connections with the other provinces.

He had more up his sleeve than he let on.

Feronia was another. The High Queen of Terrene and I had met on multiple occasions over a drink or two.

I needed a second, and for now, it was Alekxander. The others feared him, and that was exactly what I wanted—to inspire fear and to force obedience.

His methods made me wonder what his court was like. I imagined they trembled when he entered the room, sinking to their knees and kissing his boots just to be spared his cruelty.

He was an artist. On the outside composed and unfazed by anything I asked him to do. On the inside, the wheels in his head turned, deciding who and what to use as his medium.

I had never seen anything like it.

"When the offender is found, I want you to make an example out of them for the others to see. Show them that I can be a just ruler to those who do not cross me." I stretched the muscles in my neck. "Have you found a way to nullify the barrier spell between the realms?"

"Any trace of it died with the old kings who cast it. A fitting way to make sure those with diluted blood stayed far away from their precious civilization." His face twisted with disgust, the resentment he still harbored toward the Light Faye plain as day.

I had heard different variations of what was done to his kind leading up to their war. It was a wonder he hadn't killed every single one of them yet.

He knew it wouldn't please me if he did.

"When I find what you're looking for, I'll bring it to you. For now, we should plan as if the moon is your only advantage."

"No. It would be impossible to sustain my rule if I'm only able to move between realms one night of the month. I want them both."

"Then you shall have them. Like everything else."

His answer did nothing to help my growing agitation. My Vassal had come up empty-handed. I could sense it.

I finished off my wine, battling the urge to hurt someone, knowing I needed to stay my hand—to keep some sort of control over myself, or there wouldn't be anything left for me to rule. Nothing for me to play with. No power for me to claim while I awaited the council's judgment on Arwen.

"I don't have everything. If I did, I'd have Riven's power. I wouldn't need to wait for the barrier spell to be found. I could pull it down myself."

"She'll give in."

CHAPTER NINETEEN

RIVEN

Vanira smacked the back of my hand with a wooden wisp, leaving a tingling red welt behind.

"You're doing that wrong. If you're going to serve the high-Faye, you need to do it accordingly. When you finish the beading on my dress, start on my fireplace. It needs to be cleaned. And don't forget to shake out the drapes and make the bed."

She left the room before I had the chance to remind her that I wasn't a servant—though it wouldn't have done any good.

I awoke in my cell this morning without my ration of bread and water, and anytime I had a moment to rest, a bucket, broom, or mop was thrown my way.

My muscles burned with fatigue, my stomach ached, and I was exhausted.

The small scraps of food Kora had been sneaking me were hardly enough, but I'd never ask her for more—not when she was already putting her neck on the line for me by leaving the occasional wash bucket in my cell late at night, or having a pot of clover broth ready for me when I needed it most.

We never talked about it. We didn't need to. But I hoped she knew I thanked her with every fiber of my being.

I undid the stitch that had offended Vanira and started again, sliding silver and clear beads into a pattern of a flower.

At first, she hated the idea of a floral pattern.

We don't have flowers at the House of Wind. They look ridiculous, she sneered at me with that nasally *I'm-better-than-you* voice—but what was ridiculous was not having flowers in the House of Wind.

After she really looked at my design, one we often used in Terling when we stitched with thread and not beads, she finally decided she liked it, and it would make her stand out from the others in her court—as if being a queen wasn't enough.

I finished one petal and moved on to the next,

draping the hem of her gauzy gown on my lap while I did.

As much as the tops of my hands stung from her reprimands, I enjoyed this work compared to many of my other assignments. It reminded me of the days when Fin's mother taught me to mend clothing and blankets, my father utterly helpless with such things.

For the first ten years of my life, I wore pants with uneven legs and tunics with crooked hems, until she finally took pity on us—though not without pointing out how much simpler it would be to sew a dress.

She never forced it more than that.

My father told her that if I wanted to wear pants, then I would. His word was final, but even then, I knew he would have preferred I wore a dress to pants like the other women in the village.

It would have saved me a lot of criticism and fighting growing up… among other things.

I paused my stitching and looked over the work I had done, deciding Fin would be absolutely flabbergasted by the beading I had to choose from.

I imagined what it would be like to wear something so elegant, though I was certain I would stick out like a sore thumb if I did.

My gaze shifted above the fabric to my reflection in Vanira's crowded vanity mirror. It wasn't anything like the small, tarnished thing I used on occasion back home, which had only ever distorted what was really there.

For the first time in my life, the image staring back at me was clear.

I reached up to touch the faint speckling of freckles on my face, more prominent than I had ever realized, tracing them from my cheekbones to the bridge of my nose before letting my thin fingers fall to the point of my chin.

Aside from a few faint scars I had earned from sparring with Knox, my complexion was clear, though my face was narrower than the reflection I was used to. My nose was straight with a subtle point, and my lips were full—perhaps a little too full.

They might have been soft if not for the dryness and chapping from dehydration.

I leaned closer to the mirror, to the stranger staring back at me, close enough to see specks of green and yellow in my brown eyes, close enough to spot the strands of gold in the curls I had always thought were just a dull brown.

Was this reflection that of my mother's—or of Fallon's?

My stomach twisted, and the glimmer in my eyes dulled the longer I looked.

I returned my gaze to the stitching on my lap and

went back to work before someone could find me sitting still. The last thing I needed was more chores on my shoulders when I finally had some semblance of a plan in place. Not much of one, if I was being honest with myself. But something was better than nothing.

For starters, I wanted my dagger back. Even if it couldn't do much damage, it was important to me—a gift from my father on my fifteenth birthday, made by the village blacksmith who owed him a favor after he helped his son fix a destroyed wagon wheel on his way to pay the month's tithe. Without my father's help, their cottage would have been burned down from sheer spite for being late on the payment.

Although he had refused the blacksmith's offer of services at first—saying he simply wanted to help and that it was within his means to do so—he was eventually cornered during a late night at the drinkery into confessing what he truly wanted.

A gift worthy of his daughter.

Black steel, acid-dipped to create subtle designs in the double-sided blade. The hand guard was made of worn bronze, and the grip and pommel were wrapped in tight ebony strips of fragrant leather.

It was the blacksmith's finest work, one he gloated about often when he saw me visiting Alma in the village square.

In other words, it was irreplaceable, and I wasn't leaving without it.

I tied off the final silver bead and set my needle aside, placing the dress on its hanger by the fireplace to dangle before I began shaking out the heavy velvet curtains to disperse the lingering dust the Commander's glamour didn't penetrate.

Once the panels were secured, allowing what was left of the morning light to filter in, I finished the rest of Vanira's requests while I considered where Alekxander kept the blade when it wasn't on him—among a few other things that had been troubling me.

Like that buzz in my ears I had been hearing—barely noticeable when I first arrived. Now, it was almost a roar.

Was it connected to the Commander's magic? A side effect from being in their realm for so long? Even now, I could feel a faint note of it vibrating through me, like a caress to my bones.

I beat out the lumps in Phelan's pillow as if it were his face that I plunged my fists into, then laid it back down on the bed with the other three, each slipped in satin.

There was another question that I hadn't yet found an answer to, nor was I sure I wanted one, as I propped my knuckles on my hips.

Why did it feel the way it did when Alekxander

touched me? I didn't feel it with anyone else. Not in the Mortal Realm. Not here.

I shook my head and began replacing the charred wood and ash in the cold fireplace with new logs. When I was finished, I wiped my hands on my thighs and grabbed the nearby tin bucket, catching myself on the mantel as I stood—nearly falling over from a wave of dizziness.

The sooner I made it down to the kitchen, the better.

Alekxander would be meeting with Demetrius right about now, giving me the chance to do what I needed in the meantime, while the bucket of soot provided an excuse to wander without drawing suspicion.

I closed the door to the chamber behind me and scanned the hall that led to more of the royal rooms. The Houses of Wind, Flame, and Tide were in this wing, while the Houses of Terrene and Nightfall were on the other side of the corridor.

The halls that branched off held Faye with high-ranking positions in their provinces—war chiefs and advisors.

Further parts of the castle, glamoured to look newly built, accommodated the rest of the arrivals—servants and companions, mostly. The Wildlings, at least the worst of them, thankfully, continued to stay out in the wood.

The Commander had insisted on filling the castle for the spectacle that was meant to be my death and his reign at the start of Solstice. I only hoped that if it got that far, I'd live long enough to see the look of disappointment on his face when he realized just how wrong he was about me.

If luck were on my side, I would be gone before then.

I made my way to the main corridor and kept my head down, carefully stepping over the creatures still passed out from last night and avoiding as many claws and teeth as possible.

It was an effort not to stop and gawk now that I was close enough to really see them—close enough to feel their earthy breath around me as I went, my footfalls muted, though still loud enough that a few roused.

With how sharp their hearing was, I probably sounded like cattle crashing through a cottage full of dishes to them. Especially to the high-Faye, who were poised and well-versed in everything they did.

"If she's the Commander's prisoner, why does she have free roam of the castle?" One of the Wildlings muttered as she unstuck her cheek from her arm.

"Do you have to be so loud?" The male beside her rubbed his antler against the couch he lay sprawled across, stretching out a hoofed foot with a groan that nearly stopped me in my tracks. "My head is killing me.

She's stuck here like the rest of us. Where is she going to run?"

My jaw tightened at the reminder I didn't need, and when I reached the hall on the other side of the corridor without incident, I allowed myself a proper breath.

Like the others, the hall was adorned with thick wooden doors and bright crimson banners, its ruby-colored rugs framed in golden fringe reflecting the steady glow of gilded candelabras—illuminating the space as the sun might have, had there been windows in this section.

"Mortal." I jumped at the sound of Morgan's tightlipped voice before I could reach Alekxander's door.

"You seem to be lost." She glared at me, pointing back the way I had come with a slender finger.

"My room is that way. The flowers in the vases need to be changed out and the room swept. When you finish, you can fetch me and my ladies some sustenance."

I gritted my teeth and swallowed back the curse I had for both her and her ladies.

"Now." She grinned wickedly, twirling a sandy blonde curl around her nail as she waited for me to obey.

Glancing back at Alekxander's door, I shifted the heavy bucket between my hands and reluctantly retraced my steps while Morgan's biting gaze prickled at my back, distracting me from the emerald-hued hand that shot out and caught my ankle.

The creature yanked, sending me skidding across the floor with the bucket of ash.

I landed on my elbow, splitting it against the stone on impact, the bucket clattering noisily as I cupped my hand over the burn with a whimper and forced myself upright, glaring at the goblin who snickered through the cloud of ash.

"Uh-oh. Better clean that up before the Commander sees."

CHAPTER TWENTY

THE GOLDEN VEINS glistened in the light filtering down from the glass dome after I had finished scrubbing them —for the *second* time today.

I set my brush down and rubbed the ache out of my fingers, more than ready to be done with today's chores.

Wiping the sweat from my brow with the back of my hand, I stood with my brush and bucket and moved to the base of the throne to begin scrubbing more of the wretched scuff marks that only seemed to grow in size.

My knees met the ground at the same time the heavy doors to the room swung wide.

In a flurry of chatter, the royal Faye, their advisors, and the war chiefs filed in for their daily progress meeting, flanking both the Commander and Alekxander, who fixed their sights on me as they approached, making no attempt to avoid the spots I had just scrubbed.

My spine turned rigid when I met the Commander's gaze, his gross smirk crinkling the scar over his eye, triggering a deep-seated fight-or-flight response within me that I resisted.

I didn't need the look on his face spelled out. I'd seen it on men's faces plenty of times when Fin and I went on evening walks after serving stew, only to be openly harassed by the town drunkards.

We never gave them the satisfaction of acknowledging them. Though, on a few occasions when I'd been out by myself, ignoring their behavior disgruntled them enough that they became belligerent—believing they had the upper hand over me.

They didn't.

Demetrius stepped over my outstretched arm as I worked, making his way up the steps to his throne.

Alekxander did the same, settling into his usual seat positioned to the side, while the others found their places in the half-circle of high-backed chairs Vassal had made me pull out earlier, each of them sitting with their own province.

It didn't take long before Dorian strolled in with the rest of the harem, draping themselves over both the Commander and Alekxander.

I kept my head down and continued to scrub as Siobhan positioned herself on Demetrius's lap, placing his hands against the bare skin of her backside where her thin dress didn't cover.

Dorian was clad in the same fabric, his pants practically see-through as he stroked the Commander's shoulder and bicep, grimacing down at me as if he couldn't believe I was even allowed in the room.

The feeling of the Dark Faye's eyes burned into me as he relaxed back into his chair, his fingers twisted into the nut-brown curls of a Faye female seated on the ground between his long legs, her head resting against his thigh as she stared off in a daze.

His other arm hung over the back of his seat, his thumb rotating the bulky golden rings he wore in different directions, while, like the others, he waited for Demetrius to begin.

I rinsed my brush and focused on the task at hand, as if it were only me in the room, though keeping my head down hadn't worked much for me today. I'd been tripped this morning, bitten while serving lunch, and stabbed with a fork shortly after.

The castle was abuzz with nervous energy, more so than usual.

At first, I thought it had to do with the arrival of the Zephyr, a high-ranking group of performers gifted to the

Commander in a grand gesture by Phelan and Vanira, no doubt to show superiority over the other provinces.

I had heard talk about them throughout the day from gossiping Faye.

They moved like the wind itself—more than just beauty and grace, they were the embodiment of femininity, trained in the art form since childhood.

I realized shortly after, around the time the blunt edge of teeth sank into my finger, that the rise of uneasiness had nothing to do with them and everything to do with me.

They were beginning to feel the effects of captivity, taking it out on anyone within reach, and I wasn't entirely sure I blamed them. Not when I saw firsthand the toll it was taking on Rowan and the others—their magic siphoned, something as personal as their own souls, ripped away.

The fact that any of the Faye could willingly support something like that was abhorrent. Yet here they were, flocking to the Commander's side, offering gifts of servitude and loyalty to avoid scrutiny.

As much as I hated it, I understood. It was survival.

I saw it every day in Terling.

The poor fell to their knees to kiss the boots of the wealthy, hoping they might get something out of it instead of fighting back. Some—like Boromir and his cousins, who hung around to fulfill the deeds the higher-ups were too good to get their hands dirty with—enjoyed it.

Some, like Alekxander.

Bile rose to my throat when he tilted his head, his gaze sliding over me as if he knew I was thinking ill of him.

Not even Jeremiah was capable of the kind of cruelty Alekxander was.

"As I was saying, the land on the northernmost side of my—of *your* kingdom. I would like to keep my reins on it if at all possible. I have it on good authority that there are citizens in that location beginning to cause an uproar over the change of leadership. If you grant me permission, I will crush them on your behalf, if only to further show how committed I am to your reign."

Seraphine snorted. "Oh, please. You just want to keep your land."

"Silence." Demetrius raised his palm in the air. "Does anyone else have anything to be addressed?"

I dipped my brush into the bucket of gray water and began on a new mark, tuning out their bickering where I could.

None of it was new information, just the constant push and pull of the power that remained between the kingdoms—soon to be dismantled until there was nothing left for them to fight over.

Demetrius picked up a shell the size of his fist and turned it over in his hand, one thick black brow inching up his pallid face.

"And what is this?" he asked, glancing toward Viktor, who smirked as if he knew something the rest of the room didn't.

"In my province, there are stories of creatures that live in the deepest parts of the sea that visit our beaches in the middle of the night. They leave behind pieces of themselves. *Reminders* to our kind that they exist. If you hold it to your ear, you can hear them whispering to you."

"And what would they whisper?"

"Your darkest desires," Viktor crooned. "Victories to come."

Without hesitation, Demetrius lifted the smooth shell to his ear, his face growing with contentment the longer he held it there.

"To a long reign, my king."

I stopped when the all-too-real possibility dawned on me: *if Demetrius became king of the Faye Realm, what would that mean for the Mortal Realm? What would stop him from taking over ours next?*

Gods. The walls started to push in on me.

We weren't ready. The Mortals had no clue what they were up against.

Alekxander narrowed his eyes, and I drew a steady breath, scrubbing the floor harder as I fought to keep myself together—resisting the urge to hurl the damned brush at his head the longer he stared down at me from his perch.

I refused to let them see me panic.

I'd wait and figure this out later in my cell—how to convince Terling to help save the Mortal slaves, how to free the Faye from Demetrius's power and restore their magic without giving my life for it, how to prevent him from setting his sights on my home.

All of it.

There had to be an answer right in front of my face— one that I wasn't seeing.

"You know who I haven't gotten a gift from." Demetrius leaned back onto his throne, malice dancing in his dark orbs as he repositioned his hands around Siobhan. "*Alekxander.*"

The weight of Alekxander's gaze disappeared as he answered, "I imagine my loyalty is gift enough."

There was a flash of amusement over the Commander's face. Not anger at Alekxander's answer and obvious lack of something tangible, but amusement followed by something else. Something that made me want to retreat into my own skin.

"Haven't I been a kind and gracious ruler over these last few weeks? Allowing you to bathe in the spoils of freedom in my kingdom. A *new* kingdom. With me as your ruler, there will be no limit to what we can accomplish together."

There was a beat of tense silence before Phelan boasted in agreement, and the others followed suit.

"Speaking of being kind and gracious… Riven," he muttered, the sound of my name sending my pulse skittering. "You'll never guess what my Vassal came across in your cell just now."

Dammit. I ground my teeth together. An idiot. I was a *damned* idiot.

I rose from the floor and tossed my brush into the bucket. Dirty water splashed over the rim as I stared up at the male with a mask of calm, clutching my hands tightly at my sides so he wouldn't see the shake in them.

"You've been quite the deceiving little one, haven't you? Stealing from right underneath my nose?"

I kept my face blank, not revealing anything as I waited for him to disclose what was found before I accidentally betrayed what wasn't.

"I see you've gone mute all of a sudden. No witty

comebacks for me today?" He frowned as if he were disappointed. "Allow me to refresh your memory."

One of his Vassals appeared at the double doors just as he snapped his fingers to summon it. In its clawed hands, it held a small satchel.

Its mouth spread into a razor-sharp grin as it sleuthed its way toward the throne, not bothering to hand the bag to Demetrius but instead tossing it to the floor at my feet, where four kitchen knives clattered out.

"Now, what exactly did you think you were going to do with… a kitchen knife?" he barked, his laughter loud and cruel. "A pathetic attempt, when you know you can't harm the inhabitants of this castle. *You*, however—I can do a great deal to harm you. You've grown far too comfortable in your role, and it's past time you were reminded that you are not a guest but a prisoner."

Shit.

A whimper breezed past my lips when the Vassal advanced, lashing out at me without hesitation, the high-Faye leaping from their chairs and backing out of its path as I stumbled over myself.

I knew what to do. *How* to beat this. I just had to focus.

I dodged the blow meant for my stomach and pivoted on my feet, ducking my head under another quick swipe of its claw before lunging for one of the knives on the floor.

Rolling over my shoulder, I landed in a crouched position.

Shadows, I breathed. That's all this was. A dance with shadows in the forbidden wood.

Vassal let out an animalistic snarl, the two slits in its face vibrating with the grotesque sound that made every one of my hairs stand on edge as it reared back to come for me. My eyes widened with horror as I found my footing and darted out of its way at the last moment.

Its body tumbled into an empty chair, shattering it upon impact.

Demetrius was on the edge of his seat, excitement growing on his face as he watched me with crude fascination.

A quick glance told me he wasn't the only one thrilled by what was unfolding.

Looks of both uncertainty and captivation lit the room as the Vassal shot out its clawed fist at the same time I raised my blade, catching it at the bony joint in its elongated wrist. It shoved me backward, and the serrated edge cut through the thin layer of its skin and tissue, spraying a tar-like substance onto my neck and chest.

I hissed through my teeth and yanked my blade back, stumbling into Phelan's hands—only for him to shove me forward again, arms crossed over his chest and his eyes alight with enjoyment.

This was a *damned* game to them.

A sharp claw caught in my arm, forcing a ragged scream from my throat.

Vassal's teeth were only inches from my face, snapping together with breath that was rotten and foul as I managed to get my foot between us and push it away.

Staggering back with my hand pressed to the wound it left me with, I dragged my eyes to Seraphine's in a silent plea for help.

Adrean's. Bellinor's. Viktor's.

Not one of them flinched.

Not one of them even tried to fight against the Commander's magic.

I whipped my head toward Vassal just in time to catch it in the same spot on its wrist before it could connect with my face. It forced me back, wedging me between its sunken chest and a column that dug into my back.

I glanced at Alekxander, unfazed in his seat.

It was a fool's hope that any of them would help me as my body began to buckle under the weight of this creature.

"No!" I cried, reaching forward with the last of my strength and sinking my nails into the side of its eyeless face, slicing down the thin membranous skin until it shrieked and pulled away, freeing my knife from its wrist.

I couldn't keep this up. I'd die if I did.

Another jab came at me, missing as I lunged to the ground, sliding on my knees through the onyx puddle between its legs and cutting through the putrid tissue and meat on its thigh before I shot back to my feet.

I twisted, sweat plastering my hair to my face as I plunged the point of the knife into its side where I thought a kidney might be, and took a step back with a heaving chest—hardly registering the elbow that connected with my jaw, sending me to the ground with a hard thud.

Pain spiderwebbed through my head and neck as I got to my knees, rolling out of the way just before its foot could connect with my face.

White and black spots burst in my vision, making it impossible to focus as I fought to blink them away, only able to make out a blurred version of the creature moving toward me.

I pushed off the balls of my feet from the crouched position I was in and crammed my shoulder into its concave ribs, not giving it another chance to lash out.

Bone came into contact with bone, making a sickening crunch that, for once, didn't come from me.

It lumbered backward, and without further thought, I picked up another knife from the ground and ate up the distance between us, shoving the point of it deep into its chest, where black blood spilled over my hands and arms in thick torrents.

They laughed.

"Just like a Mortal to think that would work," Feronia said to Phelan and Vanira, her golden eyes pinned on me.

I blinked up at the monster that had been tormenting me for weeks.

I knew that a stab to the heart wouldn't do much— but I hoped removing it would.

Yanking my blade down, I sliced open its flesh further and replaced the blade with my hand. The warm, wet feeling inside its chest made my stomach curl as I wrapped my fingers tightly around the one thing that moved and ripped its steady beating from the cavity with a roar of my own—as raw and violent as I could muster.

CHAPTER TWENTY-ONE

It wasn't long before the sound drew lesser-Faye and Wildlings from the corridor, wide-eyed and gasping at the sight of Vassal lying lifeless on the ground, while I stood drenched in thick black blood that reeked of rot.

My chest heaved, and my muscles shook as I held the knife in one hand and its heart in the other, waiting for the guilt. The remorse. *Anything*, as I stared down at the creature I had just killed.

What I felt instead was almost worse.

I dropped the heart from my hand, and the tender tissue bounced on the stone, rolling to the bottom of the Commander's throne—much like that damned grape had rolled to my boot.

Gods, what was this place turning me into?

A wicked look formed in the Commander's eyes, so black that there was no longer a shred of white around them as they flicked between me and the now-lifeless heart, contemplating how he'd punish me—how much he truly needed me.

Siobhan jumped from his lap, snatching up the lesser-Faye female who clung tightly to Alekxander, blissfully unaware of what was happening, while Dorian ushered them from the throne and into the growing clusters.

Alekxander leaned forward, resting his elbows on his thighs. His skin was paler than I recalled as he watched Demetrius, waiting for what he'd do next.

Maybe this would be it. Maybe I wouldn't get a chance to save anyone after all.

Maybe I wouldn't get to see my home again, either.

Maybe I'd die here today.

I dragged my eyes over them—Faye and Wildling alike—watching as they worked themselves into an uproar, and what I felt wasn't that tug in my chest or the buzz in my ears, but fear. As raw and real as it had been the day I entered this realm.

Bellinor and Adrean moved Seraphine back when the creatures began shoving against one another, Viktor standing firm in the crowd not far from them with his hand resting on his sword.

My throat tightened as my gaze shifted to the silver-haired Faye male who had narrowly stood up for me in the courtyard, offering me a nod—his familiar green eyes carrying, like Viktor's, that look which told me he wouldn't leave.

Dorian and the rest of Demetrius's harem lingered at the edge of the growing frenzy, grinning from ear to ear with wicked satisfaction as they passed coin among themselves, making sure I saw it as they did.

A tsking sound drew my focus to Phelan, who chuckled darkly. His nostrils flared, and any attempt to veil my uneasiness vanished as Demetrius clutched his throne, his knuckles turning white and his gaze swirling with power.

The air in the room shifted into a static weight that pressed against my skin as silence fell around me. I kept my chin high, my fingers tight around the slick handle I held, my heart pounding so hard and so fast I knew he could see it—that he could hear it.

"Perhaps this has been enough excitement for one day," Alekxander sighed, as if he had better things to be doing at the moment.

"Not nearly," Demetrius said, his lips twitching as he stood and, like a predator about to pounce on its prey, took his time descending each stair.

He stopped in front of me, and before I could draw a

full breath, the overwhelming sting of metallic wrenched it away.

A crushing pressure built over my chest, constricting my lungs as I snapped my hands to my throat, clawing at it with such viciousness that my nails broke, their jagged tips slicing into my flesh as I struggled for the tiniest sliver of air.

My eyes widened, vision pulsing at the edges when none came.

When I thought I couldn't take another second of this, the pressure on my lungs eased, dropping me to my knees in relief as I gasped—so deeply I thought I might vomit on his spotless shoes.

The scent of warm copper filled my nose between each heaved breath, blood soaking into my tunic as I wiped the sweat from my upper lip with a trembling hand, attempting to collect myself.

Do not stand. Stay down.

I should have listened to that inner voice.

I didn't.

I stood, facing the male who was no different than Jeremiah—a bully, disgusting and repulsive in every way.

"Did you enjoy that power trip?" I rasped.

Demetrius's jaw went slack, and Alekxander was at his side in a whirl of shadow and smoke.

I had been entirely mistaken if I thought I had seen the Commander mad before now.

His mouth twisted into a snarl, revealing sharp white teeth, as a blast of power hit me in the chest, launching me backward into weightless suspension before slamming me into a column.

My spine cracked against it, then my head, the pain ringing through my skull so violently that my vision left me as I collapsed to the ground at its base, colors and shapes bursting behind my eyes as I tried desperately to move—to push myself up from the elbow I'd landed on.

Blood filled my mouth, and tears I didn't try to hide rolled down my face. I had barely slid my knees beneath me before Demetrius was there again, lifting me with phantom hands of magic and hurling me into a wall, scattering the creatures below.

I landed with a pitiful thump and tried again to move—my arms, my legs, *anything* to get away from the male who was over me within seconds.

He seized me by the throat with the pads of his fingers and dragged me to the stairs of his throne, dropping me onto them. The sharp edges bit into my back—a pain that was nothing compared to the fiery split of my skull.

"Nothing to say now?" He crouched with his face inches from mine.

I blinked up at him and gritted my teeth as a river of blood flowed from my nose and over my mouth, trickling onto the obsidian rock. My lips twitched with defiance, acceptance of my fate, as I spat a wad of runny blood at his face.

He began laughing, the kind of laugh a small child who mutilates animals for fun might have had, before running his tongue over the crimson spatter. "I'm going to enjoy this."

"If you kill her, Commander," Adrean spoke from somewhere in the room, "how will you obtain her power?"

The solid black in Demetrius's gaze softened, turning contemplative. I should have found relief in the hesitation, but I didn't. My chest tightened, squeezing in on itself as any thoughts of the Mortals or Terling slipped away.

No. Please, *no*. I couldn't live like this for a moment longer.

"Take it," I breathed.

No! That inner voice rang out, and I stuffed it down, praying for a swift death in its place.

Demetrius's grin turned wild as he began cleaving into me, giving no warning beforehand.

It felt as though I was being ripped apart at the seams as my back arched, the bolt of power hitting my chest with such force that something deep within me broke.

No! That voice erupted through me in panicked desperation—reaching for me as I closed my eyes and let myself glimpse the remnants of the future I might have had, latching onto vivid images of my husband cutting wood, breaking only long enough to wrap me in his sweaty arms.

I imagined Fin surrounded by healthy children who looked just like her, and my father—white-haired and smiling as he laughed.

He'd be so disappointed in me for giving up, but I couldn't keep doing this.

Tears dripped down my temples, mixing with the blood and sweat that already saturated my hair. My spine cracked, reverberating through me, and a wet gasp left my mouth. The warmth in my body began leaving, too, along with the pain.

This feeling wasn't so bad anymore.

I let my head fall back to the stone step and savored my final breath. But Death was cruel and unkind, refusing to let me leave this wretched realm as more pushed its way into my mind—decadent tastes and mouthwatering smells, vibrant colors and luxurious textures—images of a life that didn't belong to me, but to someone else.

I opened my lids with the last of my strength, and my vision was flooded by a blinding light unlike anything I had ever seen before. It was beautiful and warm, pulsing around a golden strand that was tethered to my chest.

A shuddering sob worked through me as I watched Demetrius reach down and wrap his fingers around the glimmering thread, my body telling me to fight, *screaming* it at me with a voice so deep I knew I had no choice.

So, I held on.

With everything I had, I held on, and when he tugged that strand of light within me, everything went dark.

Cold water surged up my blood-crusted nose and flooded my throat, jolting me awake to find Phelan standing over me with his brows drawn tight, watching as I sputtered and choked.

I instinctively went to my side to spit it out, but the pain was so immense it stopped me, pounding through my back and head as darkness encroached on my vision, threatening to pull me from consciousness with each movement I made.

"Wake up." He leaned down and gripped my face with a rough palm. "I think it's time we talked."

The sound that tore from me wasn't natural as I tried to push him away, spitting out mouthfuls of water and blood. Every inch of me felt sore and wrong, as if all my bones had been broken twice over and bound back together with weak twine.

He let go of me and straightened, waiting for me to fully rouse.

My hand shook as I tenderly explored my shredded throat, searching the empty throne room lit by scattered candles when I remembered what had happened… what I had seen.

I touched the part of my chest that felt as though it had been pried open, my gaze dropping to the nasty pool of drying black on the floor behind Phelan once I was certain we were alone.

"That was a good show you put on." His head tilted in a manner that had me wishing I could move. "Had I known Demetrius wasn't entirely full of shit about you, I would have had a *much* different plan in place."

"What?" My lungs burned as I gaped up at him.

"I'm here to make a deal with you. When you decide you're done fighting for your life, come and find me."

"What is—what is that supposed to mean?"

"It means anyone who doubted his claims about you before no longer does. You're a weapon. The product of Fallon herself. A damned *beacon* to the Old Kingdom. If they aren't trying to claim your power for themselves, they'll try to kill you before someone else has the chance to do so. A severe oversight by Demetrius. He thinks we're all his willing subjects," he chuckled. "He has no *fucking* clue what he just stirred up in this castle."

He placed his hands on his hips, inhaling deeply as he studied me—so thoroughly I could feel his gaze pressing against my body.

"I'm offering you a way out," he said, more serious now. "Pledge your fealty to me, and I'll let you live in my province, so long as I have access to your power at all times. Your life will be tethered to mine—but it will be a life. I'm already working on a way around the barrier spell. As soon as it's down, we can leave."

I blinked up at him, my head pulsing with the effort. "No."

"*No?*" He raised a brow. "They'll hunt you. Pick your bones when they've finished with you. Don't be small-minded about this, Riven."

"Let them." I slumped, no longer having it in me to keep my head up.

There was no considering his offer. I belonged to no one. If I wouldn't be free, then I would be dead. There was no in-between.

"We'll see how long that lasts."

CHAPTER TWENTY-TWO

THE COMMANDER

I leaned back, shifting Siobhan on my knee as I dragged my eyes to the Dark Faye.

"You know who I haven't gotten a gift from?" I said his name, waiting for the slightest flicker of discomposure.

"I imagine my loyalty is gift enough." His fingers trailed along Aislin's umber jaw in a soft caress as he turned his icy glare to me.

I could hardly blame him for his lack of interest in this meeting when he had her practically humming in his hands.

My cock twitched, the scent of her release making my mouth water as my thumb grazed the thin fabric between Siobhan's plump ass cheeks. I had told her to feed the female a few berries, not the whole damned bowl.

I parted my lips, ready to close out the meeting so I could tend to… more pressing matters, when my attention was drawn elsewhere.

My Vassal had found something.

"Haven't I been a kind and gracious ruler over these last few weeks?" I asked, letting my gaze linger over the room. "Allowing you to bathe in the spoils of freedom in my kingdom? A *new* kingdom. With me as your ruler, there will be no limit to what we can accomplish together."

"Gracious indeed, my king," Phelan chimed in.

"Speaking of being kind and gracious…" Siobhan shared a tense look with Dorian before wrapping a slender finger in a lock of my hair in a poor attempt to distract me. "Riven, you'll never guess what my Vassal came across in your cell just now."

Her eyes met mine, dull and expressionless, revealing nothing as she rose from the spot she had been scrubbing and tossed her brush into the bucket of dirty water.

"You've been quite the deceiving little one, haven't you? Stealing from right underneath my nose?"

No answer.

"I see you've gone mute all of a sudden." I raised my brow. "No witty comebacks for me today?"

Still no answer.

Fine.

"Allow me to refresh your memory." I snapped my fingers, and my Vassal appeared with a satchel at the throne room door, tossing the bag and its contents into a scattered mess on the ground as it approached.

"Now, what exactly did you think you were going to do with… a kitchen knife?" I laughed aloud, the room following suit. "A pathetic attempt, when you know you can't harm the inhabitants of this castle."

My skin pebbled with anticipation, her fear thick enough to taste.

"*You*, however," I said, my voice low, "I can do a great deal to harm you. You've grown far too comfortable in your role, and it's past time you were reminded that you are not a guest but a prisoner."

I nodded, sending my Vassal forward.

Faye leaped from their chairs, scattering as Riven stumbled, then dodged, ducking and rolling over her shoulder with one of the kitchen knives now in tow.

She was calculated, even as her eyes widened on my creature that barreled toward her, shattering an empty chair into pieces under its weight when she darted out of its way.

Alekxander had said that she knew her way around a dagger. *This*, however, I hadn't been expecting.

I dug the tips of my fingers into Siobhan's thighs, my excitement growing along with the others who watched with rapt fascination as Vassal aimed for her throat, its wrist catching on the edge of her knife as a sensation I wasn't wholly expecting pressed against me.

I snapped my gaze to Alekxander, who fidgeted in his seat. Then to Seraphine. Viktor…

My Vassal waited for my wishes, but now I grew curious.

Continue.

Onyx blood sprayed over Riven, saturating her as she hissed through her teeth and wrenched the knife free from my Vassal, stumbling into a grinning Phelan, who shoved her forward without hesitation.

Her wide eyes skimmed the room as her chest rose and fell in sharp bursts, the tops of her breasts glistening in the candlelight as true panic settled over her.

The thud of her heart became deafening as my creature struck her arm, wringing a scream from her throat that pierced the room.

Divine hell, I could listen to that sound on an endless loop.

Siobhan dropped her hand to my engorged length and began to stroke it through the fabric of my pants. But I could sense it in her, too. It was deep. If only a sliver. It was the reason she was trying to distract me, whether she realized it or not.

That *fucking* cunt. How did she do it?

I reached out to the creatures in the room, watching each one of them as I did. As I felt for that fucking tie that bound them to her just like it bound their ancestors to Fallon.

My face reddened with heat, and I snatched Siobhan's wrist to keep her from working me.

How many of them knew? I pushed myself further, pressing in on their emotions and coming up empty-handed.

They were fighting against me.

The urge to protect Riven was ingrained in them, even if they refused to acknowledge her influence.

I tensed my jaw and focused on her, pinned and fighting for her life.

How had I not seen it before?

"No!" she cried out, sinking her nails into my Vassal's face.

Continue, I ordered.

The bones in Siobhan's wrist flexed beneath my hold as I watched her turn the tables. As I reinforced every ounce of Divine magic I had pulsing through these ruins to hold the Faye and Wildlings in place.

"Just like a Mortal to think that would work."

Feronia laughed aloud before snapping her mouth closed along with Phelan and Vanira.

Riven tore the heart from my Vassal's chest, the roar that she expelled too familiar for my liking as its body fell to her feet and a swath of Faye and Wildlings flooded in through the entrance of the throne room.

She stood, covered in thick black blood and rot, shaking uncontrollably as she dropped the heart from her hand.

I was wrong. It wasn't an ember easily stoked. It was a full-fledged flame.

Siobhan jumped from my lap when I released her arm. She and Dorian grabbed Aislin and cleared out as Alekxander leaned forward, resting his elbows on his thighs. The growing crowd frenzied as they began to place bets on what I'd do to Riven for her insolence.

Good. Not all of them recognized it then. Not yet.

I gripped the armrests of my throne and sent out a wave of metallic static that silenced them, every muscle in my body tense as I stared down at her.

She didn't even attempt to hide it anymore.

"Perhaps this has been enough excitement for one day."

"Not nearly." I ignored Alekxander and stood, descending the stairs until I was directly in front of her. Any restraint I'd had to keep from ripping out her throat disappeared as I drew the air from her lungs with minimal effort, holding it just beyond her reach.

Her eyes went wide, filling with tears as she reached for her neck—clawing at it until it bled, until she had stripped it raw, until I could see that flame being doused out.

The alarm in the room grew, and I released her, unable to pinpoint where it was coming from. Feeling the tether between her and them strengthen, I dropped my gaze back on Riven, gasping for any amount of air she could get in.

She wiped the sweat on her lip and stood. Defiant even now. "Did you enjoy that power trip?"

My face twisted into a snarl at the audacity of this creature.

A whirl of shadow and smoke appeared at my side, and I pinned Alekxander in place, blasting Riven backward and into a column.

The sound of flesh and bone against stone was not nearly satisfying enough as I stalked toward her, ripping her from the ground with magic and slamming her against the wall before she could even try to stand.

Her body hit the floor, and I was there in an instant.

I flexed my jaw as I watched the fountain of red sputter from her nose and mouth. The need to feel her in my hands outweighed the need to use my magic as I reached down and yanked her up by the throat.

The warmth of her slick skin reminded me too much of the battlefield as I dragged her to the stairs of my throne and dropped her onto them.

"Nothing to say now?" I crouched close enough that I could hear her punctured lung deflating.

Her lips twitched, and she spit a wad of runny blood onto my mouth.

My cock nearly erupted as I belted with tight laughter. *Oh*, I was going to kill her. "I'm going to enjoy this."

"If you kill her, Commander, how will you obtain her power?"

Fuck.

I could say that I wanted it. The truth was that I needed it.

Her power was the key to tearing down the wall, but my time here was limited with her alive. There was already talk of the Old Kingdom arising in hushed whispers among the halls of this place.

How much longer would I have left if she remained?

"Take it," she rasped, and I thought for a moment that my ears were deceiving me.

I stood, able to feel that barrier of resistance drop— the only thing between me and what was *rightfully* mine.

Static crawled down my arms as I pried into her,

using minimal effort to pull her very essence to the surface.

My eyes widened as golden light filled the room, and when I comprehended what she harbored—Fallon's checkmate—I reached for it.

Her power swelled when my fingers closed around the wispy strand, vibrating the bones in my wrists. The surge was like nothing I had ever felt in my life… and it was *mine*.

Light leached into my skin, surrounding each digit as I imagined all of the things I could do with it, my pulse jumping with excitement as I tugged, only to yank my hand back with a hiss when it scorched my palm.

I narrowed my eyes and reached for the dulling thread again, only for it to slip through my fingers when it began to disappear.

"*No!*" I roared, snatching her up by her tunic when it faded entirely.

My chest heaved. Everything I had worked for—*everything*—was in my hands. I had it in my hands!

"*No!*" I screamed, dropping her lifeless body back to the stairs and swiping my knuckles over the lingering blood on my mouth.

"Out! Now!" The walls shook with my command, and both Faye and Wildlings bolted for the door, unable to move fast enough as I snarled in Alekxander's direction.

"You," I growled, my nostrils flaring as I stalked toward him. "Start explaining yourself, or I swear to the Divine Kingdom I will rip your spine out."

I seized him by the collar of his tunic. There was no fear in the male. Only amusement as he brushed my hand away from him with a slow grin.

"Please, did you really think I'd let you kill the girl?" He straightened the front of his shirt and slid his hands into his pockets. "You can't claim her power if she's dead."

I raised my brow, not the idiot he thought me to be. "Is that why you were fighting against me even after she offered it up?"

"Hmm…" He strolled over to her body and peered down at it. "You were so focused on everyone else in the room you didn't see the moment she changed her mind. I was simply trying to do you a favor before it got as far as it did. Now," he continued with a laugh, "your entire kingdom has seen you fail firsthand. Not only that, but you've fueled the very thing you were seeking to prevent."

He knelt and ran his fingers through her blood-drenched locks, admiring the glistening sheen they left behind with a tilt of his head.

"And I'm just supposed to take your word that you were trying to stop me for my own benefit and no other reason?"

I sucked my teeth, watching as he rose to standing, his fingertips teasingly rubbing against one another as he faced me. "You've been asking me the same question since I arrived here, Commander. Here is my answer: Be it by your hands or mine—I want the Light Faye to suffer for what they've done to my kind. If you can trust anything, trust that."

Turning on his heel, he meandered toward the open doors, tossing a final sentiment over his shoulder as he did. "I want this as much as you do, if not more. Do not doubt my loyalty. It is the only reason I am here."

CHAPTER TWENTY-THREE

RIVEN

I had fallen in and out of consciousness a dozen times or more, each attempt to get up sending my muscles and bones into a spiral of agonizing protest as I shifted to my hip, unable to do more than that before tears filled my vision and my chest stuttered painfully under the unbearable weight that lingered there.

It was real. *Everything* Demetrius had claimed was real.

I held up a hand that lacked the elegance of the Faye and ran my swollen eyes over it, touching the blunt arch of my ear afterward as old thoughts found their way back into my throbbing head. I had been avoiding them because I didn't want to believe I wasn't me. Not Faye. Not Mortal. But an object made of flesh.

My father—my mother—were my memories of growing up even mine? If I wasn't Faye, and I wasn't Mortal, where did I fit?

I'd been so certain—of myself, my wants and needs, the life ahead of me. But now I was second-guessing everything. Why fight if what I was fighting for wasn't even real? If my life wasn't my own? If, even after escaping this place, I'd be hunted for something I never chose to be?

I wiped the remnants of tears from the corners of my eyes. The ache in my head had grown dizzying as I felt along the spaces between my ribs with shaky fingers, cupping my hands over my mouth to muffle the sob that broke free when I pressed a little too hard.

How much more could I take of this? *How much*?

My throat tightened, and a strange calm settled over me with the realization that there had been a moment when Demetrius held me within his magic—that I had felt at peace. I could go back to that. I could feel it again.

The thought was enough for me to pull myself to standing—barely. My legs shook beneath me as I made my way to the knife I had used on Vassal, sniffling when I picked it up.

This could all be over in a few seconds. Just a few seconds, and I'd be free.

"You'd really give up?"

I didn't need to turn to see who it was that spoke.

"Why?" Alekxander strode out of his own darkness, coming to a stop in front of me. His night-colored waves pushed into a mess away from his face, revealing shadowy circles that formed under silver-flecked eyes.

"Why not?" I rasped, placing all of my focus on that shimmering edge.

"You'd give up that easily? You'd truly let him win?"

"Would he be winning?" I pressed my lips into a tight line. "If I died, wouldn't that mean whatever power I held would go with me? No one else would be able to get their hands on it, including Demetrius. Would that truly be considered giving up? Or would it be doing the world a favor?"

He shook his head slowly, his throat bobbing as he looked me over with tired eyes, lingering on the wet fabric that clung to my bruised skin and thin frame, the old blood crusting over wounds and staining my clothes.

I flinched when he took a step forward, his body freezing and eyes going wide when I directed the blade to the pulse in my neck.

"Don't," I warned through clenched teeth.

He moved forward in a dark blur, seizing my fist with one hand and my soggy braid with the other. I lost my footing as he yanked me against him, my legs buckling beneath me when I could no longer hold my weight.

My body turned rigid from the abrupt contact as he twisted my wrist until the blade fell, clattering to the ground at our feet, leaving me staring up at him with a slack jaw.

My whimpers were hardly audible, my lips trembling as hard as the rest of me as I waited—held captive by the hands of the one creature in this castle who was reviled more than Demetrius himself, if that were even possible.

The High King of Nightfall. Of Shadow and *Death*. A creature capable of untold atrocities and… he *held* me.

Confusion twisted my face as his grip around my hand loosened, and a breath slipped past my lips as I watched the tips of his fingers smooth over my wrist with a tenderness I didn't think him capable of—sparks trailing in their wake as they grazed the chafed skin on my shoulder, the bruises along my collarbone, and the ache in my jaw.

"Try something like this again, and—" I tore my face from his fingers, only for him to yank me back by my braid, the sensitive skin on my scalp throbbing with dull pain.

He pressed the corner of his mouth against my temple, pinning me to him as he breathed, "Test me. I dare you, Riven." His voice turned lower, softer, squeezing my insides until the pain in my lungs was the least of my worries. "Don't let them break you."

"Why do you even care?" I whined through gritted teeth and wet eyes as I clung to him. "I'm so tired. I can't—"

"Hold on a little longer," he muttered against my skin. "Just a little longer."

Hold on a little longer.

It was all he said before leaving me there, staring off into a void of empty darkness, to trace the parts of me he had touched while I questioned why he cared and what he got out of me staying alive if it wasn't the power I held.

I wiggled my fingers at my side, as I had been doing for the last few days while I lay still on the ground, testing myself between the dull haze of nightmares where I dreamed of being trapped in the skull weaver's nest—its sharp claws tearing into me while its young feasted on my heart—only to be pulled to the soggy moor that called my name, dragging me beneath the silent black water.

When I finally breached the surface in those dreams, I would find myself back in Demetrius's hands, alone in that throne room where he choked the life from me—or on that damned field of dead soldiers, where I sank to my knees and screamed at the scarlet sky.

Over and over, I screamed, cursing Demetrius and his brother to death until my throat bled—until a raven's feather drifted down on the wind to remind me that I wasn't alone, even in my darkest moments.

It was the reason I kept my eyes closed. The reason I let myself drift away even now.

Wake up.

No. I fought to stay, not caring that he was a figment. I needed him. I needed to *feel* him. To feel something. *Anything.*

Wake up. The soft presence urged—not quite a voice, not quite a touch—more like a pressure slipping behind my eyes, winding its way into the hollows of my mind.

My lashes fluttered, my lids heavy with exhaustion, as the scent of sweet butter and warm bread filled my cell, pulling me fully from my dreams.

"Riven," Rowan whispered my name, her voice fracturing from somewhere nearby as she muttered beneath her breath, "Gods—you look like shit."

"Go away," I croaked, reigniting the dry pain in my throat.

"No."

I cracked my eyes to see her standing at the door of my unlocked cell, her silver strands unbound and resting over her shoulder in the dim light as she looked down at me.

"I'm sorry…" She released a heavy sigh. "I'm sorry we weren't there for you when you needed us."

"It's better that you weren't." I closed my eyes again, hoping that she'd leave so I could go back to sleep.

"What's on your mouth?"

I scrunched my brows and trailed my tongue over the bitter corner of my lips, tasting what remained of the weeds I had been chewing. "Clover."

"How much of it did you eat?"

I shrugged and rolled to face the wall. Her slender hands stopped me, yanking me upright so fast that the room spun, and I almost vomited right in her perfect Faye face.

"Sit. Up," she ordered. "We need to get this bread in you."

"I'm not hungry," I protested with a groan.

"Are you going to eat on your own, or are you going to make me force it down your throat?" Her porcelain fingers flexed around my bicep in warning.

I raised my hand to block some of the candlelight from view. "Where in the hell were you when I first got here?"

"I don't have anything for you to drink. We'll have to make do with this." She let go and plopped down beside me, reaching beneath her top skirts and pulling out a satchel full of bread and cheese.

My mouth watered at the sight.

"You should go, Rowan. If the Commander catches you down here, he'll—"

"Get over himself?" She arched a brow, more focused on loading the cloth in her hand with food than what he'd do to her.

"He'll kill you," I amended, my chest caving with the thought.

Her lips tilted as she pushed the food toward me. "He'd have to catch me first."

"I'm serious."

"I am, too." Her grin disappeared, and she frowned at the tiny cloth square. "You should have seen Albert trying to get up the stairs to you… we all were."

My throat tightened as I stared at her, considering that maybe they were trying to fight for me after all. Maybe standing firm and not retreating was the best they could do.

"It's a wonder he didn't give himself a heart attack with all of those spices he's been sampling lately," I mumbled half-heartedly.

She raised her eyes to mine. "You know you don't have to do that, right? We know you're strong already.

You don't have to keep putting your walls up all the time —at least not around us."

I shook my head. My walls were all I had left.

She watched me fidget for a long moment and then flicked me on the shoulder with minimal bruising. "It's a good thing you're beginning to heal like one of us. Or these would look a lot worse."

"It's the clover." I broke off a fluffy piece of bread and popped it into my mouth, audibly sighing as it melted on my tongue.

"The clover helps—" She paused. "Wait, you don't still think you're Mortal, do you?"

"No." I swallowed, chewing another bite as I said, "That hope was long gone the moment I saw—"

"Your power?" She tilted her head. "Most Faye don't come into their magic until their twenty-fifth year around the sun. Not fully. You'll start showing more signs of it the closer it gets."

But I wasn't Faye. I was an abomination—trapped here like the rest of them and unable to do anything about it.

I sucked in a deep breath and expelled it.

"Keep eating," she urged. "You've taken too much clover."

"Is there such a thing as too much clover?" I asked facetiously and shoved another piece of food into my mouth, nearly choking myself on it when a chunk went down the wrong pipe.

"Geeze," Rowan laughed. "She can kill a Vassal with one hand, but she can't conquer eating cheese and bread at the same time."

"Says the girl who forgot my water." I leaned in on her shoulder, letting her take some of the weight I couldn't hold any longer while I coughed, pressing my hands tightly to my side when my lungs protested.

Gods, I wished broken ribs healed as fast as cuts and bruises.

"So, do you have a plan then?" she asked as I devoured the last cube of cheese and wiped the crumbs from my hands, leaving them as a snack for any mice that might find their way into my cell tonight.

"I thought I did. Now I'm not so sure," I admitted.

When my stomach settled and my mind felt less foggy, I said, "I didn't know you could take too much clover."

"It's a finicky weed. There is a fine line before it becomes deadly. I take it you skimmed some from the kitchen?"

"I'm sorry." I shook my head, ashamed of myself. It had been many years since I had to resort to stealing. I never thought I'd see myself doing it again—but to survive, I didn't have much of a choice. Even if it meant stealing from those I cared about.

"It's okay. Kora left it out in case you needed it. She knew you'd be too stubborn to ask. Of course, she'll have herself a fit when she finds out you ate it all." She laughed, and the guilt I felt began to fall away as she nudged me. "Speaking of which, if you're feeling up to it, you should come to the kitchen. There's something we want to talk to you about."

I sat straighter, deciding now was as good a time as any to try to stand.

Carefully sliding my legs beneath me, I pulled myself to my feet, teetering to the side just as Rowan jumped up to catch me. She hauled me upright with a strength I envied, my body spasming as I latched onto her with a hiss through my teeth, not daring to move again until the worst of the pain had subsided.

"I didn't mean now. You're still too weak to go out there."

"Nah, I feel phenomenal." I ground my teeth.

The lingering sting in my muscles began to fade as she looped her arm around mine, helping me from my cell and up the stairs that led to the main corridor. With some reluctance, she gave me space when we reached the top landing, and I took a deep, controlled breath, preparing to take my first step alone.

I straightened my back, gasping quietly as I moved forward, following her down the brightly lit corridor crowded with Faye and Wildlings setting up banners and floral arrangements for the Solstice dinner.

It was also a tradition in the Mortal Realm to hold a feast for family and neighbors on the first night of Solstice.

Masks were decorated with thin paints if you could afford them, and flower crowns were worn. There was music, dancing, and crafts. The celebration would last for weeks at a time if we were lucky.

It had once been my favorite time of the year.

Not anymore. Not after this.

The edge of my boot snagged on an uneven stone, causing me to misstep into Rowan, who was close enough to catch me if I fell but far enough not to draw suspicion.

I glanced around to see who witnessed me stumble— who I needed to mentally mark to stay away from until my strength was back.

Most of them hardly acknowledged me.

Some, however, did something I wasn't entirely prepared for…

CHAPTER
TWENTY-FOUR

ROWAN WRAPPED her arm around my lower back when I didn't move any farther, my legs frozen in place as I tried to understand what was happening, and led me down the stairs to the kitchen.

When we hobbled through the doorway, Albert's brown eyes widened, and his right hand, like the others, went to his chest.

I glanced around, wondering if I was going mad on top of everything else… but Isra did the same, nearly dropping a crate of potatoes in the process.

Kora did a double take at the two before swatting them both with her hand towel. "Stop that, you hear me? She's got enough to deal with right now. She doesn't need you two adding to the mix."

"Eh." Rowan readjusted her grip around my waist and moved toward the stool Kora was pulling out. "She'll survive. It's in her blood, after all."

I couldn't help but glare at her as she sat me near a tray of cut-up vegetables.

"How are you feeling, child?" Kora asked, filling the space in front of me with more food and a cup of steaming broth before preening me with her fingers.

"What does that mean?" I asked quietly, avoiding her question as she lifted my arms, checking the healed spots Vassal's claws had left behind and placing them back at my sides.

"Don't you worry about those two."

"Rude." Isra cupped both palms over his heart. "Those two are standing right here."

"It's not just them," I muttered, and her hands stilled on the nape of my neck. "Others are doing it, too."

"Upstairs," Rowan added. "More than I expected to see so soon."

I fixed my gaze on Albert, the pot behind him boiling over as he stared—*motionless*. His skin was so pale I wondered if he was the one we should have been concerned about.

"What aren't you telling me?" I asked.

Isra hesitated, and when no one answered, he blurted, "It's the symbol of the Old Kingdom."

I raised my brow, waiting for him to divulge more as Kora finished inspecting my scalp, but silence stretched as she placed my braid back over my shoulder—until finally, Albert took pity on me.

He let go of a tight, trembling breath and removed his cap from his short white hair. "Fallon didn't just leave behind a weapon. She left behind an heir."

"And you think that's me?" I pressed my hand to my side and barked out a laugh, pinching my lips closed when they didn't join in.

I waited for the punchline of the joke—for one of them to say they had been mistaken. When they didn't, I unstuck my tongue from the roof of my mouth, unable to swallow the lump that formed in my throat.

It wasn't fair.

None of this was fair.

It was only weeks ago that I was living a normal life in Terling, and the most I had to worry about was surviving the drought. Not this. I didn't ask for *this*. I didn't *want* this.

Hold on a little longer.

I could feel Alekxander's fingers against my skin and his breath on my face as if he were in this room, whispering those damned words to me. I hated him. *Hated* this. I wanted to scream. To run away. To go home.

I closed my eyes and placed my hands on the table

next to the plate Kora made for me, forcing myself to drag air into my sore lungs before I looked back up at them.

"What was it you needed to tell me? Or was that it?" The words tasted as bitter as they sounded.

"Are you seriously not even going to consider—"

"Rowan," Kora warned.

Rowan snapped her mouth closed, her jaw tightening as she stared at me before shutting the kitchen door when Albert and Isra began clearing items from the table.

Kora smoothed out sheets of parchment in varying sizes, and I picked up my cup of broth, wedging my foot beneath my thigh as I scanned the first page, realizing it was a map of the castle, marked with passages and exits —the grounds far more massive than I had initially thought.

Albert sat down a stack of worn books next to the dust-heavy scroll Isra was unrolling. "We've done some digging," he began.

"And some eavesdropping," Isra added.

"We know what the scouts are searching for," Rowan said, addressing the room. "It's called the *Infernal Tribulations*. It was used to torture prisoners in the olden days for information."

I stared down at the scroll, pinned at each corner to

reveal a smudged drawing of a chest with three locks on it.

"How did you come across this?"

"The library. There are a ton of scripts just lying around. I suppose the Commander wasn't smart enough to limit his glamour to the necessities." Isra rolled his eyes, as if the oversight were plain sloppiness on Demetrius's part. "His loss, our gain."

"Yes, but why is it here? For anyone to pick up?"

"Silly girl." Kora added a piece of bread to my still-full plate. "Don't you know whose castle this once was?"

"I'm sure I could take a wild guess." I sucked my teeth as I ran a finger over the long-dried ink, wondering what it would look like if there wasn't a glamour over it.

"How did you even get this down here? Why are you risking your lives to help me? Sneaking me food and water is bad enough—but this?" I repositioned myself on the stool when my side ached too much. "You're no better off than me if Demetrius finds out you're helping me."

"Careful, dear." Kora winked at me. "One might think you care about us vile creatures you despise so much. Now, where were we?"

"The Infernal Tribulations." Rowan rested her elbow on Albert's shoulder. "It's been used throughout history

—mostly on the Dark Faye. I couldn't find when or how it was created, only a mention of it being lost or hidden after the War of Light and Dark. The Commander is planning to announce his intentions with it over dinner tonight."

My heart leapt to the base of my throat. "They've found it then?"

"We don't know." She frowned.

"What does it do?"

Isra retrieved a paper from beneath the scroll and set it on top of the others. It was a drawing of a creature with no face. No form. Nothing more than black smoke, if you could call it that.

"The box contains a Wraith caught thousands of years ago by Azrail himself. It wasn't until recently that it was discovered again and used as a weapon. Whoever holds the box controls it." He pointed at a worn inscription. "Its goal isn't so much to kill as it is to break down the bearer for information. It was a proficient way to find Dark Faye in hiding during those times. It's unclear what else that entailed."

I grimaced. "Why were the Dark Faye hated so much? Were they really worthy of all of this?"

"No," Kora answered, her face twisting into a frown. "They wanted to coexist. The Light Faye wanted to control them. When they couldn't, they persecuted them."

A shiver ran the length of my spine. Coexisting with something that had the stomach for killing the way Alekxander did—the way he *enjoyed* it—I couldn't imagine it.

I closed my eyes and recalled the sounds of terror that had filtered down into my cell the night of the explosion in the abandoned wing… and then what I found the next morning when I went to start my chores. The bodies he left behind in a ragged mess. The way blood pooled under my boots as I watched him wipe his hands clean with a linen and toss it to the ground.

He hadn't said anything when he realized I was present. He hadn't even bothered raising his head long enough to acknowledge me before leaving me there, my hands trembling at my sides as I looked at their faces, contorted with fright—Demetrius's latest request of him when no one came forward to claim responsibility for their actions.

I hadn't been any more used to what he was capable of than I had been the night he killed Erik and Sibble.

I sipped from my cup and wondered what they would have done if Alekxander hadn't shown up. If they would have had any restraint or left me in pieces like Sibble wanted. It was a recurring thought that frequented my mind during the nights in my cell.

Wouldn't that make the Light Faye just as capable of what he was—as the Dark Faye were when they were around?

I glanced at Rowan. She was small like me, only she had meat on her bones. *Muscle.* What I'd look like if I had three square meals a day, maybe.

I had never heard her say anything out of malice or spite. I had never seen her do anything repugnant or manip-ulative, nor had I seen the others do so. But I still knew that even though they were hidden beneath the surface, each of them had their own versions of claws and teeth.

They were one and the same. The Light Faye were just better at hiding it.

"Up next." She took the scroll and drawing from the table, replacing them with a scribbled list of names as I nibbled on my bread. "These are the kingdoms you need to watch out for..." She continued, reviewing names and titles while Isra and Albert presented their thoughts and comments on them.

Don't let them break you.

I closed my eyes and set my bread down, feeling a spark of the determination I had when I vowed to myself that I would make Demetrius regret luring me here. The anger outweighed the fear—the *hopelessness* I had felt when...

I could still feel the sharp edge against my neck.

How could I have let it get that far?

Kora placed her hand on my shoulder, and I opened my eyes, finding Rowan's golden-green gaze already trained on me as I asked, "Can you tell me more about the clover?"

"What do you want to know about it?"

"You said it was finicky. How much is too much, and what happens if you take it?"

"Well, like you found out this morning, a handful will put you on your ass for a day or so. Sometimes, it will cause hallucinations. Most of the time, it will just feel like the worst hangover you've ever had. If you double the amount you took—which I *don't* recommend—it would incapacitate you entirely. Your heartbeat would slow to a near stop, as would your breathing. Some have died from it."

There it was. My chance.

"Can you get more without anyone noticing?"

"I'm sure, but—"

"Get as much of it as you can." I brushed off the disapproving sound Kora made. She could chastise me about taking too much later.

"What do you plan to do with it?" Albert ran his fingers over his chin, curiosity fresh on his face.

What did I plan to do with it? Escaping was no longer enough. I wasn't scared anymore. I was pissed. It was the only thing left.

I had a plan in place, and I would follow through with it. I wanted my dagger back. I would continue to play the game, pretend to be the damsel, be the entertainment for Solstice, and face the Wraith. But I would not let Demetrius break me. I would not let him win.

Kora had once said she thought I could defeat him… I was going to do so much more than that.

"I'm going to kill him."

Rowan clasped her hands behind her back, her gaze hard but approving. "Good."

"We will stand with you." Kora slipped the treasonous evidence across the table for Isra to hide.

I took a chunk of bread and shoved it in my pocket for later before finishing off my broth in a final gulp, setting my cup down as I slowly slid from my chair. The pain was still there, but what Kora had put in that batch helped dull it immensely.

"I'm going to go see what else I can find on the Infernal Tribulations."

Rowan started to reach out to offer me help, and I raised my hand, stopping her.

"No," I breathed, not wanting her to be seen with me more than she already had. "Thank you, but I have to do this on my own."

She pinched her lips together, looking me over as apprehensively as the others before stepping aside so I could pass.

My tongue felt heavy as I stalled at the door. "Please be safe… all of you."

CHAPTER TWENTY-FIVE

My legs shook as I made my way up to the corridor, now adorned with such finery it felt as though I had stepped into a painting.

The doors I passed were decorated with wreaths of roses and greenery woven together, the arched alcoves heavy with furniture veiled in gauzy ivory curtains.

Long dining tables stretched the length of the hall, golden plates and folded linen napkins nestled among garlands of white roses and lamb's ear, while above me the ceiling dripped with the same tangled blooms, their strands cascading at uneven lengths from the thin strings that bound them.

I pivoted around Faye scooting in chairs tied with

silken sashes as the nearby sconces and candelabras gleamed, their surfaces freshly buffed.

Even the old candles had been replaced with new ones, all in preparation for the dinner where Demetrius would reveal my looming fate to the high-Faye—who, I imagined, were all too eager for his announcement.

More cautious of my footing now that I no longer had someone walking beside me, I slipped past a Wildling setting out food and continued toward the library. Every step was deliberate, faltering only when Vanira's voice boomed across the corridor with complaints about the decorations.

Phelan dismissed her before she could cause any more of a scene and, as if he could sense my presence, his dark eyes found mine.

The corner of his mouth turned up as he muttered something indistinguishable, stirring that thing deep in my gut that kept me from danger—his offer hanging in the air like a blade about to come down on my neck.

A sound of disgust caught in my throat. If he really thought I would say yes to him, he had another thing coming.

I shifted my gaze from his and skirted around a column to the door I needed, letting out a breath of relief when I found the room empty.

Wedging a chair under the knob, I began searching

for something to use as a weapon—considering Vassal had sacked my cell and Alekxander seemed to have a thing for mine, leaving me with whatever I could find in here.

I scanned the shelves and furniture, deciding on a silver letter opener lying on an old desk in the corner. It wouldn't carve its way through a chest, but it might give me a head start if I needed it.

Tucking it into my waistband, I began pulling down old tomes and settled in to read through them—or at least attempted to. Most of the texts were indecipherable, the letters looping and swirling within one another like a dance in a language I had never seen before.

Closing one book and opening another, I flipped through stiff pages until I stopped on an illustration of a snake coiled around itself in a cave. It was massive, its scales slicked in what looked like an onyx substance.

Below, a smaller image of a broken fang was accompanied by more unreadable text, while the page alongside it depicted a female in a ball of light with no other explanation—not one I could understand, anyway.

The next passage was more of the same—illustrations and muddled words.

I closed the thick leather cover with a sigh and relaxed my head against the shelf—the same shelf I had smashed myself into in an attempt to get away from Alekxander.

My hand went to the laces on the front of my binding, and before I could let myself be sucked down that rabbit hole, I placed the book on top of the others I had set aside to sneak into the kitchen later tonight. Though, I wasn't entirely sure how I planned to move them without being noticed.

With any luck, the Faye and Wildlings would be swept up in tonight's celebrations and not paying me any attention.

The candlelight around me flickered, drawing my attention to a slight breeze that dropped the temperature in the room, despite both the door and window being closed.

Carefully, I sat up and glanced around, yelping when a text fell from the top shelf, landing next to me with a loud thud and a cloud of dust.

My pulse spiked, and my heart battered itself against my ribs as I rested my hand on my waistband and stood with little enthusiasm, lifting the damaged tome by its spine and stilling when a key fell out with a metallic ping.

Picking it up, I turned it over in my hand, studying it and then the book, when the gilded text began to flake from the pages, leaving behind moth-eaten holes where there had been none only seconds before.

The glamour *faded*—rotting away before my eyes until only the remnants of an ancient spine dangled from my fingers. Then it turned to dust.

My brows pinched. *What in the hell was I supposed to make of that?*

I wiggled my fingers against the gritty sediment left behind and looked up at the other books that had stayed intact.

Why only this one?

I pinched my bottom lip between my teeth, unable to dwell on the thought. My time was limited in here as it was, and finding the lock for this key was just another thing to add to my list.

I scooted the stack of books under the settee with my boot, hoping no one found them before I could return and unwedged the chair from the door before going back out into the corridor.

The key felt heavy in my pocket as I snatched a bucket of soapy water from an occupied servant, using it as an excuse to knock on Alekxander's door. When he didn't answer, I pushed it open to a room that was nothing like the dungeon of doom I had expected.

The thick velvet curtains were drawn to one side,

allowing shimmery waves of evening sun to shine through the decorative pane of the giant window, illuminating a four-poster bed with an elaborate canopy adorned in elegant designs and golden tassels, positioned in the middle —not much different from the others I had been in—except his looked as if it hadn't been slept in a single night.

The white silk sheets and crimson duvet were still crisp and untouched, a heavy contrast to the writing desk, where the only sign anyone stayed here at all was the mess piled atop it.

I closed myself in and set the bucket down before I could lose my nerve, starting there.

The top drawer was surprisingly empty, while the second was locked. When the key in my pocket wasn't a match and the letter opener was too big, I searched beneath the scattered papers for something small to pick it with, stilling when my eyes caught on the page in my hand.

My mouth went dry.

Demetrius didn't plan to just rule over the Faye Realm—he planned to wipe out the Mortal one to expand into. I had been right to worry. Nothing would be left behind when he was finished.

I set aside Demetrius's plans for the Mortal Realm and moved the rest of the clutter, clearing the way for a better look at the giant map sprawled beneath.

"Shit," I muttered. I had known there was more my entire life—I just didn't know how much more.

I dragged a finger from the Mortal village of Terling, through the wood, to the ruins of this castle.

The province of Terrene was the closest to us, illustrated with thick forests and large lakes, identified by an emblem of a leaf within a water drop that mimicked the tattoo I had seen on Feronia.

Bordering their lands was the Kingdom of Tide and Flame.

Tide was much bigger than Flame—most of their land not land at all, but grand waterfalls that cascaded into a rendering of a city not far from the water's edge— while Flame lacked both greenery and water in their province.

It was dry and flat, butting up to steep cliffs marked with the Kingdom of Wind's emblem: a water drop with three curved lines.

It, too, was void of forests but held massive valleys and mountains along its outer border, where a landmass nearly as big as the four kingdoms combined lay unlabeled and barren to the eye.

The Mortal Realm was hardly existent compared to the Faye one—maybe fifty villages. Some were bigger than I could have guessed, but none of them were big enough. It would take Demetrius less than a week to clear it out—*days* with Alekxander on his side.

My chest tightened with the thought of starving families out in the streets… *helpless*.

There was no way of knowing if my father still fed them. If he was even still alive. If Fin and Knox were okay.

I had been gone for weeks now. The drought would have dried up any remaining streams in Terling. Gardens would be long dead, and the game would be deeper in the wood.

Gods. I needed to get out of here.

I put the papers back and began opening empty side tables and chests, looking under the bed and in the closets, searching every inch of Alekxander's room—only to come up empty-handed.

No lock. No blade.

The meeting in the throne room would be over soon, and the castle would begin preparing for tonight's Solstice kickoff. I could slip in and try the doors on the first and second-floor walkways while they were occupied—see if I could find a lock for the key in one of those rooms, at least.

I picked up the bucket and made my way out into the hallway, stopping when the air around me chilled, pebbling my skin as it had when the book fell from the top shelf.

My hand slid from the knob as I looked around the empty wing, setting the bucket down again just as the embroidered panel at the end of the hall swayed.

Hesitantly, I went to the detailed image of the castle, unmarred by time and treachery, and reached out, shifting it to the side to reveal a door hidden behind it— just as massive as the one that led into the throne room.

I checked over my shoulder to make sure no one was watching, then prodded the lock with my fingers. The key I had was far too small for it.

Taking a chance, I pushed on the doors, and they cracked open to the first room I had come across when I arrived here—one of the unmarked spaces on the map we had gone over in the kitchen.

The drape fell closed behind me as I stepped inside, my boots crunching against the glass that had once made up the domed ceiling, startling a small flock of birds into flight through the ivy- and rose-covered opening above as I stopped in front of the granite throne.

The weight of who had once sat upon it was enough to leave me fumbling as I took in its raw beauty, untouched by Demetrius's vile magic.

I could almost feel her staring down at me—the daughter of Azrail and Evaline, the product of true love between gods—and I was supposed to believe I was somehow worthy to take her place.

A cruel joke, indeed.

I shook my head at the ridiculousness of it all and followed the familiar path until I found myself where I had once been rooted by my boots.

It felt like so long ago that I had stumbled into this place—like I had been trapped in these ruins for months, not weeks.

A part of me itched at the memory of that day as low voices reached me from below.

Daring a peek around the corner, I saw Demetrius and Alekxander standing in front of the jagged throne.

Demetrius didn't look happy.

CHAPTER TWENTY-SIX

DEMETRIUS RAN a hand through his stringy hair, adjusting his gilded crown and straightening his pristine tunic like a nervous tick. "The girl is mine. They know what will happen to them if they try to take her for themselves."

"So, you've said." Alekxander stood with his hands clasped in front of his waist and his shoulders relaxed.

"Her cell has been fortified. No one can touch her in there so long as they have the intent to do her harm. If I need to, I'll make an example out of one of them at tonight's dinner."

"Phelan would make a good candidate."

"Phelan has been *nothing* but loyal. Someone the rest of you could learn from." Demetrius scowled, and the scar over his eye crinkled with the gesture. "Maybe I should have made a deal with him rather than you."

"Maybe." The Dark Faye's lips kicked up, amusement glittering in his silver eyes. "I think you'll find he lacks in certain areas, though."

A beat of silence passed between the two while Demetrius paced in deep thought and Alekxander perched on a stone stair, looking every bit the black-hearted monster the others cowered from.

The last living descendant of Azrail…

I could still feel the whisper of his fingers against my skin as he held my broken body in his hands.

I ran my fingertips over the trail of tingling heat they left behind, a faint flush creeping up my neck as I decided Phelan wasn't the only one playing games in this court of nightmares.

"Dress her up. Show everyone she is my prize. *My* prize only. Tomorrow, she will start the Infernal Tribulations. I want them to be drawn out. I want her to know she fucked up. She can't keep what is rightfully mine for much longer. She will break in front of everyone—"

"And if she doesn't?" Alekxander tilted his chin toward the rays of sun streaming through the glass ceiling, basking in the warmth they offered, his shadows hidden from sight.

"Then *you* will break her for me," Demetrius stated plainly.

Alekxander snapped his gaze back to him, and my heart twisted painfully as I watched the male in white storm out of the throne room toward his private quarters.

When the crippling feeling passed, I retreated into the cover of the arch before I could be seen, pressing my back against the cool stone with a shaky exhale while I waited for the sound of Alekxander's steps to recede.

Once I was certain he was gone, I hurried to the door diagonal from me and slipped inside, silently closing the door behind me.

The room, lit by a crack in a small windowpane, was cluttered with old paintings draped in sheets, forgotten beneath shrouds of dust. There were no obvious locks lying out… but my gaze caught on something else.

I went to the large frame half hidden in the back corner and tugged the sheet the rest of the way down.

The fabric gathered at my feet as I stared at the woman with full lips, crooked with a vengeful grin, and an angular face that somehow worked with her small chin and large eyes.

It was me… but it *wasn't*.

Her skin was paler, her hair radiant white despite the dull paint used, and between her breasts, she wore a key strung by a thin golden chain that looked a lot like the one I had in my pocket.

The signature at the bottom read, Our Queen, our salvation. Fallon.

Drawing in a breath, I tugged away what remained of the coverings, sending dust into a thick cloud that swirled around me and choked the air.

Coughing into my hand when the last sheet dropped, I stepped back for a better look.

My fingers trembled as I reached out and touched the male's thick, dark brow, tracing over his silver eyes and high cheekbones. It could have been a painting of *Alekxander*. The differences between the two were nearly undetectable.

His presence was the same—dark, deadly, *commanding*—but this male's lips were a tad thinner, and a faint dimple rested in the middle of his chin, something Alekxander didn't have.

Keir, High King of Nightfall. The Queen's—

"You seem to enjoy getting caught by me, *Fawr o un,*" Alekxander drawled from behind me, the sound of his voice winding me tight and drawing me up by my spine. "Tell me, has anyone ever told you that eavesdropping is considered to be rude?"

I dropped my hand from the painting and turned to face him, noting the absence of a dagger at his waist as soft tendrils of night drifted from his black tunic, cloaking his shoulders.

His eyes fixed on mine as he crossed his arms over his chest and slouched against the threshold, as if he'd been standing there for a while. When I didn't respond, he arched a brow, and the effort it took to drag my gaze from his was nearly painful.

My mouth was too dry, my throat too tight to speak, as Demetrius's parting words to him hung in the air, making the room feel even more carious than it already was.

"Will you make it hurt?" I asked at last, my voice barely audible.

"Do you want me to make it hurt, Riven?" My ribs constricted, squeezing my battering heart when the warmth of his knuckles lifted my chin, forcing my face up to his.

Of course, I didn't want it to hurt. I didn't *want* it to happen at all.

I cupped my hand over his, bracing myself as he slid his knuckle down the curve of my jaw. His hand opened beneath mine, fingers tenderly exploring the healed marks on my neck, as if he couldn't help himself.

The contact was enough to draw a tight sigh from my lips.

I didn't know what this deep-rooted thing was that I

felt when he touched me, bewitching me into believing there was some semblance of safety in his presence.

But there wasn't.

I pushed his hand away, wincing as I stood straighter. "Who was he?"

He glanced at the spot where I clutched my side, hesitating before going over to the sheets piled on the floor and draping one over the image of Keir.

"He led the Soldiers of Exodus during the Great War. They were allies."

"*Allies*?" I echoed.

Alekxander nodded and pressed his hands into his pockets. "Yes."

"Why then? Why have you chosen to fight with Demetrius against the Mortal Realm? To—" I pinched my lips closed, realizing my mistake.

"You've certainly been snooping." He leaned in ever so slightly, his grin darkening and his eyes sparkling with vivid light as he flicked them between mine, waiting for me to divulge anything else I shouldn't have been privy to.

He looked almost disappointed when I didn't.

"It's true," he admitted. "After you relinquish your power, Demetrius will use it to break down the magic enforcing the wall and take the Mortal Realm. Most of them won't know what has happened until it's too late."

I clenched my fists at my sides. "What did he offer you that made you so willing to help him?"

He swept his gaze over me, inhaling a deep, deliberate breath and expelling it as he said, "You wouldn't understand."

"Try me."

"From the moment I stepped foot in these ruins, Demetrius became the most powerful being in our world. *He* has the final say in what happens, Riven. Not me."

"That's not a good enough answer. How can you just sit by and let him take over like this?" I was seething now, my fists shaking. "Wasn't that the whole point of the Great War? To stop tyranny. That's what he is. A tyrant. And you all are just so eager to fall in line behind him. It's pathetic—"

His hands were wrapped around my throat before I could get another word out, a low, guttural growl reverberating from his chest as I folded my fingers around his wrists with wide eyes.

"Careful," he snarled, his glossy teeth only an inch or two from my face. "Who are you to call the Faye pathetic when it was *you* who was so willing to end it all for an easy way out? If I hadn't been there to stop you, you would be dead. *You're* the one who is pathetic, Riven. A coward. Not us."

His fingers flexed, narrowing my airway, and in a

matter of seconds, it felt like I had gone from being in front of Alekxander to being back in the throne room at Demetrius's mercy.

Shadow wafted from him, swirling around us in viscid wisps that blocked out what little light shone from the window as his pupils flared, fixed on mine.

I slammed my fists against his chest, and when he didn't budge, a horrid squeak escaped my throat.

"Tell me, Riven. Are you willing to fight now? Now that you're faced with *Death* himself?"

I reached down, grabbing the meager excuse for a weapon from my waist when I couldn't take anymore, and stabbed it into his shoulder, forcing him to let go of me.

He stepped back and prodded the wound with a lewd sound. "You'll have to fight harder than that if you plan to survive me."

Was that what he was trying to do? Scare me?

I gasped hoarsely, my chest heaving as I delivered a kick to his unguarded crotch.

He snapped forward, clutching himself with a sharp curse before I slammed my knee into the side of his face, driving the letter opener into him.

Blood coated my fingers as I leaned into his ear, tangling my other hand in his silken hair as I said through clenched teeth, "The thing about death is that you can only threaten someone with it so many times before it loses its effectiveness. When I first arrived here, I was a coward. Now I've become something I can barely recognize. It is you who should be fearful, Alekxander, *High King of Nightfall*."

I twisted the blade deeper into his flesh, and he sucked in a breath.

"Unlike you, I don't plan on rolling over like a little bitch for the Commander."

I unwound myself from him and put distance between us, watching as he stood with a salacious smirk tilting his mouth, then wrenched the blade from his sternum.

He wiped the flat of it against his muscled thigh, cleaning it with methodical swipes. "When the time comes, I will make it hurt worse than anything you've ever felt before. I will tear into you with my claws and pull your heart from your chest until you beg me to stop, Fawr o un. I *won't* be a face you forget so easily."

His words lingered between us like a decadent promise as he stalked toward me to hand the blade back, the steel slipping from his fingers with casual disregard, unbothered by the punctures I'd left him with.

His heavy-lidded gaze lingered over me—unhurried—before he turned, leaving me alone in the room, every nerve in my body alight as I stared after him.

CHAPTER TWENTY-SEVEN

I TURNED, doing as Kora directed after Alekxander left me to roam the halls absently until it was time to come back down to the kitchen.

It felt like I was miles away as I thought about those paintings, Alekxander's threat, the key, Demetrius, and my plan. The weight on my shoulders grew heavier with each passing second as I dropped my arms to my sides when Kora finished sewing me into what could hardly be considered a dress.

I stepped off the small stool with a sigh, gliding my fingers over the thin, sheer fabric—white to match Demetrius's usual ensemble—while she wrapped a coordinating sash around my waist and knotted it into a bow at the back, securing the front panels that barely kept the swell of my breasts from spilling out the middle and sides.

I pressed my knees together, my legs equally bare thanks to the overly obnoxious slits on either side of my hips that stretched from my waist to the material puddling on the floor.

It was a power move, no doubt. To make me feel vulnerable.

"What's wrong with you, girl?"

"It's nothing," I mumbled.

"It's something." She tugged at the front panel in an attempt to cover me more. "Come on. Get it out."

"Were you able to get any more clover?"

"Yes." She fluffed the fabric. "But that is not what's got you all solemn like."

I sucked my bottom lip between my teeth, releasing it with a frown as I said, "She looks like me—not just a little bit, but an *exact* copy."

Kora's graying brow lifted as she began messing with my curls, twisting them with her plump fingers to revive the life within them.

"Fallon," I clarified when she didn't respond. "I found her portrait in one of the rooms I was in today. I guess… I just thought that when Demetrius said I looked like her—" I reached for the curl she had just finished with, studying it and then letting it go, thankful that at least my brown hair was my own.

"Well, it only makes sense. Doesn't it? She made you, after all."

"I just don't get it. How could she have made me? My father tells me the story of my birth all the time." I had it committed to memory.

"I don't know," she said, her frown matching mine. "Magic is a funny thing. Fate is even funnier. I imagine all will be revealed when the timing is right—what's important is that he is your father in your heart. That's all that matters, my girl."

I nodded. Only a few weeks here, and Kora already knew the thoughts that afflicted me before I could even voice them.

"There was another painting... one of a man. He looked like Alekxander."

Her fingers stilled. "Keir."

"Keir," I repeated. "Is that all? Is it not odd he and Alekxander are also identical?"

"It would have been Alekxander's great grandfather's grandfather or something like that." She finished what she was doing and stepped back to admire her work.

"Here's the wine." Rowan emerged from the back storage with Demetrius's personal bottle selection, stopping in her steps when she laid eyes on me. "You look—"

I glanced down at myself, my cheeks hot with embarrassment as I crossed my ankles to give me some added coverage. "Naked."

"Beautiful," they said in unison.

"You're just missing one thing." Rowan handed me the bottle, and I inspected it for any obvious sign of tampering while Kora retrieved a flat box hidden beneath a linen and passed it to her to open.

She extended it to me, and I stared down at the headpiece resting on a silk pillow.

It was breathtaking.

Each side was decorated with black feathers and twisted gold, resembling the gnarled branches of the forbidden wood. I reached out to touch the gems that adorned it but stopped, afraid I might break it if I did.

"I—I can't wear this."

"You can…" Rowan grinned mischievously.

"And you will," Kora finished for her, plucking it from the pillow and placing it in my hair before I could refuse any further.

Their eyes gleamed as they looked at each other, then at me. Instinctively, I clutched the bottle of wine to my chest as though it could shield me.

"Your bruises are gone." Rowan brushed her fingers over my shoulder.

I noticed their absence when Kora was setting me up to bathe at Demetrius's request. It was a small blessing I was able to run a cloth over my skin without collapsing from the pain.

All this time, I had thought it was because of the clover I healed so quickly. Not once had I considered it could be for another reason.

How could I have?

My stomach turned leaden. I wished my bruises weren't the only thing that healed fast enough to disappear, but the damage done to my back as well. It wasn't like I planned to wander around Terling, exposing it to everyone… but *Knox* would eventually see it.

Would he be able to look at me the same? Would he still want to touch me?

I blinked away the wet lining my lashes and cleared my throat. "They aren't all that's gone." I wiggled my toes against the porous stone. "Why can't I have my boots again?"

"Ah, you can thank the High King of Nightfall for that one." Kora laughed.

"We heard someone kicked him in the balls today." Rowan picked at her nails with a wide smirk. "I bet he just *loved* that."

"He deserved it." I rolled my eyes and surveyed the bottle in my hands once more. "Do you think he'll taste it?"

Kora shrugged her shoulders and unscrewed a tin of pale pink rouge, dipping a finger into it before buffing it into my cheeks and lips. "Not sure. It's why we're starting small."

"That's reassuring," I groaned.

"It's not too late to stop this. I can still dispose of the bottle." Rowan put a hand on her hip.

"No." I turned to her when Kora put the lid back on the tin. "This might be our only chance to get the upper hand over him. It needs to be done. And…" Until the others could fight back, too, this was all we had. *Me.* I cringed at the thought, and Kora's satisfied hum drew me back to them.

"A creature worthy of all the fuss she's been getting, wouldn't you agree?"

"I thought Faye couldn't lie?" I forced out a sarcastic laugh, but it died in my throat, replaced by the rise of bile from nerves that wound tighter the longer I waited to be summoned.

"I didn't. You can ask me anything you desire, and I'd have to tell you the truth if I choose to answer."

I narrowed my eyes on her and thought of the one thing a lady always lies about. The one thing I had been most curious about during my time here. "Okay then. How old are you?"

She nearly choked, her cheeks turning as red as mine while Rowan belted out a laugh, speaking through gasps as she said, "You trapped yourself with that one."

"I'm serious." I blinked at them. "If you can't be killed—does that make you *immortal*?"

"No. It doesn't." Kora sighed, glaring at Rowan, who had her fingers pressed to her mouth in a hopeless attempt to muffle the laughter still shaking her shoulders. A strangled snort escaped anyway, earning her another glare. "Though it feels like it at times."

"Do you think—do you think I'll live a long time, too?" I reached for the blunt arch of my ear without thought.

"That I cannot answer." She placed a hand over mine, cupping it in hers and pulling it away. "Did you know Fallon didn't have pointed ears either?"

"No. I didn't."

She nodded and took the bottle from me, lifting the label ever so slightly to mark it before laying it with the rest due to go out soon. "Neither did her parents. I don't know what manner of creature you are, dear. Nor do I know how long you'll live. Or what awaits you when you return home—should you decide that is what you want. What I do know is you are here for a purpose.

When you enter the room, we can feel it in our bones you belong with us. Some are just more willing to admit to it than others. We don't need pointed ears to tell us that, and you shouldn't either."

"You've been avoiding it since you got here. Maybe try embracing it for once," Rowan said softly when she'd finally collected herself, though the tilt of her chin made it feel more like a challenge than advice as she sprayed me with something sweet-smelling.

The fine mist settled over my skin, clinging to me while I considered how I was supposed to embrace something I'd never wanted in the first place.

"He's ready for you." Albert appeared at the doorway. "Gods, Riven. You look—"

"Ethereal." Rowan placed the decorative glass bottle down and tucked the loose strands of silver back into her cap before extending her arm for me to take.

"Are you ready?"

"No," I breathed, wrapping my fingers around her bicep anyway.

Demetrius wanted to make it known I was his, and playing the part was in my best interest: keep him happy, show the others they couldn't touch me. It could work in my favor, but I had to play it carefully if I wanted this plan to succeed—if I ever wanted to taste freedom again.

We ascended the narrow stairs, pausing just before reaching the top.

"Are you sure you want to do this?" Rowan asked with a grimace, her gaze fixed ahead. "We can find another way."

"There is no other way." I dropped my arm from hers, any remaining aches and pains thankfully blanketed by nerves as I moved ahead. "I'll be fine."

I wiped my hands over the mesh wrap at my waist and lifted my chin, taking the last stair to the corridor alone, where stringed music drifted down on a wave of invisible magic, rising in a crescendo over bursts of loud laughter as I stared in awe.

The room shone with candlelight flaring high above in grand chandeliers that sparkled like diamonds.

Tables overflowed with food and wine, while white rose petals covered every surface, swept across the floor by skirts of fine ivory silks and linens.

The high-Faye and Wildlings had long since surrendered to the music, grinding against one another with reckless abandon, their masks of gold and silver gleaming in the warm light offered by the sconces.

And in the middle of it all stood Demetrius, a crooked crown resting atop his head, wearing a white silk tunic buttoned to the neck with a frilled collar and matching trousers pressed with sharp creases.

His hair was pulled back, making the hollows of his cheeks more pronounced as his gaze found mine—a sickening smile curling onto his lips, making me wish I could scrub myself raw with steel wool as the spinning in both the corridor and the throne room came to a stop.

Conversation quieted, and eating halted as the attention of the room fixed on me.

I wanted to turn and run—to hide in the dungeon until I was forgotten—but I couldn't. I *wouldn't*. For them. For me. I moved forward, my heart thundering beneath my ribs with each slow step I took.

Their eyes locked on mine, and I felt as if I were being swallowed whole—trapped in the deepest part of the moor, unable to come up for a breath while twisted fingers held me down and kept me in place.

My steps faltered as panic began to prickle at the base of my spine, the mounting tightness in my chest interrupted by Alekxander when he stepped out from the parting crowd and into my path, offering only a broad hand and nothing more—no facetious comment or presumptuous smirk.

My gaze skimmed over him, tracing the golden paint across his lids and cheekbones in place of a mask before drifting down to the dark jacket that bared his lean chest and stomach, revealing the fading bruises I'd left behind.

My cheeks heated when I boldly allowed myself to

look lower, not missing a single detail of the black pants that hugged his long legs or the muscles that peeked out from beneath his belt.

"You healed fast." I cleared my throat and took his hand, feeling more like myself as I looked away despite that annoying jolt that ran through me.

He didn't respond as we approached Demetrius—who grinned as if he'd won something of value—and I assumed that he was still cross with me about stabbing him… *again.*

I dipped my head obediently, my eyes flashing up in time to catch the gilded gleam of a collar. My fingers screamed in protest as I squeezed Alekxander's hand, drawing back on instinct.

A collar.

A *damned* collar.

Every inch of me said to fight. To stop him. To not allow this.

The pain in my fingers sharpened, biting deep until it nearly tore a yelp from me as Demetrius clasped the thin band around my neck.

I blinked the dampness from my lashes as my lungs pulled tight, each breath reduced to a shallow inhale that burned from the inside out.

My gaze shifted to the High King of Nightfall in a

silent plea, but his eyes stayed fixed ahead, the muscle in his jaw ticking.

His grip cinched tighter around my fingers, stinging heat radiating through them as I gaped at his hold—realizing it wasn't *me* squeezing his hand. It was *him* squeezing mine.

Before I could question it, Demetrius looped the delicate chain tethered to my collar around his knuckles and wrenched me away. "Come. Let's show them they will never have what is already mine."

CHAPTER
TWENTY-EIGHT

THE METAL CLUNG TO ME, shifting ever so lightly with each step as Demetrius guided me to conversation after conversation while I tried to hang on to his words. Tried to retain any information that might have been useful. But I couldn't. I couldn't think a moment past the rattle of the chain.

Naked and collared.

I was ashamed. I was—

"Move," Demetrius growled into my ear. The chain tightened, and his hands gripped the bare sides of my hips, shoving me forward before I even realized I'd stopped.

I needed to get out of my head—to focus. I clasped

my hands at my waist and ran my thumb over the lingering tingle in my fingers from Alekxander's grasp.

Anger. That's what I needed to feel right now—*not* shame.

I took a shallow breath as we approached the High Queen of Terrene.

"Lovely little show you put on for us, Commander." Feronia giggled drunkenly into her goblet as she adjusted the skirts of her gown.

Like her, it was impossibly stunning, with a long ivory train edged in gold and a low, scooped neckline revealing the inky black designs adorning her rich brown skin—tattoos most of Terrene had, if not all.

She ran her fingers over her pointed ear, pushing back the straight, silken strands that fell the length of her upper body, and adjusted the golden mask she wore— close enough now that I could see the glint in her eyes that matched it.

"I thought you might enjoy the display. Sometimes, it's good to remind those around you of what doesn't belong to them." He wrapped a finger into one of my curls possessively before dropping it to my bare shoulder.

I was glad I skipped on the additional ration of food Kora tried giving me, or it would be all over the floor.

Feronia tilted her head back with laughter. "Oh,

Commander, there is no doubt here that she belongs to you. I am eager to see how she fares tomorrow. You may have her power sooner than you think."

"I agree." There was triumph in his words.

"I couldn't help but notice smoke out in the distance from my balcony last night. Are there others coming to see what you have planned for her?"

"It is my armies you speak of in the distance. They will arrive over the next few days to await my command."

"Oh?" The Queen of Terrene expertly hid a look of concern, whereas I couldn't. "What command?"

His grin widened, and I knew exactly what command it was.

His plans were *already* in motion.

"Any command I wish." He ran a finger down my spine, and the ground seemed to tilt beneath my feet as I fought to keep my composure. "Excuse us."

I pressed a hand to my stomach, willing myself not to pass out as we moved on to Phelan and Vanira, the conversation passing in a blur—I hadn't even noticed when she slipped away, leaving us alone.

"How did you enjoy my gift?" Phelan asked, his voice steeped in arrogance.

"They were... entrancing." Demetrius shifted from

beside me. "Not like the females I usually surround myself with."

"We acquire them from their mothers when they're young. Only a select few match the sought-after traits among those in our province," Phelan began. "If you start training them young to be as you wish, the qualities tend to stick. A sentiment I wished reached more of the females around here."

I tuned them out and glanced at the others, unsure how much longer he planned to keep this up when it seemed we had already met everyone of importance, each playing their part to garner favor where it was needed.

My thumb stilled over the bends of my fingers when my gaze locked with Alekxander's from where he sat, sprawled in the farthest corner, lazily nursing the drink in his hand while Morgan went out of her way to reclaim his attention.

Part of me couldn't help but hope it was the tainted wine meant for Demetrius he'd been draining since we parted ways.

"Are you enjoying yourself, Riven?" Phelan asked, startling me. It was the first time anyone other than Demetrius had spoken to me since I'd left the kitchen. "I imagine you're missing your home in the Mortal Realm."

"I am," I admitted, dragging my eyes to those who

danced—dipping and turning with enviable elegance—so I didn't have to face the arrogant male who had been staring at my breasts for the past ten minutes.

It made me wish I'd seen the Zephyr perform earlier at the big dinner.

I'd been hoping for a glimpse of them all evening. Though, by the way Phelan spoke of them, I imagined they were locked away in their own dungeon. Or maybe they simply weren't interested in these kinds of affairs.

Demetrius clasped his hand around my wrist and led me again, not to another painfully bland conversation, but into the flurry of dancing Faye and Wildlings.

His palm flattened against the bare skin of my lower back, pulling me against him and holding me in place while his other hand stayed wrapped in my chain, crushing my fingers in his grip.

I frantically scanned the others, watching how they moved before attempting to mimic them.

Dancing wasn't something I'd ever learned. I was clumsy and underprivileged, never given the same opportunity to master it that the wealthy side of Terling had.

The panic on my face must have been obvious, because the smile Demetrius gave me when I placed my hand on his shoulder was one that almost made me forget he was the villain in this story.

"Follow me." He started slowly, moving in four-step increments until we fell into rhythm with the others, who tried and failed to mask their stares, colliding with one another in their distraction.

My heart pounded, my eyes wide as I struggled to keep up—wondering if this was how a small animal felt just before the predator that had been stalking it finally pounced.

Without warning, he spun me out, pulling me back in until I was smashed against his chest.

"You should know tomorrow marks the start of your trials," he said, and I bit my tongue, keeping silent as he went on. "Many have faced them before. Only one has ever walked away. I'll give you another chance, Riven—give me your power, and I will make it quick for you. I'll show the realm you call home mercy in the days to come. You have my word—it will remain untouched."

"A word I should trust even after my death." I narrowed my eyes. "Say what you will about the Mortal Realm, Commander, but it taught me never to trust a creature as wicked as the Faye."

His good brow raised, and I couldn't help but stiffen, bracing for a painful blow or metallic sting, unsure whether I had intrigued him or pissed him off with my statement.

"I suppose it's a good thing I am no Faye. I am a Divine being—or have you forgotten already?"

The still-healing soft spots on my head and ribs ached in answer.

"Even so," I countered, watching the blue wings of a Wildling flare out behind her as she spun, enraptured by her beauty. "You'll find that once you cross the wall, the Mortals aren't ill-prepared to stand against you."

"Ah." He chuckled, and I drew my face back to his. "Iron weapons and fake potions. It's been hundreds of years, and the Mortals haven't changed their ways. You'd think they'd consider a different tactic after being cast out. One with more merit."

"What do you mean, *cast out*?"

"Lack of education really is a problem on that side of the wall." He sighed, dragging his black eyes over mine —desolate and cold—before adding, "All beings began as Faye. Did you know that?"

He spun me before I could answer.

"We wiped most of them out during the Great War, and what was left of the lineages became watered down over time. Any who weren't considered pure or were different were sent away or hunted down for tainting the bloodlines, and a wall was erected to keep them away."

He dipped me as he clarified, "Mortals were once pure-blooded Faye. But now they are the product of everything undesirable about the race. Even the Wildlings are considered above them."

My jaw locked as I glared up at him. "For someone so *Divine*, you certainly enjoy the destruction of others."

"I do." He stopped us, turning me to face those who were still dancing. "But so do they. I could walk away from you, let you live, but they wouldn't. Not after what they've seen."

His hands tightened around my arms. "Life is about one thing. *Power.* They aren't your friends, Riven. If it wasn't for my protection, you'd already be strung up on a wall somewhere in this castle, or worse—you would think you would be grateful for it."

He released his grip on me, and my breath hitched when his fingers began tracing across the uneven skin on my back.

"Try not to get eaten," he muttered, unhooking the chain from my collar just as Adelram approached.

I didn't stick around—not even to see why everyone was so taken aback by the Advisor of Tide. Not even to fully register that Vanira's sister, Cordelia, was on his arm and not Morgan, who was still attempting to lure Alekxander into her bed, as I wove my way through drunken chatter and toward the library.

I stopped when a soft hand touched my shoulder,

turning around and nearly punching Seraphine in the face before she caught me by the wrist.

"Good reflexes." She released me, her grin fading into something more serious as she said, "I wanted to check on you—see how you were doing after… whatever that was."

"I'm fine." My voice cracked, and she looked far from convinced.

"Did he say what awaits you?"

"He told me enough."

She nodded and ushered me out of view behind one of the columns before tearing a strip of fabric from her dress. I blinked down at it, unsure what she wanted me to do.

"Clean yourself up before they see," she urged.

I ran my fingers over my cheek, feeling the tears that had gathered there, before taking it from her and dabbing the corners of my eyes so I wouldn't ruin Kora's work. "Thank you."

"You're welcome." The candlelight reflected off her golden mask. "Are you ready for tomorrow?"

"I don't have much of a choice but to be." I frowned, crumpling the fabric in my hand.

"In Flame, we train the Troops of Inferno to expect the unexpected. Never trust what you see and hear—only what you can touch."

"And if you can't touch it?"

"Then you burn a hole through it." She glared point-edly at the Commander, who was still engrossed in conversation with Adelram.

"I'll try and remember that."

"I told you my father left for the War of Light and Dark when I was little." She blew out a breath. "I didn't tell you that he never returned from it. At first, it was hard to accept. I was thrust onto the throne and expected to know and do things that shouldn't have been within my power then. I thought I would be much older before that day came." She paused. "I guess what I'm trying to say is, I don't blame you for being hesitant, is all."

"Hesitant?" Half of this realm wanted me dead; the other half expected me to resurrect the Old Kingdom because they thought I was Fallon's heir. Then there were those who just wanted me to suffer for the hell of it. "Hesitant isn't the word I'd choose."

She perked up when Adrean approached us, offering her his hand. "May I have this dance, my queen?"

"Hang in there," she said to me as she laced her fingers with his. "And remember what I said."

I watched as Adrean effortlessly swept her out onto the floor with the others, captivated by their grace. One melody turned to two before I made my way toward the library—the room empty as I slipped inside, reaching underneath the sofa to find the books I'd set aside were gone.

My brows pinched as I sank to my knees and searched again, but the space was empty.

I stood and went to the parts of the bookshelves I remembered taking the tomes from, running my fingers over the empty spots where they had once sat, noting that they hadn't been put back either.

My throat tightened as I considered the very real possibility that I was being watched more closely than I'd thought—that Demetrius might know what I'd been up to.

"Fuck." It was always one step forward and two steps backward with this damned place.

I placed my hands on my hips and paced for a moment, gathering myself before I made for the door. Any longer in here, and someone would be sent to come find me. It was already odd that Demetrius was letting me wander so freely, collar or not.

My fingers brushed the metal at my throat. Showing them I belonged to him was one thing. He could have kept me chained at his side for the display, but letting me wander without the excuse of chores—something else was going on.

CHAPTER
TWENTY-NINE

I MADE sure Demetrius had eyes on me, Alekxander too, as I moved through the crowd to a card table where two plum-skinned Wildlings played for a box of emerald beetles, not sure I wanted to know what the winner planned to do with them when the time came.

"She ran off. It was embarrassing to watch." Morgan's ladies stood not far behind me in hushed gossip. "It's a loveless marriage. What did she expect?"

"Still, it's tasteless. Why stay together if all you do is fight?" One of them snorted.

"They share a son. Perhaps it's for his sake," another answered.

I edged toward Viktor's table, having a pretty good

idea of who they spoke of when I didn't see Phelan or Vanira at each other's necks.

The High King of Tide laughed, drawing my gaze as he entertained his advisor with magic tricks—his smile contagious to those around him, aside from Adelram, who looked as if he had more than coin tricks on his mind as he watched Morgan flirt her way around the room.

I supposed there wasn't any more space on Alekxander's lap, since he and Demetrius were stretched out in an alcove with Siobhan and three others lying across them.

Dorian, thankfully, paid me no attention as I made my way closer, stepping aside when Adrean spun Seraphine into her brother's arms.

Bellinor's spine was less rigid than usual as he belted out a husky laugh—the first sign of joy I'd seen from the male as he twirled her toward the Wildlings gathered to watch, their hands clapping in time with the rhythm of their footfalls.

For a moment, it was easy to forget we were all captives in one way or another. It was easy to forget I was supposed to revile these creatures.

"Did you hear? There is a Mortal outside the castle walls."

The words were no more than a whisper to my ear as I whirled around to the empty space behind me.

If there was a Mortal outside, I could save them before it was too late. Before they're trapped here like the rest of us. I could send them home with a message for my father. I could tell him I was alive.

Seconds. It only took *seconds* for me to gather the sheer panels of my skirts and take off for the courtyard.

My bare feet thumped against the petal-covered stone, the sound echoing off the walls behind me as I ran the side passages—needing to reach them before any of the Faye did. Before the Wildlings in the wood. Before Demetrius or Alekxander.

I banked down a hallway and barreled toward the double doors that were propped open, not stopping until I reached the dimly lit courtyard where I stared wide-eyed at the empty entrance and the path that led out to the side lawn.

Was I too late?

My chest heaved as I struggled to take the next step. As I begged the forgotten gods to lend me the strength to get around the Commander's magic.

"Hello?" I shouted, desperate for an answer. "Please, if you can hear me say something."

A burst of pain stung my upper arm, forcing a ragged scream from my throat. I clasped my hand over the slick wound and turned, searching the patches of darkness for my attacker.

Another slice found the bare flesh of my thigh, and I stumbled.

It was deep. Too deep. I could feel the blood pouring from the wound, an unfathomable, teeth-chattering ache settling into my bones where the worst of it was.

I blinked wildly, trying to get my eyes to adjust to my surroundings before they could lash out again. The doors I came from were too far away for me to reach. I had no weapon. *Nothing* I could use to defend myself with.

Another jolt of blinding pain erupted over my shoulder blades.

It was a trap. And like a damned idiot, I fell for it.

The back of a hand came from nowhere, cracking across my jaw and sending me to the gravel with a hard thud. Suffocating pressure exploded in my ribs as I curled in on myself, wheezing.

I could have screamed.

I'd come so far—I was so *fucking* close to making it out of this place.

Shaking my head, I laughed at my own stupidity—at the painfully dull edge of irony.

How many times could one be tricked?

"Is something funny?" A female voice came from the shadows in front of me—one I hadn't yet heard.

I forced myself up, no longer caring about the blood seeping from my wounds or the searing burn that radiated from them when I was fucked regardless. "Alekxander is going to be so pissed he didn't get to be the one to kill me."

"I'm not scared of the Dark Faye."

"You clearly haven't seen him in a bad mood then." I wiped the sweat away from my brow.

"Will you be laughing when your entrails are pulled from you?"

I smirked, doubting anyone would be doing much of anything if their entrails were pulled out. "Maybe if you'd stop talking, we'd find out."

"Fine by me—"

I swung my arm back at the voice, my elbow connecting with a nose and cracking it before I bolted for the door, reaching into the glow of candlelight just as a broad hand reached back, yanking me into the safety of the castle walls.

"Run!" Alekxander snarled, shadow flaring violently from his shoulders as he released me and stalked into the darkness without hesitation.

I backed away, my eyes wide and my leg shaking so badly I could hardly keep it under me as I turned, doing as he said.

I didn't stop when I burst into the corridor, startled gasps erupting around me as I shoved my way through.

I didn't stop at the stairs either, nearly tumbling down them as my bare feet skipped frantically over the steps, my chest burning as I threw my weight against the kitchen door and fell into Rowan's hands before I could take another step.

She gripped my bicep while Albert snatched a cloth from nearby, pressing it firmly to my back to staunch the bleeding as he called out for Kora.

"Yes, what?" Kora waltzed in with a sack of vegetables, setting them down the instant her eyes met mine.

"Move her to the table," she ordered quickly. "Keep pressure on the wounds."

"Alekxander." I drew a sharp breath through my teeth as Kora eased me into the place she had cleared, the ache from my wounds deepening until a cold sweat dampened my skin. "He's still out there. We need to tell someone."

"Don't you worry about him, you hear me." Kora frowned, eyeing my arm. "We need to stitch this one."

"Here." Albert slid over a small wooden box and took my hand in his, his other still pressing against my back.

"I've got it." Rowan took the lead when Kora hesitated, removing the lid and readying the needle and thread. "Have you had stitches before?"

I squeezed Albert's hand, crying out when she pinched my skin closed and drove the point in—the bite nowhere near as painful as the wound itself.

"Don't leave me hanging."

"Uhm..." My voice shook as badly as the rest of me as I tried to focus, breathing in through my nose and out of my mouth in slow, steady pulls. "I fell out of a tree."

"Why were you in a tree?" Albert urged.

"It's silly—I was chased by some boys when I was a kid. They were throwing rocks—and—I stayed in it until they left, but I slipped on my way down." I swallowed. "A jagged branch caught me on my leg. I had to stitch myself up before my father could see what happened."

"Why in the hell would they do that?" Rowan asked, a sharp edge to her voice.

"Her leg needs some too." Kora blotted the blood above my knee.

"Uh—bullies. They were just bullies." I didn't have it in me to go into the real reason when all of my focus was on staying upright.

The door behind me closed, and Kora straightened with a scowl. "You have some nerve. Some *damned* nerve, do you hear me!"

Albert's hand tightened around mine, and he cursed under his breath.

"Out," Alekxander commanded, and I flinched at the hoarse sound of it.

"No way. She needs us." Rowan bared her teeth, her sticky fingers stilling against my skin as she challenged him.

My heart sank in my chest. Creatures had been killed for less in this castle.

I straightened my back, ready to jump in front of her if I needed to.

"The Commander has summoned everyone to the throne room," Alekxander growled, each word clipped and harsh. "Go upstairs. Find Isra and keep your heads down—*don't* make me ask again."

We were caught then.

I let go of Albert and steadied myself with the table's edge, afraid I'd take him down with me if I dropped.

Demetrius knew we had tried to poison him.

Albert dabbed my back with the saturated rag and placed it down, gently nudging my chin with his knuckle. "It's okay."

I shook my head. It wasn't okay. *None* of this was okay. But they went anyway, each one leaving with reluctance as Alekxander came to my side.

"He's going to kill them." I turned to go, too. Maybe I could explain it was my idea. *My* fault.

"No." Alekxander caught my wrist, holding me in

place, and the tingling I'd grown used to when he touched me was drowned beneath the crushing force of guilt in my chest as he muttered, "They'll be fine."

"I don't believe you." I jerked away, my eyes blurring with heat as I looked up at him.

He was so focused on my arm that I didn't think he'd heard me.

"I said *no*. You wouldn't make it up the stairs in this condition—quick healing or not."

He wiped his hands on Rowan's clean cloth and picked up the needle hanging from my wound, beginning where she'd left off. I winced, pressing my lower back against the edge of the prep table and digging my nails into the ridges of the wood with each repeated prick of the point that followed.

"Unless you want to end up on the floor…" He tied off the end and clipped the thread. "Don't hold your breath."

I ground my teeth, wanting to snap at him—to tell him how much I hated him for allying with Demetrius, for letting him collar me. But my tongue stayed stuck to the roof of my mouth, and it took effort just to draw my next breath, to focus on each nauseating beat of my heart as his thick, dark lashes swept over me.

His nostrils flared, and he nudged the fabric over my

leg aside with two fingers that grazed the inflamed skin. "She should have started with your thigh."

I dropped my head to look for myself, following the crimson trail that led from the kitchen door with sluggish eyes as blood trickled steadily down the curve of my calf, pooling beneath me.

Any attempt Kora had made to clean me up had been pointless.

"Oh." The room tilted to the side, and then, somehow, I was sitting on the prep table.

"*Hey*, look at me."

I fought to keep my eyes open, even as his fingers stroked unrestrained lines down my jaw and neck, breaking the gilded collar and freeing me from it.

"Riven." He wound his hands in my hair and brought me forward, pressing his mouth against my temple. His breathing was quick and harsh. *Panicked...* or maybe it was me that was panicking.

I could hardly concentrate on anything beyond the uneven thump in my ears and the heavy weight in my head, certain I could curl up right here and fall asleep.

The gash on my leg must have been even worse than it looked.

"Riven, I *need* you to look at me."

I leaned into him, unable to resist how good it felt as

the faint, decadent brush of a feather slid across my mind —followed by a bitter taste forced into my mouth.

Not clover—something else.

Gritty and foul.

It didn't cure the velutinous feeling but shoved me into semi-alertness—just enough to see my sweaty fingers digging into the front of Alekxander's bare chest.

"Good." His hands covered mine, those silver eyes darting over me with a trace of discomposure as he set my palms flat on the table at my sides before carefully peeling the blood-soaked panel away from my thigh.

I jolted forward, stopping him when the wound traveled higher than I wanted him to see.

He glared at me, and my stomach pitted when I knew I had no choice but to let him stitch it.

I muttered a curse under my breath and released his hand, leaning back and bracing myself on the table as I fixed on the texture of the grain beneath my fingertips, rather than the way his hand traced the curve of my hip, gathering the fabric of my dress before pausing for a brief moment.

He cupped the back of my knee, gently pushing my legs apart while keeping me covered—just barely—as he raised my leg and placed my foot on his knee.

I closed my eyes tightly and bit down on the meat of

my tongue, anticipating the pain that didn't come when he plunged the needle into my flesh.

"What did you give me?" I breathed, my voice wobbling.

"Draedon," he said evenly as he tugged against the thread. "It will keep you numb and alert long enough for me to do what I need to."

His hand moved further up, tenderly touching the back of my thigh, and I grew dizzy for an entirely different reason.

I wasn't numb. The pain, yes—but *him*. I could feel him.

I sucked my bottom lip between my teeth and let my head roll back, praying he would be done soon as I fought the urge to look at him—to watch him sew me up as if he'd done this a million times before, to ask why I felt this way when he touched me… or if maybe he felt it too.

His fingers moved further—tauntingly, *teasingly*, whether he meant for them to be or not.

A sigh escaped my lips and he stilled, stopping just shy of grazing the traitorous part of me that ached with a throbbing heat.

What in the hell was wrong with me?

I sat up straighter. My face and chest flushed as I kept my gaze low, avoiding meeting the steel in his eyes.

"Finished?" I cleared my throat.

He snipped the thread and lowered my leg back onto the table. "I need to check your back."

"I'm sure it's fine." I yanked my dress into place and slid off the edge, Alekxander's arm coming out just in time to catch me around my waist before I could fall.

"Easy," he breathed into my hair as I clung to him, my head resting against his shoulder while I waited for the room to stop spinning.

The scent of him—I *knew* it, but I couldn't pin it.

"The Draedon helps, but you've still lost a lot of blood."

A bitter laugh left me unexpectedly, and I shoved away from him. "Don't pretend to care, High King of Nightfall. It doesn't suit you."

The corner of his lips kicked up with anything but amusement. "Turn. *Now.*"

"Fine." My nostrils flared.

I didn't want to stay down here a moment longer with him—not when I still needed to find Rowan and the others. To make sure they were okay. To get far away from this male. Far away from that *damned* feeling.

"Are you going to kill them too?" I asked as I turned. "My attacker—are you going to kill them like you did Erik and Sibble?"

"Yes," he said, his voice softer.

"Are you going to enjoy it?" My throat tightened, and I pulled the gilded piece from my head, lifting my blood-crusted curls from my back.

The ends were stiff between my fingers as I waited for the feel of his hands against my skin or the yank of needle and thread.

Neither came.

He had seen them—they all had.

My scars weren't some carefully kept secret, not with the tunic I wore every day torn open at the back and my binding the only thing keeping it together.

So why was he just staring at them?

I chewed my lip and dropped my hair, forcing down the embarrassment and humiliation that followed the stretch of silence.

"I guess we're both monsters," I rasped. "Just for different reasons."

CHAPTER THIRTY

Whether he could lie or not, I didn't trust Alekxander's word, and I'd be damned if I spent another moment with him in crippling silence.

Leaving him there, I dragged myself up the stairs and moved through the empty corridor with a limp while I fought the weight of my eyelids. When I reached the doors to the throne room, I stalled, fearing what I might find on the other side.

The scent of lilac permeated the air—faint enough that I pushed forward, the doors opening to reveal a room filled with spectators whispering among themselves, none of them sparing me or my disarray a glance as I wove through, searching for a wisp of silver hair or a white beard.

I thought my mind might have been playing tricks on me when my eyes landed on the ladies of Zephyr, sitting on their knees in front of the jagged throne, their delicate fingers coated in dried blood and wrists bound in chains as they slumped forward in defeat.

Alekxander brushed past me, ascending the stairs to the throne and leaning in to whisper into Demetrius's ear.

"Good," Demetrius said, his mouth set in a grim line. "Leave him locked in his room."

I watched, engrossed, as Alekxander took up space before the performers, who trembled as they held one another close.

The floral scent in the room grew to near choking as I realized this *wasn't* about the bottle of wine.

"It's come to my attention that my declaration on Riven wasn't clear enough for some of you." A weight pressed down on me, the gross tang of metallic power assaulting my senses as Demetrius stood and straightened the ruffle on his tunic sleeves. The entire room shifted uncomfortably under the pulse of it—of him. "Tonight, I will make it clear."

The green-skinned goblin at my side began to buckle, and I reached out, wrapping my arm around his and lending him some of my strength despite the snarl on his face when I caught him off guard.

The ladies of Zephyr sobbed, drawing both our eyes

back to them as they tried and failed to console one another while Alekxander looked down at them, his face void of emotion and his hands tucked into his pockets as if this were just another task.

"An attack on what belongs to your king is an attack on the king himself and will be treated as such." Demetrius scanned the room. "As we move into the Solstice celebrations this week, I hope this isn't forgotten again."

My gaze flicked between the two and my teeth clenched as the realization settled in—the reason Demetrius had let me wander tonight. Why he had me dressed the way I was.

It wasn't just a declaration.

I was bait.

"If you have any final words," Demetrius said as he sat back down on the jagged throne and plucked a grape from the bowl beside him, popping it into his mouth with a raised brow. "Now would be the time."

I felt as if I were back home in Terling, *powerless* as I stared up at the wooden scaffold while Jeremiah sucked at the yellow of his teeth with sick satisfaction.

Thick, dark shadows swirled into the room, my gut urging me to close my eyes and not watch what was about to happen.

"May you never have the girl's power for yourself."

The Faye female in the middle raised her chin, and Alekxander tilted his head back.

His throat worked as he summoned darkness around him, gathering it into murky masses that filled the space with the stench of a tomb while he searched the night sky, as if waiting for the stars and the moon to speak to him.

"Alekxander." Demetrius snapped forward in his seat, the Vassal positioned in the corners of the room snarling with impatience.

And then, as if a veil had been pulled from my eyes. It was no longer the High King of Nightfall I watched with terror, but the feared Dark Faye the Commander wielded as a weapon.

Silver flames danced in his dead eyes as they found mine—a monster worse than anything this room had to offer.

Every hair on my body stood on edge as I stared back, unable to believe this was the male who had tended my wounds only moments ago, that I could even let something like *him* touch me.

With a flick of his wrist, a scream tore through the crowd—violent and raw, as the sharp edge of shadow sliced through bone and flesh.

I released the Wildling's arm and screamed again, cupping my hands over my mouth as I stepped back—

bumping into those behind me, pushing and shoving to escape. But no matter how hard I fought through the growing haze in my head and the deadening weight in my limbs, I couldn't move fast enough.

I don't know at what point my body stopped trembling, when I fell asleep, or when I ended up here—staring at the crimson stain on the floor, glistening in the silvery rays that shone through the glass ceiling above.

I had been silently standing in this spot, trying to understand, trying to accept this cruel joke that had become my life. Everything I had faced since leaving home—the first time I felt the sting of magic, and the last. Every strike from Vassal. The hunger and isolation of the dungeon, where I had learned to find comfort. The tricks and humiliation. Being so close to giving up. Being used as bait.

No normal person had to survive life this way.

I shook my head and wiped away what dampness remained on my cheeks, glad the castle was in a deep slumber for what came next. I knew what needed to be done, and I couldn't wait for it any longer. I couldn't allow anyone else to die because I was too much of a coward to make a move.

What if it was Kora who was next? *Rowan*? I pulled the letter opener from my waistband, hoping the wine would be taking effect by now. *Hoping* I was quicker than Demetrius tonight.

I raised my chin and met the eerie glow of a predator's eyes sitting in the shadows.

My knuckles turned white as I stared the male down from where I stood, not sure how long he had been watching me from the impenetrable darkness.

I had managed to stab him before. More than once. I could do it again. Pull his heart from his chest and *squeeze* it until it burst through my fingers this time.

"If you could see yourself now, you'd have no doubt you were a direct descendant of the gods above." His voice was a low, and smoky rumble through the room, coming from all directions at once and sending my heart to my throat.

"The gods have been gone a long time," I breathed, forcing my eyes to stay open despite the exhaustion, afraid that if I closed them, I'd see the faces of the Zephyr—of Eric and Sibble and the countless others he had executed. "I don't fight for them."

"Who do you fight for, then, if not for them?" He leaned forward into the dim moonlight, one arm braced on his muscular thigh.

I averted my gaze, bringing it back to the spot on the

floor I had been so focused on. "For those who need to be fought for. For those who deserve a fair and just life."

For my home. For his home. For everyone and everything in need of a chance they were never given. To leave this place and never have to look back.

"Spoken like the true heir to the realms." He stood, stepping out from the cover of shadows and coming forward. His black tunic was misbuttoned, and his hair was in more disarray than usual. "You won't succeed tonight. Go back to your cell, Riven."

"No." I flexed my fingers around the thin metal in my hand.

He shook his head, glancing down and rolling the sleeves of his wrinkled shirt to his elbows. "Don't make me tell you again, Fawr o un."

"Stop calling me that." I bared my teeth and lunged forward with my knife first, just barely missing the plane of his cheek as he pivoted out of the way.

"What would you have me call you?" He narrowed his eyes on the spot of my thigh that was beginning to bleed through my pants.

"You can call me by the name my mother and father gave me at birth." I shot forward again, stopped when he caught me by the arm.

A cry stuck in my throat as he dug his fingers into my stitches, stealing the air from my lungs.

"You're so much more than that." He released me, and I staggered back, blood dripping onto the stone at my feet as I glared at him with disgust.

"You should have closed your eyes," he said quietly.

"Closing my eyes wouldn't have changed anything. They didn't deserve to die. Not like that." My voice cracked. "It didn't have to be like that."

"How should it have been?" He paused. "There is no kind way to go about death, Riven. I made it quick, which is more than what they deserved."

"I'm so sick of hearing the cruelty in this world explained away so easily. As if the excuses make it right. You have Demetrius's ear. You could have offered them a fair trial."

"They *attacked* you. Do you really think I'd let them live?" He cocked his head, his dark hair falling over his brow when he did. "That's not how things work here. You know better than that—just like you know you aren't getting past me."

I pressed my lips into a thin line and ran at him, pouncing before I could change my mind.

The tip of my blade met the flesh of his neck just as his hands found my waist, slamming me into the column behind him. Stone bit into my spine as he pinned my wrists, holding me there while I gasped, my cry lost between us as he tightened his grip.

"If you face him, Riven, you *will* die. Do you understand me?" His voice was low, almost desperate, as if my death meant something to him. "If you go into his chambers, you will not come back out."

"I was always going to die," I whimpered, smashing my forehead into his mouth and wincing at the sharp ache that shot through my skull.

He let go, stumbling back with a furrowed brow and wiping away the small bead of blood forming at the corner of his lips.

"No matter what path I take." I swallowed, knowing the truth. "It will always end with my death."

There was never any way to avoid it. It was over for me. If I succeeded in killing Demetrius, I'd still have to look over my shoulder for the rest of my life. I'd be a danger to those around me. Any hope I had of returning home to my old life was nothing more than a delusion at this point. If it wasn't a Faye or Wildling, it would be Arwen, or another lackey sent down from the Divine Kingdom.

"No." He licked his lips. "*No.* It's not your time."

"I guess we'll find out—" I made for the door, but he sidestepped, not allowing me any closer to Demetrius's rooms.

"I *heard* you." The darkness in the room rippled.

"Begging for death when he had you in his grasp. I heard your pleas for me to end it."

My brow rose, thumb caressing the warmth of the handle in my hand. "My father would tell me stories of *Death*. He wasn't something to fear—but a friend. One who held your hand when you walked to the Veil so you weren't alone. Tell me, Alekxander, what have I done to offend you so? That even the smallest kindness would be denied to me?"

His lips parted, yet no words followed as he stared at me.

"And I was praying to Azrail," I said. "Not you."

I glanced toward the doors, and the moment his eyes followed mine, I struck.

My blade sliced through nothing but air, and before I could try again, he grabbed me—yanking me back against his chest and locking his arms around my middle while I thrashed, kicking out and slamming my heel into his shin.

A sharp curse ripped from his mouth, and he dropped me, allowing me to spin around—only to have him catch my wrist in a vise-like grip, twisting until the letter opener slipped from my grasp and clattered to the floor.

I latched onto his hand with a strangled noise, weakly prying at his fingers as he angled closer with a low snarl.

"I have faced down armies with my bare hands, Riven. Your tricks won't work on me."

"And yet you're trapped here just like the rest of us." I glared up at him. "How tragic."

His lips twitched. "It's a small price to pay. And I'd pay it over and over if it meant I got the chance to stand here."

Tears gathered in the outer corners of my eyes as I tried to wrench away from the hold he had on me. "You're no better than the Commander."

He brought his chin up, proud, as he spoke through clenched teeth. "No. I'm so much worse."

He let go of me, the light in his eyes gutting as his gaze dropped and a pulse of his power slipped through the cracks of his normally composed exterior, making me wonder exactly how much of it he was hiding—and why as he added, almost half-heartedly, "Now get back in your cage before I put you there."

I bit my lip, my pride hurt more than anything as I glanced between Alekxander and Demetrius's door. "I hate you so much."

He ran a ring-clad hand through his hair and over the edge of his alabaster jaw. "I know you do—they all do. It makes things so much easier."

He brought his tired eyes to mine once more before

turning away, muttering quietly, "Nice touch with the wine. Try a little more clover next time."

CHAPTER THIRTY-ONE

I‌F I ‌HAD a coin for every time the High King of Nightfall left me fumbling for words, I'd be able to move my father to the rich side of Terling.

"I hate him. I hate him so much."

"Now that's a little dramatic, don't you think." Kora tied off the new bandage on my arm before yawning into her hand. "Finish your broth. We need to get as much in you as we can before your first trial."

I frowned down at my cup. "What about the wine? Are you not worried he'll tell?"

She laughed and sat down beside me. "I imagine if Demetrius knew, we wouldn't be sitting here dwelling on it."

"Maybe." I pulled my knee to my chest and rested my chin on it. "I thought that's why he summoned the castle to the throne room. I thought he was going to kill you for helping me."

"Well, don't fret, girl. I'm alive and well. We all are." She glanced down at my arm and scrunched her nose. "Minus a few cuts and bruises. Drink your broth."

"Kora—I'm serious." I blew out a breath, unsure of why she would trust someone like him.

"I am, too," she countered. "We all have homes we want to get back to. Families waiting for us. I have a sister who needs me. Albert and Isra have a son who is waiting for them to return. So, if it means getting my hands dirty to make it happen, then so be it. I'll be glad to say I had some part to play in a bigger story. *Your* story."

"I can't let anyone else die," I muttered more to myself than to her after a moment. It was too much. I had seen it almost every day in Terling, and now I was seeing it here. This world was disgusting, dark, and violent, and it was sucking me into its depths. "I can't bear it."

"You should be concerned with your own life. What you did was reckless. It wasn't part of the plan. You'd be dead if the High King hadn't been there to stop you, and all this fighting would have been for nothing."

I sighed. "I thought I could do it. I managed to kill a Vassal, to stab Alekxander more than once, too."

Her brows rose as she belted with tired laughter. "Oh, child. If you stabbed Alekxander, it's only because he let you. As for the Commander's armies, they are just a bunch of mindless brutes. More brawn than brain. It's their numbers that do the damage."

I dropped my leg, feeling now like those accomplishments didn't mean much—I was an idiot for thinking I had a chance.

"You will get your opening, girl. You just need to be patient. Stick to the plan. You may not have your magic yet, but you have tenacity. I'll give you that."

Patience. *Tenacity.* I nearly laughed. I hadn't had much patience before I left Terling, and I had even less now that the trials were beginning today. It meant my time here was coming to an end, whether by my terms or the Commander's.

I sipped from the greasy broth and set the cup back down, holding my hand over the warm steam and flexing my fingers.

Weapon. Heir. Where did *Riven* fit in all of that?

"Where did you get that?" I pinched my brows, recognizing the book Kora pulled out to thumb through.

"It was in the stack brought down last night."

"I didn't—" It must have been Rowan. "Are you able to understand any of it?"

"Bits and pieces." She grimaced and reached for the plate of jelly scones left out, shoving one of the bigger ones before me. "It's in the old language. The best I can tell is that the serpent's fang is some sort of weapon—or tool. That part is unclear."

I picked at the golden flakes of the scone and frowned, doubting I would find a serpent in this castle, let alone its fang as I thought of the map Rowan had laid out a few days ago.

I still needed to find the lock that fit the key in my pocket, and there were still places off the main castle that I hadn't checked. Maybe I could find more information than what the library had to offer.

If this castle was Fallon's, maybe there were other things hidden in plain sight.

"I should get going before the castle starts to wake." I finished off my broth and stood, wrapping my scone in cloth to take with me. "Thank you—for everything, Kora."

"Hey, now." She reached for me, her pale blue eyes glistening as she gently patted my hand. "This isn't goodbye."

I forced a small smile onto my face for her sake and left. I needed to move. If I didn't, there was a good chance I'd let myself sink into a panic, and that wouldn't be good for anyone.

So, I went forward, skirting the early morning shadows with light steps so I didn't draw any attention to myself. It didn't take long until I made it to a section hidden in a wing far off from the rest of what I had already explored.

Like Fallon's throne room, it had remained untouched by the glamour. The further I went, the more unstable it became. Cracks ran through the walls, and holes gaped open in the floors where sections of the ceiling had caved in from above, leaving rotten beams jutting out at odd angles.

I reached out and pulled down a dense cobweb. The fact that this wing still stood was extraordinary.

Within a few more feet, the darkness became impenetrable, and I could no longer see in front of me. I started to turn back but hesitated when a feeling in my gut urged me forward—followed by a gust of cold air that howled through the hall, nearly knocking me on my ass.

I grabbed the nearest object and braced myself, my hair caught in the billowing surge, whipping across my face and stinging my cheeks and eyes. The walls groaned around me, and for a moment I was certain they would cave in.

The noise grew too loud, too overwhelming as I

squeezed my eyes shut, curling around the fallen rafter and holding tight until it stopped—as abruptly as it had begun, leaving me blinking at the empty space.

Flames burst to life along the walls in giant torches held in place by bolts, leaving me slack-jawed as I gawked at the hundred or so of them that lit the path before me.

Shit.

Sweat beaded on my brow as I glanced back to where I had come, then to where I was going, hating to admit it, but I kind of missed that damned bird. Luckily, it was smart enough not to enter the ruins of an eerie, enchanted, fucking castle—*unlike me.*

I blew out a breath and followed the invisible tug I felt. The stale scent of animal fat wafted around me in smoky tendrils as I went, my back stiff and my hands clammy as I clutched them at my sides, moving with caution.

I doubted Alekxander would hear me if I stumbled into one of the more questionable Wildlings—or that he'd even come to my aid after last night.

The hall ended at a set of doors untouched by time, and hesitantly I approached, pressing against the wooden panels. When they didn't budge, I eyed the lock and retrieved the key from my pocket, which felt heavier than usual as I slid it in.

A click sounded, and the doors opened.

I stepped back from the darkened entrance, a chill running the length of my spine as I reconsidered how smart this was. But that tug—that deep, ancient tug I felt inside me—was different from the one I'd felt when I admired the creatures of this realm… different from when Alekxander was near… when he touched me. I had to go.

I moved forward, and the large candles that sat upon the stone floor and on ledges lit on their own when I entered the room. The massive chamber came to life before my eyes, and it felt like an old drum began beating inside my soul as I drank in every detail of it. Touched by magic, but not Demetrius's. It felt different than his—more than a glamour, but something else. As if it had been frozen in time and someone might return at any moment.

Books lay stacked and open on tables, while quills and dried ink wells sat forgotten beside messily scribbled letters and a giant game left mid-play—mountains jutting high and valleys dipping low.

Fancily tufted chairs rested askew near the stone fire-place, which roared to life, and off to the side a couch waited with a thin blanket and decorative pillow draped across its cushions.

Balls of crumpled paper littered the floor, filling a

small basket nearby. And towering over it all were walls lined with shelves that held more books than I could have ever imagined—*thousands* of them, far more than what was in the library.

Finally able to move—able to do anything other than stare with my mouth wide open—I began looking. For what, I didn't know, but this key had found me for a reason. I was here for a reason.

I started with the giant round table in the middle of the room, running my fingers through the dust on the finished wood top before picking up one of the pieces that resembled a soldier. The metal was cool in my hand. *Heavy*.

I narrowed my eyes on the board, not a game at all, I realized, but a map. I sat the figure back down, beginning to understand.

My father's stories mentioned rooms like this one. Where wars started and ended among kings and queens.

I chewed on my lip, feeling them move around me even though I couldn't see them—the memories that weren't mine, yet somehow were. It was as if Fallon herself stood here, *guiding* me.

I slumped my head, and the loose pieces of my braid fell over my shoulder as I glanced over the neat lines of soldiers on foot and horseback, their banners held high to distinguish who was who.

It was the Great War.

I could still feel the dry heat on my face from that day, *smell* the rot of the bodies cooking in the high sun around me, and hear the buzz of flies on flesh.

They were so prepared—and for what? I touched the part of the map that hadn't yet been marred by Arwen and wondered if they had gone into battle aware they wouldn't make it back out.

I frowned, knowing I couldn't do what she wanted from me… I didn't know how to, *nor* did I want to. This was too much to expect from someone. I wasn't an heir. I wasn't the descendant of the gods. I was caught in the middle of an age-old revenge plot, and I didn't want anything to do with it.

This *wasn't* my fight. She had to understand.

After Demetrius was dead, I'd leave this place behind and forget it ever existed. I'd let my father know I was okay, tell him and the others how to protect themselves, and then go before I could put them in danger. The Mortals… the Mortals on this side of the wall would have to be saved by someone else.

The further I got from here and the ones I cared about, the better. And when the time came—when my power showed itself—I would stamp it down and hide it.

A gentle draft caught my attention, lightly scattering

the paper forgotten on the table and sending some of the sheets to the floor at my feet.

I picked one up, flinching when the ancient text recoiled from my fingers, the unreadable wording changing into the language I had known my whole life.

CHAPTER THIRTY-TWO

I HAD LOST track of time, having fallen prey to the lure of this room and its contents as I leafed through letter after letter between Fallon and the High Kings, outlining their plans for the upcoming battle. I couldn't pull my eyes away, no matter how hard I tried or how much I rubbed at the dryness in them, still exhausted and weak.

I repositioned myself on the couch and picked up the final piece from the stack I had collected and started to read.

There is strength in the realm if you stick together as one. Equal. Hold steadfast in your beliefs. Follow your hearts in my absence, and all will be well. Do not let him win. Do not become what he claims. You are the creations of Azrail and Evaline, meant to build a world of wonder and enchantment—a future to be proud of. Show strength.

We will meet again, even if in another life.

My brows pinched, and I flipped the sheet over to the back, certain that couldn't be it.

When it was blank, I leapt from the couch in search of more—anything that would tell me what happened next, *needing* to know how it ended.

But I did know…

My chest tightened, and I slid the book I had begun to retrieve back into its place on the shelf before slouching against the horizontal slats.

She fell with the others. She couldn't beat Arwen. Even after uniting the realm under one rule—a fair and just rule. Even after planning for every possible outcome.

She had armies, *power*, kings for allies—she had prepared for *years*, and she still fell.

All I had was *tenacity*.

"You chose wrong!" I shouted into the empty space, feeling utterly defeated as I cupped my hands over my face and mumbled into them, quieter, "You chose wrong."

More time went by than I cared to admit as I stayed slumped in that position. How long exactly, I wasn't sure.

I raised my head to the windows at the far end of the room to find that day had given way to night at some point, which meant it was nearly time, and with heavy steps, I went to them, opening the latch and pushing them wide to see the sky and breathe the air before I faced what awaited me in the throne room.

The silver sphere hung high, nearly full, casting its light down on me as I let my eyes close and focused on the warm breeze caressing my skin.

My wounds weren't healed, but they were better. My other injuries were nearly undetectable at this point but the blood loss from being attacked had taken a heavy toll on me.

Kora was right. Thinking I could face Demetrius last night in my condition—or in any condition—made me a fool. I could hardly stand when I was facing Alekxander. The fact that I thought I had a chance was laughable.

Did I have a chance tonight? Against what waited for me inside that box.

I opened my eyes with a sigh and looked out over the darkened shapes of the treetops, the hills, and the clouded night sky. The beauty of the stars peeked through the fluffy masses, and I wondered if Azrail and Evaline were looking back.

We hadn't found any other mentions of the box, nothing that would help me prepare for what lay in wait inside of it, and Alekxander still had my blade, leaving me to go in empty-handed.

I reached to close the window when my gaze snagged on a black feather resting on the sill. I lifted it, twirling it between my fingers, certain it hadn't been there a moment ago—*had it?*

Uneasiness settled low in my stomach as I slid it into my waistband and latched the windows shut, closing up the room and locking it behind me as I made my way back to my cell to prepare.

The halls were quiet, empty of creatures as I descended the narrow staircase to the musty dungeon. Lighting the short candle, I retrieved the tiny box left out for me to find and glanced over the clean bandages inside, silently thanking Kora as I stripped away the old one from my arm and quickly replaced it.

I stuffed the used wrapping into the box and pulled

my hair back into a less tangled braid, checking that my binding was secure, then ensuring my boots were properly laced up to my knees and my leather sheath was strapped snuggly to my thigh.

Blade or no blade, I needed any reminder of home I could get—any semblance of comfort to help me through.

Only one thing was missing.

I kicked through the hay on the ground, searching for the piece of charred wood I had taken the last time I cleaned Morgan's fireplace. When I found it, I knelt, coating my fingers in its ashes and dragging them from my eyelids to my cheekbones.

Demetrius wanted me to be broken down, weak enough for him to take what he wanted from me. I wouldn't give him that chance.

"Hear me. Protect me. Guide me," I whispered up to the gods, needing far more than a little camouflage for a traipse in the wood.

The dungeon door scraped against the stone floor, and my heart sank, my stomach hollowing as I stood and wiped my hands on my pants before facing one of Demetrius's Vassals.

I followed it up the stairs, each step weighted with dread as we neared the top, where more waited, the slits in their faces vibrating as they scented the air.

They opened the doors to the throne room, where Faye and Wildlings stood in tense clusters along the walls and balcony. The floor below lay bare, and any trace of what had happened to the Zephyr had long since been erased.

I stared ahead, catching glimpses of Kora and Rowan in the crowd as I went forward.

Viktor offered me an encouraging nod when I passed by him and his sister, and Seraphine reached out to touch my arm.

"Remember what I told you," she whispered, her fingers slipping away from me.

Never trust what you see and hear. Only what you can touch.

I planted my boots in front of the throne, and that wicked grin set my skin on fire as I stared up at Demetrius, bearing that promise I had made to myself the day I crushed that damned grape under my foot.

"What in the Divine hell have you done to your face?" He narrowed his soulless black eyes on me as he stood, descending the stairs and stopping at my side.

"I suppose I could ask you the same thing," I retorted, tight-lipped as I kept my focus ahead of me.

The back of his hand collided with my face, splitting my bottom lip against my teeth as my head snapped to the side. I squeezed my eyes closed and breathed through the ache until the buzz in my ears faded.

"Enough," he shot back.

"Oh—I'm just getting started, *Demetrius*." I straightened up, not bothering to wipe the blood from my mouth and chin, not wanting to ignite the blaze in my lip any further when I was certain there would soon be more to follow.

He gripped my shoulder, digging into my collarbone until it felt like it would splinter beneath the pressure of his fingers. "I won't miss that mouth of yours when you're gone."

Alekxander shifted in his seat and leaned forward to watch, his thumb twirling the golden rings he wore as he did, my pain no doubt getting him off.

I sucked in a breath and dropped my gaze to the ground when the throb from Demetrius's grasp became too much. My eyes watered, and my cheeks stung with heat… but I wouldn't cry out.

"You might not—but they will." I flexed my fingers at my sides, knowing damn well I should be keeping my mouth shut as the air around us charged with static.

He released me and clasped his hands behind his back, clearing his throat as if his perfect feathers hadn't just been ruffled.

"We'll see if you're still joking by the end of this."

He beckoned two fair-skinned servants who carried in a large box draped in black linen. They set it before me and slipped away just as Demetrius yanked off the cover and tossed it aside.

It was identical to the picture I had seen, sans the smeared ink.

Three bulky locks hung from different points on the chest, black spikes jutting out between them. The darkened wood had seen better days, its surface worn and scarred, while ancient text was scrawled across the front and sides, not unlike the markings I had found in the books and letters from that room.

Overall—it was a bit *underwhelming*.

"Welcome to the beginning of the end, Riven. The Infernal Tribulations," he addressed the room. "Lost for hundreds of years, it was a weapon used on prisoners of war to extract information about escapees and plots. It breaks down even the strongest of minds, withering the weak ones within minutes."

He returned to his throne, casting Alekxander a glance of pure wickedness as he sat, adding callously, "Its last known use was during the War of Light and Dark—on your *father*, wasn't it, Alekxander?"

The muscle in the High King's jaw ticked as he turned his gaze on Demetrius, who reclined in his seat like a giddy child.

My mouth went dry as I watched Alekxander, careful and contemplative. His dark waves slid over his brow when he cocked his head, revealing the golden hoops glinting at the delicate point of his ear.

It felt as if the entirety of the room held its breath, waiting to see how he would respond.

"I suppose if that's what you've heard, it must be true," he muttered.

"Hmm..." Demetrius studied him before turning back to me. "Let's begin. My patience is nearly gone."

The tension in the room thickened as I mentally listed all the reasons I had to do this, my knees trembling when I reached for the chest—stilling when I heard the strangest voice, a dreadfully *frightening* voice.

Riven. It called to me, turning the blood in my veins into ice as I stared down at it, unblinking. *The girl who seeks to free the realms.*

Its allure sucked me in until it was the only thing that existed.

Riven.

"Riven—" A hand closed around mine before I could touch the chest, its warmth pulling me back from that disembodied presence that threatened to devour me where I stood.

I looked up at Alekxander, unsure when he had left his seat or why he looked so tired. His throat bobbed, and

I flinched—caught off guard by the stinging slice to my palm that followed.

Blood pooled on the surface of my skin as he guided my hand over the box, hesitating a moment before turning it over.

"I'm sorry for what happened to your father." My voice cracked.

Alekxander closed his eyes… and after every terrible thing he had done, even as he squeezed my hand firmly in his, letting my blood fall onto the text below, my heart ached for him *and* for his father.

CHAPTER
THIRTY-THREE

The text came to life with a yellow glow, and the world around me slipped away.

I dropped my hand to my side, my fingers tingling from the wound on my palm as I glanced around the empty throne room.

Riven. The haunting whispers rode an icy gust of wind, winking out all light but what the moon offered.

Silence fell, and I took a step back from the opened chest.

"Hear me. Protect me. Guide me," I said into the darkness, my words echoing back at me... but they weren't my words at all. They were someone else's.

"Show yourself," I demanded, whipping my head around.

"Oh, Riven. You really are pathetic, aren't you." My face paled when the female figure prowled out of the darkness. "Look at you. You look like you've seen a ghost."

"H—How is this possible?" I watched with disbelief as she—as I came forward. Her thick brown hair twisted into a loose braid that hung over her shoulder while fawn-colored eyes stared back at me.

Every detail, down to the freckle, was identical to my own.

"Why do you look like me?"

"Why do you look like me?" she mocked. "How is this possible? Why me? Do you ever get tired of hearing yourself whine? I mean, really? You've been stuck on repeat since you arrived here. Given things Mortals and Faye alike can only dream of, and yet, all you do is complain."

I pivoted on my feet, still trying to comprehend what was happening as she grinned.

"What?" She clicked her tongue against her teeth. "Did I strike a nerve?"

"No," I breathed. "I was just waiting for you to finish."

Her grin broadened, making my skin crawl. "There's that sarcasm. I was wondering when it would show itself."

"It never left," I answered seamlessly.

"Now, see, I don't believe that for one minute. I know the truth, Riven. You do, too. We're the same, after all."

I tensed my jaw as she came closer, my hand going to my empty sheath on instinct. "If you know the truth, then by all means, enlighten me."

She stared at me for a moment, as if contemplating which truth to share.

"You're scared." She began circling me. "*Terrified.* You cry yourself to sleep every night until you can't breathe because you know, deep in your very core, you aren't good enough. You weren't good enough in Terling, you aren't good enough here. And you're going to die. Not good enough."

I shook my head, letting everything she said roll off me. If this was the tactic the Wraith used to make prisoners of war crumble, it would need to try harder.

"They didn't want you. They wanted what you offered them. Not one of them stood up for you when it mattered most. They would have let you bleed out on that post. Poor Riven—spent her entire life chasing the approval of others, trying to fill the void left by an absent mother, helping them before she ever helped herself. Or did she?" She laughed, sharp and cruel.

"What was the story you told the others? Oh, yes—

you climbed the tree to get away from bullies. But we know the truth, don't we? You and me. The real reason Jeremiah hated you so much."

My throat tightened. "We had to eat."

"I don't think his brother saw it that way."

"It was survival."

"Hmm…" she purred. "You don't have to lie in here. Not to me. I've done the worst. Seen the worst. *Hell*—I am the worst. The worst this world has ever witnessed. And now I'm here to show you all the terrible things you are, too… You know, when they woke me, I thought it would be another tedious task for information, but I was wrong. The Commander really has it out for you."

She sucked her teeth. "Anyway. Where were we? Ah —right. You'll have to forgive me. I'm a little rusty."

Stretching her arms and rolling her neck, she began again, "How does it feel, Riven? To know it was all pointless? That every path you might have taken would have led you here—to those who hate you even more than the Mortals. To those who would see you dead for their own gain?"

"Feels a lot like a monologue with no ending in sight."

"You want an ending? I'll tell you your ending. Better yet, I'll show it to you." She moved with a blur of speed, not giving me the chance to step out of her reach before she could latch onto either side of my face with her hands.

Her touch sucked the breath out of my lungs, turning me inside out and bending my mind painfully to her will as I screamed, fighting to keep her out.

"That only makes it worse." She grimaced. "Let. Me. In."

"No!" I shouted when my knees began to buckle.

I wouldn't let her in. *I couldn't.* If I did, there was no telling what she would find. How she would use it to her advantage. I had to fight. *I had to.* I bared my teeth, desperately trying to hang on.

"I said, let me in!" she hissed, and a dark void that left me fumbling for my next breath rolled over me. My chest squeezed, and any control I had was now gone as my knees cracked against the stone.

I slumped over—shaking, lost, *scared.* I was everything I had been the first day I stepped into these ruins. Any sign of strength, real or feigned, faded the moment she let go of me, her laugh echoing viciously in my ears as she knelt with a smile plastered to her face. To *my* face.

My stomach twisted. I—I couldn't bear to look at her.

"Ah, there she is," she said in a singsong voice, the razor-sharp edges of her presence slipping behind my eyes and grazing the threshold of my mind as if it were a gate—prickling the base of my skull and gliding down the back of my neck, as though she were digging her claws deep into my flesh, branding me.

I closed my eyes when they began to sting, tears mingling with ash as they rolled down my cheeks and pooled at my collarbones.

"Let's start, shall we?"

"Go screw yourself." I sniffled.

"Now, that's no way for a lady to speak."

It was Alma's voice. Aged and sweet—but I was no fool.

Believe none of what you hear and see, only what you can touch.

I kept my eyes closed.

"I saw you, Riven. I saw the blood on your hands. Did you feel any remorse for that boy? Do you ever even think of what you did to him?"

"I had no choice."

"We all have choices." The voice changed, and a sob broke from me. It was so perfect, so right. My fingers flexed at my sides, itching to reach for him—for my father.

"I'm disappointed in you."

"Father," I croaked, keeping my lids squeezed tight.

"I raised you to be good. To do the right thing."

"I am good." I sucked in a hoarse breath. "I'm so sorry."

"Are you?" I bit my lip at the sound of the next voice.

"I think you liked it—trying so hard to hide the real you from the others. But I see you, Riven. And I'm not the only one. I saw you when you broke that boy's jaw, felt the satisfaction radiating from you—the same satisfaction you felt when Erik and Sibble were torn to pieces right before your eyes. A darkness hidden beneath the surface."

"No."

"You thought they deserved it. You enjoyed it."

"No!" I shouted back as he leaned in, close enough, I could smell wood chips.

"Didn't you think the same thing about Alekxander when you plunged your blade into his heart? When you felt the warmth of his blood on your fingers. *Smelled* it even."

My teeth ached from clenching my jaw so tightly.

"You're broken. Damaged goods." The sound of my own voice returned, and I opened my eyes, cupping my sweaty palms over my mouth to muffle a cry as I looked at the version of myself standing in a puddle of blood, her tunic ripped from her shoulders as she stared down at me—empty, dead in the eyes.

"Here. Let me show you the monster you've become." She turned, and I cried out when I saw the plane of her back. It was nothing more than strips of flesh torn away, barely hanging on, with welts running from the nape of her neck all the way down to her tailbone.

It was no wonder Alekxander couldn't even speak when he stared at them. He was disgusted.

"The Commander will have your power, and there isn't a thing you can do to stop it. That is your ending."

No. I dropped my hands to my sides and clenched my fists. I knew what to do if I couldn't get out of here. I was resolved in the decision if it meant keeping what I had away from someone else.

She clicked her tongue. "We both know you don't have what it takes to go through with it. You never did. You couldn't do it in the throne room, and you couldn't do it all those summers ago, either—not even to grant your father one less mouth to feed. Stuck in this loop of never-ending pain. You do it to yourself, you know, with all this whining and self-loathing. Just let it go. Free yourself by giving the Commander what he wants."

"No," I said, dropping my head.

"Hmm, maybe not today—but you will. I've never met a soul I couldn't break—well, maybe one. A particularly *vulgar* one at that. Speaking of, have I told you how much I enjoy ruining surprises? And I know the best surprise yet. I'm utterly shocked you haven't figured it out for yourself." She paused. "Look at me when I'm speaking to you."

I tilted my head up, tears flooding my vision as I locked onto her, pulled into another reality—one worse than anything I could have imagined.

My hands flew back to my mouth, and I gagged into them, unable to endure the sight of bodies strung across the ground and impaled on giant pikes, in various stages of rot, while black beetles tunneled through organs already being feasted upon by rodents.

Creatures from both realms worked in endless lines, their emaciated bodies slick with sweat from the searing heat rolling off the flames that roared through the mountain's cracks—casting long shadows within their merciless glow, drenching Demetrius in light as he sat enthroned on the jagged cliff, crowned in bone while he surveyed his Empire of Death and Flame.

This... This is what he planned to do with my power —not to rule, but to destroy the realms in their entirety.

I twisted towards a ragged cry, unable to do anything but watch as a Vassal nailed a living male to a thorned spire.

Blood poured from his wounds, mingling against dirty skin, his face so battered and swollen it was nearly unrecognizable. But I recognized it. I knew his face as well as I knew my own.

"Stop!" My voice was raw with terror as I screamed, fighting against whatever held me in place, desperate to help him—to pull him down from the spikes that pierced his skin.

I watched helplessly as the Dark Faye was disemboweled with a swipe of razor-sharp claws, and it felt as if my soul were being ripped from my body—my heart crushed into a thousand pieces as I screamed for him to look at me, to raise his head one more time so I could see the silver inferno I knew burned within his eyes.

"Stop! Stop it!" I shrieked, dragged back to that empty room where I stared wide-eyed at the twisted version of myself, grinning triumphantly.

My chest pounded, my body shook uncontrollably as I fought back vomit.

"Good." She snapped her fingers and vanished into thin air.

The room rippled around me, and I was back—twisting my hand into the breast of my tunic as I gasped for air, desperate to latch onto anything that felt real while the eyes in the room raked over me.

"Welcome back." Demetrius chuckled, and I shot him a look that silenced him before I rose from my knees, my hand trembling uncontrollably as the cut in my palm healed before my eyes as if it had never happened.

"Riven," Alekxander said my name under his breath, drawing my attention to him—right where he had been when I left.

He started to reach for me, and I jerked back.

"Don't touch me," I hissed.

All I could see was the version of him from that damned box. The flames. The heat. The rot that lingered long after the lilac had faded. Their cries for help. Alekxander. I felt him die. I felt it—I *felt* him die.

"Are you done now?" Demetrius leaned forward in his seat. "Give me what is owed to me, and this will all be over."

I glared up at him, now fully aware of the extent of what he was capable of and what he planned. "My answer is no. You will never have it."

CHAPTER THIRTY-FOUR

I DIDN'T SLEEP. I didn't eat the moldy bread, drink the putrid water, or go to the kitchen. I didn't sneak off to that room or plot how to get my knife back—I just sat, hugging my knees tightly to my chest while staring into the darkness of my cell. Wondering if it stared back. Waiting for that version of me to make herself known, as if her reach went beyond the box, as if she'd latch her fingers into my skin and drag me back.

My chest burned, and my eyes blurred with lingering tears while I questioned everything. *Everything* that I was.

Was I really like them? A monster? I considered leaving Phineas about a dozen times before I realized it wasn't even him I chased after.

Part of me had been relieved when Alekxander stopped Erik and Sibble. Covered in their remains, I still found some shred of justification in it.

I wanted to hurt the Dark Faye, too. The way his blood felt on my hands—I wanted to kill him. I wanted him dead at my feet, along with Demetrius. To feel their life slip through my fingertips when I did it.

These weren't thoughts I would have had before coming here. Even if they truly deserved it, it wasn't my place to decide what happened to them.

This realm was becoming a stain on my soul. I wiped away the wet ash on my face with the sleeve of my tunic and rested my temple on a knee.

I knew the box was designed to do this—to make you question everything and tear you into pieces, to play tricks on your mind. I just hadn't expected it to work so well. I hadn't expected so much of it to be true.

My stomach growled. I wasn't sure if I could keep food down right now, nor did I want to face the others. They'd want to know what happened, and I still wasn't ready to face it myself—what I had seen in the end: a future built on the blood and bones of this world.

I gave in to the heaviness of my lids, only to yank myself back awake when the image of Alekxander on a spire of thorns found me—like it had every time I started to drift into sleep.

The planes of his face were all wrong, those entrancing eyes dull and lifeless.

My throat still felt raw from the way I had screamed for him, needing him to take another breath for me. I had never needed something so much in this life. I didn't understand it. As much as I hated him, it shouldn't have affected me the way it did.

He was horrible and depraved, everything that was wrong with this world. And maybe, at that moment, wanting him to be okay was just another of the many reasons I was officially messed up.

But somehow, somewhere along the line, he had done just as he promised—clawing his way into my chest until I had grown comfortable with the hate I felt for him —giving me something to focus on when I needed it most.

For that alone, I suppose I should be thankful.

Gods, I needed to shake this off and focus. The first trial was rough, but it didn't break me. I was still here, *still* standing—sitting. For as long as I had breath in my lungs, I wouldn't let Demetrius win, and that damned box just gave me an entirely new reason to keep going.

They could hate me all they wanted, but I wouldn't let them fall. I wasn't a monster. I was the daughter of the most amazing man this world had to offer, and he raised me to believe in good. I had to give them the chance to believe in it, too.

I stood, wiping the last of the soot from my face and brushing off the hay clinging to my pants before taking the stairs two at a time. At the top, I kept to the edges of the room so I wouldn't be noticed.

Most of the castle's inhabitants had already turned in, no longer as amused by the celebrations as they had been before the Zephyr's execution. Still, decorations hung, and food and drink remained for those drawn to the night —Viktor among them, his laughter a welcome sound that drew in the company around him.

I reached the kitchen stairwell just as Rowan emerged, a gilded tray piled high with meats and vegetables wobbling in her hands as she noticed me. "Hey. I was just about to drop this off and come check on you."

"I'm fine. I was coming to see if there were any updates."

She eyed the part of my lip that was swollen. "We've gotten through a few more pages, but it seems like it just keeps on repeating itself. Albert is down there now with his notes all over the table."

"Maybe we are looking into the wrong book," I sighed. "We're running out of time."

"I know." She frowned. "We will get this figured out, and then—"

"And then Alekxander."

"*Alekxander*?" She raised a silver brow.

"If the trials fail. I overheard the two of them talking about it."

Rowan pivoted, mumbling something under her breath and switching the tray to her other hand. "Are you able to take this to Phelan's room for me?"

I blinked at the ridiculous amount of food. "Some meal for someone who is supposed to be a prisoner."

"Yeah, well. Apparently, he's found his way back into the Commander's good graces. There's talk going around about what happened. He claims he had no part in it."

I took the weight out of her hands, not entirely sure I believed he had. Not after the offer he made me.

She untied the apron around her waist and slung it over her shoulder. "Don't trust anything he says."

Nodding, I went to turn, stopping when I remembered the other reason I was on my way to the kitchen. But she was gone before I could ask about the wine… and it looked like Morgan was on her way over to me, no doubt with a list of chores.

I adjusted my grip on Phelan's tray, raising it to cover my face as much as possible as I made my way to his room, deciding I'd ask him for the truth myself—pry it from his throat if I had to.

When I got to his door, I didn't bother knocking. I shoved it open and went inside, where he stood practically naked at a cherry wood serving hutch, pouring amber liquid into a crystal glass.

I looked away, heat rising to my cheeks instantly.

"Well, what do we have here?" The arrogance in his voice was grating as I sat the tray down on the nearest short table.

"I heard you completed your first trial today. Sorry, I missed it. I seem to have been… otherwise *detained*," he continued. "I plan to be there for the next one."

"I'm sure you do." My throat was tight as I raised my chin, keeping my eyes away from his body.

"Does my attire bother you?"

I glared at the High King of Wind then, wearing only a thin sheet wrapped around his waist. His bronzed muscles were on display, and dark brown hair swept back from his face, which had notably more stubble than it had the last time we had spoken.

"No," I lied.

"Good." He looked the length of me before tossing a handful of sugared nuts into his mouth. "What is it you want, Riven? Certainly, it wasn't to bring me my dinner."

I cleared my throat, keeping my eyes on his as I said, "I want to know why you did it."

"Do you really think I had anything to do with that?"

He huffed a laugh, leaning back against the hutch on his elbows, the sheet at his hips drooping more than necessary to reveal the deep V of his pelvis. "It was messy. If I wanted you dead, I'd have done it myself and spared you the chance to live your life in my kingdom."

I shifted uncomfortably, pressing my knees together. "I'd still be a prisoner."

"Yes—but you'd be my prisoner." He sipped from his glass. "You'd have everything you ever wanted or needed. All I'd ask for in return is unlimited access to your power. I'm not a bad guy, Riven. I simply want what's best for my people, and I tend to have a temper when I don't get what I want."

"Say's every villain ever."

He ran his tongue over his lips and came closer. Close enough, I could feel the heat radiating from his body as he reached up and touched my check, wiping away some of the missed ash with a brush of his fingers before frowning down at my lip.

"If you're so convinced I tried to kill you, why are you here? Speaking to me as if you're my equal. Better yet. If you're so convinced, I wish to do you harm… why are you *wet,* Riven?"

"What?" I backed away from him with a squeak, nearly knocking over the tray I had just set down. "I'm not—I—"

"It's nothing to be ashamed of." He crossed his arms over his chest, swirling the liquid in his glass as he watched me.

"You're disgusting."

"Am I? I'm a High King, Riven. I think I can be anything I want."

"Not for long if Demetrius gets his way," I reminded him.

He raised a brow. "I suppose that all depends on you."

"Where is your wife?" I steadied my voice, hoping he heard the disgust I purposely laced in it.

"I imagine she's somewhere contemplating my death. Or maybe she's fucking Adelram again. Who knows? The woman is a corrosive poison—much like her damned sister." The corner of his mouth kicked up. "Now that we've concluded I had nothing to do with the plot on your life, was there anything else you wanted from me?"

"No." I let my glare linger before I turned to leave, only to collide with the impossible hardness of his chest, sending me back with a curse and a flash of pain through my nose and mouth.

I cursed, staring up at him as I prodded my face, still not used to how fast the Faye could move.

"Take these." He extended his hand, and my brows

pinched together as I looked down at the berries in his palm, recognizing them as the ones Siobhan and Dorian usually ate before they disappeared into Demetrius's chambers.

"What are they?"

"Passion berries, though I've heard them called by many other names."

"Absolutely not. I have no interest in being your—" I could barely say the words. "*Sex slave.*"

"It's not for me, Riven. It's for you." His jaw feathered. "And they aren't sex slaves, just so you know. They're willing participants. These just help make it more… pleasurable for them."

He shoved them into my hand. "After the arousal wears off, the other side effects kick in. You'll sleep better than you ever have."

I blinked, still confused by what he wanted from me.

"You scream at night," he clarified. "It's become a regular occurrence, and some of us would like to get some shut-eye in this gods-forsaken castle."

"Oh." As if my cheeks couldn't turn any brighter. "I didn't know."

He moved out of my path. "If you decide you require your *other* needs met, you know where to find me."

I sucked in a breath. Despite the overall embarrassment of this encounter with the High King, I kept my face blank and reached for the lip of the tray I'd brought in, flipping it to the ground with a loud clatter. "Enjoy your dinner."

Satisfied, I slipped the berries into my pocket and shut the door behind me, slumping back against it as I waited for the heat in my cheeks to fade.

If it wasn't Phelan... then who?

My head began to ache the harder I thought about it, but I feared the other stuff would get in if I stopped. I pulled a berry from my pants pocket and studied it for a moment.

Did I really scream at night?

The lighting in the hall dimmed, and I tilted my face up, watching as the corners of the decorative banners and runners flaked away—disintegrating before my eyes, just like that book had.

And then, with a single blink, everything returned to the way it had been.

I deposited the berry with the others and stepped away from the door, narrowing my eyes on the two figures speaking in the shadows of the opposite hall, certain the box was still having its fun with me when one disappeared completely in a flash of silver.

Not just disappeared, but—I couldn't explain it. It was there one moment and gone the next, leaving me staring at the other silhouette.

A gut-wrenching ache surged in my chest, and I stepped back, bumping into Phelan's door when I realized it was Alekxander.

It felt as if I were watching him die all over again.

He started toward me, but before he could cover half the distance, I was already fleeing for the safety of my cell.

CHAPTER THIRTY-FIVE

I DIDN'T EAT the berries. A choice I now regretted as I scrubbed the floor, the muscles in my arms burning with fatigue and my lids so heavy I could barely keep them open.

I shifted my knees and started scrubbing the scuff mark at a different angle, knowing that going into this evening's trial half asleep wasn't wise, but taking the sex berries Phelan offered me last night was even less so.

I'd gotten maybe an hour of sleep after I turned in—two if I was lucky. Most of the night I'd spent staring at the ceiling of my cell until the flame of my candle guttered out, trying to summon any comfort I could among the frenzy of nerves that kept me awake, real or not.

But there were no waterfalls. No lush green mountains or rolling fields of flowers. Only death. Every time I closed my eyes, that was all I saw: a version of the world with no hope, no salvation. A world so awful that not even the figment of my raven dared to rescue me from it.

Pressure built in my head, tugging my thoughts toward a faint sensation that reminded me of digging, as if the Wraith were once again scraping at the threshold of my mind, fighting to get back in.

I was afraid that if I looked up from where I scrubbed, I'd see that version of myself weaving maliciously through the Faye and Wildlings left mingling after lunch, its presence lingering over me like an icy shadow I couldn't escape.

There was no mention of the tribulations or the fang when I returned to that room this morning, searching for ways to resist the creature that resided within the box, for weaknesses it might have—finding nothing more than what we already knew. But there were so many books that I imagined it would take me weeks to make a dent in the collection, and time was already against me.

I considered asking for help. Kora hadn't given me any reason not to trust her, nor had the others… but I needed this one advantage to be mine. Something I had in my pocket no one else did—just in case the time came when it was all I had.

"Did you see the way she looked at the Commander?"

I slumped, keeping my head down and ignoring the whisper just as I had ignored the others surfacing around the castle all day.

"She'll break, and then we can finally go home. Just wait," another said, and I pressed my lips into a tight line, keeping my focus on one of the smaller marks on the floor left from last night's celebrations.

"She doesn't deserve that kind of power. She's no heir," a Wildling sitting on a settee sunbathing her feathered wings in the sunlight muttered.

"She can't even figure out how to use it." Dorian laughed, the two members of Terrene beside him joining in.

"She isn't one of us. It isn't her place."

"Who does she think she is?"

I flipped my braid over my shoulder and ground the bristles of the brush into the stone, scrubbing harder, trying not to let their words get to me as the handle splintered in my grip—snapping against my palm and carving a gash into my skin.

A shallow breath puffed between my lips as I forced myself to breathe, studying the small cut before I tossed the remnants of the brush into the bucket and wiped the blood away with the hem of my sleeve.

I dragged my sluggish gaze to Alekxander, seated on the opposite side of the room, the dark circles beneath the dull flames in his eyes making me think he hadn't slept any more than I had.

"I'm over here." Morgan wrapped her long fingers around his wrist, positioning herself so her breasts were pressed against his shoulder as she scowled at me from her perch. Her nose scrunching up as if she could smell the grime on my skin from where she sat.

If his power was truly death, I wondered if he knew his own. If he could sense it in the air the way I could. If he could see it before it happened, as I had.

I wrenched my attention away when it became too painful... too real to look at him. Because even if he couldn't feel it or see it, I could. And if Demetrius had his way, it wouldn't just be Alekxander who would meet that terrible fate, but everyone in this room.

Those icy claws dug in again and I grabbed the bristled part of the brush, starting on a new mark, needing to stay busy—needing to keep it out.

"Too bad she can't use her power to remove that scuff mark."

The room erupted with laughter, and I had finally had enough.

I slammed the brush into the bucket, not caring about the splash that spread across the floor as I stood, glaring at each one of them before retreating to the nearest stairs and slumping beneath the archway where I was out of view.

Weight pressed down on my chest, suffocating me to the point of pain. Tears brimmed in my eyes, and my body trembled as I gasped quietly in the shadows, feeling her digging in, her voice whispering my name.

No, no, no. This is real. I was here. Leave me alone, please leave me alone.

I found every detail I could latch onto before it could slip away: the stinging pain in the palm of my hand, the itch from my mostly healed stitches, the porous texture of the stone my bare shoulder pressed against, the scent of rose and ale lingering in the air, the way the sunlight seemed to absorb into the walls and floor, yet reflected off the gilded veins beneath my boots.

I counted the doors. *One, two, three, four.* Counted the decorative spindles of the balcony. *Fifteen, twenty, thirty.*

My pulse began to slow and the crushing weight faded some as I wiped away any trace of tears, reminding myself once more that I was here, and I was okay. *This was real.*

"Better?"

I jerked my head toward Viktor, who stood in his usual kingly stance. The smile I was so certain never left his lips, nowhere to be found.

"I'm fine," I lied, pushing myself off the wall and straightening the hem of my tunic.

His brows furrowed. "You're not fine."

I cleared my throat, struggling to keep my composure. "How—" My voice cracked, and I tried again. "How do you do it?"

"How do I do what?"

"Laugh? *Smile*, when there's so much wrong? I don't get it. I keep trying, and… I just don't get it."

"Walk with me." He held out his arm for me to take, and I peered down at the sword he wore at his side, then at the matching dagger, its hilt encrusted with sea glass— both weapons he could reach before I had the chance to blink.

He followed my line of sight and shifted on his feet as he added, "I am no danger to you, Riven."

I fought a frown, wishing that were true as I wrapped my arm around his and let him lead me onto the walkway.

"It wasn't always like this." He tilted his head toward the open throne room below and stopped. "When I was a boy, my parents would tell my sister and me stories of a time when the realms weren't two but one—when we were one. Before prejudice took hold of the lands and divided us."

He swiped a hand through his carelessly brushed, sun-bleached hair and down the back of his tanned neck. "It's hard to believe now, but we are capable of so much more than this. I choose to believe there's a better future for us—not as two realms, but as one. Reunited, the way it was always meant to be. The way it was before Fallon's death."

He looked at me then, and I could have sworn the waves of the sea collided in the crystal blue of his eyes. "I have hope. It's why I laugh when no one else does. It's why I smile."

"Hope can be a fleeting thing." I pressed my lips into a tight line, watching as he plucked a freshly misted rose from the bush that cascaded over the banister.

"Hope is just the beginning. The rest is up to us." He twirled the flower between his fingers and offered it to me.

Tiny droplets of water rolled over the velvet petals as I took it... studying it in silence.

"After all this time, do you still not understand who you are, Riven?"

I glanced up and my jaw hardened. I was tired of hearing this speech. "I do."

He raised a groomed brow. "I don't think so."

My chest burned with the repetition. "I'm a weapon created by Fallon. Neither Mortal nor Faye. I—"

"We can *feel* you. Have you asked yourself yet why it is you can feel us?" He held my gaze. "There is a divide happening in this castle. Those who will follow you when the time comes and those who won't."

"You're wrong." I tried to pull away from him, but he held my arm in his too tightly.

"You are the chosen one—"

"I'm not."

He let go then and placed a finger beneath my chin. "You are the direct descendant of the gods. The heir to both realms. The one who is going to reunite us, Riven. The Faye and Wildlings are finally beginning to believe again because of you—because of what they see inside you. You're not just some revenge plot. And if you need proof…" He glanced down, dropping his hand to the hilt of his long sword.

My heart stuttered in my chest when I followed his eyes with my own. *The flower*… The droplets were no longer on the rose petals but suspended in the air above them.

How was this possible?

I opened my mouth, and before I could find my words, the glamour around us failed, just like it had when I left Phelan's rooms.

The walls crumbled into remnants of what they once were, and the floor beneath our feet cracked. The flower I held withered into nothing, as did the ones cascading over the balcony railing—pieces drifting softly to the floor below, where others held out their hands to catch them.

Then it was back.

"Did you just see that?" Viktor's eyes went wide with wonder, as if the failing glamour were more mind-boggling than the water droplets that somehow separated themselves from the ivory petals in my hand.

Alekxander pushed Morgan away and rose from his seat, disappearing into Demetrius's personal quarters while everyone else in the room stood frozen, mystified by what had just happened.

After a few moments, he reappeared.

"Tonight's trial will be postponed until tomorrow…" His eyes met mine. "Celebrations will resume as previously planned out on the side lawn."

"Tonight should be interesting." Viktor grinned. "Consider what I've said, Riven." He placed a hand over his heart and inclined his head. "We are long overdue for a ruler like you. While *some* may prefer to wait until you are ready to accept your fate, I have no such inclinations."

CHAPTER THIRTY-SIX

I FOUND my way down to the kitchen, where Kora hovered over a fresh batch of broth while Albert stirred a simmering pot of vegetables, and Rowan showed Isra her secret to rolling out the perfect dough for sweet rolls.

"The pin doubles as a weapon when you're in a pinch," she joked with him.

"Why so glum, girl?" Kora sat on the stool next to me. "We should be celebrating, not moping."

My eyes were sore from staring at the bead of broth clinging to the rim of my cup for so long that it had almost completely dried. Celebrating was the last thing on my mind.

I sighed, glancing over at her, uncertain what to divulge when it all weighed so heavily.

When I had only just begun to accept I was a poorly thought-out weapon of some sort. The idea I was also—I couldn't bring myself to say it, let alone think it.

It was clear Alekxander and Viktor had spent a little too much time around one another, though I never seemed to see them together for longer than it took to give a general greeting before moving on. I had never seen Alekxander with anyone, really. Aside from Morgan —and the figure he was speaking with under the cover of shadow.

I set my fork down. She was right. The wine was working. The glamour was weakening, which meant maybe the rest of Demetrius's magic was too. It was a small victory, but a *victory*, nonetheless. I forced on what I could of a smile. "I didn't sleep much, but I'm fine."

She reached out and cupped my hand in hers. "You're going to get through this. We all are." She frowned. "If you want to talk about what happened—"

"No," I cut her off. "I don't. I just want to forget about it."

She nodded, grim understanding etched into her features. "If you change your mind then. How are your wounds?"

"Better." I sat up. "I can't really see the one on my back, but my arm and thigh are mostly just irritated welts now. I took the bandages off them this morning and pulled what remained of the thread."

"If I could ring that male's neck."

"Get in line." Isra brushed by me for a sack of flour.

"So…" Rowan snatched a cube of cheese from my plate and tossed it into her mouth. "Did you have a good chat with Phelan? High King of *I'm better than everyone else in this castle.*"

"I don't think he had anything to do with it." I ran my fingers over the healed cut on my arm. But if what he said was the truth, then it meant whoever attempted to kill me was still in this castle—and they didn't care about Demetrius's threats. "Could Alekxander have been wrong about the Zephyr? Could they have been innocent? I elbowed one in the face hard enough it would have bruised and none of them showed any signs of being hit."

"I wasn't wrong." I nearly knocked my broth over when I heard the deep lilt of his voice from behind me. "But it's good to know you're paying attention, Fawr o un. The Zephyr took part in your assault. It wasn't Phelan who sent them out there, though. There was someone else present. Unfortunately, they disappeared, which is why I'm here."

"To use her as bait again?" Albert slammed his hand down on the table.

"Because it worked so well the last time." Rowan scoffed. "Hasn't she been through enough?"

I kept my eyes low and wrapped my fingers around my cup, focusing on the warmth radiating into my palms.

Their protests and bickering became background noise as they fearlessly stood up to the High King… but I didn't hear what they said. I couldn't feel grateful for their defense.

I only felt a painful sting in my chest as I drifted further away. The painful sting of his presence *and* his death. I had been avoiding him… but now…

That voice that was too cold and too wrong called my name.

My spine turned rigid. The hairs on my body rose, and my skin dampened with sweat. I sucked in a breath, fighting it.

They can't see. They can't know what awaits them if we fail.

My lungs burned, and Rowan grabbed my arm with a look of concern on her face, startling me. I blinked at her, trying to remember what it was that had upset them.

"I'll do it," I said finally, keeping my back to Alekxander. "I don't have a choice in the matter."

"Good. I'll be back to collect you when the sun sets." He paused. "Get her ready."

No one moved when he left… or even breathed too loudly, as if the world would break if we did. *Bait.* My hand went to my neck. *Would there be another collar? Would I have to bear Demetrius's touch again?* I shook my head and stood. It had to be done.

"We're going to be okay. It'll be okay—" I glanced at each one of them.

"What if you get hurt worse this time?" Isra slumped against Albert's side. "What if you walk into a trap and you don't walk back out?"

"Then I suppose I'll crawl."

Kora clicked her tongue. "We prepare for the worst. Let's get more clover together. Bone needle and thread just in case." She nodded and went in the direction of the cabinets.

Rowan massaged her temples before looking at Isra and Albert. "I want you two to take care of the wine. Have it sent to his quarters with dinner—two bottles this time."

They split off after she gave the order, her hand skimming over her waist for something that wasn't there.

"Rowan…" She glanced at me, but the question stuck in my throat.

I narrowed my eyes, watching as she shoved a silver piece of hair back under her cap. Not entirely sure I wanted the answer, I settled on the next best thing. "Do you think you can distract the High King of Nightfall?"

She grinned, not missing a beat. "How long do you need?"

"As long as you can give me."

She headed for the door, and I turned to Kora, taking a bundle of cloth from her and spreading it across the table to tear into strips. The rims of her eyes glistened, but she said nothing.

"What can I do for you?" I asked, and she looked up, surprised.

"You are about to willingly walk yourself into a trap —and you want to know what you can do for me?"

"Yes… you've done so much for me. All of you have. If it hadn't been for Demetrius making Alekxander bring me down here…" I sighed, knowing the truth all too well in the way my clothes hung on me, in the way the aching in my belly had eventually stopped—and what that meant. "I would have died a long time ago. So, if there is something I can do for you," I glanced at Albert, who was carefully funneling clover oil into an uncorked bottle while Isra critiqued how he was doing it, "any of you. Please let me know."

"The only thing we need from you is to survive." Kora patted my cheek and went back to tearing strips. "Just survive, girl. We are so close now."

The sound of a fight breaking out filtered its way down from the corridor. *Now* was my chance. "I'll be back."

I had to give it to Rowan—she knew how to make a distraction when it was needed.

Papers were scattered across the floor, chests gaped open, and furniture shifted while I tore through Alekxander's room, dragging the bedding to the floor and running my hand beneath the mattress before heaving it onto its side. Maybe a little *too* thorough in my search for my dagger, but I wanted what was mine, and I wasn't leaving until I found it.

I ran my hands along the underside of his bedframe and over the floor, looking for any weak boards. Then I began taking paintings from hooks on the walls and checking the backs, not bothering to put them back when I finished.

He didn't have my dagger in the throne room, which meant it had to be in here somewhere, and I wasn't giving up as easily as I had the last time I was in here.

I felt the underside of his desk, sliding my palms along the wooden surface until I felt the sharp prick of metal.

Yes! I got to my knees and freed it from the leather mount holding it.

Relief rushed through me as I turned it over in my hand with a hum, missing its weight. Just in time, too —the commotion in the corridor was dying down, which meant it was time for me to get the hell out of here.

I cracked the door, making sure the path back to the kitchen stairwell was clear before I inched out and—

"There you are."

Shit.

I slipped the blade into the sleeve of my tunic as best I could without drawing attention to it, then turned to Vanira.

"I have some things that need tending to," she said, glaring down at me with a grimace.

"I have orders from the Commander to stay in the kitchen." I closed the door behind me.

"Yes, well…" Her brow arched. "You aren't in the kitchen now, are you?"

"What is it you need?"

"Some of the beading on my dresses have come loose, and you are the only servant in this castle who knows how to do a proper hand stitch."

I bit down on my tongue and signaled for her to lead the way back to her rooms, figuring if this were a trap, I was at the very least armed with more than tenacity this time.

She opened the door, and I half expected to see her husband posted up on a piece of furniture in only a sheet —or less—as she directed me toward her vanity, where a silver gown was already laid out, the bottom draped over a chair with missing pieces of the flowers I had sewn in days ago.

"Needle and thread are in the same place. I'd like to wear it at tonight's celebration now that we're allowed to wear our house colors again. The white was becoming boring. So, if I were you, I'd hurry."

I lifted the skirts and sat down in the vanity chair, expecting her to leave the room like she usually did. This time, however, she sat lazily on a nearby bench and watched as I gathered what I needed from the drawer.

My stomach churned uneasily as I began, removing the imperfect stitches and replacing them with new ones. I knotted each delicate bead into place, waiting for a smack to the back of my hand if I placed one she didn't like. It never came, which put me even more on edge.

"Who taught you?"

I didn't look up as I answered, "My friend's mother."

"Don't you have a mother for such things?"

"No." I looped in another bead. "She died giving birth to me."

"It would explain your lack of elegance," she muttered, and I hissed when I missed the fabric, pricking my thumb instead. "If you get blood on my dress, I'll have you scrubbing it as well."

My nostrils flared as I wiped the droplet away on my thigh and began again, holding back every foul thing I wanted to say.

"My sister is the same way, unfortunately. I keep thinking she will grow out of it, but she hasn't. It's a shame, considering our mother went to great lengths to ensure we had every opportunity to get ahead in life— and more. She even made sure we had a place waiting for us in the Zephyr. It's how I met Phelan. Our marriage was the saving grace that got me out of it."

I pressed my lips together, more focused on the shapes I was making than on her life's story.

"My sister, however, simply didn't make the cut," she continued. "She'll be considered an embarrassment for generations to come—a label that's hard to outrun." She pouted her glossed-over lips. "Even so, it's incredibly unsettling. I'm doomed to a loveless marriage while she flaunts herself around this castle on any arm she wants. Do you have any siblings?"

"No." I finished the work on her hem and held it up for her approval. She stood, coming to my side to inspect it.

"I suppose that's both a blessing and a curse. Eventually, they begin to covet everything you have, and if you don't put a stop to it, they will never learn their place." She nodded, tapping her long, polished nails on the vanity top. "I have more in need of being fixed, but this will suffice for now. You're excused."

CHAPTER
THIRTY-SEVEN

When I returned to the kitchen, Kora and Rowan hung over a map of the castle grounds in tense conversation, neither one of them acknowledging me when I sat down on the stool with a heavy sigh.

I watched as Kora dragged her finger between two inked marks with a contemplative hum. "This one, too. I don't like the way it's set up. The tents are too close to each other."

"If she got cornered…" Rowan twisted up her mouth while she thought and then drew a line. "She could go out this way. It's an open area. It would give Alekxander a chance to get to her if something happened, and it's far enough away from the tree line that Valda wouldn't try anything."

"I wouldn't be too sure. The moon is almost full."

I raised my brow. "Who is Valda?"

"She represents the worst of the Wildlings." Rowan glanced up from the map. "You grew up with stories of the diamoria ravaging your borders. I grew up with stories of her."

I could feel the color drain from my face. "Oh…"

Rowan shook her head. "You'll be fine. She knows what will happen if she comes near you."

Right… because it worked out so well the last time Demetrius threatened the realm.

"It'll be okay." Isra placed a hand on my shoulder, and I frowned, doubting it as I leaned forward to memorize the routes they had drawn out—the turns I should take and the corners I should avoid, while they continued talking strategy.

"Okay, that's the last of it," Albert said as he folded over the cover of the platter sitting in front of him. "Wrap it up so the others don't see."

"Do you have any questions, girl?" Kora asked, and I shook my head as they began to clear the map away. "Good. We'd better get you ready then."

I flexed my fingers in my lap as my throat tightened, reminding myself to stay calm—because if I didn't… I pressed a hand to the back of my neck, feeling that icy sensation settle deeper.

Shaking off the dread that followed, I stood and made my way to the dry storage area, where a bucket of warm water and a cloth awaited me, stripping away my clothes and placing my dagger atop them.

After letting my hair down, I picked up the cloth and dabbed at the marks on my arm and thigh, cleaning the small cut on my palm, which had already begun to heal, before scrubbing the rest of my body.

Dipping the cloth once more, I wrung out the excess water and wiped away the sweat and dirt from my face and ears.

When I was done, I wrapped myself in a linen cloth left to the side and reached for my tunic.

"You leave those clothes, girl." Kora wandered in, holding something black in front of her. "The Commander wants you dressed in scarves again."

I frowned, not wanting to go through another night with my body on display.

"Don't fret." She unrolled what she held. The same dress, but different. *Altered.* "We made a few changes I thought you might prefer."

"But the Commander—"

"Screw the Commander. He's locked away in his rooms nursing the clover hangover of the century, thanks to those two lads in the other room. Now, we've already gone over the best routes if you need to flee. We have bandages if you're hurt, and I've got a fresh pot of broth on." She pressed a palm to my damp cheek. "We've thought of everything. Stay where Alekxander can protect you. Try to enjoy yourself. Gods know you deserve it. Just… come back to us safely. Then we'll regroup and plan for what awaits you tomorrow. The clover is working, Riven. A few more days, and you'll have your time with the Commander… we all will."

I smiled, barely, but it was there. I could feel the ghost of it against my lips as I thought of home, of how good it would feel to finally be able to leave this place. But my smile faded, and reality settled in like it had every time I let myself look forward to it.

Home would be short-lived for me.

"Let's get you dressed." She dropped her hand from my cheek and prompted me to let go of my linen and hold out my arms while she wrapped me tightly in the sheer fabric, which glimmered in the candlelight like stars in the night sky.

"Can you tell me something?" I asked, and she arched a brow, doubling down on the layer over my breasts. "*Anything*. Something I don't know about you."

She contemplated my question and then grinned slightly. "I was born in the Mortal Realm. My twin sister and I are considered *Halflings*."

I tilted my head, running my eyes over the points of

her ears sticking out from beneath her kitchen cap, mostly hidden by the crinkles of her hair. "How is that possible?"

"It happens more than you'd think. We were lucky we were found before the Mortals could toss us into the nearest stream or worse." She wrapped my hips and signaled for me to step onto the short stool. "You asked before how old I was—would you believe Rowan is older than me? We Halflings don't age the same as full-blooded Faye."

I blinked, attempting to wrap my head around that. "But—your mother and father. *Halfling* or not, they were your parents."

Her hands stilled, and then she continued knotting the back of my dress until there was no question I wouldn't fall out of it. "Mortals don't see Halflings as children. They see us as monsters. Not all of us are lucky to be saved with the wall in place, but those who are find a new home. One that accepts us with open arms no matter how pure or impure our bloodlines are."

"What's it like? Your home, I mean."

When she finished, I stepped off the stool, and she began undoing the tie in my hair and raking her fingers through my curls. "Explaining it would hardly do it justice."

"The freshest air imaginable," Albert said from the

doorway, holding the hairpiece I'd worn the last time. "A night sky you wouldn't believe, and a city so alive it takes your breath away. It's like nothing you've ever seen."

I wiggled my toes beneath the black fabric pooled over them—more of an actual skirt tonight than a few poorly placed panels. "Maybe one day I will. It sounds beautiful."

"I sure hope so." He placed the golden band in my hair and twisted the curls around my face with his fingers. "I'd hate to think our journey together ends with this castle."

"Me too," I admitted with a sigh.

He took the maroon rouge Kora handed to him and dabbed it across my cheeks and lips.

"You know what, honey!" he called to the other room, where Isra answered. "Bring me the other two containers."

Isra came in quickly, swapping out the rouge with another tin before sliding a band of sheer fabric that matched my dress up both of my arms, creating detached sleeves that hung loosely at my sides.

I couldn't help feeling thankful there wasn't a mirror nearby, doubting I'd recognize myself if there was, as Albert swiped thick gold over my upper and lower lids, taking a brush from the other tin after and drawing a thin line of black coal along each lash line before stepping back.

"What do you think?" he asked the other two that lingered over his shoulder.

"Perfect," they agreed.

"Let's get you some shoes on. He's waiting." Kora retrieved a set of black heels.

"I get shoes this time?" I snorted sarcastically and raised my skirts, allowing her to slide them on me.

"They are no good for running. You'll need to kick them off if it comes to it. But Alekxander will think twice before messing with you tonight." She stood, staring at me for a moment. "You look as I've always imagined you."

I pinched my brows together, and before I could open my mouth to question what she meant, I was wrapped into a group hug.

"It's a good thing my ribs don't hurt anymore." I groaned beneath their Faye strength, only making them squeeze me tighter.

And tighter.

"This isn't goodbye," I reminded them.

"Never goodbye," Albert whispered before they released me.

"Never," I repeated as I grabbed my leather sheath,

strapping it tightly to my thigh where it was mostly hidden before sliding my dagger into place.

"Shall we?" Kora held out her hand for me to take, an olive branch of comfort as we went back into the kitchen, where Rowan sat on the edge of her workspace with her arms crossed over her chest, glaring at the male who sat fearlessly in the chair nearest to her. His black boot propped up on a crate while he leaned back with his hands clasped behind his neck, waiting for me.

"Took you long enough—" He paused, and our eyes met for a slow, painful second before I tore mine away, and Kora gently let go.

"I thought I caught your scent in my room." He cleared his throat and stood, reaching out to touch the thin sliver of my blade that the dress didn't cover, careful not to graze my thigh as he did. "You should have just asked for it back, Fawr o un."

His voice was rough and sensuous at once, tightening every muscle in my body, whether I wanted it to or not.

"Would you have given it to me?" I kept my gaze low.

"No." He held out his hand for me to take, and I fought the urge to look up at him, afraid of what I might see if I did.

"I told you to stop calling me that." I gathered up the mesh panels of my skirt in my hands so I wouldn't trip on the stairs as I pushed by him. "I know the way. I don't need your help."

Rowan barked with laughter as I breezed by her, leaving the room and heading up.

After a moment, Alekxander followed, thankfully keeping his distance, though it did nothing to ease the unbearable weight of his gaze on my back as we left the main corridor and entered a narrow hall that opened into the courtyard, the doors braced with elaborate vases.

Beyond them, candelabras lined the gravel path in endless rows, burning a trail toward the side lawn. My steps faltered as I stared ahead, considering the last time I'd entered this courtyard—the trap I was never meant to walk away from.

I glanced down toward the mostly healed marks peeking out from beneath my dress, the light pink of them reflecting the moonlight above as warm knuckles grazed the back of my arm.

My lips trembled, and I thought I might not be able to take in my next breath as I closed my eyes and pressed a hand to my chest, where it felt as though a sword were sticking straight through it.

I am here. This is real.

"Look at me."

"I can't." I shrugged away from him, away from his

touch that was both decadent and foul, pulling me in and repelling me at the same time.

"If I'm attacked, will you save me?" I asked, wrapping my arms around myself, as if somehow they would help keep me together—knowing that he didn't have a choice in the matter if he wanted to stay in Demetrius's good graces.

I wondered if he knew how *pointless* that was.

Dread swirled in my gut, and I squeezed my lids tighter, not letting it in any further than it already was.

"Always," he whispered.

I nodded and made my way down the gravel path to the lawn, thick with beige tents and brightly colored ribbons. If he and the Commander wanted bait, I'd give it to them the best way I knew how.

Alekxander's gaze lingered as I located the crates of wine and ale, pouring myself a drink while I watched Viktor bellow with laughter, leaping barefoot around a fire as smoke and embers swirled high above his head.

The creatures around him did the same, keeping time with music that was nothing like the elegant tunes I had grown used to, but wild and provocative—twirling between tents and along pathways near the buffet tables, where Phelan sprawled drunkenly across a log in conversation with a fox-faced Wildling who absently bobbed his head while sucking down the foam from his mug.

Vanira lingered on the opposite side of the fire, glaring at the king with all the interest of someone who wished to be anywhere else.

Tossing back a hearty gulp, I gagged into my hand as the overly sweet, too-thick liquid I filled my goblet with slid down my throat, the heat already crawling up the back of my neck and prickling my cheeks.

Gods, how did they drink this stuff?

I glanced around, catching a glimpse of Feronia moving between two tents. Coughing into my hand, I quickly followed after her, stopping at the corner and peeking around the canvas to see her speaking to her general and advisor.

I eased my way to the other side, where I could hear better, and plucked the bud of a white rose from a pot to inhale, hoping I looked more interested in the flowers than them.

"It failed twice already. That could mean this is almost over," her advisor said quietly.

"I wish the fool would just kill her already," the other grumbled, and I couldn't stop myself from flinching. "He's already declared he can rule without her power. The sooner she's gone, the sooner we can leave this place."

"If you really believe that, then you are the one who is a fool," Feronia clipped out. "This is only the beginning. The Commander will lace us up with pretty promises to keep us docile, but he has no true plans to let us go home. Not for long anyway."

I took another sip of my wine, my eyes practically crossing as I fought to get it down.

It was no shock Terrene wanted me gone. Most of the castle did, but… I frowned, waiting for them to slip up with information about my attack. When they didn't, my focus shifted to where Morgan and Adelram argued before he grabbed her arm and led her out of sight.

Making sure no one was watching, I followed after them, stopping just short of the candlelight spilling from the tent's opening he had taken her into.

CHAPTER THIRTY-EIGHT

"I just don't understand." Morgan sniffled into a handkerchief. "Why are you here with Cordelia when you should be here with me? I'm so tired of waiting for you to want me back."

"I just need a little longer," he pleaded, running a hand through gelled tousles of short brown hair. Handsome in the firelight glinting off of his bronzed jaw, but not nearly worth the fuss he had been getting.

"No. I refuse to sit back and watch while you parade Vanira's sister around on your arm. If it weren't for me, you wouldn't have the position you're in now. Or should I remind you? I can have my brother take it away just as easily as I had him give it to you. Let his war chief choose your replacement when we return home."

It was now making sense why Vanira said what she did about siblings coveting what you had. I had seen Cordelia on Adelram's arm *several* times recently, and if what Phelan said about his wife was true, Adelram was courting a lot more than just Morgan and Cordelia.

I wondered if the other females would still swoon over the muscular male if they knew what an ass he was. I shook my head and took another sip of my wine. He'd out himself eventually at the rate he was going.

"Stop." He straightened his satin doublet. "You're being ridiculous. I don't have any choice but to court the other kingdoms. Your brother would be onto us if I didn't, and his approval is something I'll never have. You know that as well as I do—" There was a pause. "Please let this go."

I was looking for information, but not this kind. I glanced back at the fire to find Feronia and the other two gone. In their place, a Wildling in wooden shoes perched on a stump, piping a whimsical tune through his flute while two drunken goblins sang along.

Who else did that leave?

"Is there a reason you're spying on me?"

"What?" I whirled around and slammed into a wall of muscle, sending ale splattering over both my dress and the male I collided with as his mug slipped from his hand and tumbled to the ground.

"I'm so sorry!" I started to bend over to pick it up, but he stopped me.

I blinked up at him, his green eyes flaring with intrigue.

"You," I breathed. I hadn't seen much of him since the day Dorian and Siobhan had spoken so ill of me. Only bits and pieces.

"My apologies." The corner of his lips kicked up in a familiar way.

"You're spying on me. I want to know why." I darted my eyes to Feronia and then back to Enver… rather, the *empty* space he no longer stood in.

"I'm not." I kept my free hand within reach of my blade, and she noted the motion, stepping closer.

"If I were you, I'd be careful who you decide to listen in on. You may have fooled some of the others into believing you are something more than what you are, but not me. Not my kingdom either. You are not one of us. You stink of the Mortal Realm, and I'll be damned if you think you will ever belong on this side of the wall."

My nostrils flared, and the heat in my cheeks grew. "That's not what I think."

"I highly doubt that." Her head tilted, and she locked onto me with golden eyes.

"There you are!" My heart jumped into my throat when Seraphine appeared out of nowhere, placing her arm over my shoulders and shooting a look of warning at the Queen of Terrene, holding it until she turned away with a snort.

"I see you've finally decided to join in on the fun." She nodded toward my mostly empty goblet when Feronia was out of sight.

I flexed my fingers around the cup, wondering if she knew she probably just saved my ass. "I figured why the hell not. I made it through the first trial, cheers to the next. May it be something *actually* worth my time." I tapped the rim against hers.

"Bullshit." She leaned in closer so only I could hear her. "You don't have to pretend you're okay, Riven. If you want—"

"*No.*" I stopped her. "I don't. Not now. Not later. Not ever."

She pressed her lips into a thin line. "It wasn't real."

I blinked at her. "How do you know?"

She dropped her arm from my shoulders. "I guess I don't. I can only go by what I heard about the trials when I was a child. I'd eavesdrop on my father's meetings with the Royal Council. Usually, by the second one, they had whatever information they needed, and then they—It was terrible what they did to the Dark Faye. They didn't deserve it."

"Maybe not all of them," I said under my breath, not able to see Alekxander moving within the shadows but able to feel him. "Do you really believe they're all gone?"

"I don't know what I believe." We started walking toward the main fire. "When the Troops of Inferno came back, their numbers were decimated. For over two hundred years, we've mourned that day with silence in the Kingdom of Flame. I remember when the news arrived that they were on their way back. I waited at the front of the crowd by the gate for my father. Bellinor, too. It didn't take long before day gave way to night, and those who were still left waiting for the remainder of them to arrive realized they wouldn't be coming."

She looked up, watching the embers float by above us as if she were reading a message only meant for her. "The battle lasted for nearly a moon. They said the ground rumbled beneath their feet, and darkness descended, plummeting those left fighting into silence. The Dark Faye had all gone when it lifted, and the Light Faye assumed victory over them. Over two hundred years and Alekxander is the first one to make himself known to the world. If anyone has the answer to that question, it's him."

I dropped my gaze to the ground, imagining what it

must have felt like for them. Without my father, I would be lost. "I am sorry about your father, Seraphine. Two hundred years—is a long time to mourn."

Watching her from the corner of my eye, I could hardly believe she had been a child during Light and Dark. She didn't look much older than me, but the way she spoke—and the way she held herself—gave it away.

"If it wasn't for Adrean, I wouldn't have made it through. He was there for me through it all, especially when I just needed to talk about it." I stopped, and so did she. "I know it's a different situation, but maybe if you just—are you okay?"

She nodded toward my hand, my knuckles white from gripping my cup so tightly. I opened my mouth, but my words failed me. I didn't understand why everyone wanted to talk all of a sudden, why they couldn't just leave it be.

I forced a breath, not letting myself yield to that mounting feeling of ice, clinging to anything I could— the crackle of the logs, the faint flutter of flames popping to life, nearly drowned out by the music.

Closing my eyes, I pushed myself further—hearing more than I ever had before: the pads of bare feet on the earth, the labored breathing of those prancing in the circle, the impossible thumping beneath their chests. Not a buzz in my ears after all, but their hearts.

It was exhilarating.

My eyes shot open, and I couldn't stay away from them any longer.

"Come on." I set my goblet down in the grass and kicked off my heels. Grabbing Seraphine by the wrist before she could push me any further on the matter, I led her to the edge of the growing circle.

"Have you ever danced to Wildling music before?" She raised a brow, handing off her cup to Bellinor as we passed by him.

"Nope." I grinned over my shoulder at her, and any weight in my chest dissipated the closer I got to the flames—the closer I got to the *creatures* surrounding the flames.

The Solstice celebrations in the Mortal Realm didn't compare to those here, but dancing with a friend at least once was tradition. Tonight, Seraphine was my friend. *They* were my friends.

We stepped into the formation, and she promptly twirled me into the arms of another, twisting and hopping from foot to foot. I mimicked her, dipping in and out of the clusters the others formed until Seraphine reached out, intertwining her fingers with mine and pulling me closer. She laughed, flinging me in another direction and passing me to Faye and Wildlings alike.

I took Viktor's hand in mine, his long, tanned fingers

enveloping my thin, delicate ones as we spun, the notes of strings and flutes riding a wave of magic. He smiled, so handsome and kind, and I couldn't help but smile in return, tossing my head back to gaze at the night sky that spun with us, the specks of light moving at a dizzying speed.

My body swayed with a mind of its own, abandoning any thought of safety or plot as he let me go, passing me to the next pair of hands. It was thrilling. *Freeing.* I felt alive—more alive than I ever have.

Sweat dampened every inch of me, my bare feet one with the earth as I spun away, raising my hands into the air and bending at the waist. I moved from side to side, then leaped—caught and lifted. Weightless, I stared down, the ends of my hair spilling around Phelan's face as I sucked in a breath.

"You're a natural," he muttered as he lowered me to my feet, then twirled me out and back in. "A *damned* natural."

The scruff of his hard jaw grazed my cheek as he unwound me once more, letting me spin over and over on the tips of my toes, my unbound curls bouncing against my bare shoulders and sending a shiver racing down my spine that pebbled my skin as my fingers slipped from his.

Adrean jumped into formation nearby, dipping

Seraphine in his arms with a smile, while Bellinor laughed from the outer edges of the circle, less stiff than usual as he watched them with a drink in his hand.

It didn't take long before I was swept into the rough arms of a giant, the feeling of tree bark scraping against my skin as I stared wide-eyed, my head tilted back so I could take in his magnificence.

The creature chuckled when I missed a step, the sound deep and coarse, much like his beetle-ridden limbs that flung me out. And then I was in Viktor's grasp again, meeting his soft eyes with my own as he lifted me into the air, above the flames that grew to an impossible height.

I couldn't help but laugh. *Really* laugh. It felt as if I was flying. As if I had wings of my own as I spread out my arms while he spun us.

It felt as if—as if I was *meant* to be here. As if I was somehow tethered to them or them tethered to me.

My feet touched the ground again, and I was pulled from the chaos, panting as I gaped up at the male who coiled me tightly against the solid plane of his chest. It was the first time I had really let myself look at him since he sliced my palm open to be bled.

The High King of Nightfall stared down at me with eyes so bright, so alive, I couldn't move. I didn't *want* to, as I let him hold me against him—one hand pressed to the damp arch of my lower back, the other resting between my shoulders.

The feeling of his skin against mine... *gods.*

My lungs squeezed and I tore my gaze from his, landing it on my hands, planted firmly against his chest. The beat beneath them mimicked my own out-of-rhythm one, thrumming into my very bones.

Yet all I could think about was the sound of that beat ceasing.

Letting him touch me was a mistake. A terrible, *horrible* mistake.

My hands began to shake, and I pulled them away, tucking them against myself as I reached for my next breath. Fear. Hate. *Panic.* I couldn't focus on just one feeling as that haunting voice rose around me, drowning out the whispers from those who cast alarmed looks in my direction.

My skin tightened, suffocating me as the flames from the fire bellowed out of control, reaching for the sky as if reaching for an escape.

My eyes widened. *This couldn't be me. I wasn't doing this.*

Riven.

I snapped my head toward the voice, able to see her, see *me,* through smoke and ember. Her smile was too wide, too vicious to be mine. The flames flared again,

Faye and Wildlings fleeing as I shoved away from Alekxander, freeing myself from his hold just as Seraphine whispered into her husband's ear.

Adrean started toward me, and I retreated a step, stumbling into Viktor, who mouthed something I couldn't hear. Their words muffled as I grasped at my chest, struggling for air, feeling as if I were being sucked back into that box against my will.

Alekxander's fingers grazed my arm, and I ripped it away. I could smell the blood. I could hear their screams. I could… I… My gaze dragged over him—broken and battered, just as he'd been on that spire.

Distorted laughter rose around me and that twisted version of myself drew closer, the Faye and Wildlings oblivious to her presence as I gathered my skirts and bolted down the narrow path between the tents Rowan had laid out for my escape, crashing into anyone who didn't move aside.

I had barely reached the gravel trail leading to a side entrance of the castle before I was yanked back, bracing for the sharp sting of claws or teeth sinking into my flesh—for the crunch of bone or the blunt force of being hit or thrown.

"No! Don't touch me," I shouted, flinging my arm back into Alekxander's waiting hand.

He pulled me close, winding his arms around me and

taking my weight on himself while I gasped for air. While I tried to calm the painful ache in my chest.

"I am here. This is real," I sobbed against his shoulder, my tears soaking through his night-black tunic. "I am here. This is real."

CHAPTER THIRTY-NINE

THE WARMTH of Alekxander's fingers drew my chin up to meet his gaze, a turbulent sort of gaze I didn't understand as I blinked the dampness from my lashes away, his eyes dropping to the spot in my chest that hurt the most, as if he could see the shard sticking out of my heart.

"I'm right here," he said as he placed a broad hand on either side of my face and dipped his head lower, so we were level when he spoke. "I'm okay—I'm alive."

He took my hand in his and placed it over his heart despite my mumbled protest, forcing me to feel the life within it, thrumming beneath the pads of my fingers in strong, steady beats.

My throat tightened as I pinched my brows, darting my eyes between his. "How did you—I didn't—I—"

He pressed his forehead to mine, his dark waves falling forward to tickle my cheekbones as he slid his hand into my hair, cradling my head. "I'm right here," he assured me again, his warm breath whispering over my lips. "I'm okay. I'm not dead—not yet."

Some part of me silenced, pacified by the way he held me as I shook my head, fighting the urge to surrender to it. To him.

I didn't understand. I didn't understand any of it. I hated this male with every ounce of my being, yet all I wanted was for him to be okay.

I clenched my teeth together so tightly that my jaw ached, letting the resentment I felt for him rise above everything else.

His body tensed, and he released me, stepping back as if he remembered how much he hated me, too.

My keeper—*not* my friend.

He placed his hands into his pockets, that blank mask of his falling back into place as thunder rumbled and bright white light cracked through the sky, illuminating the ground beneath our feet.

My heart skipped in my chest as I looked up at the static charged clouds, inhaling the earthy scent deep into my lungs. A scent I'd longed for.

Another loud crack, and I backed away, turning and racing out into the darkened field where I could be far away from Alekxander—far away from the others. Where I could just be.

The Wildlings stirred in the tree line—spindly arms and eerie eyes peeking from the brush as they watched, my feet padding through soft blades of grass while thunder rumbled through me like life itself.

And then it happened.

The first drop of rain rolled down my flushed cheek, quickly followed by more that drenched my hair and dress as I came to a stop, tilting my head up and letting the warm shower fall over me, letting it wash away the pain. The *fear*.

It was an end to the drought. A chance for Terling to survive. For gardens to regrow and streams to rush back to life. A chance for the young and old. *For my father*.

I raised my palms at my sides, letting the water pool and drip from my fingertips, letting the distant sound of Faye rushing for cover under the tents fade as I fixated on the pattering of drops hitting metal and canvas, displacing gravel on the paths and gathering in thin streams that flowed from the roof of the castle, splattering into mud at the bottom.

Each rumble of thunder and crack of lightning rooted me to that ancient feeling thrumming to life beneath my ribs as I opened my eyes, my gaze clashing with Alekxander's, the distance between us blurring from the onslaught of rain.

He stood as still as a statue, his jaw flexing as night curled around him and water trailed harsh lines down his face, gathering at the hollow of his throat—his tunic clinging to every dip and bulge of lean muscle beneath it.

Rowan helped me peel away the rain-laden layers of my dress, letting it fall to the stone with a wet thud before wrapping me in a heated linen. My skin pebbled on contact, the peaks of my breasts hardening with each shiver that ran through me as I pulled my dripping hair to one shoulder and twisted it out.

"I wasn't thinking." I plucked the gilded piece from my head and handed it off to her. "I'm sorry if it's ruined."

"Because I'm just so mortally offended you got it wet." She shook her head with a broadening grin. "I'm just glad you're safe."

I twirled a wet curl around my fingers, watching as she dried it off and closed it back into its box. "Me too."

"So, are you going to tell me about your night, or are you going to leave me to guess?"

I frowned, not sure I even knew where to start or how to explain what had happened—how it felt. The dancing. The storm. *Alekxander.* "There was a moment tonight when I felt as if—I don't know. It feels silly now that I'm saying it aloud."

"It's not silly. Tell me."

"Tonight, when I was dancing... I didn't expect to feel the way I did. It was like I was connected to everything around me... like I belonged."

"And that's a bad thing?" She raised a brow.

"Yes—*No.* I don't know."

"Did you learn anything new?" She shoved a jellied scone into her mouth.

"No." I shook my head and scooted out a stool, sitting down on it. "Nothing useful. Feronia caught me listening to her conversation with her advisor and general. I think it's safe to say she won't be warming up to me anytime soon."

"She's had a stick up her ass since she arrived. I suppose she's earned it, though. Perhaps more than anyone."

The corner of my mouth kicked up, and I reached for a sweet of my own, taking an oversized bite and wiping away the crumbs that fell to my chest when I did.

Rowan looked at me funny, and I wiped at my chin, too, just in case some of the jelly made its way there.

"What?" I asked. "Is there some on my face?"

"No." She smiled. "Did you kick or stab anyone noteworthy tonight? Perhaps a certain High King with dark hair and silver eyes?"

"Does wanting to count?" I swallowed back another sugary bite and sucked away the stickiness left behind on my fingers. "My head is throbbing."

Worry pinched her brows, and I quickly clarified that it was because of the wine that was apparently far stronger than what we had in the Mortal Realm.

"Here you are, hungover and eating pastries in the nude. If only he could see this." She flashed me her teeth.

"Demetrius would have my head for sure—I'm going to need you to show me how to make these before I go home. The town I live in would love them. We usually make stew, but maybe we could make these too. Give them out during—sorry," I breathed when I noticed the grimace etching its way onto her face. "I'm rambling. It's the wine."

"You're still going to go back to the Mortal Realm?"

I pulled my linen tighter. "I have to."

"I guess I just thought maybe you would stay here with us."

"I can't." I slid off the stool and began to gather the clothing Kora had left clean and folded on the table for me. "They'll never stop hunting me. If I stay, I'm as good as dead. If I go, I at least have a chance. I need to get back home. To ensure my father is okay and then, I'll have to keep moving."

"We can protect you. You're one of us. You said it yourself—you felt like you belonged tonight."

I shook my head and slid my pants on. "The wall is weakest during the moon. When I know my father is safe, when I'm safe, I'll visit. I promise."

"No." She crossed her arms. "He's going to kill me for this, but I don't care. You deserve to know, and he should have told you when he had the chance."

"Told me what?" I dropped my tunic in place and pulled the linen free with narrow eyes. "Who?"

"The High King. There's more. I wanted to tell you sooner, but he forbade me from it. You can't leave because—"

"I know," I sighed. "He already told me. The castle is dividing itself into those who will follow me when the time is right and those who won't. Which is just plain ridiculous."

She tilted her head like I had missed something completely. "And you're still going to leave?"

"Yes."

"We need you. Now more than ever, and you're just going to abandon us?" I dropped my eyes from hers, unsure what else to say to make her understand that Fallon chose wrong. That I wasn't capable of what they thought I was.

"You are not only the rightful heir, the ruler over both realms, but also our protector—our uniter," she said evenly. "Just like Fallon before you."

I slid on my binding and began tightening it, yanking the laces and pulling them taught before tying them off and putting on my boots to do the same.

"I was raised Mortal. Brought up on fairytales and horror stories about this side of the wall. We don't have kings and queens. No magic. I haven't the first clue on how to be what you want from me, and a weird golden string tethered to my chest doesn't change that. I will do my best to send you home, and then I will do my best to survive." I strapped my sheath to my thigh and put my blade back in its place. "That is all I can promise you."

"He didn't tell you everything then. If he had, there would be no doubt you'd stay."

"There is nothing more for him to say." The throbbing in my head grew into a splitting ache. "This isn't my home."

"Some queen you're turning out to be." She turned to leave without another word, slamming the door behind her hard enough to rattle the glass bottles in the room.

I flinched at the noise that echoed through the empty

kitchen and sank back down on the stool, rubbing at my temples.

Life had been a lot simpler when I only had to worry about finding food and paying tithes.

I hadn't meant to upset her. The last thing I needed was to lose the few allies I had... though they were more than that. I cared about them as much as I cared about Fin and Knox. As much as I cared about Alma.

They had become family.

I folded my arms on the tabletop and dropped my cheek onto them, drained and exhausted as I fought the rush of anxious thoughts.

Tomorrow would be my second trial, and we were still a long way from finding anything useful in the texts.

Sitting up, I shoved my hand into the cubby beneath the table, pushing past Albert's hoard of secret spices until my fingers brushed the book with the serpent on its cover.

I opened the tome and flipped through until I found the page with the fang, its margins marked with ink from their late nights spent down here, trying to figure out what some of the words meant.

My stomach sank the longer I stared down at it, unable to help wishing the text would reveal itself to me like the books in the war room had.

I chewed my lip, considering... There were still a

few hours until sunrise, and I imagined most of the castle would already be turning in for the night. I needed sleep, but—sleep could wait.

I tucked the book under my arm and blew out what remained of the kitchen candles before heading up the stairs and peeking around the top arch to see who was still awake.

The corridor was mostly empty, aside from a few Wildlings snoring under tables and Phelan, who had passed out between the legs of one of Morgan's ladies.

I shook my head, hoping he had at least spared Vanira from seeing where he landed, and made my way to the abandoned part of the castle with quick steps, slipping into the ancient chamber and locking it tightly behind me.

Flames flared to life at my presence, lighting the room as I held the book out in front of me and opened it wide.

"Thank the gods." I exhaled in relief when the text began to transform, wasting no time in taking up residence in a chair before the fireplace to read.

CHAPTER FORTY

I STOOD ON THE FIELD, *dressed in armor that reflected the sun's harsh light.*

The air was dry enough to split my lips and chap my cheeks as I looked out, expecting the carnage I had grown so used to—flags that once stood for something great, ripped and forgotten, their tattered cloth jutting from bloodied corpses piled high.

Instead, there was nothing.

A flap of wings sounded from above, and I tilted my chin up, blocking the sun with my hand to see what manner of bird flew about, casting shadows with outstretched wings on the cracked ground beneath my feet.

I only got a glimpse of its black feathers before it disappeared, but I knew it was my raven.

When I dropped my gaze again, I no longer stood on an empty stretch of unmarred land, but at the front of a silent battalion.

My heart caught in my throat as I looked around at the faces staring back at me—a never-ending line that stretched to my left and right of armored males and females with their hands on the hilts of their swords, some far too young to be in a place like this.

I stepped out from the front to find that their numbers continued much further than I was capable of seeing as they waited, eyes wide, breathing calculated.

A trumpet sounded in the distance and the beat of my heart ramped up, churning bile in my stomach as I saw what stood before us only a short distance away.

Clad in white and gold steel, the Commander stood before his army of Vassal—just as frightening as ever, their numbers easily matching, if not exceeding, our own.

Dust rose in thick clouds as the creatures dug their claws into the earth, preparing to charge at us.

Every tiny hair on my body lifted in response—I knew how this ended.

Desperately, I tried to get the attention of my company, pushing and pulling them, screaming until my throat was hoarse and bloody for them to run—to save themselves before it was too late.

They didn't listen, didn't acknowledge me, as I fought to make them move, to make them look at me.

"Run! You have to run!" *I glanced over my shoulder to see the Commander grinning ear to ear as he began to advance.*

"Run!" *I screamed and screamed.* "Please!"

They didn't budge.

I wiped the tears from my face and took my place in line, drawing the heavy sword from my waist with shaky hands as the others had done, readying myself for the inevitable impact when a rumble of hooves erupted on the ground behind me.

My lips parted—a flag of delicate silk whipped in the dry wind as Fallon rode to the front with her head held high, her horse rearing back and kicking its legs as it neighed loudly.

"Do not be fearful!" *she addressed us, her white hair falling in wisps around her face and her helmet tucked beneath her arm as she drove the pole she carried into the ground.* "Do not show weakness. Today, we stand as one. We show Arwen just how wrong he is about us. We are not a civilization to be toyed with—*no*. We are so much more than that. We are the creations of Azrail and Evaline, the true gods of this world, and today we fight for them! For our future! For the right to be free of the tyranny of a false god!"

Fearless cheers erupted around me as those beside me raised their swords high, unwavering even as the horde of nightmarish creatures began to close in.

Fallon turned her horse, setting her helmet firmly on her head before lifting a sword of her own and leveling it at the Commander. The grin that curved her mouth was darker, more wicked than his, and in that moment I realized—she wasn't frightened. Not even as they closed in.

None of them were.

I tightened my clammy grip on the hilt of my blade and braced.

Jumping awake, I knocked the book from my lap to the floor with a loud thud as my chest heaved, sweat dampening my skin while I struggled to regain my sense of time and place before pulling the blanket from my lap and standing.

She had to know they didn't have a chance.

My fists clenched at my sides and my eyes caught on the morning rays filtering across the floor. I needed to go before anyone noticed I was gone—before Alekxander took it upon himself to start putting the lock back on my cell again.

I picked up the book that had fallen and set it on a small tea table, turning to leave—then stopping when I noticed another book sitting there as well. One I hadn't gotten out.

In fact, I didn't remember putting the blanket over me either…

The heavy tome nearly slipped from my fingers when I lifted it, opening its coarse leather cover to loose pages filled with scribbles that resembled a journal entry.

My brows scrunched when the text warped, turning readable beneath my thumb.

After a harrowing journey through the mountain pass, my mate has finally returned to me with a weapon capable of destroying the false god. I didn't believe it until I saw the fang for myself. Within seconds of picking it up, I felt my power nullify. Imagine what a weapon of this magnitude could do to Arwen himself. It would be foolish to believe we could beat him in a fair fight. At least with the serpent's fang, we have a chance.

It was a weapon then.

And should I fall in the impending battle, I've made preparations to ensure it will not be in vain. There is a temple, deep in the wood, where I have sown my magic. I bound it to my own rib bone, as my mother and father once did to create the inhabitants of this world.

What I have created is far superior. Born of flesh and bone.

— Called upon when the world is no longer something to celebrate but reviled. When the land has turned on itself and begun to wither, when kings fight for themselves and not for the hearts of others...

This being will usher forth a new era of freedom and just rule over the world, taking my crown as their own. Their strength and power will rival any God who dares to challenge our world again, and maybe they will do what I could not. Maybe they will succeed in protecting it.

My throat tightened as I closed the cover, feeling as if I might vomit from exhaustion—or pass out. Maybe both.

I stood when my head stopped spinning and located more books with identical spines on the back shelves, poring through them until my fingers ached from flipping so many pages—journals from when she was younger, details of her life and those around her. How she learned to wield her magic on her own. How she united them. Her hopes and her dreams.

I closed the book I held and set it with the rest—a carefully laid-out map to guide me. Something Fallon hadn't had while she navigated the world on her own. I could use what she wrote, rule as she did and learn to wield my magic just like her.

My fingers trailed over the cover as I swept my gaze around the room, weighing if this was what I truly wanted. Weighing what would happen if I failed—if I *succeeded*.

Making my way to the doors, I locked them tightly behind me and headed for the kitchen. It was too late to chase sleep, not that I'd be able to anyway. I needed to let the others know what I had found.

I stepped out of the ruined wing, avoiding the large crumbles of stone and debris on the ground and slinking through shadows behind columns to avoid being seen the closer I got to the corridor, doubting the Commander would be in his rooms for another day.

It was more likely he'd put on a show to pretend everything was fine with both him and the glamour.

When I rounded the corner, I caught a glimpse of Vanira and Adelram speaking and jerked back out of sight, holding my breath and praying they hadn't noticed me.

There was no explaining why I had wandered to this side of the castle. The best excuse I could come up with was that I'd been searching for cleaning supplies, which felt as unbelievable as it sounded.

After a long moment, I released the breath I'd been holding and dipped my head back around the corner, certain that if Vanira had heard me, she would have made it known.

"How could you let this happen? We were so close to being rid of my sister," she seethed at him, her fingers coiled tightly into the front of his sapphire doublet. "You would have had Viktor's crown for yourself, and Nodin would have taken Phelan's place on the throne. Now we are right back where we started."

"Get a hold of yourself." He glanced down and plucked her hands away. "All great plans come with minor hiccups. We can still get rid of your sister and have everything we've dreamed of. We just need to try again."

Viktor's crown? Phelan's throne? Killing her own sister? How in the hell was I supposed to do what Fallon wanted from me if there was always a plot to kill or be killed?

"I had it tied up in a neat bow for you." She began pacing. "We were so close."

Adelram grabbed her by the front of the dress she wore with one hand and pulled her to him. "It's not over yet. We will have what we want. And when we do, you will finally be my wife. No more of this sneaking around."

He leaned down, sliding his tongue into her mouth with a kiss that made my cheeks heat as much as the realization that Adelram had never wanted Morgan to begin with. He was only using her to get close to the crown.

I had to warn Viktor.

CHAPTER FORTY-ONE

THE EDGE of my boot clipped an uneven stone when I was too lost in thought to pay attention to where I was going. My feet tangled, and before I could reach out to catch myself, claw-like fingers wrapped tightly around my bicep, yanking me upright and pushing me forward with a snarl.

I regained my footing and glanced around, wondering why it wasn't Alekxander who had come to collect me, deciding it was probably for the best, since I still wasn't entirely sure if I could look at him… if I even *wanted* to look at him.

"I take it the Commander requests my presence?" I asked pointlessly, expelling a shaky breath and moving forward with Vassal close behind me, my hand on the hilt of my blade in case it decided to lash out.

There was nothing more sobering than being ushered like a lamb to slaughter by a creature of nightmares.

We turned down a small hall branching from the corridor and made the long walk to the throne room, where Phelan and Demetrius sat at a dining table, picking at their lunch as they conversed.

I stumbled forward with a hiss when the blunt tip of Vassal's elbow struck me in the back, sending a sharp pain splintering through me.

"Touch me again," I said as I whirled around, "and I'll—"

"You'll do nothing." Demetrius didn't bother raising his face to me as he scarfed down a hunk of juicy meat, my mouth watering and my stomach cramping as I watched the grease run down his chin.

"Hungry?" He grinned spitefully.

"The moldy ration of bread and the piss-poor excuse for water has me pleasantly full. Anything else and I'm sure to pop." I glared at him. "What is it you've summoned me for?"

Phelan hid his silent laugh behind the rim of his goblet as Demetrius cracked open the rib cage of a roasted pheasant, pulling the crimson heart from its chest and sliding it between his teeth.

"Where have you been all morning?"

I hesitated, choosing my next words carefully. "Working on my morning chores."

"Is that so?" He sucked down his wine and leaned back into his chair, those dark eyes of his swirling and contemplating as they went the length of me, stopping on my dagger. "You don't look as if you've been doing chores all morning."

Phelan set his cup down and angled forward with his elbows on the table. "If I had known her whereabouts were concerning you, my king, I would have enlightened you to the fact she was in my rooms, making and remaking my bed until it was done right."

My gaze slid to the High King, and I tried my best to hide any sign of confusion on my face as both he and Demetrius studied me.

"Did you finally get it right?" he asked, running his teeth over his bottom lip with a grin. "Even a small child could have figured it out by now."

I nodded my head, afraid my voice would deceive me if I spoke.

Demetrius contemplated, picking a piece of green lettuce from his teeth with his pinky nail before shifting in his seat. "Very well, then. I want you to know that your trials will resume today. There were matters I needed to attend to personally yesterday, but I can no longer put it off. The week of Solstice is almost over, my army is nearly complete, and my patience is long gone. Not many make it through the second trial with the Wraith. I have high hopes this will all be over soon."

I ground my teeth. "I wouldn't be too sure about that."

He leaned forward, the black in his eyes no longer fluid and swirling but hard and insentient as that disgusting sting of metallic began to pound at my senses, churning the bile in my gut and forcing my knees to wobble.

I dropped my head, focusing on drawing my next breath before he decided to rip it from my lungs like he had before, but my brows pinched, my attention now on the stone at my feet as it began to crumble and wither— the glamour fading and then returning.

The feeling pressing down on me was gone too, leaving me with a throbbing skull in its place.

Grateful the wine was still working, I looked up at him, ignoring the sweat dripping down my temple as I took in the pallor of his skin and the circles under his eyes I hadn't noticed when I entered the room.

Clearing his throat, he sat up a little straighter and undid the top button of his tunic as he collected himself —and I realized something: Demetrius didn't have enough power to harm me *and* keep the glamour up for the others.

I kept my mouth closed, not wanting to push him any further than I already had.

"Perhaps you should bow," Phelan said, *testing* me. "He is the king, after all."

The Vassal behind me came forward with its too-long limbs dragging on the ground at its sides, forcing my heart to leap into my throat as I reached for my blade.

"There is no need for that." Phelan stood, putting his hand up to stop the attack as he cockily strolled to my side.

"Play along," he whispered, knocking one of my boots out from beneath me before raising his voice, loud enough now for Demetrius to hear. "Kneel."

My knee hit the floor and my cheeks burned with humiliation, but I had no choice. Despite the thundering in my chest and the roaring in my ears that drowned out their laughter, demanding that I stand, I had to play along —to see this through to the end.

"Commander." I bowed my head and stood, resisting the urge to punch them both in their smug faces.

"I'll see to it she gets back to work." Phelan bent at the waist with a flourish of his hand, snatching my wrist in his iron-tight hold. "My king."

He straightened and tugged me toward the open

doors where Alekxander stood, his gaze unreadable as he took in the High King of Wind's hold on me.

"Alekxander, it seems you've come just in time to miss all of the fun we've been having."

"What a *pity*." The Dark Faye grimaced as Phelan dug in and dragged me forward, regardless of how hard I pulled against him.

"Oh, and Riven…" We stopped when Demetrius addressed me. "Consider me *letting* you keep the blade a kindness."

I swallowed, nearly losing my footing when Phelan snatched me back to his side.

"Did you find it?" Demetrius asked Alekxander before we were out of hearing distance, my arm twisting as I was dragged forward.

"Let go of me!" I slammed the heels of my boots down when we were far enough away, ripping myself free from Phelan's grasp.

He smirked, just like he had the first time he spoke to me. As if he was intrigued. As if I was only here to entertain him and nothing else.

"You're welcome." He leaned against the corner of the settee he had passed out on just this morning, crossing his arms over his chest as he looked down at me, all too pleased with himself.

"For what?" My hands balled into fists at my sides as

I debated whether to run him through with my blade or simply kick him in the dick.

"For saving you," he said with a chuckle, and my mouth gaped.

"If it weren't for me," he continued, "you'd still be in there, and you and I both know you haven't been doing chores—If I were you, I'd close your mouth before I give you something to put in it."

My lips snapped shut, and in a blind fury I swung at his face, my knuckles colliding with the force of a rock wall as his hand closed around my fist.

He knocked my arm aside, and I stumbled back as he took a step closer, towering over me in height.

"I am not the High King of Nightfall, my dear. Lash out at me again, and I'll break both of your arms." He reached out, fingers toying with the tired braid resting over my shoulder. "Then I'll break both of your legs."

"Screw you." My voice trembled as I watched him inhale a deep, deliberate breath through his nose, his eyes sparking with something that reminded me of hunger.

"Now? Or later?"

I didn't answer him. Not as my pelvis tightened to a near painful point and my mouth went dry. Not as I found the fullness of his lips curving to one side more appealing than they should have been.

"When I told you that you would have anything you

needed if you came to stay in my kingdom, Riven. I meant *anything*."

My eyes darted up to his. "I don't need anything from you."

He stood straighter. "We Faye are driven by the most basic of instincts. If we have needs, we fill them. If those needs aren't met, we become… *reckless*."

"I'm not Faye," I clarified. "And since we are on the topic, I thought Faye couldn't lie."

"Oh, but you are one of us. More and more every day." He lifted my arm in his hand, glancing down as he ran a thumb over my flesh. "I noticed it last night by the fire. It should be impossible with the Commander stifling all magic. But it seems the more time you spend among us, the more it shines through… And I *didn't* lie. I sent my servant to fetch you to make my bed hours ago. How was I supposed to know she never found you?"

I rolled my eyes, dropping them to where his thumb was, not seeing what he was talking about until he tilted my wrist enough that the candlelight glinted off it. It was subtle, but it was there—a faint sparkle embedded in my skin that was otherwise invisible without the direct lighting.

"I still have months until my twenty-fifth year around the sun." I withdrew my hand from his.

He narrowed his eyes. "Your power becomes *mature*

at that age—you had to have felt it coursing through you last night. The fire dancing with you. The earth singing under your bare feet. Even the wind and rain came when you called."

"Impossible," I whispered.

"Come to my kingdom, Riven. I'll show you how to control it. I'll show you an entire world you've yet to see. A world even your wildest dreams couldn't capture."

I shook my head. "No. I've already told you that I won't be your prisoner."

"What if you were something else?"

"My answer is *no*."

He shot forward, fingers digging into my arms with impossible strength as he locked me against him. "You're going to make me *beg* to have you, aren't you."

"Take your hands off her!" Alekxander's voice boomed through the corridor in a low growl, and Phelan quickly backed away from me, allowing me the chance to escape.

Kora and Albert practically jumped out of their skin when I came barreling through the kitchen door, not able to move quickly enough to get away from Alekxander and what was unfolding upstairs.

"Gods. You gave us a fright!" She pressed her hand to her chest.

"Sorry." I brushed past them and went to the boiling

pot of broth that was ready to come off the fire, plucking it up so that it could begin cooling.

"Where have you been? We need to start preparing you for the second trial." Albert watched me as I went back and forth, getting a cup to fill and checking the bins Kora had put together for me, making sure they each had enough supplies in case I needed to be stitched up or worse.

"Demetrius requested to see me." I paused, mentally counting the bandages. "The wine is working better than we thought. He tried to use his magic on me, and he couldn't—but there's more. I was able to read that book, as well as a few others I found—the journals Fallon left behind… I know what she wants from me."

They shared a quick look of apprehension as I continued, updating them in a long-winded ramble about everything I had learned from the day Fallon arrived at this very castle as a child to her end.

I told them about the plans I found on Alekxander's desk to tear down the magical barrier and take over the Mortal Realm, and about the future I saw in my first trial.

Pulling the key from my pocket, I also told them about the war room and what was within it. About my dreams. The memories that weren't mine.

I told them everything, not holding any of it back.

"There was no mention of the location of the fang,

but it is a weapon. I also found no mention of the Infernal Tribulations but there are far too many books in there for me to do it alone—any questions?" I raised my brow when they looked at me as if I'd grown a second head.

"Daytime will be too obvious for you to go, but I'll leave the door unlocked tonight so you can access the room. I left the journals on the tea table next to the fireplace. I already combed through the middle section, but I may have missed something." Realizing I left out an important part, I clarified the text changes.

"Oh." Albert laughed sarcastically. "Because that just makes total sense. A magic room with magic books from six thousand years ago which lights up with hot flames when you enter it. Have you met me, Riven? Have you ever seen me run for my life before? It's not pretty."

Kora smacked him on his shoulder with her hand towel. "Anything else you wish for us to know, girl?"

I filled my cup to the top and began blowing on the rising steam. "I'm pretty sure Vanira and Adelram are going to attempt to steal the thrones from Viktor and Phelan—and possibly kill her sister, too."

"Well now..." Kora gave me an approving look. "You've been busy."

CHAPTER FORTY-TWO

There was no turning back. It didn't matter how prepared I was or how many times I checked the kitchen supplies—standing at the doors to the throne room always had the same effect on me.

I had managed to hide my fear during the first trial, but now that I had tasted even a glimpse of what awaited me, there was no more hiding it as the doors opened, revealing a room already filled with anxious spectators.

My fingers trembled as I curled them into my palms and straightened. With any luck, it would become tangible enough that they'd choke on it as I walked past them, toward the box nestled at the base of the throne where Alekxander stood idly beside it.

"What?" I asked flatly, meeting Demetrius's gaze

from where he perched on the jagged rock. "No speech today?"

The despicable grin on his face widened as I strolled to a stop, and he gestured for me to begin.

Alekxander stepped forward, and I pulled my own blade, slicing my palm open before he could have the satisfaction of doing it himself.

Either I'd make it out of this, or I wouldn't. I only hoped it was the former as I held the stinging wound over top of the charred lid of the chest, avoiding the torrid feel of the Dark Faye's gaze against my skin, and in a jarring, gut-twisting, bile-raising second—*I was alone.*

Minutes passed—maybe even hours—as I stood silently with my blade drawn, listening to the faint drip of water puddling somewhere in the room.

At first, it made me uneasy, then calm. Now, my teeth were grinding against one another with each plop that echoed off the walls.

It didn't help that I was tired or that being back here kept what happened during my first trial fresh in my mind.

"I was wondering when you'd be back," she said, her voice emerging from the shadow creeping along the edges of the room. My knuckles turned white as I waited for her to step out from their cover. When she did, my mouth went dry. "I thought you might prefer this form to my other."

"Why?" I asked her—*him.*

"Because, Riven, it's my job to break you, and the High King may be just what I need to do it." Her voice turned to the dark velvet of the male's.

"You're way off." I snorted. "Nice try, though."

He stepped closer, hands tucked into his pockets. "We'll see about that, Fawr o un. I've stayed with you since our first meeting, watching and gauging your responses to the future I showed you. Finding your weaknesses. Some, it seems, you aren't even aware of."

I lunged out with my blade when the Wraith came within reach, turning into a puff of smoke and reforming behind me. "You can't harm me, girl. I was forged from the darkest parts of the Veil itself. Carved from the great oak of the wicked. I am eternal. I am the never-ending stain on every soul who has passed through those gates, and I will continue to thrive in the minds of others long after you fail. And you *will* fail, make no mistake."

I flipped my blade over in my hand and slid it back into its sheath. "If I'm being honest, we've already done that speech. Got any new material?"

He laughed aloud and circled to my front, stopping close enough that I could feel his breath on my face, his eyes softening as he pushed a loose curl behind my ear and muttered, "I was afraid you'd never look at me again, Fawr o un."

My lips parted as his knuckle traced the curve of my jaw, pulling me closer.

"I was afraid I had lost you," he said, dipping his head, and my heart caught in my throat when I felt the brush of his lips against the side of my neck.

"This isn't real," I breathed.

"It is. It's been real from the moment I laid my eyes on you." His hand found my cheek, cupping it in a caress as he brought his face back to mine. Heat enveloped me, and my body stiffened. This was a trick. *A terrible*, cruel trick. "Don't you feel it? Feel me?"

I flinched away from him when he began laughing again. "I almost had you there for a moment, didn't I?"

"Not for a single second," I bit out, trying my hardest to not let the sting I felt show on my face.

"Have you asked yourself why his death affected you so?"

"His death wasn't what affected me. It was the manner in which it was delivered. No one deserves to die like that. Not even him."

He smiled. "Right. Well, I suppose you can figure it out for yourself. What I'd really like to talk about is what you were up to today. Sneaking around corners. Watching those private moments between Adelram and

Vanira. Now, that's not very becoming of someone who is supposedly the future of the realms. I wonder what Knox would say if he knew what you had been up to. I wonder what your father would say if he knew you let a married male touch you. That you might have even liked it when he did."

He moved closer, silver eyes dragging over me with agonizing slowness. "Almost as much as you like it whenever I touch you. Whenever Jeremiah's brother touched you."

"I don't know what you're talking about." I bristled then.

"No? But that was the deal, wasn't it? A loaf of bread in exchange for a kiss?"

I kept my mouth closed, not letting him exploit me any further than he already had. I knew the truth. The details were practically singed into my skin. My first kiss —stolen away from who it was meant for. Turned violent, and if I hadn't fought back—

"Is that what you tell yourself?" Alekxander changed. "How you justify what you did? You asked for it, Riven. Practically *begged* me for it in those tight pants."

Warren ran his tongue over thin lips, and the vomit I was fighting back found its way out as I bent forward, emptying the contents of my stomach.

"I told you no." I spat at his feet. "And I meant it."

We went round and round for hours, the Wraith chiseling away at me, reminding me of every bad thought or feeling I had ever had. Every horrible memory I had buried deep down. Feeding me images that made my mind seize up painfully until I wanted to give up—I almost did as I lay on the cold stone, staring up at the glass ceiling, lost to myself and my surroundings.

His voice had faded out some time ago, along with everything else—ripped away with a smile or laugh, a tender stroke of his fingers, or a carefully placed jab.

I didn't bother wiping the blood running from my nose, pooling at the nape of my neck and dripping onto the floor. I didn't have the energy to. I only closed my eyes, unable to hold them open any longer.

After a while, the scent of Jeremiah's breath tainted the air around me, his footfalls heavy as they approached. "I've been waiting to knock you down off that high horse of yours."

Tears rolled over my cheeks, soaking my temples further as I sobbed, feeling as if I was back on the scaffold where he whipped me until the flesh separated from my muscles.

"Stop," I begged, unable to take anymore.

"You want this to stop? You know how to stop it. Give your power to the Commander. Relinquish your future and any claim you have over the lands. Give up, Riven. Give up, and you will never know pain like this again."

"I can't," I said, my lips trembling.

"You can."

"No," I whimpered, and the Dark Faye knelt, taking my hand into his with a heart-crushing gentleness.

"Give up, Fawr o un." He wiped away my tears, my blood. "Give up, and you will never have to bear the evil this world has to offer."

"But *they* will."

"You don't owe them anything. Let go."

My body went limp, and he placed my hand over my chest with a victorious smile.

Let go. Let go, and this would all be over.

I wasn't good enough for them. I never would be. I wasn't some savior, a uniter of realms, or a descendant of the gods. I wouldn't free them, nor stop Demetrius from enslaving them. I couldn't change the future. I was done.

I had nothing left.

You're not done. Get up. Fight.

My throat tightened as I tried to push it away—that

voice, that feeling that always seemed to find me at my darkest.

I didn't want to listen to it. I wanted to close my eyes and lie here until it was all over, but it was persistent, a whisper at first—now deafening, thrumming through me like its own entity.

I ground my teeth together, my legs shaking as I shoved them beneath me, my back nearly giving out under the strain of standing.

Alekxander's eyes flashed with unease as he watched me straighten, backing away from me as if I should be feared, not him.

He shook his head, and with a final smile, he dug those claws in, ripping me raw and ragged as I watched the life leave his eyes. As I watched the bruises on his face and body appear, just as they had every time I looked at him since the first trial.

Cuts, both shallow and deep, emerged across his body.

"No!" I stumbled forward with my hands out and caught him as he dropped to his knees, knowing what came next.

My chest squeezed, and my eyes widened with horror when phantom claws sliced through his middle, spilling his entrails onto the ground between us.

"No!" I wailed, reaching down into the slick gore and

trying desperately to put him back together, screaming when I realized I couldn't.

"No! Please no! Please! *Please!* No!" I cupped his cold face in my sticky hands, wrapping my blood-soaked arms around his torso and holding his limp body against mine in an attempt to offer him a final shred of comfort.

My pleas for him to be okay muffled into his tunic as I sobbed, stilling when his shoulder shook beneath my cheek.

I blinked away the tears clinging to my lashes and carefully pulled away, feeling as if I'd been slapped as I watched him laugh.

"That's the feeling of your soul cracking in two." He leaned in with a tilt of his head. "Give the High King of Nightfall my warmest regards, will you? It's been an awfully long time since we've had the chance to chat."

The apparition disappeared, and I found myself on my knees in front of the box, unable to do anything but blink as the room stared at me.

I couldn't move. I *couldn't*—I glanced up at Demetrius, his stupid smirk crinkling the scar over his eye, and wondered if he had the faintest idea of just how much I was going to make it hurt when I killed him.

The trembling in my body halted as I stood, a fire stoked to life somewhere deep inside of me—not broken, but fucking pissed—and when this was all over, I'd dismantle that damned box piece by piece.

"Will that be all, Commander?" I asked calmly, despite the urge to rip out his windpipe.

He angled forward, clearly expecting me to emerge in a much different state than I was in. "Tomorrow will be your last day on this earth. I suggest you remember that during tonight's celebrations."

"I'll think of nothing else."

His face twitched as he waved his hand to dismiss me, and I made my way back to the one place I knew had answers.

CHAPTER
FORTY-THREE

My FINGERS ROVED over each sentence until they were stiff and sore. There was little time until I was needed back in the kitchen, but something had been bothering me. Now, even more since the trial.

That is the feeling of your soul cracking in two. I shook my head and tossed the journal down when I came up empty-handed, searching for the one with a thicker binding. The one that mentioned Fallon's lover—her *mate.* I overlooked it, thinking it wasn't anything of value to learn about, but I remembered those words clearly.

What did they mean? Why was the Dark Faye the key to breaking me? I hated him more than I ever thought possible. He was going to take down the wall and destroy my home. He was going to help the Commander enslave the world—*and then he was going to die.*

My chest ached. *There had to be answers in this damned room. There had to be.* I put the journal down and went to another, thumbing through until I found the passage I was looking for.

> *After a harrowing journey through the mountain pass, my mate has finally returned to me with a weapon capable of destroying the false god.*

No, not that one. I flipped over a few more sections.

> *Today, he begged me to stay and not go through with it. He begged me to let all of this go—the war, the prophecy. I could feel it breaking him in two, as if my soul were cracking down the middle. My mate. So worried about losing me. I had never known a bond so strong was possible. Tieran can't even speak to what we share—something no one had seen before, not even he himself, who has traveled the world over.*

For this reason alone, we made the short journey to the temple. In secret, we bound ourselves with the sacred oath of marriage, vowing not to go another day longer without being husband and wife. Deep down, I know both my mother and father would approve.

When we finished the ceremony, it was he who helped me sow my magic—plucking my rib away and replacing it with one of his own so Arwen would be none the wiser. A move of deception I pray will work.

Now, lying here with him, watching his chest rise and fall as he sleeps, I can still feel all he bears on his shoulders. See it in his dreams. Hear it in his deepest thoughts, even when he thinks I cannot. The fear and pain swirl in my gut as if they were my own. And yet, they will turn into something entirely different when he finds I've put measures in place to keep him away from the battle—that I've been slowly pulling away from our bond and fortifying my mental walls to keep him in the dark about my *plans.*

It is the only way I can protect him, because in truth, as much as I long for my parents to return, as much as I love my kingdom and hope for victory—it is Keir who will break me in the end. If I were ever to bear the loss of him, of my raven, it would be to bear the loss of the other half of my soul, and I would not survive it.

I set the journal down and began to pace back and forth, cradling my hands in front of me as I rubbed my fingers roughly against one another. Keir was her *mate*. In all this time, I hadn't put it together. Her *mate*. Not just her ally, but the other half of her soul. The High King of Nightfall.

This couldn't be possible. Alekxander couldn't be my —*mate*. He couldn't be my *raven*. He was evil and cruel. A murderer. I hated him, and he hated me. It was a lie. It had to be. The dreams. *The feather*. I pressed my hand to the ache in my chest.

It couldn't be true. Because if it was, then it meant… I cupped my hand over my mouth, the ache deepening as I told myself it was just the Wraith trying to get in my head. It was trying to do what it was meant to do.

I glanced toward the door, snatching up the journals that mentioned Fallon and Keir being mates and burying them in the furthest corners of the shelves so the others wouldn't find them.

My elbow knocked into a small vase on the window ledge when I spun around, sending it smashing against the ground with a loud crash.

"Dammit!" Shards of every shape and size scattered across the stone, glimmering as I got to my knees to pick up the big pieces first.

Coming back here was a mistake. I still needed to find Viktor. I didn't have time for this—tomorrow might very well be my final day. If I failed in the trial or in my attempt to kill Demetrius, all of this would be for nothing. I should be getting my affairs in order, not letting that damned apparition worm its way into my head.

I blew out a breath, running my teeth over my bottom lip as I considered that maybe all this searching was for nothing—that there wasn't anything to find. Fallon wouldn't have used the Infernal Tribulations, and she hadn't been around by the time Light and Dark happened.

A shard of glass pierced the side of my finger, cutting it open and forcing me to drop the other pieces I had already collected with a curse. Warmth trailed down to my knuckle, dripping into a small crimson puddle on the floor as I plucked the shard free, pinched the wound closed, and glanced around for something to wrap it with.

Surely, there would be bandages in a war room.

I started to stand, stopping, when the puddle began to move—bleeding a path beneath the bookcase where it disappeared.

My jaw went slack as I eyed the massive section, grabbing hold of it and pulling until it began to budge.

The bottom scraped loudly against the floor, sending a puff of thick dust shooting out from the cracks as I swung it open to a space that was shallow and dim, only a few feet wide if that.

I snatched a small torch from the wall, its flame flickering to life, and took a cautious step inside, where more books and scrolls lined the area—appearing far older than the ones I had been reading since finding this room.

At the very back was a chest sitting on a narrow table, a withered scroll tied with twine atop it. I secured the torch to the wall and picked it up, careful not to bloody it as I undid the knot to unroll it.

It wasn't Fallon's handwriting I had become used to as I read the first line, but another's. I blinked, reading it again for a second and then a third time.

"Gods," I said quietly. It was a letter—addressed to *me*.

My lungs burned as I ran through the corridor and descended the stairs to the kitchen, clutching the rolled-up leather pouch in my hands.

"I found it!" I said as I burst through the door, sweeping bowls and plates aside with my arm before laying it down.

Rowan reached out to open it, and I stopped her.

"Don't," I panted. "Only I can touch it. It's why Fallon fell. She couldn't use it during the battle. It made her too sick."

They blinked at me, my chest heaving at a dizzying pace.

"God's child. You need to sit." Kora came to my side, the look of alarm growing on her face.

"No. I can't. There's too much I still need to do. I—" The ground moved beneath my feet, and Albert was there to steady me. "I can't."

"When was the last time you slept?" Kora asked as she placed a hand on my forehead. Her frown deepened as she barked at Albert, "Sit her down. Don't leave her side."

Albert did as she asked, moving me onto a stool and raking his fingers through my braid and down my back in comforting strokes.

Rowan was there, too, piling a plate with more food than I had had in the entirety of my stay here. "Eat."

"I can't. I have to find Viktor," I breathed, fingers digging into the tabletop as if it would somehow keep the room from spinning.

"Viktor can wait." She took my injured hand in hers while Kora handed her some of the clover salve she had made to spread onto it before wrapping it tightly. "What is it you found?"

Leaning forward when she finished, I pulled the ivory dagger made of the serpent's fang from the pouch, leaving it on the table for them to see.

Rowan picked up her rolling pin and poked at it. "If it was too dangerous for her to use, what makes you think we're going to let you use it?"

I shook my head. "She made it so I could. The magic she used—" The room tilted again, and Kora shoved a cup of broth into my hands.

"We will deal with the fang later. Rowan, lay something over it and see if Isra has delivered the wine yet." She helped Albert prop me up. Every ounce of energy drained from me as she guided the cup to my mouth. "Drink."

"Wait." I reached out to stop her. "Rowan, I'm sorry for the way we left things. I—"

She embraced me in a tight hug that rivaled even my

father's. "I shouldn't have said what I did to you." She squeezed even harder. "I had no right, and I didn't mean it. If you want to go home, then I respect your decision. But if you choose to stay, I promise you will do everything Fallon meant for you to do and more."

That was the problem. I bit down on my tongue and placed my hand over my pocket, where I could feel the part of the scroll I kept... *What good would it do to choose your future if it had already been chosen for you? If you already knew how it ended?*

She released me from the hug, leaving the room as Kora urged the cup in my hands back to my mouth. I sipped from it, scrunching my nose up when the bitter taste hit me. "What is this?"

"We use it back home. It'll perk you right up, don't you worry," she assured me as I moved my tongue around, taking another small drink while she watched. "I knew you weren't sleeping—I just didn't know how bad it was."

"Can you blame her?" Albert brushed the hair off my face.

"Just one more day," I reminded them.

"And then what." Kora angled against the edge of the table. "You can barely stand."

"I'll be fine." I finished off the broth, which she

promptly replaced with another piping spoonful—this one more bitter than the last.

It wasn't until about halfway through that I began to feel like myself again. The dull ache in my head had lessened, and the fatigue in my muscles waned as well, but there was no telling how long the effects would last before I wound up in the same situation again.

I needed to sleep.

I rubbed the heaviness from my eyes just as Isra and Rowan appeared at the door with empty crates in their arms.

"Told you she'd be fine," Rowan purred, offloading what she carried onto a table while Isra did the same.

He rolled his eyes playfully at her. "Rowan said you found it?"

Nodding, I reached for the linen covering the pouch, pulling it off and retrieving the dagger. It was heavy in my palm, smooth to the touch, and impossibly sharp at the tip. I could only imagine what Keir had to do to acquire it.

"It's larger than I thought it would be." Albert leaned in for a closer look. "Where did you find it?"

"It was hidden in that room." I set it down and picked up a piece of bread to chew on.

"What's the plan?" Isra asked, handing a tray of meat

off to Kora, who placed it down with the rest of the platters that were piling up for tonight.

"Stick the pointy end in the Commander. Hope for the best."

"No." He grinned. "I mean tonight, tomorrow—*after*. What's the plan?"

I looked at the dress that hung on the wall waiting for me, knowing it meant I'd be playing bait again tonight.

"There won't be another trial tomorrow," I said quietly. "I wouldn't survive it. I'll find a way to get close, and then I'll strike."

"And then?" Rowan asked, hopeful for the answer I could no longer give her.

"And then your magic will be returned, and you'll be free to go home."

"I guess we better start getting you ready then." Isra undid the tie in my hair and began brushing his fingers through it to loosen up the chunks of braid and work through the knots while I retrieved a folded piece of parchment from the cubby beneath the table.

"There's just one more thing…" I took a deep breath. "If I fail tomorrow, you'll need to find safety as far away from here as possible. No one will be spared from what he is planning, but just maybe you'll have a chance to live a little longer than the others."

Isra's fingers stilled as my words settled over the room like the soured truth they were.

I held out the letter for Kora to take. "If you find you have the chance, could you see that this makes it to my father? He deserves to know what happened. That I never meant to abandon him."

She took it from me, pausing before sliding it into her apron pocket. "You don't worry about us, girl. We are survivors—I'll see he gets this if it comes down to it."

CHAPTER FORTY-FOUR

I watched both the Faye and Wildlings twirl gracefully in dance and conversation, enjoying the spoils of drink and food—creatures that I had been raised to hate and fear, and a realm that had chewed me up and spit me out on numerous occasions.

Yet, I couldn't find it in myself to revile them the way I had only weeks ago. Not when they were everything I had been raised to believe and more—and less. Some of them becoming friends during my time here, some of them becoming allies…

I had thought my final night among them would bring me relief, but as I clutched my chest, I felt anything but that.

It was as if by leaving, I was losing a part of myself in the process.

But what choice did I have?

Adelram coughed, drawing my attention to where he and Cordelia sat while she patted her nose with a pouf, creating a cloud of thick powder around them.

He shifted, his gaze fixed on Morgan and her ladies who lounged together on the far side of the room, and I couldn't help but feel pity for her now that I understood how deeply Adelram's deceit ran.

Viktor sat a short distance away, one leg crossed over the other, as he spoke to the group gathered around him about a time when he was younger.

I moved closer, listening to him go on with an enthusiastic wave of his hand.

"I kid you not. They took both my clothes and my weapons when I jumped from the cliffs." He grinned. "Half of Tide saw what my ass looked like that day."

"What did your mother and father think?"

"Let's just say there were only a scant number of times my parents were mad, and that wasn't one of them. We laughed about it over dinner." He glanced up, blue eyes meeting mine, and his smile widened. "Turns out my sister paid them their weight in gold to trick me—If you all would excuse me, there seems to be a lady in need of tending to."

He stood with the grace of a High King and came to my side, taking my hand in his and dipping to kiss the back of it.

"I didn't mean to interrupt."

He kept my hand in his as he straightened. "I was finished. What can I do for you?"

I dragged my gaze to the open floor, where few still danced, with more elegance and restraint than the night before.

He shook his head, his smile disappearing as if he knew what I was thinking. "This won't be your last dance, Riven. There will be many more we share."

"Maybe," I whispered under my breath as he led me forward, and we joined the next formation as if we had been there the whole time.

"What's on your mind?" He twirled me out and back into the salty scent of his embroidered tunic.

"Adelram," I said quietly. "I overheard him speaking of a plot to take your throne."

"I'm aware of it," he breathed calmly into my hair. "I have been for some time now."

I jerked my face up to meet his, certain I hadn't heard him correctly.

"Don't look so surprised." He scanned the room around us before continuing, "I may be young, but I make up for what I lack in age in other areas. He's been angling for my throne for years, using my sister to climb the ranks. It's nothing more than a desperate grab for power."

"And you're just letting him?" I blinked in disbelief.

"Keep your enemies close, Riven. It is the true game of kings and queens—one you'll need to learn sooner rather than later."

"Vanira is part of it. They plan to marry when it's all said and done."

The muscle in his sun-kissed jaw feathered. "Now *that* I didn't know."

"Just be careful. Please."

"Me?" He acted as if I had wounded him. "You're the one about to face down with the Commander."

"I'll be fine." I bit the inside of my cheek, the icy drag of a claw raking down the nape of my neck, digging deeper the more I tried to ignore it. "I have tenacity on my side."

He belted with laughter as he spun me in rhythm with the others twirling around us. "*Tenacity*. I like that. You wear it well."

The tension in the corridor shifted as Demetrius entered from his throne room with Alekxander at his side. Our eyes clashed, and my heels tangled beneath me, the tenacity I claimed to have wavering as I tore my gaze from the silver hold of his.

"It looks like our fun has come to an end." Viktor pulled me upright, his body rigid as we slowed to a stop. "Remember what I said. This isn't the last dance we will be sharing, Riven."

He bowed his head, abandoning the floor before I could thank him, and when I began to do the same, I found that I couldn't—that my legs felt as if they were stuck in a pit of mud, my chest cinching tighter as panic prickled at the base of my skull.

The room dimmed, gutted by a chill-inducing silence, broken only by the haunting whispers of my name that grew louder—a deafening chant echoing around the creatures unaware of what was happening.

The dizzying circles they spun slowed, blurring into swaths of color and distorted glimmers of jewelry that bled together as my name was called once more.

Riven.

My heart clogged deep in my throat as I spun around to search for an escape, only to be met by an abrupt silence as I stared up at Alekxander, who stood with his hand out for me to take.

"Dance with me," he said softly.

I hesitated, sparing a cautious glance toward where Demetrius sat sprawled out on a settee before shaking my head. "No."

Challenge glimmered in his eyes. "I wasn't asking."

"Maybe not. But my answer is still the same."

He caught my hand before I could turn away and pulled me to him, curling his fingers into mine and placing his palm against the small of my back. I tensed, knowing what it was he felt there.

"What are you doing?" My cheeks flared with embarrassment—*shame*—as the music died down before starting again, gentle and slow.

He didn't recoil from me like I had expected, nor did he look at me with disgust.

"What does it look like I'm doing?" He grinned so faintly I nearly missed it as I dragged my gaze away and scanned the room, waiting to hear the voices again—to feel the terrible, icy drag down my spine that accompanied them, or to see that awful version of Alekxander before me.

When they didn't come, I stifled any further protest and placed my hand on his arm, letting him lead us into the space quickly abandoned by the Faye and Wildlings, who chose instead to watch what I was sure was some new angle he and Demetrius were playing.

My chest ached as I inched my eyes back to his, finding the sliver of strength I needed to look at him—to truly look at him.

His muscles stiffened beneath my touch as I slid my hand farther up his arm, my fingertips grazing the silk collar of his black tunic as I took in every detail before it could be ripped away again.

His jaw tightened, and I fought the urge to touch that too—to reach into his sable waves, to trace the delicate point of his ears—unable to help but wonder if Keir and Fallon had danced like this.

His palm slid down the curve of my back, pebbling my skin and drawing a sigh from me as I asked, "How did you know?"

"How did I know what?" He caressed my hand with his thumb.

"Last night," I reminded him, a slight shudder running through me. "You knew."

"I'm a Dark Faye, Riven. We can see and feel things the others do not."

"*We*?" I tilted my head back, my curls slipping off my shoulders and falling down my spine. "That's all? Was there another reason?"

"Should there be another reason?" His silver-flecked gaze traveled over the warm flush spreading across my chest and face, settling on my lips.

"No." My mouth turned dry.

Nodding, he raised my hand above my head and twirled me, hooking his arm around my waist and gathering me to his chest, my back pressed securely against him.

"Just because I can't lie doesn't mean I don't know when you do." His breath warmed the shell of my ear, and I found myself leaning into him as we swayed. "I can smell it on you."

He brought his hand up and rested it along my collarbones—above the thundering beat of my heart that was almost enough to make me forget we weren't alone… *Almost* enough to forget what he was capable of doing with the hands that held me, that he could enjoy it when he did.

"I think you do lie," I muttered unevenly.

"Oh?" He spun me out and back in so that I was facing him, guiding my hands to the back of his neck as we swayed. "And what am I lying about?"

I opened my mouth to speak, unable to find my voice when he laced my fingers into his messy hair and began dragging the tips of his own down my arms and back to my waist, *every* inch of my body tingling with the sensation they left behind.

The corner of his lips kicked up. "You were saying, Fawr o un?"

My throat grew tight as the music came to a bitter end, and, after a brief hesitation, we stopped as well— neither of us moving when the next instrumental began.

His grin faded when I let my hands fall away from him, taking a step back.

I could speak the words, but what would they matter?

"Riven—" He started to reach for me, but I stopped him, my voice breaking as I thanked him for the dance and turned, needing space—needing to understand what in the hell was wrong with me, why I kept letting myself be pulled in by him.

I wove through the crowded corridor and slipped into an empty section of the dimly lit hall, slumping against the wall and closing my eyes when I was certain I was alone.

The chill from the stone seeped into my shoulders, anchoring me while I considered how Fallon was able to block Keir out—how I could do the same.

I pulled my hair off my neck and blew out a tight breath when the sound of footsteps neared. "Please," I begged. "*Please* just leave me the hell alone—"

My heart leaped to the base of my throat, my lashes fluttering open when his hands found either side of my face, cupping it in warmth as his chest heaved against mine with harsh pulls of air.

"I can't." He shook his head—his lips so close that I could almost taste them before they were gone again, abrupt distance consuming the space between us.

"I highly doubt that." Cordelia's obnoxious giggle rounded the corner, and my mouth went dry as I snapped my head toward her and Adelram.

Her voice—how had I not heard it until now?

She slammed her mouth shut when her gaze clashed with mine, realizing her mistake.

"It was *you...*" I pinched my brows together, able to see it now that I was close enough—the faint tracing of old bruising on the bridge of her nose from the break I had left her with.

It was almost completely healed.

How had I missed it? How could I have overlooked something so blatantly obvious?

She released her grip on the advisor's arm and backed away a step, nervously darting her eyes between me and Alekxander, who cocked his head to the side, curiosity furrowing his brow.

"You don't understand," she blurted. "She didn't give me a choice. She—"

Adelram turned to her, and in a calculated burst of shadow, Alekxander seized his arm, preventing him from swinging.

"She?"

CHAPTER FORTY-FIVE

THE COMMANDER

My temples pulsed with the exhaustion of the power drain on my body. It was only a matter of time before the others would see the glamour I put in place was beginning to fail and, with it, the nullifier I put on their magic.

I rolled the seed of a grape around on my tongue while I listened to Feronia speak of her kingdom with great detail and passion like she always did, only retaining bits and pieces of what she said.

I was growing tired of this nonsense. If they truly didn't believe I knew who was trying to curry favor with me, hoping I decided not to take their kingdoms after all, they had another thing coming. I wanted them all. If only for a short reign. No matter what they did or how they did it, they would not divert my path. I was set in my decision.

The ache in my temples had become unbearable, and my crown felt heavier than ever. *Tomorrow*. I only needed to wait one more day to claim her power. I didn't just want it anymore; I needed it—not only to bring down the wall but to secure my place here.

Being away from home for as long as I had was starting to take its toll. I could feel my light being sucked away, as if I were being drained from the inside out—something that hadn't happened during the war.

It was *odd*.

I spat the seed onto the floor and picked up my goblet of wine, swirling its contents and allowing the sweet notes to hit my palate before drinking.

It was inferior to what we had in the Divine Kingdom. Even their best reserves fell short by comparison.

Here, however, I could drink as much as I wanted without anyone batting an eye at me. They were always so worried about achieving perfection that the whole kingdom forgot what it was to retain any semblance of joy or self-indulgence.

I leaned back, resting my arms over the velvet sofa while Siobhan traced her fingers along the outline of my cock. Her allure was hardly enough to keep me from noticing how rigid Alekxander was, his expression darkening as if he'd tasted something foul.

I followed his gaze to where Riven stood, her hands clenched tightly at her sides.

My jaw flexed as I shoved Siobhan away from me. "Go join the others. I'm tired of you."

She obeyed, collecting her skirts and slipping off as I took another drink from my goblet, narrowing my eyes and extending my mental reach toward the middle of the room.

The shields protecting Riven's mind were down just enough for me to feel the dread and defeat that weighed on her—that damned Wraith having achieved in two trials what I couldn't in four weeks.

There was something else, though… I could sense pieces of her guarding it. Protecting it.

I tried to feel some semblance of accomplishment as I watched her, frozen in place and practically shaking. I didn't.

"Go tend to our prisoner. It seems she has forgotten this is a party."

Alekxander didn't hesitate. He stood, closing the distance between them with long strides before stretching out his hand to her.

My curiosity only deepened the longer I watched

them, expanding my senses to him as well—stopped, as always, at the damned edge of his mind.

I pushed myself harder, fighting against his resistance until my vision began to tunnel, forcing me to back off.

"The gardens are grander than anything you've ever seen before—"

"I imagine the gardens in my bath house are grander." I took another drink, tired of hearing Feronia speak. "Phelan, I'm curious. What are your thoughts on Viktor?"

He grinned crookedly and set down his goblet. "Young. Inexperienced. He's never seen war or any hardship for that matter."

I located the High King of Tide on the sidelines, effortlessly charming his way into a card game as I asked how it was that he came to rule.

"His parents walked into the sea and never came back," Feronia said, for once offering something of value from her lips. "There were whispers that they went mad, and that the sea lured them to their deaths."

Interesting.

I dragged my tongue over my teeth, weighing whether I needed him alive when all was said and done. Adelram had assured me he would fall in with the others, but I wasn't convinced. If he had never faced true authority, there was a chance he would resist it.

"Yes, well. I believe most of our parents went mad after Light and Dark."

"Is that so?" I raised a brow and shifted my focus to Phelan. Still unsure if I could trust him, I plucked another grape from the blue-mosaic bowl and dropped it into my mouth, chewing and spitting out the seed as I caught the faint scent of something sweet in the air.

I dragged my gaze back to Riven, and a bitter knot twisted in my stomach as she and Alekxander danced, her back pressed against his chest and her skin flushed with the contact.

"Have you ever smelled anything like it?" Phelan lounged back, nostrils flaring as he scrutinized them as closely as I did.

"Once," I muttered when she stormed off, my fingers flexing around the neck of my goblet, forever unable to grasp how Fallon had made her into her image.

Even her damned pheromone pattern was the same. A scent as unique as a fingerprint—one I found myself longing for a little too often.

"What about Flame?" I asked. "Did you believe Seraphine when she pledged herself to me?"

"Not one bit." Phelan crossed his legs, and Feronia rolled her golden eyes. "But I doubt she is stupid enough to make a move against you. Not this far from home."

I waited to see if Alekxander would go after Riven

while I considered if the assassins would follow me if Seraphine and Adrean didn't return, needing to tie up as many loose ends as possible in the coming days.

A loud crash of dishes drew my attention to one of the Faye from the kitchen. Thin. Pretty. Not overdone like some of them. I had seen her a few times, but she never seemed to linger long enough for me to really look at her.

"What province is that servant from?"

"She was here before mine arrived." Feronia filled her goblet to the brim.

"Perhaps she's one of Tide's," Phelan added.

"Perhaps." I narrowed my eyes on her as she quickly cleaned up her mess and disappeared.

I wouldn't mind seeing her in my rooms tomorrow, serving me personally as a consolation prize.

My length twitched to life with the thought as I glanced back to find Alekxander had conveniently vanished. Nodding to my Vassal, I sent it to track him.

He had been loyal to me thus far... I only hoped, for his sake, it continued.

"Are you concerned at all with the talk of the Old Kingdom surfacing?" Feronia asked, flinching when I snapped my head toward her.

"The Old Kingdom is dead."

She wiped her hands along the emerald satin of her gown. "Yes, I know. I was just—"

"It has been six thousand years, Feronia," Phelan sighed. "Any talk of the Old Kingdom is just that—*talk*. The likelihood of anyone attempting to rise up—especially after Alekxander's *decorative* displays around the castle—is hardly something to worry about."

He glanced in the direction Riven had walked off in. "If I were to worry about anything, my king, it wouldn't be the provinces that have already sworn their loyalty to you. It would be the Dark Faye and whatever it is he's planning."

"Are you so sure about that?" I glared at him.

"You're an incredibly smart being, my king. So, I won't bother insulting you by assuming you haven't noticed how he looks at her—or how he postures when she's being harmed."

"Alekxander did say he wanted her for himself when he arrived here," Feronia added with a sip of her wine.

"If I may be so bold, what is it you have over him to make you so certain he won't double-cross you?"

I grinned then. "What I have over him is everything he holds dear. His very reason for existing. He won't cross me any more than you will, Phelan."

Tired of this conversation, I stood, raising my goblet

in the air to address the corridor. "Tomorrow is the final night of Solstice celebrations."

The room quieted.

"With it, Riven's final day alive," I continued. "I know that this has been a hard transition for some of you. Some of you were more hesitant in the beginning than others—but I have faith that we will learn together and grow together. When I have what belongs to me, I will drop the barrier. I will send you home to your provinces to let it be known that there is a new ruler, a new kingdom, and a new world. Together, we will usher in a new era of reign. A prosperous one. May it bring us a year of unyielding growth and understanding, my friends."

"What about our magic?"

I snapped my eyes in the direction of the question. "Prove yourselves to me, and you will have anything you can possibly wish for."

Alekxander cleared a path through the corridor, two Faye in tow and Riven following closely behind.

I took a drink of the bitterly sweet wine, noting the lack of claps and cheers as they approached—the room silently waiting for the same explanation I was.

"Is there a reason you have the Advisor of Tide and his date in shadow bands, Alekxander?"

He kicked Adelram behind the knee, forcing him to kneel before me. "It seems these two have been busy."

"Have they now?" I arched my brow.

"I didn't have anything to do with it," Adelram gritted out. "I—"

"Silence," I cut him off, sliding my attention to Riven, who stood tall despite her frailty, looking at me as if I were the mud on the bottom of her boots.

"Do you have proof?" I asked Alekxander, ignoring the urge to have one of my Vassal smack her around some for the fun of it.

Cordelia began sobbing into her hands, and the fact that she and the advisor were up to something was all too apparent as I rubbed my fingers against my temples.

Setting my goblet down, I approached them. "Start talking, or I'll tear your tongues from your throats."

Adelram's eyes widened ever so slightly before he darted them to Vanira, who was attempting to slip from the room unnoticed.

"Stop her!" I ordered my Vassal with a snap of my fingers.

"No!" Adelram shot forward with bound hands, and Alekxander yanked him back by the back of his neck, forcing him down to his knees again with ease.

"Bring her to me," I demanded.

Phelan stood, coming to my side as his wife was being dragged toward us. "Now, what in the hell does my *wife*, her *lover*, and her *sister* have to do with one another?"

"Lover?" Cordelia shot Vanira a sideways look, and I couldn't help but grin. This evening was turning out much different than I had imagined.

"Tell them, Vanira." Something hideous sparked in the Dark Faye, reminding me I made the right choice in allying with him in the coming days.

"Tell them how you invited the Zephyr here with orders to kill Riven. To keep the Commander from what he is rightfully owed. Tell them you instructed your sister to lead the plot so when she was caught, it would result in her death." Alekxander released the hold he had on Adelram and kicked him forward, thick shadow beginning to pulse from him. "Let us not forget the part where you, *Adelram*, planned with Vanira to stage a coup to kill the Commander, take Viktor's throne for yourself, and remove Phelan to replace him with his son."

I laughed through my teeth, sighting Viktor moving forward within the crowd for a better look. "Well done, Alekxander."

"How could you?" Cordelia sobbed. "You wanted to kill me? Why?"

Vassal released Vanira, nearly dropping her on her face.

"Why not? I hate you!" She sneered, turning toward

her husband. "And I hate you! Always running around with your whores. I can see you! Just like I can see you, Cordelia. Always wanting everything I have for yourself. It's pathetic—so, yes. It was me, and if it wasn't for that stupid cunt—"

Before she could get another word out, Alekxander had her bound with shadows, mouth included.

"It seems you were innocent after all," I muttered to Phelan. "Lock them in their chambers. Keep them separate, and tomorrow, we'll enjoy more than one death."

I waved my hand through the air, and the music resumed, the Faye and Wildlings returning to the celebrations I had so graciously laid out for them as my Vassal began dragging the three away despite their best efforts to fight.

Riven, however, remained in place, staring at me with open disgust.

"Is there something you wish to say?"

"Cordelia was a pawn in this. Just like the Zephyr were."

"And?" I raised a brow.

"She doesn't deserve to die."

"Since when did prisoners get an opinion on these matters?" Feronia laughed from her seat. "Poor girl doesn't know when to stop."

"Shut up, Feronia," Phelan warned as I took a step

closer to Riven, looking her over ever so slowly as the ache returned to my temples.

She didn't cower like the rest of them, but I could still smell her fear. Taste it like a thick coating of bitter-sweet sugar.

My fingers twitched at my sides, longing to feel the flesh of her throat crushed between them again.

This female. This fucking carbon copy of Fallon herself.

Resisting the urge to touch the damned scar along my eye, I yanked her up by her hair instead, her fingernails digging into my flesh as she blinked up at me, refusing to make a sound.

For a moment, I wondered if forcing her to kill Cordelia would be a far worse punishment than sending her in for another trial with the Wraith.

She was more like Fallon than she knew, willing to help those who would do her more harm than good. I was doing her a favor by ending her life.

"She will die." I pulled her close enough that only she could hear me. "But not before you. Count down the hours, Riven. It is all you have left before I destroy everything you've ever loved or cared about—starting with your father."

My other hand found the soft skin of her throat as if it had a mind of its own.

I could end her. Right here. Right now. I could snap her delicate neck and throw her to the floor.

My power pulsed through the room as I looked into her tear-rimmed eyes. Beautiful. Fearsome. *Fragile.* The light behind them could be easily extinguished if I pushed just a little harder.

My fingers dug in, fighting back her pulse.

We had been here before.

I let my eyes close, allowing myself to be drawn back to that memory on the day of battle—the moment I held Fallon just like this, before she sliced down my face with her short sword.

"Let—them—go." She fought for breath in my hands.

"My king." I opened my eyes to see Alekxander standing at my side, a hand I hadn't felt placed on my shoulder with a warning to stop the pulse before I was weakened any further.

CHAPTER FORTY-SIX

RIVEN

"My king." Alekxander intervened, placing a hand on Demetrius's shoulder. "Look around you."

A blind fury crept into Demetrius's darkened features as he took in the room, releasing the pressure around my neck and allowing me to collapse to the floor at his feet.

I cradled my throat, my lungs protesting the violent bursts of air I took in as I watched the bastard slip off, shutting himself in his rooms, where more of his miscreants stood guard.

My legs were under me, carrying me forward in a fit of rage before I could think anymore on it—only to be stopped by Phelan, his arm wrapping around my shoulders and hauling me back before I could make it more than a few feet.

I thrashed against him, struggling to break free of his grip so I could go after Demetrius. So I could kill him. Here and now.

"Let me go!" I screamed, uncaring that my throat felt as if hot coals were being poured down it as I lunged forward.

Phelan yanked me back by my arm and shoved me around to face the room. "Look."

I froze, my breath puffing between my lips in harsh bursts as I stared at them—Faye and Wildlings alike, their fists clutched to their chests, some with their hands wrapped around the hilt of their weapons as if they had been prepared to use them only moments ago.

"Do you feel that?" he asked under his breath.

"Yes." I freed myself from his grasp, feeling it with every fiber of my being. "I do."

I slammed the dungeon door and paced back and forth, fingers flexing at my sides as my body practically vibrated with the need to tear the Commander's heart out through his throat—to feel his blood slick my fingers.

My father. *How dare he threaten him.*

How dare he! I hissed through my teeth as the feeling

in my chest grew, swirling into something I had only ever felt a fraction of before. Something powerful.

I gripped the iron slats of my cell and closed my eyes, letting it build, imagining every horrific thing I would do to Demetrius when I got my hands on him.

The dungeon door scraped against the stone floor, and the shadows around me stirred.

"You're in the wrong room." I didn't recognize the sound of my voice. It was dark. Threatening. A voice of someone or something that wasn't entirely me.

"No," Alekxander purred, closing the door behind him. "I think I'm in exactly the right room."

The candle flared, and the walls began pressing in, stealing the air in the space and leaving it thick. *Heavy.* I tightened my fingers around the iron bars of my cell, able to hear the start of a fracture forming within them. "Get out."

He laughed, low and mocking, the sound of it slithering seductively over my flesh. "No. I don't think I will."

"What in the hell is wrong with you?" I turned, nostrils flaring as I looked at the male who relaxed against the wall with a reticent smirk on his face. "Why can't you just leave me alone?"

His jaw tightened. Alarm flashed through his eyes as they skimmed over me and then my *cage.*

"I'm not leaving you." He straightened and began rolling the sleeves of his tunic to his elbows, more serious now. "Not until you calm down."

"Calm?" I was seething. My teeth clenched so tightly they ached.

He prowled closer, shadow unfurling from his shoulders and clinging to the floor of the dungeon like a valley mist. "At this very moment, your power is pulsing through the castle at a rate that will drain you by the hour. If you don't stop, you will not survive it, Riven."

Power. What good was having power if I couldn't wield it? Couldn't use it to tear down these walls. To tear Demetrius's head from his shoulders.

"Stop. Just stop *pretending* like you care what happens to me and leave."

"No." He was close enough now that I had backed myself against the bars of my cell, my shoulder blades throbbing in protest. "You need to focus, Fawr o un. Pull it back in."

"Stop calling me that," I said, my voice cracking.

He raised his arm, resting it on the bar above my head as he stared down at me as if he were searching for something.

"Stop."

I battled the familiar tug in my chest when he

reached up, brushing the hair that had slipped into my face over my ear—a commanding feeling deep within me that I had once been so fond of when I needed it most, caressing the deepest parts of my mind with the softness of a feather until it was all I could focus on. Until it was all I wanted to cling to.

It was him. *It had* always *been him.*

"There she is," he whispered, his fingers traveled down the shell of my ear, my jaw, tilting my chin up to his.

I sucked in a sharp breath and smacked his arm away. "Are you happy now?"

He shook his head and slid his hand into his pocket, the other one still lazily resting against the bars above my head. "I'm anything *but* happy."

"How long have you known?" I glared at him.

"How long have I known what?"

"Was it when you arrived? When you staked your claim on me? Was it when you left me to be starved and beaten? When you made plans to tear down the wall and take the Mortal Realm—my realm?"

His brows drew together and I leaned closer, feeling his body stiffen—as if he knew what I would say next, the truth that had been tearing me to pieces since I learned it.

"At what point did you learn that I was your mate—and that you didn't care?"

His eyes narrowed on the curls that had fallen over my shoulder before he pulled away, slipping his other hand into his pocket. "A while."

I wrapped my arms around myself. Tired. So *damned* tired.

My mate. My raven.

Neither of which thought I was worth saving.

My chest caved, and I closed my eyes, feeling the warmth of each tear as it rolled down my cheeks—as if they were nails being driven into my heart.

He had known. This entire time, he had known.

Making me fight. Begging me to hang on, just so he could watch me suffer. Giving me a shred of peace and comfort, only to take it away. Invading my mind. My emotions.

"Please leave." Something permanent in my heart cracked, the pain worse than anything Demetrius could do to me.

Could he hear it? *Feel* it?

His fingers brushed against my temple, so softly I barely felt them.

"Alekxander…" I opened my eyes when I heard the sound of the door, fixing my gaze on the dwindling flame in front of me. "You should have let me die."

The door closed, and I was alone.

My sobs broke through the dimming room, and my hand went to my throat as I slid down the slats of my cell to the floor, holding myself while I wept.

I had searched for him for what felt like my whole life. He was there when no one else was or could be in the way I needed. Not knowing if he was real, I still let myself imagine what life would be like with him.

I let myself *love* him—that piece of him that found me when I was broken, bringing me back each time.

I loved him. I...

I pushed my hair back from my face and wiped the tears from my eyes, forcing myself to breathe. I didn't need him. I didn't want him. And I sure as hell wasn't going to let him hurt me like this.

My raven, my mate—he was neither, and I wouldn't let him distract me. Not when I was this close to ending the Commander and getting the hell out of here.

I unsheathed my blade from my thigh and inspected the edge with my finger—still as sharp as the day it was forged as I stood and placed it on the table.

Retrieving the gilded hairpiece from my head next, I set it beside the blade, thankful that Kora had left my clothes here and not in the kitchen.

My gown dropped to the floor, and for the final time, I dressed.

For the final time, I'd wear the tattered clothes I arrived in—either to face my death or to burn them after I defeated Demetrius and returned home.

I pulled my father's torn tunic over my head, bunching the back of it and securing my binding to my midsection before drawing it tight.

My body was thinner than it had ever been—fragile and weak-looking on the outside, but on the inside, it felt strong. Powerful.

As if my muscles were being rethreaded from within.

The fine shimmer embedded in my skin was more prominent, too, catching the candlelight as I turned my hand over to find that my fingers were more slender, longer even.

The changes were subtle. *Slow*... but they were there, growing each day as if the Commander's attempt to pull that gilded thread had triggered something inside me.

I finished dressing, strapping my blade in place before stepping into my cell and lying down.

I hardly remembered falling asleep—only that it had been a paralyzing kind of sleep, one that rode the edge of life and death.

It was so deep that I didn't move. Didn't rouse. Not even for the soft stroke of fingers across my cheek, chasing away the nightmares and replacing them with the comforting lull of darkness that held me in its depths—keeping me there until the faint drag of the dungeon door startled me.

Not enough to fully wake, but enough to know someone had come into the room.

"I figured I might find you here," the male whispered.

"Were you seen?" I thought perhaps it might have been Alekxander's voice that reached through the haze.

"No."

"Good," he said.

"You know you can't stay down here. He'll notice your absence."

Silence stretched.

"Have you found a way to stop the final trial?" the male asked.

"No. I need you to stay out of sight until Fenris returns. Keep the castle wall down and unguarded for the others. It's the only advantage we have."

The warmth of my tunic rose over the curve of my shoulder, covering my back.

"The barrier would have killed you. You know that—right?"

"Find the others, Enver. It's time we prepared."

~

I jumped awake at the sound of the dungeon door closing and rubbed the heaviness from my eyes, blinking absently into the darkness outside of my bars as I plucked a piece of hay from my hair.

After a moment, I stood, feeling my way out of my cell to the short table to light a new candle. Flame took to the wick, and shadows flickered to life along the walls while I braced my hands on the table.

My face felt swollen from crying, and my throat was still tender as I filled my lungs with a steadying breath. Whether I lived or died today, it was almost over. I only hoped that, whatever happened, I did it with grace.

I grazed my hand over my pocket, feeling for the folded parchment, then checked the sheath strapped to my thigh to make sure my blade was still in place. When I was satisfied, I wiped the cold sweat from my neck and squeezed my trembling fingers together until they stilled.

The wave of nerves faded, and I went to the far side of the dungeon, yanked the hidden sewage grate from the ground, and pulled out the leather pouch that held the ivory dagger.

Staring down at it, I wondered how something so simple could be the answer to the freedom of the realms. I didn't understand it as I tucked the only weapon worth something into my boot and tossed the pouch down before kneeling and scooping the ash I kept into my palm.

I smeared it over my lids and down my cheekbones, not bothering to say a prayer this time.

The only one getting me out of this was myself.

CHAPTER FORTY-SEVEN

The corridor was lined with clusters of Faye and Wildlings gawking at me as I made my way toward the throne room, my back stiff as I approached the doors that were already propped open in anticipation of my arrival.

Pushing past the hesitation and the thick scent of lilac, I entered the room with my hands clenched into fists at my sides and my head held high.

Demetrius sat on the jagged throne, ankles crossed while he lounged back as if today were no different from yesterday or the day before. Only today, he was paler, *smaller* than I remembered.

Faye wrapped their fingers tightly around their weapons, and creatures nodded at me reassuringly— offering faint whispers of encouragement as I moved through them toward the male with a crooked grin spreading across his face.

"I've been waiting for you." He slid his eyes over me.

I glanced toward the exits to make sure they were clear and that Rowan and Kora stood where they were supposed to, while Albert and Isra settled into position near the stairwells.

Doing a quick count of the Vassal in the room as I came to a stop in front of him, I spotted Adelram on the second-floor walkway—Cordelia and Vanira beside him, bound and gagged with cloth and chain.

The Vassal flanking them snarled as Phelan inched closer, positioning himself near his wife while he scanned the creatures in the room with a grim tilt to his mouth.

"Better late than never," I breathed, landing my gaze on Alekxander last—reclining with his arms lazily draped over the back of his usual seat next to Demetrius, not bothering to acknowledge me.

I bit down on my lip, hoping he could feel the hate— the resentment I felt for him—as I said, "There will be no trial today."

"Is that so?" Demetrius placed both feet flat on the ground, rising from the jagged throne and descending the stone steps.

I didn't waver when he stopped in front of me.

Didn't cower as I looked into his black, soulless eyes.

I wanted him to strike me down.

To use up his power until there was none left—until he was weak enough that the others were released from his hold.

Until he was weak enough to be killed.

The foul taste of metallic power licked at me, scraping me away layer by layer, forcing me to slump and shake.

I shot Seraphine a look of warning when she stepped forward, and she moved back beside Bellinor and Adrean.

Some of the others shifted, too—*Feronia* among them.

The tether Demetrius held over them, the one that kept them in place, was already thinning.

His face flushed as he threw more of his power at me, my knees finally giving out beneath the force and smacking against the floor.

I resisted as much as I could, refusing to fall any farther as I reached for my blade, feeling his power wane when I slashed it across his shins with a quick flick of my wrist before I could pass out.

The wounds closed before they even had the chance to bleed, hardly garnering a reaction from him as I pushed back to my feet, knees bent and legs braced as I held my blade in front of me.

"What's wrong, Commander?" I drew a sharp breath and wiped away the sweat gathering at my temple. "Not feeling it today?"

His face twisted into a snarl as he held up a fist and a wave of metallic power hit me so hard my boots slid against the stone, compressing my chest and making my body feel as if it would fold in on itself.

If I could have screamed, I would have.

My feet left the floor, and I was flung back, covering my head before it could connect with something. My hip and shoulder cracked off a wall, and I fell to my front, busting my chin and mouth on the stone surface.

Maybe this wasn't such a good idea.

Wiping the coppery trickle from my face, I forced myself to take a breath, flinching through the sensation that filled my lungs as I struggled to stand—falling when my arms and legs went out from beneath me, completely sapped of their strength.

Alekxander shot from his seat when Demetrius began walking in my direction, and I realized I no longer held my blade.

Frantically, I searched for it at the feet of the surrounding Faye and Wildlings, pulling myself onto my hip with a hiss through my teeth and scooting away from him, praying for any spark of magic or power to reveal itself to me.

He lifted his boot and aimed it at my face. The edge of his sole clipped my jaw, sending me back to the ground with a bolt of fire shooting through my head and neck.

My tongue was pinched by my teeth closing shut and blood spurted all over the white and gold-marbled stone as I stifled a cry, not sure how much more I could take.

My vision filled with spots when another burst of his power hit me—weaker than the last.

I dug my fingertips into the stone until it faded—and with it, the glamour that held the castle together. Only a flash of the crumbled ruins that lay beneath, but enough to pull the Commander's attention away.

"What a shame." He dropped his blackened gaze back on me. "I had so many plans for your power."

He raised his boot again, and I braced.

When the blow didn't come, I peeked around my outstretched hand and my eyes went wide with shock.

Demetrius blasted Alekxander backward, and the sound of his spine cracking against the stone resonated through the room.

I pulled myself up, wiping the trickle of blood from my chin as I searched the cloud of sediment, waiting until the plume of dust settled enough to reveal his silhouette.

A flutter of wings came from above, followed by a raven's caw that drew every gaze in the room to the glass dome aside from mine.

The cloud thinned, and I could have sworn I heard the faintest sound of relief escape Alekxander as he got to his feet and wiped away the thick swath of dust from his shoulder with a smirk.

He glanced at the crumbled wall behind him, unimpressed, before sliding his silver-flecked eyes to me, taking in the planes of my face—my lips, my eyes—letting them linger before his jaw set and a petrifying sound tore from his mouth.

My pulse raced, and if it were even possible, Demetrius turned a shade paler as Alekxander relaxed his shoulders—unfazed by what had just happened—before sliding his hands into his pockets and strolling toward him.

"I wonder," he hummed. "Have you checked on your armies today, Demetrius?"

The room shifted uneasily, and I forced myself to my feet, the muscles in my thighs and back trembling under the strain as the Faye and Wildlings stumbled over themselves to retreat.

Alekxander cocked his head to the side, stopping

mere feet from the male as he muttered, "It seems the Vassal within these walls are all you have left."

"How exactly do you figure?" Demetrius snarled, a flush of crimson already creeping back into his cheeks.

"I'm glad you asked." Alekxander removed his hands from his pockets and rolled the sleeves of his dust-heavy tunic to his elbows. "While you've been busy tongue-fucking anything with a pulse and guzzling down poisonous wine, I've made a few moves myself."

Shadows cracked through the room in smoky tendrils that clung to the floor.

A hooded figure to my left dropped his cloak, and my eyes widened as Enver stepped forward, drawing an onyx sword from his waist and sending it spinning through the air before pulling his own.

Alekxander caught the blade just as two more figures to my right shed their cloaks, revealing black leather and golden armor beneath.

Viktor yanked his broadsword free next, and Seraphine and the others followed suit, as if they had been waiting for this moment.

My heart beat so violently in my chest that I had to fight back the urge to vomit when I realized what was about to happen.

The Vassal around the room shrieked in high-pitched

unison, swarming to shield Demetrius as he retreated into them.

"If you think you have a chance against me, think again." Demetrius waved his hand, and the glamour dropped, the castle crumbling into ruins around us.

"You forget who you're speaking to," Alekxander purred, running his thumb along the edge of his blade before lifting his silver gaze back to Demetrius. "I am the High King of Nightfall. The Commander of the Exodus. The protector of the Veil and the deliverer of death. I am older and stronger than any born into this realm—and I didn't come alone."

The room flooded with leather-clad figures from the abandoned wings, and madness descended.

Faye and Wildlings clashed with Vassal, their cries ringing out around me as I struggled to find my footing —to focus on one thing after the next.

Bellinor shouted, and I twisted toward him, barely catching the sword he flung my way. The hilt was too big for my hands. The blade itself was too heavy. The weapon clearly meant to be wielded by someone far more experienced than me.

Thick black blood sprayed across my face as Viktor cut diagonally through thin bone and flesh, kicking the severed pieces aside and driving his sword into the chest of another.

"Go!" He shoved my dagger at me with a growl, clearing the path to the base of the throne where Demetrius advanced on Alekxander, who met each deadly slice with effortless precision.

I took the space he claimed for me, dodging teeth and claws as I moved.

"I am the Commander of the Divine Armies. You are nothing! No one!" Demetrius's elbow smashed into the side of Alekxander's face, and I lurched forward as dagger-like claws drove into the flesh of my bicep, shoving me aside.

Sucking in a breath through my teeth, I swung my blade under my arm and stabbed the Vassal in the chest before slashing its neck and leaping back from the sweep of another weapon.

I fought to breathe, my hands trembling as I watched Demetrius's fist crash down on Alekxander with such force the ground at my feet rumbled.

Jagged teeth sank into my shoulder before I could move any farther, and I screamed when the points tore deep into my skin.

Alekxander snapped his head toward me, giving Demetrius the opportunity to lash out, hurling him into a column and cracking it to its base.

"I've bound beings far stronger than you, boy."

I watched, frozen, as Demetrius advanced, chains of light spinning in his hands.

My heart thundered against my ribs when I realized what he meant to do as Alekxander was swallowed by a swarm of Vassal, the creatures crawling over walls and flooding the space around him.

"No!" Panic seized me as I dropped my sword and gripped the dagger with both hands, driving its tip into the crown of a Vassal's skull before wrenching my arm free of its teeth and shoving the creature away.

My eyes snapped between the two as I lunged for my sword, snatched it up, and charged before Demetrius could finish.

The glimmering binds dissolved just as I struck, sinking my blade down on a weapon of light conjured from thin air to block me.

"Now, this feels familiar," he said with a harsh laugh that cut through the sound of steel ringing through my skull, disorienting me as I tried to keep my footing.

I twisted at the waist, yanking my arm back and driving the edge of my blade into his shoulder—only for the butt of his weapon to smack into my nose, sending me stumbling back with a sharp explosion of pain.

Tears streamed down my face when I advanced again, and the muscles in my arms protested with each lift of my blade that he knocked to the side as if it were nothing more than an annoyance.

"Give up!" he snarled.

"No!" I growled, fighting through the fatigue—through the pain. Each movement was slower than the last. "I will n—"

I sucked in a sharp breath, my eyes wide with shock as I stared down at the silver edge jutting from my side. Barely registering the feeling of steel inside of me, I reached back and yanked the dagger free, letting it clatter at my feet.

Warmth bloomed, staining my tunic red as I pressed a hand to the wound and stumbled back, unsure who had stabbed me as my own sword slipped from my fingers.

"Look around you." Demetrius hauled me forward by my tunic, his lips curling when the tip of his sword sank into my stomach with a fleshy sound, sliding to the hilt with sickening ease. "You were never going to win."

The room turned silent as I gaped in disbelief, wrapping my bloodied fingers around his hand with a horrific, wet rattle from my throat.

CHAPTER FORTY-EIGHT

"Riven!" Seraphine's scream broke through the muffle in my ears, and I forced my head toward her to find her eyes were on me and not the Vassal who slashed its claws down her front.

Demetrius shoved me back, and I fell to my knees. The blade in my gut jolted from the impact, turning the sting into a hot throb that tore through my middle until it was unbearable.

The pain was no more than an afterthought as I watched Adrean run to Seraphine's aid, only to be advanced on by two of the creatures.

My face crumpled and my vision blurred with the onslaught of tears as a strangled cry for help drew my gaze upward, where Cordelia fought for her life.

Jagged teeth tore into her—her eyes locking with mine for a single fleeting second before she was tossed over the edge of the balcony, landing on her head with a sickening thud.

Blood spurted around her, mixing into the puddle already there… a puddle belonging to Dorian.

I had never seen so much of it before—the stench of it, the taste of it.

My lids fluttered, heavy and warm as I looked down at my stomach, my hands doing nothing to staunch the flow around the hilt of Demetrius's blade.

I was dying—and it wasn't graceful at all.

"You failed." Demetrius knelt in front of me with that vile grin of his. "For every one of my Vassal killed today, there will be three more standing in their place tomorrow. I am a Divine being, and you are nothing."

He yanked me up by my hair when I began to slump. "And when I descend on the Mortal Realm, Riven, I'll make sure they know it. I'll make sure your *father* knows this was all your doing. That all you had to do was give me your power."

The edges of his blade sliced into my palms like razors as he pulled it from me, and I could have sworn my name was being frantically screamed from some-where close, the sound splintering through the weight in my head as fresh blood bubbled at the back of my throat.

I wheezed for my next breath, feeling every life needlessly slip away from creatures who didn't deserve this. The tether between me and them cut like a thread.

My fingers tingled. My chest.

"No," I said through clenched teeth, shooting my cut hands out to catch his blade before he could drive it through me again.

A burst of light—so bright it was blinding—surged forward, knocking him away from me, the last of my strength waning as I pushed to my feet.

If I was lucky, I had only seconds left.

I needed to make them count.

My boots scraped limply against the floor as I tossed his sword aside, unable to feel my legs as I dragged myself forward.

Demetrius pulled himself to his feet, more focused on adjusting his crown and wiping the bead of blood from his brow than on my approach.

His arrogance, even now, was unmatched.

Disbelief shadowed the hollows of his face as I pulled the serpent's dagger from my boot, my bloody fingers weakly slipping over its enamel surface as I gripped it.

He lifted his hand, his last attempt to use his power so feeble I barely felt it over the pain consuming me.

His mouth opened, but before he could speak another

word—before he could truly comprehend what I held in my hand, that this wound would not heal—the tip of it met flesh.

It was all it took as his fingers wrapped firmly around my wrists, his power draining away with each inch I gained until the magic he had stolen had begun returning to the Faye and Wildlings around me.

A violent roar shook the room and my eyes clashed with Alekxander's as he fought to reach me, hurling aside the hordes of creatures tearing into him with every step.

He wouldn't make it. I could see it in his eyes. He knew he wouldn't make it to me in time.

"You," Demetrius rasped, dragging me down with him as he sank to his knees. "You kill me, and he'll know. My brother will come for you."

"He'll be coming for a corpse," I whispered groggily, using my body weight to press the fang further into his chest.

Calloused hands clasped over mine, and I blinked up at Enver as he knelt by my side—careful not to touch the dagger while lending me the extra strength I needed to drive it toward the Commander's heart.

The thud beneath his ribs slowed to a stop as I slid my sluggish gaze back to his in that final second, looking into those inky pools of black as his life left him—like a flame being snuffed out.

No longer something to fear.

His skin began to turn ashen and his features sank into bone.

The crown atop his head tarnished into nothing as he looked back at me before his body shriveled into a black husk and then disintegrated entirely—taking the serpent's fang with it.

Wind roared through the room, whipping my hair around my face and drowning out the shrieks of the remaining Vassal as Enver threw his arm over me, shielding me from the gust.

I tucked my face against him, watching the creatures turn hollow just as Demetrius's had, their bodies collapsing into black sand that bounced across the stone floor.

The wind abandoned the ruins as the last one fell, and weapons clattered down—an audible sigh sweeping through the chamber as I dropped my head, bracing myself upright on trembling hands as I waited for what would come next.

Instead, warmth tingled through my middle. No longer a sting or an ache… but the strangest, most unsettling sensation.

Enver's arm fell away from me, and I lifted the hem

of my tunic, my brows knitting as I watched raw flesh weave itself back together with threads of golden light—sealing the twin wounds.

"Gods," Enver breathed, his green eyes lifting to mine as he extended his hand for me to take. "Let me—"

"No." I flinched away, terrified anything he did would make it hurt worse than it already did. "Don't touch me."

My body shook uncontrollably, sweat beading over my skin as I pressed my palm against my middle.

The warmth from the golden glow pulsed through my fingers as I stumbled upright, taking in the room that was strung with bodies—the blood that puddled around them, thickening and congealing in massive pools.

My lips trembled as I cupped my hand over my mouth—willing to take a thousand swords if it meant I'd never have to endure this.

My chest stuttered as warm, wet hands found either side of my face.

"Bring them back," I demanded, my voice breaking as I looked up at the Dark Faye, curling my fingers around his wrists.

The High King of Shadow and Death.

I didn't know what power he truly held. I didn't know where the limits lay with his magic.

I didn't care.

"Bring them back. Please—bring them back," I begged, my vision blurring with tears as the breath stalled in his chest.

He slid his gaze over my face and shook his head. "I can't."

"Yes, you can. You can. You said so yourself. You're the keeper of the Veil. You can bring them back," I sobbed.

His thumbs smoothed over the tears on my cheeks. "They knew what waited for them when they entered this room."

I dragged my eyes to Feronia, who pressed against the irreparable wound on her advisor's neck.

"May the Veil keep you," she said. "May it protect you. May it guide you to the eternal stream and fill you with the sweetest water. May it wash away your sorrows and your burdens, leaving you unhindered and new." She gently closed his eyes. "May we meet again."

My jaw flexed, Alekxander's hands slipping from my face as I went to a Wildling who reached out for help.

"It's going to be okay." I applied pressure over the claw marks on his chest, recognizing him from the day I tripped with a bucket of ash in my hands.

"I have bandages!" Kora's voice rose over the groans.

"I need some," someone called out.

I opened my mouth too, stopping before I could get the words out.

The creature exhaled, and his body went limp—his eyes glassy and vacant.

I stared at his antlers, at his furry ears, my gaze falling back to his chest where my hands hadn't yet moved because I was waiting—waiting for him to take another breath, for a heartbeat, for a cry of pain.

Rowan dropped to her knees beside me and recited the words Feronia had spoken, each syllable woven with deep respect as she closed his eyes. "May the Veil keep you."

I jerked my head toward the far side of what was once the corridor, where Alekxander's voice carried.

"May it protect you. May it guide you to the eternal stream and fill you with the sweetest water. May it wash away your sorrows and your burdens, leaving you unhindered and new." He laid his hand over the Faye's eyes before rising. "May we meet again."

We worked that way for hours, moving around each other with our heads down, until I physically couldn't bear it anymore.

I found my dagger and made my way to the front entrance of the ruins, staring out at the sky as it cast warm pinks and yellows over the hills and trees.

I didn't know how long I stood there—only that I had tried to leave a dozen times or more, feeling as if I were being pulled in two directions at once, both ending in an outcome I would never be able to outrun.

The tips of my fingers stilled over the gold-sheened scar at my hip, the match to the one Demetrius had given me, and I couldn't help but think I should have been dead. That I should have been lying on the stone floor with the others I had wrapped in shrouds.

It was all I could offer them after what they had given up: a few kind words and a dirty sheet.

Standing straighter, I flinched at the lingering pain that jolted across my stomach. A small price to pay in comparison.

"Seraphine is asking for you," Alekxander said quietly from behind me, and I closed my eyes, too much a coward to face her after what she had lost.

It was better this way. To be gone before anyone noticed my absence—while I still had the chance.

His fingers grazed my arm, a part of me still expecting them to be covered in blood.

I pulled the feather I had kept from my waistband, twirling it as I had almost every night since finding it on the windowsill. Then I let it go—let *him* go—as I watched it drift and sway to the ground at my feet.

"Stay out of my head, Alekxander," I whispered, not having it in me to speak another word more as I began walking.

A LOOK INTO
THE NEXT BOOK

My body swayed, my lips quivering as gentle fingers brushed against my chin to angle my tear-streaked face up to his.

They were warm—so *warm*.

That one simple, all-consuming touch a threat to every wall I had erected around myself to protect me from him.

"Enough, Fawr o un." His voice was hoarse, and the vivid light that sparkled in his eyes—those eyes. Not silver flames at all, but the stars above. "You've given them enough."

The Shadow Series

A tale of power and survival

Are you ready for more?

Follow the Author

Instagram

Tiktok

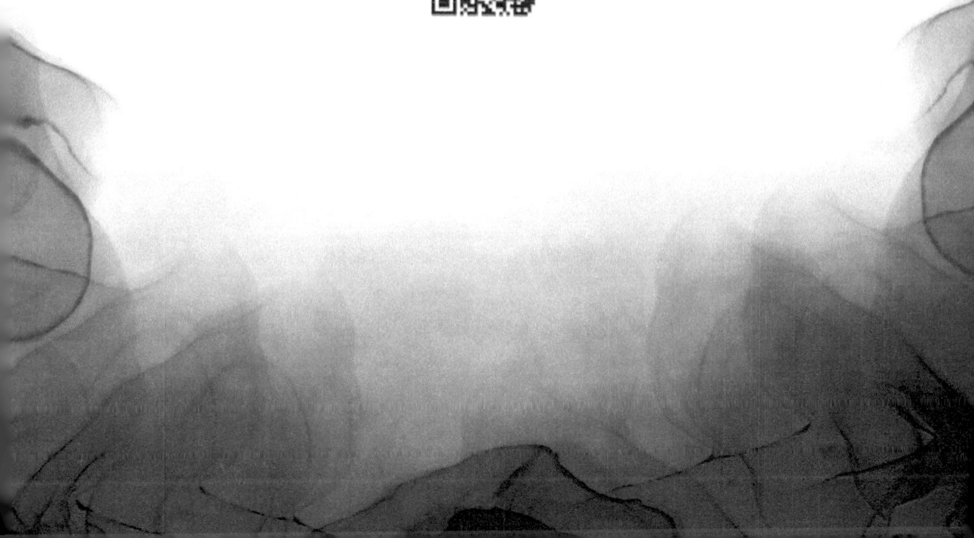

JOIN THE GROUP

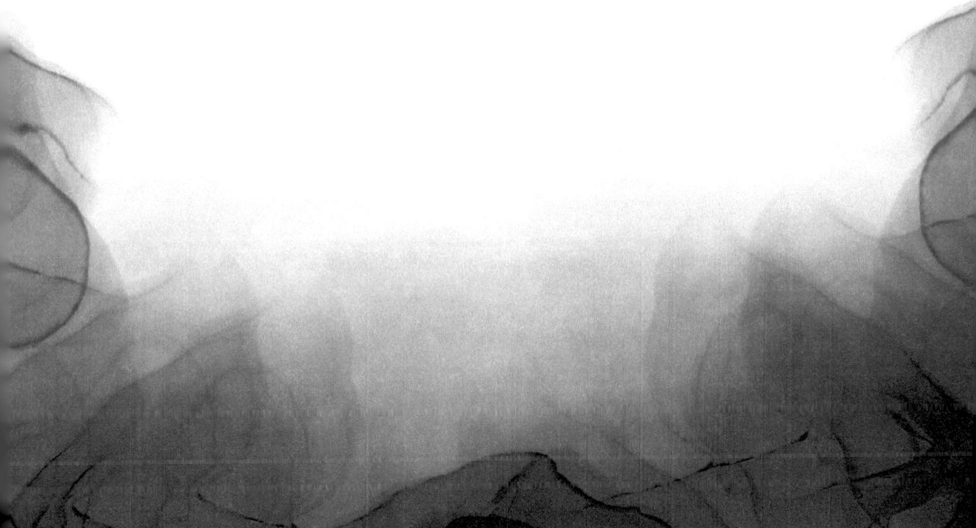

GET INVOLVED

USE

#AUTHORKATHERINEANN
#THESHADOWSERIES

TO BE FEATURED ON SOCIALS

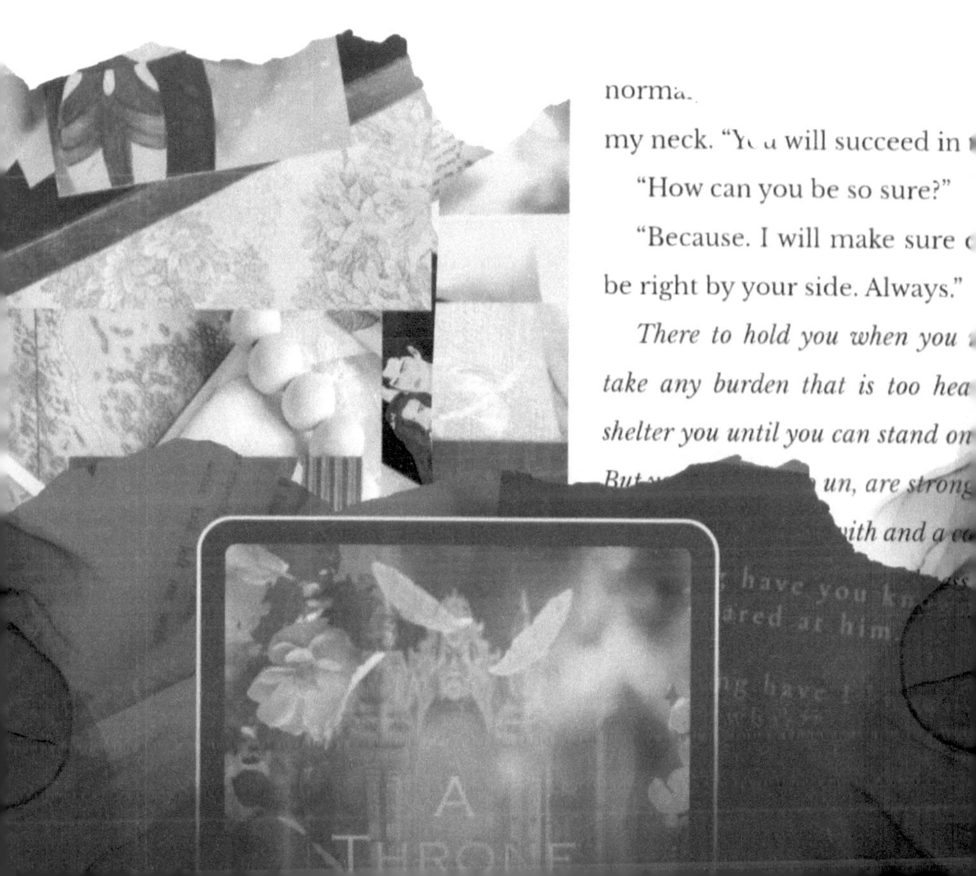

Contact

TRIGGER WARNINGS

Please be advised: this is a multi-book series designed to unfold gradually. Questions are answered throughout the narrative in order to avoid excessive exposition or "information dumping." Cliffhangers are present and are intended to build momentum into subsequent installments.

This is a **plot-driven** story with romance as a secondary element that involves the concept of **fated mates**, and the term *mate* is used frequently throughout the story. The relationship between the FMC (female main character) and the MMC (male main character) is a **toxic, slow-burn romance**. It is not meant to serve as a model for real-life relationships.

There is on-page, **descriptive adult content**

("spice") that increases in intensity with each install-ment. The cast is **large** and dynamic, featuring multiple characters, the occasional miscommunication, and supporting POVs alongside the primary narrative focused on the FMC.

This book also includes **BDSM themes**, which may not be suitable for every reader. In some cases, characters find control and comfort in these scenes as a means of reclaiming power and healing after trauma. These moments are fictional and are **not intended for educational or instructional purposes**.

Dark themes are present and detailed below for your awareness in the form of "Trigger warnings" which are a modern and valuable tool for readers and writers alike. In collaboration with sensitivity readers, a list has been compiled of potential triggers included throughout the series. However, please note that individual sensitivities vary. Despite our best efforts, some content may not be listed here.

The trigger warning list may be **updated post-publi-cation** as additional concerns are brought to the attention of the author and team. These warnings apply to the **entire series**, not individual books, in an effort to avoid unpleasant surprises for readers in later installments.

This series contains, but is NOT limited to, the following triggers:

Poverty, extreme class systems, starvation, illness, violence, detailed gore, death, murder, miscarriage, sickness, PTSD, dubious consent, humiliation, anxiety, mental health representation, public execution, public punishment, war, mass extermination of a fantasy race via world history, child death (not in detail), torture, alcohol, rape (not in detail), drug usage, BDSM themes, depression, suicidal ideation, on-page descriptive adult content, animal death (via hunting for food), spiders, blood kink, knife play, large cast of characters, unhealthy romantic relationships, rope bondage, nightmares, fantasy-based lore and religions, dehydration, marriage, supporting character pregnancy, unhealthy non-romantic relationships, miscommunication, desecration of ruins, angst, false gods, slow burn, ghosts, exhibitionism, polyamory, orgies, death of a parent, ocean swimming (including at night), sirens, waterboarding, vomiting, female rage, rough on-page adult content, shadow play, sexual punishment, multiple POVs, bipolar representation, breath play, hyperspermia, non-sexual child grooming.

Disclaimer

This is an **ADULT work of fiction**, intended for **mature audiences** only. It is not suitable for readers under 18 or for those sensitive to any of the above themes. If at any point the content becomes overwhelming or triggering, please feel free to stop reading. The story has been intentionally written with these elements to reflect the complexity, darkness, and depth of the fictional world in which it takes place.

This story exists in a **fantasy world**, not our own. The customs, behaviors, and consequences within it may differ significantly from those of reality.

Some stories aren't meant for everyone—and that's okay.

Mental Health Resources

If you or someone you know is struggling with suicidal thoughts or mental health concerns, please reach out for help. Call the National Suicide Prevention Lifeline at **988** or **800-273-8255**, or visit the NSPL website to connect with a trained counselor.

CHARACTERS

PRONUNCIATION

PLAYLIST

ACKNOWLEDGMENTS

Thank you to every reader who chose to enter this world and remain within it. To my team, sensitivity readers, and alpha and beta readers—your care, honesty, and dedication helped shape this story into what it became. I am endlessly grateful to my editor, Samantha Swart, for her steady guidance, and to my personal assistant for keeping everything moving when it mattered most. And to the character artists who gave these characters breath—tonyviento, avoccatt_art, mageonduty, coralie.renards, and magicnaanavi—thank you for bringing them to life.